ONE
BY ONE

About the author

Born in Brazil of Italian origin, Chris Carter studied psychology and criminal behaviour at the University of Michigan.
As a member of the Michigan State District Attorney's
Criminal Psychology team, he interviewed and studied
many criminals, including serial and multiple homicide
offenders with life-imprisonment convictions.

Having departed for Los Angeles in the early 1990s,
Chris spent ten years as a guitarist for numerous rock bands
before leaving the music business to write full-time. He now
lives in London and is a Top Ten *Sunday Times* bestselling
author.

Visit www.chriscarterbooks.com or find him on Facebook.

Also by Chris Carter

The Crucifix Killer
The Executioner
The Night Stalker
The Death Sculptor

CHRIS CARTER

ONE BY ONE

**SIMON &
SCHUSTER**

London · New York · Sydney · Toronto · New Delhi

A CBS COMPANY

First published in Great Britain by Simon & Schuster UK Ltd, 2013
A CBS Company

Copyright © Chris Carter, 2013

This book is copyright under the Berne Convention.
No reproduction without permission.
® and © 1997 Simon & Schuster Inc. All rights reserved.

The right of Chris Carter to be identified as author of this work has been asserted in accordance with sections 77 and 78 of the Copyright, Designs and Patents Act, 1988.

1 3 5 7 9 10 8 6 4 2

Simon & Schuster UK Ltd
1st Floor
222 Gray's Inn Road
London WC1X 8HB

www.simonandschuster.co.uk

Simon & Schuster Australia, Sydney
Simon & Schuster India, New Delhi

A CIP catalogue record for this book is available from the British Library

Hardback ISBN 978-0-85720-305-2
Trade Paperback ISBN 978-0-85720-306-9
Ebook ISBN 978-0-85720-309-0

This book is a work of fiction. Names, characters, places and incidents are either a product of the author's imagination or are used fictitiously. Any resemblance to actual people living or dead, events or locales is entirely coincidental.

Typeset by Hewer Text UK Ltd, Edinburgh
Printed and bound by
CPI Group (UK) Ltd, Croydon, CR0 4YY

ONE
BY ONE

One

A single shot to the back of the head, execution style. Many people consider it a very violent way to die. But the truth is – it isn't. At least not for the victim.

A 9mm bullet will enter someone's skull and exit at the other side in three ten-thousandths of a second. It will shatter the cranium and rupture through the subject's brain matter so fast the nervous system has no time to register any pain. If the angle in which the bullet enters the head is correct, the bullet should splice the cerebral cortex, the cerebellum, even the thalamus in such a way that the brain will cease functioning, resulting in instant death. If the angle of the shot is wrong, the victim might survive, but not without extensive brain damage. The entry wound should be no larger than a small grape, but the exit wound could be as large as a tennis ball, depending on the type of bullet used.

The male victim on the photograph Detective Robert Hunter of the LAPD Robbery Homicide Division was looking at had died instantly. The bullet had transversed his entire skull, rupturing the cerebellum together with the temporal and the frontal lobes, causing fatal brain damage in three ten-thousandths of a second. Less than a full second later he was dead on the ground.

The case wasn't Hunter's; it belonged to Detective Terry Radley in the main detectives' floor, but the investigation photos had ended up on Hunter's desk by mistake. As he returned the photograph to the case file, the phone on his desk rang.

'Detective Hunter, Homicide Special,' he answered, half expecting it to be Detective Radley after the photo file.

Silence.

'Hello?'

'Is this Detective *Robert* Hunter?' The raspy voice on the other end was male, the tone calm.

'Yes, this is Detective Robert Hunter. Can I help you?'

Hunter heard the caller breathe out.

'That's what we're going to find out, Detective.'

Hunter frowned.

'I'm going to need your full attention for the next few minutes.'

Hunter cleared his throat. 'I'm sorry, I didn't catch your na—'

'Shut the fuck up and listen, Detective,' the caller interrupted him. His voice was still calm. 'This is not a conversation.'

Hunter went silent. The LAPD received tens, sometimes hundreds, of crazy calls a day – drunks, drug users on a high, gang members trying to look 'badass', psychics, people wanting to report a government conspiracy or an alien invasion, even people who claim to have seen Elvis down at the local diner. But there was something in the caller's tone of voice, something in the way he spoke that told Hunter that dismissing the call as a prank would be a mistake. He decided to play along for the time being.

Hunter's partner, Detective Carlos Garcia, was sitting at his desk, which faced Hunter's, inside their small office on the fifth floor of the Police Administration Building in downtown Los Angeles. His longish dark brown hair was tied back in a slick ponytail. Garcia was reading something on his computer screen, unaware of his partner's conversation. He had pushed himself away from his desk and leisurely interlaced his fingers behind his head.

Hunter snapped his fingers to catch Garcia's attention, pointed to the receiver at his ear and made a circular motion with his index finger, indicating he needed that call recorded and traced.

Garcia instantly reached for the phone on his desk, punched the internal code that connected him to Operations and got everything rolling in less than five seconds. He signaled Hunter, who signaled back telling him to listen in. Garcia tapped into the line.

'I'm assuming you have a computer on your desk, Detective,' the caller said. 'And that that computer is connected to the Internet?'

'That's correct.'

An uneasy pause.

'OK. I want you to type the address I'm about to give you into your address bar . . . Are you ready?'

Hunter hesitated.

'Trust me, Detective, you will want to see this.'

Hunter leaned forward over his keyboard and brought up his Internet browser. Garcia did the same.

'OK, I'm ready,' Hunter replied in a calm tone.

The caller gave Hunter an internet address made up only of numbers and dots, no letters.

Hunter and Garcia both typed the sequence into their address bars and pressed 'enter'. Their computer screens flickered a couple of times before the web page loaded.

Both detectives went still, as a morbid silence took hold of the room.

The caller chuckled. 'I guess I have your full attention now.'

Two

The FBI headquarters is located at number 935 Pennsylvania Avenue in Washington DC, just a few blocks away from the White House and directly across the road from the US Attorney General. Aside from the headquarters, the FBI has fifty-six field offices scattered around the fifty American states. Most of those offices also control a number of satellite cells known as 'resident agencies'.

The Los Angeles office in Wilshire Boulevard is one of the largest FBI field offices in the whole American territory. It controls ten resident agencies. It is also one of the few with a specific Cybercrime Division.

The FBI Cybercrime Division's priority is to investigate high-tech crimes, including cyber-based terrorism, computer intrusions, online sexual exploitation and major cyber frauds. In the United States, in the past five years alone, cybercrime has increased ten-fold. The US government and its networks receive over a billion attacks each and every day, coming from multiple sources all around the world.

In 2011 a report was submitted to the US Senate Committee on Commerce, Science and Transportation, estimating that internal cybercrime was bringing in illicit revenues of approximately US$800 million a year, making it the most lucrative illegal business in the USA, exceeding drug trafficking.

Thousands of the FBI's 'web crawlers', also known as 'bots' or 'spiders', search the net endlessly, looking for anything suspicious concerning any type of high-tech crime, inside and outside the United States. It's a mammoth job, and the FBI understands that what the crawlers find is merely a drop of water in a cybercrime ocean. For every threat they find, thousands go unnoticed. And that was why on that autumn morning at the end of September, no FBI web crawler came across the web page Detective Hunter and his partner were looking at back at the Police Administration Building.

Three

Hunter and Garcia's eyes were glued to their computer screens, trying to take in the surreal images. They showed a large, see-through, square container. It looked like it was made of glass, but it could've been Perspex or other similar material. Hunter guessed each side to be approximately 1.5 meters wide, and at least 1.8 meters tall. The container was open-top – no lid – and it seemed to have been handmade. Metal frames and thick white sealant connected the four walls. The whole thing looked just like a reinforced shower enclosure. Inside the enclosure, two metal pipes of about three inches in diameter, one on the left and one on the right, ran from the floor all the way up and out the top. The pipes were sprinkled with holes, none wider than the diameter of a regular pencil. But two things worried Hunter. One was the fact that the images seemed to be streaming live. Two was what was at the center of the container, directly between the two metal pipes.

Sitting there, tied to a heavy metal chair, was a white male who looked to be in his mid to late twenties. His hair was light brown and cut short. The only piece of clothing he had on was a striped pair of boxers. He was a chubby man, with a round face, plump cheeks and chunky arms. He was sweating profusely, and though he didn't look hurt there was no doubt about the expression on his face – pure fear. His eyes were wide open, and he was taking in quick gulps of air through the cloth gag in his mouth. Hunter could tell by the fast 'up-and-down' movement of his belly that he was almost hyperventilating. The man was shivering and looking around himself like a confused and frightened mouse.

The entire image had a green tint to it, indicating that the camera was using night-vision mode and lenses. Whoever that man was, he was sitting in a dark room.

'Is this for real?' Garcia whispered to Hunter, covering his mouthpiece.

Hunter shrugged without taking his eyes off the screen.

As if on cue, the caller broke his silence. 'If you are wondering if this is live, Detective, let me show you.'

The camera panned right to a nondescript brick wall where a regular, round wall clock was mounted. It read 2:57 p.m. Hunter and Garcia checked their watches – 2:57 p.m. The camera then panned down and focused on the newspaper that had been placed at the foot of the wall, before zooming in on its front page and the date. It was a copy of this morning's *LA Times*.

'Satisfied?' The caller chuckled.

The camera refocused on the man inside the box. His nose had started running and tears were streaming down his face.

'The container you're looking at is made of reinforced glass, strong enough to withstand a bullet,' the caller explained in a chilling voice. 'The door has a very secure locking mechanism, with an airtight seal. It only opens from the outside. In short, the man you can see on your screen is trapped inside. There's no way out of there.'

The frightened man on the screen looked straight at the camera. Hunter quickly pressed the 'print screen' key on his keyboard, saving a snapshot of his entire desktop to the computer's clipboard. He now had what he hoped would be an identifiable shot of the man's face.

'Now, the reason why I'm calling you, Detective, is because I need your help.'

On the screen, the man started panting heavily. Fearful sweat covered his entire body. He was on the brink of a panic attack.

'OK, let's take it easy,' Hunter replied, being certain to keep his voice calm but authoritative. 'Tell me how I can help you?'

Silence.

Hunter knew the caller was still on the line. 'I'll do everything I can to help you. Just tell me how.'

'Well . . .' the caller responded. 'You can decide how he's going to die.'

Four

Hunter and Garcia exchanged uneasy glances. Garcia immediately clicked off the call and quickly punched the internal code to be connected to Operations again.

'Please tell me you've got a location for this creep,' Garcia said as the phone was answered at the other end.

'Not yet, Detective,' the woman replied. 'We need another minute or so. Keep him talking.'

'He doesn't want to talk anymore.'

'We're getting there, but we need a little more time.'

'Shit!' He shook his head at Hunter and signaled him to keep the caller talking. 'Let me know the second you get something.' He disconnected and tapped back into Hunter's call.

'Fire or water, Detective?' the caller said.

Hunter frowned. 'What?'

'Fire or water?' the caller repeated in an amused tone. 'The pipes inside the glass enclosure you can see on your screen are capable of spitting out fire or filling the enclosure with water.'

Hunter's heart stuttered.

'So pick, Detective Hunter. Would you like to watch him die by fire or water? Shall we drown him or burn him alive?' It didn't sound like a joke.

Garcia shifted in his chair.

'Wait a moment,' Hunter said, trying to keep his voice steady. 'You don't have to do this.'

'I know I don't, but I want to. It should be fun, don't you think?' The indifference in the caller's voice was mesmerizing.

'C'mon, c'mon,' Garcia urged between clenched teeth, staring at the line lights on his phone. Still nothing from Operations.

'Choose, Detective,' the caller ordered. 'I want *you* to decide how he's going to die.'

Hunter kept silent.

'I suggest you pick one, Detective, because I promise you that the alternative is much worse.'

'You know I can't make that decision . . .'

'CHOOSE,' the caller shouted down the line.

'OK,' Hunter's voice remained calm. 'I choose neither of the two.'

'That's not an option.'

'Yes, it is. Let's talk about this for a minute.'

The caller laughed angrily. 'Let's not. Talking time is over. It's decision time now, Detective. If you don't pick . . . I will. Either way, he dies.'

A red light started flashing on Garcia's phone. He quickly swapped calls. 'Tell me you've got him.'

'We've got him, Detective.' Excitement colored the woman's voice. 'He's in . . .' She paused for a moment. 'What the hell?'

'What?' Garcia pushed. 'Where is he?'

'What the hell is going on?' Garcia heard the woman say, but he knew she wasn't talking to him. He heard some more undecipherable whispers coming from the other end of the line. Something was wrong.

'Somebody better talk to me.' Garcia's voice raised about half an octave.

'It's no good, Detective,' the woman finally answered. 'We thought we had him in Norwalk, but suddenly the signal jumped to Temple City, then to El Monte, now it's showing the call is coming from Long Beach. He's rerouting the signal every five seconds. Even if we keep him on the phone for an hour, we wouldn't be able to pinpoint him.' She paused for a moment. 'The signal just moved to Hollywood. Sorry, Detective. This guy knows what he's doing.'

'Shit!' Garcia tapped back into Hunter's call and shook his head. 'He's bouncing the signal,' he whispered. 'We can't get his location.'

Hunter squeezed his eyes tight. 'Why are you doing this?' he asked the caller.

'Because I want to,' the caller came back. 'You have three seconds to make your choice, Detective Hunter. Fire or water? Flip a coin if you need to. Ask your partner. I know he's listening in.'

Garcia said nothing.

'Wait,' Hunter said. 'How can I make a choice if I don't even know who he is, or why you have him in that tank? C'mon, talk to me. Tell me what this is all about.'

The caller laughed again. 'That's something you will have to find out for yourself, Detective. Two seconds.'

'Don't do this. We can help each other.'

Garcia's eyes had left his computer screen and were now locked on Hunter.

'One second, Detective.'

'C'mon, talk to me,' Hunter said again. 'We can figure this out. We can come up with a better solution for whatever this is.'

Garcia held his breath.

'The solution is either fire or water, Detective. Anyway, time's up. So what is it going to be?'

'Look, there's got to be another way we can . . .'

TOC, TOC, TOC.

The sound exploded through Hunter and Garcia's phone so loudly that their heads jerked back, as if they had been slapped across the face. It sounded like the caller had slammed his receiver against a wooden surface three times to get their attention.

'You don't seem to be listening to me, Detective Hunter. We are through talking. The only word I want to hear from you right now is either *fire* or *water*. Nothing else.'

Hunter said nothing.

'Suit yourself. You don't want to pick, I will. And I pick fi—'

'Water,' Hunter said in a firm voice. 'I choose water.'

The caller paused and let out an amused chuckle. 'You know what, Detective? I knew you would choose water.'

Hunter stayed silent.

'It was obvious, really. When you considered the options you had, death by drowning seemed less awful, more humane, less painful and quicker than being burned alive, right? But have you ever seen anyone drown, Detective?'

Silence.

'Have you ever seen the despairing look on a person's eyes as he holds his breath for as long as he can, knowing death is all around him and closing in fast?'

Hunter ran a hand through his short hair.

'Have you ever seen the way a drowning man frantically looks around himself, confused, searching for a miracle that is just not there? A miracle that will never come?'

Still silence.

'Have you seen the way the body convulses, as if it was being electrocuted, as the person finally lets go of hope and breathes his first mouthful of water? The way his eyes almost bulge out of his skull as water enters his lungs and he slowly starts to suffocate?' The caller deliberately breathed out heavily. 'Did you know that it's impossible to keep your eyes shut when you're drowning? It's an automatic motor reaction when a person's brain is starved of oxygen.'

Garcia's gaze returned to his screen.

The caller laughed one more time. This time a relaxed giggle. 'Keep on watching, Detective. This show is just about to get much better.'

The line went dead.

Five

All of a sudden and with incredible speed, water started jetting out of the holes on both pipes inside the glass enclosure. The man tied to the chair was caught by surprise, and fear made his whole body jerk violently. His eyes widened in complete desperation as he realized what was happening. Despite the gag in his mouth, he started screaming, frantically, but on the other side of the screen Hunter and Garcia couldn't hear a sound.

'Oh my God,' Garcia said, bringing his closed right fist to his mouth. 'He's not bullshitting. He's going to do it. He's going to drown the guy, goddammit.'

The man kicked and wiggled ferociously inside the enclosure, but his restraints wouldn't give an inch. He couldn't break free no matter what he did. The chair was solidly bolted to the floor.

'This is insane,' Garcia said.

Hunter stood still, his eyes unblinking, staring at his computer screen. He knew that from their office there was absolutely nothing they could do – except maybe collect evidence. 'Is there a way we can record this?' he asked.

Garcia shrugged. 'I don't know. I don't think so.'

Hunter reached for his phone again and got the LAPD switchboard.

'Punch me through to the head of the Computer Crimes Unit, *now*. This is urgent.'

Two seconds later he heard a ringing tone. Four seconds after that the phone was answered by a baritone voice.

'Dennis Baxter, LAPD Computer Crimes Unit.'

'Dennis, this is Detective Hunter from Homicide Special.'

'Hello, Detective, how can I assist you?'

'Tell me, is there a way I can record a live webcam broadcast that I'm watching on my computer right now?'

Baxter laughed. 'Wow, is she that hot?'

'Is there a way or not, Dennis?'

Hunter's tone knocked the play out of Baxter's voice.

'Not unless you have some sort of screen recording software installed on your computer,' he answered.

'Will I have one?'

'On an LAPD office computer? Not as standard. You can put in a request and IT will install one for you in a day or two.'

'No good. I need to capture what's on my screen right now.'

A split-second pause.

'Well, I can do it from here,' Baxter said. 'If you're watching something live over the net, just give me the web address. I can log into the same website and capture it for you. How does that sound?'

'Good enough. Let's try it.' Hunter gave Baxter the sequence of numbers the caller had given him minutes earlier.

'An IP address?' Baxter asked.

'That's right. Aren't they traceable?' Hunter asked.

'Yes. That's actually their main purpose. They work almost like a license number plate for every computer connected to the net. With that, I can pretty much tell you the exact location of the source computer.'

Hunter frowned. Could the caller have made such a silly mistake?

'Do you want me to start a trace?' Baxter asked.

'Yes.'

'OK. I'll get back to you as soon as I get anything.' He disconnected.

The water was already reaching the man's waist. At that speed, Hunter calculated that the man would be completely submerged in another minute and a half, maybe two.

'Operations said that there was no way they could trace the call?' Hunter asked Garcia.

'That's right. He was bouncing the signal all over town.'

The water reached the man's stomach. He was still trying to wiggle himself free, but he was steadily losing energy. He was shivering even more now. A combination of uncontrollable fear and the water temperature, Hunter guessed.

There was nothing Hunter or Garcia could say, so they both went eerily quiet, watching death rise inch by inch around the man on their computer screens.

The phone on Hunter's desk rang again.

'Detective, is this for real?' Dennis Baxter asked.

'Right now, I have no reason to believe it isn't. Are you capturing it?'

'Yeah, I'm recording it.'

'Any luck with tracing it?'

'Not yet. It can take a few minutes.'

'Get back to me if you get anything.'

'Sure.'

The water reached the man's chest, and the camera slowly zoomed in on his face. He was sobbing. Hope had left his eyes. He was giving up.

'I don't think I can watch this,' Garcia said, moving from behind his desk and pacing the room.

The water reached the man's shoulders. In a minute it would be past his nose, and death would arrive with the next breath. He closed his eyes and waited. He wasn't trying to break free anymore.

The water reached the underside of his chin, and then, without any warning, it stopped. Not a drop more came out of the pipes.

'What the hell?' Hunter and Garcia looked at each other for a second and then back at the screen. Surprise etched on both their faces.

'It was a goddamn hoax,' Garcia said, approaching Hunter. A nervous smile on his face. 'Some nutcase pulling our chain.'

Hunter wasn't so sure.

At that exact moment the phone on Hunter's desk rang again.

Six

The sound of the phone ringing cut through the silence like thunder ripping through a night sky.

'You are very clever, Detective Hunter,' the caller said.

Hunter quickly signaled Garcia one more time, and within seconds the call was being recorded again.

'You almost had me fooled,' the caller carried on. 'I thought your concern for the victim was quite touching. Once you realized there was no way you could save him, you picked what seemed to be the less sadistic, less painful and quicker death of the two choices I gave you. But that was only half of the story, wasn't it?'

Garcia looked confused.

Hunter said nothing.

'I figured out the hidden reason behind your choice, Detective.'

No reply.

'You realized I was about to pick fire, and you quickly interrupted me and chose water.' A self-assured laugh. 'Water would've given you hope, right?'

'Hope?' Garcia mouthed the word, frowning at Hunter.

'The hope that when, and if, you come across the body, maybe your—' the caller put on a silly voice

'*—super-advanced, high-tech forensics lab* could uncover something. Maybe on his skin, or hair, or a trace of something under his nails or inside his mouth. Who knows what microscopic clues I might have left behind, isn't that right, Detective Hunter? But fire would've destroyed it all. It would've carbonized his entire body and everything else with it. No clues left, microscopic or not.'

Garcia hadn't thought of that.

'But if he drowns, the body is intact.' The caller moved on. 'Death comes from suffocation . . . skin, hair, nails . . . nothing gets destroyed. It's all there ready to be analyzed.' The caller paused for breath. 'There might be a million things to find. Even the water in his lungs could provide you with some sort of clue. That's why you chose water, isn't it, Detective? If you can't save him, do the next best thing.' The caller let out an animated laugh. 'Always thinking like a detective. Oh, you're no fun.'

Hunter gave himself a subtle headshake. 'You were right the first time around. My concern was the victim's suffering.'

'Of course it was. But . . . just in case I'm right, guess what? I was already prepared for it.'

The man on the screen had reopened his eyes. He was still shivering. Despite the darkness, he looked around himself, waiting . . . listening.

Nothing. Not a sound. The water had stopped.

Behind the gag his mouth twisted into a shy smile. A glimmer of hope returned to his eyes, as if it all had been just a bad dream . . . a sick joke. He swallowed hard, closed his eyes and tilted his head back, as if thanking God. Tears found their way through his closed eyelids and cascaded down his face.

'Keep on watching, Detective.' There was a proud ring to the caller's voice. 'Because you're about to get the "Cirque du Soleil" of shows.' He disconnected.

On the screen the water level started decreasing.

'He's draining the container,' Garcia said.

Hunter nodded.

The water drained fast. In a matter of seconds its level had gone back down to the man's chest.

Then it stopped.

'What the hell is going on?' Garcia asked, lifting his palms up.

Hunter shook his head. His full attention never leaving the screen.

The camera zoomed out just a little, and all of a sudden the submerged portion of the pipes sprang back into life. Like a Jacuzzi bath, the underwater jets ruffled the water as they spat more liquid into the enclosure. But there was something different this time. As the colorless liquid exited the pipes and mixed with the water, it was producing an odd effect, as if the new liquid was denser than that already inside the enclosure.

Hunter leaned forward, bringing his face closer to the monitor.

'That's not water,' he said.

'What?' Garcia asked, standing right behind him. 'What do you mean?'

'Different density,' Hunter replied, pointing at his screen. 'Whatever he's pumping into that tank, it isn't water this time.'

'What the hell is it, then?'

At that moment something started flashing at the top right-hand corner of the picture. Four letters inside parentheses. The first, third and fourth were in capitals.

(NaOH)

'Is that a chemical formula?' Garcia pointed to it.

'Yes.' Hunter breathed out.

'For what?' Garcia rushed back to his computer and opened a new tab on his web browser.

'No need to search for it, Carlos,' Hunter said grimly. 'That's the chemical formula for sodium hydroxide ... caustic soda.'

Seven

Garcia felt a knot tighten in his throat. Years ago, when he was still just a uniformed LAPD cop, he'd responded to a domestic violence incident where a jealous boyfriend had thrown half a pint of caustic soda in his girlfriend's face. The boyfriend fled the scene but was arrested five days later. Garcia still remembered helping the paramedics strap the girlfriend down to the gurney. Her face was just a mess of raw flesh and burned skin. Her lips looked like they had melted onto her teeth. Her right ear and nose had totally disintegrated, and the solution burned holes into one of her eyeballs.

Garcia looked at Hunter over his computer. 'No way. Are you sure?'

Hunter nodded. 'I'm sure.'

'Sonofabitch.'

The phone on Hunter's desk rang again. It was Dennis Baxter from the Computer Crimes Unit.

'Detective,' he said in an anxious voice. 'NaOH is caustic soda. Sodium hydroxide.'

'Yes, I know.'

'Shit, man. That stuff is highly corrosive. Many times worse than acid. If somebody is dumping sodium hydroxide into that much water, for now, the solution will be over-diluted and not very strong, but soon . . .' He went silent.

'It will turn that whole thing into an alkaline bath,' Hunter finished the sentence Baxter couldn't.

'That's right. And you know what that will *do*?'

'Yes, I know.'

'Holy shit, Detective. What's going on?'

'I'm not sure. Did you manage to trace the transmission?'

'Yes. It's coming from Taiwan.'

'What?'

'Exactly. Whoever is doing this . . . he's good. It's either a hijacked IP address or he stole one from a Taiwanese server pool. Bottom line . . . We can't trace it.'

Hunter put the phone down. 'We can't get him through the Internet transmission either,' he told Garcia.

'Shit. This is messed up, man.'

The man on the screen started shaking again. But this time Hunter could tell it wasn't from fear or cold. It was excruciating pain. The solution was getting stronger and starting to corrode his skin. His mouth opened wide to release an agonizing scream that neither Hunter nor Garcia could hear. Secretly, both detectives were relieved by the lack of sound.

As more and more caustic soda was added to the mixture, the water started gaining a faint, dull, milky color.

The man closed his eyes and started shaking his head violently from side to side, as if having a seizure. The alkaline bath was starting to scrape away his skin like an electric sander. It took only a few seconds for the first pieces of skin to be ripped from his body.

Hunter rubbed his face with both hands. He had never felt so helpless.

As more and more skin started to float around the tank, the water began to change color again. It was now going pink. His entire body was bleeding.

The camera zoomed in on something else floating inside the enclosure.

'What is that?' Garcia asked, pulling a face.

Hunter pinched his bottom lip. 'It's a fingernail. His body is dissolving.'

The camera zoomed in on another one, and another one. The solution had already dissolved his cuticles and most of the nail beds on his fingers and toes.

The water was getting bloodier. They couldn't see through it anymore. The man's face, though, was still above the water line.

The victim had lost control of his body, which was now shaking incessantly, guided only by pain. His eyes had rolled back into his head. His mouth was contorted into an excruciating shape. His teeth were relentlessly grinding against each other, and he was now bleeding from the gums, nose and ears as well.

The water was starting to boil.

The man convulsed for the last time. His chest kicked forward so violently it looked like there was something inside it, trying to explode out of his body. His chin fell to his chest, submerging his face under the bloody water and sodium hydroxide mixture.

There was no more movement.

The camera zoomed out, showing the entire glass enclosure.

Hunter and Garcia couldn't find any words. They couldn't look away either.

A few seconds later a message flashed across their screens.

I HOPE YOU'VE ENJOYED THE SHOW.

Eight

The LAPD's Robbery Homicide Division's captain, Barbara Blake,
wasn't easily intimidated and, after so many years in the force, very little ever shocked her, but this morning she sat in absolute silence inside her office on the fifth floor of the Police Administration Building with a disbelieving look on her face. The office was spacious enough. The south wall was taken by bookshelves crammed with hardcovers. The north one by framed photographs, commendations and achievement awards. The east wall was a floor-to-ceiling panoramic window, looking out over South Main Street. Directly in front of her desk were two comfortable-looking leather armchairs, but none of the three other people inside her office were occupying them.

Hunter, Garcia and Dennis Baxter were all standing behind Captain Blake's desk, staring at her computer monitor, watching the footage Baxter had captured from the Internet minutes earlier. The Operations Office had also already sent Hunter a copy of the recorded telephone conversation between him and the mysterious caller.

Captain Blake listened to the recording and watched the entire footage without uttering a word. At the end of it all she looked up at Hunter and Garcia, her face paler than moments ago.

'Was this real?'

Her stare jumped to Baxter, who was a big man, none of it muscle. He was in his forties, with curly fair hair, a plump face made heavier by a double chin, and a thin mustache that looked more like peach fuzz.

'I mean,' she said. 'I know that nowadays CGI technology can make anything look real. Can we be sure that this whole thing isn't just digital and camera trickery?'

Baxter shrugged.

'Well, you're the head of the Computer Crimes Unit.' The captain's voice went hard. 'Tell me something.'

Baxter tilted his head to one side. 'I just captured the whole thing moments ago after getting a call from Detective Hunter. I haven't really had time to analyze it, but at first look and on gut feeling – it's real.'

The captain ran a hand through her long jet-black hair before allowing her stare to return to Hunter and Garcia.

'Too complex and bold to be just a hoax,' Hunter said. 'Operations couldn't trace the call. The caller was bouncing it around town every five seconds.' He gestured to Baxter. 'Dennis said that the Internet transmission came from Taiwan.'

'What?' Captain Blake faced Baxter again.

'It's true. What we had was an IP address, which is a unique identifying number given to every single computer on the Internet. With that, we can easily pinpoint the host computer. The IP address used was assigned to a server in Taiwan.'

'How can that be?'

'Easy. The Internet makes the world a global market. For example, if you want to set up a website, there is no law that tells you that you have to host it in America. You can search the net for the best deal, and have your website sitting in a server absolutely anywhere – Russia, Vietnam, Taiwan, Afghanistan . . . it makes no difference. Everybody can access it just the same.'

Captain Blake thought about it for a second. 'No diplomatic relations,' she said. 'Not only does the United States have no jurisdiction, but even a diplomatic approach, such as calling the server company and asking for their help, would fail.'

'That's right. He could've also hijacked the IP address,' Baxter added. 'It's like stealing number plates from a car and putting them on yours to avoid being caught.'

'Can that be done?' Captain Blake asked.

'If he's good enough, sure.'

'So we've got nothing?'

Baxter shook his head. 'Though I have to admit that we're limited in what we can do at the Computer Crimes Unit.' He pushed his wire-rimmed glasses up the bridge of his round nose. 'Our investigations are usually restricted to crimes committed using computer-stored information, or sabotage to computer-stored information. In other words, database and information hacking – from private individ- ual computers to schools, banks and corporations. This kind of thing isn't really what we deal with.'

'Fantastic,' the captain said, not impressed.

'The FBI Cybercrime Division, on the other hand,' Baxter said, moving on, 'is a much more powerful unit. They deal with every kind of cybercrime. They even have the power and the equipment to terminate any internet transmission made from within the US territory from their office.'

Captain Blake pulled a face. 'So you're saying that we should get the FBI involved?'

It was no secret that the FBI and any police force in any American state didn't have the best of relations, no matter what politicians and heads of departments said.

'Not really,' Baxter replied. 'I was just stating a fact. There's nothing the FBI can do now. The transmission is over. The site is dead. Let me show you.' He pointed to the computer on her desk. 'May I?'

'Go right ahead.' Captain Blake pushed her chair back a couple of feet.

Baxter leaned over the captain's keyboard, typed the IP address into the Internet browser's address bar and hit the 'enter' key. It took only a few seconds for a web page to load: ERROR 404 – PAGE CANNOT BE FOUND.

'The site isn't there anymore,' Baxter said. 'I already set up a small program that carries on checking that address every ten seconds. If anything comes up again, we'll know.' His eyebrows arched. 'But if it does, maybe you should consider at least liaising with the LA FBI Cybercrime Division.'

Captain Blake scowled at him and then looked at Hunter, who remained quiet.

'The head of the unit there is a good friend of mine, Michelle Kelly. She's not your typical FBI agent. Trust me, when it comes to knowing about cyberspace, the buck stops with her. The FBI is much better equipped than the LAPD to track these kinds of cybercriminals down. Back at the Computer Crimes Unit, we liaise with them all the time. They aren't pretentious field agents in black suits, dark shades and earpieces. They're computer geeks.' Baxter smiled. 'Just like me.'

'I'd say let's cross that bridge when we get there,' Hunter replied, looking at Baxter. 'Like you've said, there's nothing they can do now, and we've got nothing to indicate that this is a federal case, so at the moment I see no point in bringing the FBI into this. At this early stage it will only complicate things.'

'I agree,' Captain Blake said. 'If at a later stage it becomes necessary that we liaise with them, we will, but for now, no FBI.' She addressed Baxter again. 'Could this transmission have been watched by anyone else, like the general public?'

'In theory, yes,' Baxter confirmed. 'It wasn't a secure transmission, meaning it didn't require a password to access the page. If anyone other than us came across that web transmission by chance, then yes, they could've watched it, just like we did. But I have to add that that is very unlikely.'

Captain Blake nodded and turned to address Hunter. 'OK, so we've got to assume this whole thing is real. My first question is – why you? The call went directly to your desk. On the phone, he asked for you by name.'

'I've been asking myself that same question, and at the moment the answer is – I'm not sure,' Hunter replied. 'There are basically two ways an outside call can end up on a detective's desk. Either the caller dials the RHD number and adds the specific desk extension when prompted, or he calls the RHD switchboard and asks to be put through to a specific detective.'

'And?'

'The call didn't come through the switchboard. I've already checked. The caller dialed my extension directly.'

'So my question still stands,' the captain pushed. 'Why you? And how did he get your extension number?'

'He could've gotten hold of one of my cards somewhere,' Hunter said.

'Or he could've called the RHD switchboard anytime before the call in question and simply asked for the extension number,' Garcia said. 'Hell, I wouldn't be surprised if he hacked into our system and obtained a list of detectives' names from there. He was bouncing his call signal around like a pro, and he had some sort of firewall good enough to stop the LAPD's Computer Crimes Unit from getting to him. My guess is that he knows his way around cyberspace.'

'I'd have to agree,' Baxter said.

'So you're saying that he could've picked Robert's name by chance from a list of all RHD detectives?' Captain Blake asked.

Baxter shrugged. 'It's possible.'

'Strange coincidence, don't you think?' the captain added. 'Given that a UV case like this would've gone straight to Robert anyway.'

Inside the Robbery Homicide Division, Hunter was part of a special branch. The Homicide Special Section was created to deal solely with serial, high-profile and homicide cases requiring extensive investigative time and expertise. But Hunter had an even more specialized task. Due to his criminal behavior psychology background, he was always assigned to cases where overwhelming sadism and brutality had been used by the perpetrator. The department referred to such cases as UV – *Ultra-Violent*.

'Maybe it wasn't a coincidence,' Baxter came back. 'Maybe he *wanted* Robert on the case, and this was his way of making sure he got him.'

Captain Blake's eyes widened a little, waiting for Baxter to carry on. He did.

'Robert's name has been in the papers and on TV plenty of times. He's worked on most of the department's high-profile cases for the past . . . I don't know how many years, and he usually gets his guy.'

Captain Blake couldn't argue with that. Hunter's name had been in the papers again just a few months ago, when he and Garcia closed the investigation into a serial killer the press had dubbed The Sculptor.

'Maybe the caller picked Robert because of his reputation,' Baxter said. 'Maybe he read his name in the *LA Times* or saw his face on the evening news.' He indicated the captain's computer screen. 'You saw the footage; you heard the call recording, right? This guy is cocky and challenging. He's daring. He stayed on the phone for that long because he knew we wouldn't be able to trace the call. He knew we wouldn't be able to track down his web transmission either.' Baxter paused and scratched his nose. 'He forced Robert to choose how the victim was going to die, for chrissakes, and then threw a twist into it. It's like he's playing a game. And he doesn't want to play it against just any detective. He wants a challenge. He wants the one the papers talk about.'

The captain thought about it for an instant. 'Great,' she said. 'That's all we need, a new psycho playing *catch me if you can.*'

'No,' Hunter replied. 'He's playing *catch me before I kill again.*'

Nine

Hunter and Garcia's office was a 22-square-meter concrete box at the far end of the Robbery Homicide Division's floor. It didn't have much more than two desks, three old-fashioned filing cabinets and a large white magnetic board that doubled up as an investigation pictures board, but it felt claustrophobic nonetheless.

Back at their desks, both detectives watched the Internet footage and listened to the telephone recording over and over again. Baxter had supplied Hunter and Garcia with a software application that allowed them to advance the recorded footage frame by frame. And that was exactly what they'd been doing for the past four and a half hours, analyzing every inch of every frame, looking for anything that could give them any sort of clue, no matter how small.

The camera work concentrated mainly on the glass enclosure and on the man inside it. Every once in a while it would zoom in onto the victim's face, or something floating on the bloody water. It had broken that pattern only once, when it panned right to show the wall clock and today's copy of the *LA Times*.

The wall was made of red bricks and mortar. It could've been anywhere – a basement, a backyard shed, a room inside a house or even a small garage in some godforsaken place.

The clock fixed to the wall was a round battery clock of about 13 inches in diameter with a black frame. It had an easy-to-read white dial with Arabic numerals, black minute and hour hands and a red second hand. There was no manufacturer's name on its face. Hunter sent a snapshot of the clock to his research team, but he knew that the chances of their linking it to a specific shop, and then identifying the buyer, were almost impossible.

The floor was nondescript and made of concrete. Again, it could've been just about anywhere.

The screen print Hunter took of his desktop came out perfect. The man sitting inside the glass enclosure was looking directly at the camera. Hunter had already emailed the picture to the Missing Persons Unit. The agent he spoke to on the phone told him that because of the gag wrapped tight around the victim's mouth, the face recognition software would only be able to analyze a limited number of facial comparison points. If the man had indeed been reported missing, it could still be enough for a match, but they had to wait and see. Hunter told the agent to search for entries dating back only a week. He had a feeling that the caller hadn't kidnapped and kept the victim for more than a day or two before throwing him into that glass tank. Victims kept in captivity for anywhere over forty-eight hours always showed signs of it – exhausted and drained face and eyes from lack of sleep, or spaced-out eyes from being doped. Personal hygiene also suffered considerably, and there were always the inevitable signs of malnourishment. The victim inside that tank had displayed none of it.

'There's nothing here,' Garcia said, sitting back in his chair and rubbing his exhausted eyes. 'There was nothing in that room except that water tank, the victim, the clock, the newspaper and the camera that broadcast the whole thing. This guy isn't stupid, Robert. He knew we would be recording the broadcast and then scrutinizing it to hell.'

Hunter breathed out before also rubbing his tired eyes. 'I know.'

'I, for one, can't watch this anymore.' Garcia got up and walked over to the small window on the west wall. 'The desperate, pleading look in the victim's eyes . . .' He shook his head. 'Every time I look at them I can feel his fear crawling up my skin like a fire centipede. And there's nothing I can do but watch him die again, and again, and again. It's screwing with my mind.'

Hunter was also sick of the footage. What really turned his stomach inside out was watching how the man's face had lit up with hope once he realized the water had stopped. And then, just a minute later, how his eyes burned with terrifying dread, as the liquid surrounding his whole body started burning and eating away at his skin and flesh. Hunter could pinpoint the exact moment the man gave up the fight, as he finally understood that he would never be getting out of there alive. The killer was just toying with him.

'Did you pick up anything from his tone of voice or something?' Garcia asked.

'No. He was calm throughout the whole conversation, except for when he yelled at me to make a choice. Other than that there were no angry bursts, no overexcitement, nothing. He was always in control of his emotions and of the conversation.' Hunter leaned back on his chair. 'But there's one thing that bothers me.'

'What's that?'

'When I told him that he didn't have to do that.'

Garcia nodded. 'He said that he knew he didn't, but he wanted to. He said that it would be fun.'

'That's right, and that could indicate that the victim was nobody in particular. Probably a complete random choice.'

'So this guy is just another fucking psycho, killing people for kicks.'

'We don't know yet,' Hunter replied. 'The problem is -when I told him that I couldn't make a decision because I didn't know why the victim was being held captive, the caller told me that that was something I would have to find out for myself.'

'And?'

'And that would indicate that the victim *wasn't* a totally random choice. That there was a specific reason why he was chosen, but he wasn't about to tell us.'

'So he's literally fucking with us.'

'We don't know yet,' Hunter said again before pushing himself away from his desk, checking his watch and letting out a deflated breath. 'But I'm through with this as well.' He powered down his computer. The same helpless feeling that had overtaken him when he was watching the live broad-cast returned, burning an empty hole inside his chest. There was nothing else they could squeeze out of that Internet footage or audio recording. Right now, all they could hope for was some sort of development from the Missing Persons Unit.

Ten

Hunter sat in the dark, staring out the living-room window of his small one-bedroom apartment in Huntington Park. He lived alone – no wife, no kids, no girlfriends. He'd never been married, and the relationships he had were never long term. He had tried in the past, but being a detective with the Homicide Special Section in one of the most violent cities in America had a way of taking its toll on any relationship, no matter how casual.

Hunter had another sip of his strong black coffee and checked his watch – 4:51 a.m. He'd managed only four hours of sleep, but for him that was as close to sleeping bliss as he could ever get.

Hunter's battle with insomnia had started very early in his life, triggered by the death of his mother when he was only seven. The nightmares were so devastating that as a self-defense mechanism his brain did all it could to keep him awake at night. Instead of falling asleep, Hunter read ferociously. Books became his refuge, his castle. A safe place where the ghastly nightmares couldn't breach the gates.

Hunter had always been different. Even as a child he could solve puzzles and work out problems faster than most adults. It was like his brain was able to fast-track just about anything. In school, his teachers had no doubt he wasn't like most students. At the age of twelve, after being put through a series of exams and tests suggested by Doctor Tilby, Hunter's school psychologist, he was accepted into the Mirman School for the Gifted as an eighth-grader, two years ahead of the usual age of fourteen.

Mirman's special curriculum didn't slow Hunter down. Before the age of fifteen, he had glided through their entire program, condensing four years of high school into two. With recommendations from all his teachers, and a special mention from Mirman's principal, he was accepted as a 'special circumstances' student at Stanford University. Hunter decided to study psychology. By then his insomnia and nightmares were relatively under control.

In college, his grades were just as impressive, and Hunter received his PhD in Criminal Behavior Analysis and Biopsychology just before his twenty-third birthday. The head of the psychology department at Stanford University, Doctor Timothy Healy, made it clear that if Hunter ever showed interest in a teaching position, there would always be a place on his staff for him. Hunter respectfully declined, but said that he would keep it in mind. Doctor Healy was also the one who forwarded Hunter's PhD thesis paper entitled *An Advanced Psychological Study in Criminal Conduct* to the head of the FBI National Center for the Analysis of Violent Crime. To this day, Hunter's paper was still mandatory reading at the NCAVC and at its Behavioral Analysis Unit.

Two weeks after receiving his PhD, Hunter's world was rocked for the second time. His father, who at the time was working as a security guard for a branch of the Bank of America in downtown Los Angeles, was gunned down during a robbery that had escalated into a Wild West shoot-out. Hunter's nightmares and insomnia came back with a vengeance, and they had never left him since.

Hunter finished his coffee and placed the cup down on the window ledge.

It didn't matter how tightly he closed his eyes or ground his fists against them, he couldn't shut down the images that had been eating away at him since yesterday afternoon. It was like he'd memorized every second of the footage, and someone had turned on the *endless loop* switch inside his head. Questions were being lobbed at him from every corner of his mind, and so far he hadn't come up with a single answer. Some of them bothered him more than others.

'Why the torture?' he whispered to himself now. He understood very well that it took a certain type of individual to be able to torture another human being before killing him or her. It might sound simple but, when the time comes, very few were ever able to go through with it. One needed a level of detachment from regular human emotions that few can achieve. The ones who can are referred to by psychologists and psychiatrists as *psychopaths*.

Psychopaths show no empathy, or remorse, or love, or any other emotion associated with caring for someone else. Sometimes their lack of feelings can be so severe that they will display none toward even themselves.

The second fact that was digging around in Hunter's mind like a bulldozer was the *choice game*. Why did the killer go through the tremendous trouble of creating a torture chamber capable of two horrific deaths – either by fire or water? And why call him on the phone, or anyone else for that matter, and ask them to make that choice?

It wasn't uncommon for a murderer, even a psychopath, to doubt his decision to kill someone right at the last minute, but that didn't seem to have been an issue with this killer. He had no doubt the victim would die; he just couldn't make up his mind on which was worse – burned to death or drowned. Two opposites of sorts. Two of the most feared ways a person could die. But the more Hunter thought about it, the more stupid he felt. He was sure he had been tricked.

He knew that there was no way the caller had that amount of sodium hydroxide sitting around for no reason at all. It had all been part of the game. He had said so himself. He was expecting Hunter to pick water instead of fire, for all the exact reasons he had mentioned over the phone – it was a kinder, less sadistic and faster way of ending the victim's suffering. But water would've also preserved the state of the body, and in case they came across it anytime soon, a forensics team would have a much better chance of finding a clue, if one was to be found. Fire, on the other hand, would've simply destroyed everything.

Hunter ground his teeth in anger and tried in vain to fight the guilt that was nibbling away at his brain. There was no doubt in his mind that the caller had played him. And Hunter hated himself for not foreseeing it.

The ringtone from Hunter's cellphone dragged him away from his thoughts. He blinked a couple of times as if waking up from a bad dream and looked around the dark room. The cellphone was on the old and scratched wooden dining table that doubled up as a desk. It rattled against the table-top one more time before Hunter got to it. The call display window told him it was Garcia. Reflexively Hunter checked his watch before answering it – 5:04 a.m. Whatever it was, Hunter knew it wouldn't be good news.

'Carlos, what's up?'

'We've got the body.'

Eleven

At five forty-three in the morning the back alley in Mission Hills, San Fernando Valley, would've still been cloaked in darkness, if not for the flashing blue lights of three squad cars and a pedestal-mounted power light from the forensics team.

Hunter parked his old Buick LeSabre by the single lamp-post at the entrance to the alleyway. He stepped out of the car and stretched his six-foot frame against the morning wind. Garcia's metallic-blue Honda Civic was parked across the road. Hunter took a moment to look around before entering the back alley. The lamppost's old bulb was yellow and weak. At night, if you weren't looking for it, it would've been very easy to miss the alleyway. It was located behind a quiet road of small shops, away from the main streets.

Hunter zipped up his leather jacket and slowly started down the alleyway. He flashed his badge at the young officer standing by the yellow crime-scene tape before ducking under it. He saw light fixtures above some of the shops' back doors, but none was on. There were a few plastic and paper bags scattered around, a few empty beer and soda cans, but other than that the back street was tidier than most he'd seen in downtown LA. The second half of the alleyway was lined with big metal dumpsters, four in total. Garcia, two forensics agents and three uniformed officers were gathered just past the third dumpster. At the end of the alleyway a bedraggled, dirt-strewn black man of indistinct age, whose wiry hair seemed to explode from his head in all directions, was sitting on a concrete step. He seemed to be mumbling something to himself. Another police officer was standing a few feet to his right, one hand cupped over his nose, as if protecting himself from a violating smell. There were no CCTV cameras anywhere.

'Robert,' Garcia said as he spotted his partner walking toward him.

'What time did you get here?' Hunter said, noticing his partner's strawberry-pink-rimmed eyes.

'Less than ten minutes ago, but I was awake when I got the call anyway.'

Hunter's eyebrows arched.

'I had zero sleep,' Garcia explained and pointed to his head. 'It's like I've got a cinema in here. Now, guess which movie has been playing on my screen all night.'

Hunter said nothing. He was already looking past Garcia's shoulder to the commotion around the third dumpster.

'It's our victim,' Garcia said. 'No doubt about it.'

Hunter stepped closer. The three officers nodded 'good morning', but no one said a word.

Mike Brindle, the forensics agent in charge, was kneeling down by the dumpster, collecting something from the ground with a tiny pair of tweezers. He paused and stood up when he saw Hunter.

'Robert,' he said with a nod. They'd worked together on more cases than they could remember.

Hunter returned the gesture, but his focus was on the naked male body on the ground. He was lying on his back, between the third and fourth dumpsters. His legs were stretched out. His right arm was by the side of the body, bent at the elbow. The left one was resting casually on his stomach.

Hunter felt his throat constrict a little as he looked at the man's face.

There was none – no nose, no lips, no eyes. Even his teeth seemed to have rotted and corroded away. The eyeballs were still in their sockets, but they looked like punctured, half-full, silicone bags. In fact, the skin around his whole body seemed to have been sandpapered away. But the exposed flesh didn't look red-raw. It had a pink-gray tone to it. Though shocking, it didn't surprise Hunter that much. The alkaline bath had, in a way, cooked his flesh.

Hunter stepped a little closer.

The body had no fingernails or toenails left.

Despite the total disfigurement, Hunter had little doubt it was the same man they'd seen yesterday on their computer screens. When the man had finally died, his lifeless head fell forward, submerging his face into the alkaline mixture, but not his entire head. His short brown hair was almost intact.

'He's been dead for several hours,' Brindle said. 'The body is in full rigor mortis.'

'Three twenty-six yesterday afternoon,' Hunter said.

Brindle frowned at him.

'He died at three twenty-six yesterday afternoon,' Hunter repeated.

'Do you know him?'

'Not exactly.' Hunter looked up. The three police officers nearby had moved back to the crime-scene tape. Hunter quickly gave Brindle a summary of what had happened the day before.

'Jesus,' Brindle said when Hunter was done. 'That would explain the grotesque disfigurement to the body, and the odd change of color to his flesh.' He shook his head, still shocked by what Hunter had just told him. 'So you were not only made to watch, but he forced you to choose the death method as well?'

Hunter nodded in silence.

'And you have the whole thing digitally recorded?'

'Yes.'

With heavy eyes, Brindle looked down at the tortured body again. 'I don't understand this city, or the people in it anymore, Robert.'

'I don't think any of us do,' Hunter replied.

'How can anyone make sense of something like this?'

Hunter kneeled down to better examine the body. With the strong forensic light, every detail was visible. The smell was already crossing the line into putrid meat territory. Hunter used his left hand to cover his nose. He noticed little dents on the man's feet, legs and arms. 'What are these?'

'Rat bites,' Brindle said. 'We had to scare a few off the body when we got here. There's quite a bit of food in these dumpsters. This back alley services a bakery, a butcher's shop and a small coffee shop stroke diner.'

Hunter nodded.

'We're going to sieve through most of the trash inside all four dumpsters in case the killer decided to discard something around here,' Brindle said. 'But after the story you told me, he doesn't sound like he would be that careless.'

Hunter nodded again. His gaze moved over to the black man at the end of the alley. He was dressed in ripped and stained clothes, and wearing an old, colorless long coat that looked to have survived an attack from a pack of hungry wolves.

'His name is Keon Lewis,' Brindle offered. 'He's the one who found the body.'

Hunter stood up, ready to go ask some questions.

'Good luck with that,' Brindle said. 'You know how homeless people love talking to the cops.'

Twelve

Keon Lewis was still sitting on the concrete step at the far end of the alleyway. He was about six foot four and stick-thin. His raggedy black beard seemed to be irritating his face no end. He would scratch it vigorously every few seconds. He had grimy, broken fingernails packed with dirt. His hands were scarred and blistered. One of them had a cut that seemed infected, the skin tender and swollen around a deep maroon scab. His eyes would gaze back at the scene every so often, but he would quickly pull them away and stare down at the ground or at his hands.

Hunter approached Keon and the officer standing by his side. Keon looked up, but again quickly averted his gaze. He rubbed his hands together like a cook seasoning a dish.

His lips were dry and cracked, and he kept on blinking as if he were wearing old, dry contact lenses. The physical signs all pointed to crystal meth addiction. He could've been in his thirties, forties, fifties or early twenties. Hunter doubted Keon knew himself.

'Keon?' Hunter said. 'I'm Detective Robert Hunter with the Homicide Division.'

Keon gave him a tense nod but still kept his eyes low.

The officer stepped away, giving Hunter and Keon some privacy.

'Listen,' Hunter said in a calm, non-patronizing voice. 'There's no need for you to be nervous. No one is here to hassle you, I promise. Unfortunately you were unlucky enough to find the body of a homicide victim. My job is to ask you a few questions, that's all. After that, you're free to go.'

Keon scratched his beard again.

Hunter could tell that his face had once been kind and attractive, but drug abuse, alcohol and a life lived well below the poverty line had transformed it into something very different.

'OK if I sit down?'

Keon scooted over to the edge of the step. His clothes stank of stale sweat and garbage.

Hunter sat down and let out a deep breath. 'This is some messed-up stuff, isn't it?'

'Shiiit, man, that is real fucked up.' His voice croaked as if he had a sore throat. 'What the fuck happen to him, man? Someone skinned him?'

'You really don't want to know,' Hunter said.

Keon picked at the loose skin at the back of his hand, twisting it painfully, as if trying to tear it off before going quiet for a moment. 'Say, man, you don't have a smoke, do you? I'm shaking like a bitch.'

'I'll get you one.' Hunter motioned the officer to come closer and whispered something in his ear. The officer nodded and took off toward the other end of the alleyway.

'This is a very quiet street,' Hunter said. 'Do you come here a lot?'

'Sometimes. If I'm close enough,' Keon replied, giving Hunter a sequence of quick nods. 'That's the reason I come here, you know what I'm sayin'? Because it's quiet. You don't have to fight to get a spot to crash. And sometimes you get some good food from the dumpsters, you dig? The food shops throw things away that you wouldn't believe, man.' Keon smiled a mouth full of decaying teeth. 'You have to fight off the rats, but, hey, it's free.'

Hunter gave him a sympathetic nod. 'Can you run me through what happened when you got here?'

'Oh man, I already told the cops everything.'

'I understand, and I know it's a pain in the ass. But it has to be done, Keon.'

The police officer returned with a pack of cigarettes and a box of matches and handed them to Keon. He quickly tapped one out, lit it up and took a drag so long the officer thought he would smoke the whole thing in one breath.

Hunter waited for him to exhale. 'You can keep the pack.'

Keon wasted no time in placing it inside his right coat pocket.

'So, can you tell me how you came across the body?'

Keon shrugged. 'Sure.'

'Do you know what time it was when you got here?'

Another shrug. Keon pulled back his left sleeve and showed Hunter his naked wrist. 'My Rolex is in the shop.'

The corner of Hunter's mouth curled up slightly. 'Could you take a guess? Were all the shops already closed?'

'Oh yeah, y'all. It was late, man. Long past midnight. I walked all the way from Panorama City, and it took me a while 'cos I've got a bad foot, you know what I mean?' Keon pointed down to his left foot. He was wearing a dirty old leather Nike sneaker. There was a large hole on the left side where Hunter could see two of his toes. The shoe on the right foot was a black Converse All Stars.

'Cops don't never come down here, you know what I mean?' Keon continued. 'So you never get poked or kicked while you're sleeping and told to move on. You can get a good few hours of sleep back here, and don't nobody bother you, you dig?'

Hunter nodded. 'So what happened?'

Keon took another drag, let the smoke out through his nose and nervously watched it dance in front of his face for a while. 'I never saw him until I got real close. The alley was dark, you dig? I came up to the first dumpster and checked inside. It's usually the one with the best food because the bakery dumps their scraps in there. I got me a nice piece of cornbread.' As he said that, a thunderous rumble came from Keon's stomach. He ignored it and took another drag of his cigarette. 'But before I could have a bite of any of it, I saw this pair of legs sticking out from behind one of the dumpsters. I thought it was just another brother crashing out, you know what I mean? There's enough space here for more than one, you dig?'

Hunter was attentively observing Keon's movements and expressions. His hands had begun shaking again once he started telling his story. The croak in his voice had worsened a touch. His eyes had trouble focusing anywhere for too long – a symptom of drug dependency – but the jitter in them was genuine fear.

'I thought maybe it was Tobby or Tyrek,' Keon continued. 'They crash here every once in a while too. But when I got close—' Keon scratched his beard as if it were burning his face. 'Holy shit, man, what happened to him?' His scared eyes met Hunter's. 'He's got no face. He's got no skin.' He finished his cigarette in one massive drag and stubbed it out under his shoe. 'I've seen a lot of crazy shit in my life, y'all. I've seen a few dead bodies too, but that—' his head jerked toward the dumpsters '—that's the devil's work, man.'

'Was he covered?' Hunter asked. 'By newspapers, or a piece of cloth, or something?'

'Nah, y'all. He was just lying there like a big piece of gooey meat, you know what I'm sayin'? Scared the shit out of me, man. Even the rats were half scared of it.'

'Did you see anybody else around?' Hunter asked.

'Hell no. The alley was empty.'

'Any cars parked close by, maybe around the entrance to the alleyway?'

Keon paused, his brow furrowed a little and he ran his tongue over his cracked bottom lip.

'Was there a car around?'

'Well, when I came around the corner, a truck was backing up from the alley.'

'A truck?'

'Yep, more like a pickup truck, you know the type? But it wasn't open-back. It had a hardtop over the back box.'

'Did you notice what type of truck it was?'

'Nah, man. I wasn't that close. As I said, I had just turned the corner when I saw the truck backing up and taking off.'

'How about color?'

Keon thought back for a second. 'It was a dark truck. Maybe black or blue. Hard to say from a distance. The lighting around here ain't that good, you know what I'm sayin'? But there was a big dent on the back fender. I remember that.'

'A dent? Are you sure?'

'Um-huh. I saw it as the truck backed up from the alley, on the driver's side.'

'How big a dent?'

'Big enough for me to see it from that far.'

Hunter took some notes. 'Did you get to see the driver at all?'

'Nah, y'all. Dark windows.'

'Could you tell if the truck was old or new?'

Keon shook his head. 'I can't really say, but I don't think it was an old truck.'

Hunter nodded. 'OK, let's move on. So what did you do when you saw the body on the ground? Did you touch it at all?'

'Touch it?' Keon's eyes went wide. 'Are you high, man? Can I have some? Keon ain't no fool, y'all. I didn't know what was wrong with the stiff. It could be a sickness or somin'. Some weird shit like "AIDS of the skin" or some new disease created by the government, you know what I mean? Like an experiment or somin'. Either that or the devil really is walking the streets, skinning motherfuckers, erasing their faces and dumping them in back alleys.' Keon reached for another cigarette. 'No, man, I didn't touch no dead body. I just dropped everything and got the fuck out of here, grabbed a payphone out in the streets and dialed 911.'

'You dialed 911 as soon as you saw the body?'

'That's right, y'all.'

Keon's stomach roared again. He lit up his cigarette, took another long drag and paused, looking a little hesitant. Hunter noticed it.

'Something else, Keon?'

'Well, I thought that maybe ... you know ... there was some sort of reward, or somin'. I did good, didn't I? Calling y'all down here? Remembering the truck and all.'

And that explained how come Keon was cooperating so freely.

'Yes, Keon, you did good, but there's no reward. I'm sorry.'

'Oh, c'mon, man. Nothin'?'

Hunter gave him a slight headshake.

'Shiiit, man. That ain't fair. Couldn't you help a brother out with somin'? I could do with a little help, you know what I'm sayin'?'

Another loud, longer rumbling of his stomach.

'When was the last time you had a proper meal, Keon?'

'You mean a full meal?'

Hunter nodded.

Keon chewed his lips for a moment. 'Not for some time, man.'

'OK, look. I'm not going to give you any money, but if you're hungry—' Hunter nodded at Keon's stomach '—and I can hear you are, breakfast is on me. How about that?'

Keon scratched both sides of his beard while chewing his lips again. 'C'mon, y'all. Just twenty bucks, man. Twenty bucks is nothing for y'all.'

'No money, Keon, sorry.'

'Ten, then. You can spare a brother ten bucks, can't you?'

'Breakfast, Keon. That's the best I can do.'

Keon looked down at his hands, considering. 'Can I have hot pancakes?'

Hunter smiled. 'Yes, you can have hot pancakes.'

Keon nodded. 'Yeah, breakfast sounds good, y'all.'

Thirteen

Despite having the body, Hunter and Garcia were no closer to finding the victim's identity. His entire skin had dissolved in the alkaline solution, and that meant no fingerprints, no identifying tattoos or birthmarks, if there were any, and absolutely no facial features. DNA analyses would take a few days, but even then they would only have a match if the victim's DNA had been archived into CODIS, the FBI's Combined DNA Index System, and for that to have happened the victim would've had to have been previously convicted of a felony offense such as sexual assault or homicide – a very long shot. They were also still waiting for any news from the Missing Persons Unit.

By early afternoon Mike Brindle and his forensics team had collected a small bag of hairs, fibers and debris that could prove to be of interest, but in an alleyway with four large dumpsters, all of them packed full with several days' worth of trash from a number of different establishments, no one was holding their breath for a breakthrough.

Hunter told Brindle about the pickup truck Keon Lewis had seen backing up from the alleyway. Brindle said that they had already come across two sets of tire prints. The first, and more prominent of the two, came from what looked like large, heavy-duty tires. The best impressions were just by the first dumpster. Brindle's opinion was that the prints were left by one or more of the city's garbage trucks on collection day. Hunter figured he was right, but the lab would have to confirm that.

Brindle's team had gotten lucky about halfway down the alleyway, where they found a second, very faint, partial tire mark, courtesy of a small pothole with just enough dirty water to get a section of the tire wet. The partial print didn't look to have come from a large and heavy vehicle such as a garbage truck. The problem was that by the time they found it, most of the impression had evaporated under the Los Angeles morning sun, but with the help of a special powder and a large sheet of black gelatin lifter, they were able to obtain traces of it. They hoped it would be good enough for the lab to get them something.

Hunter checked with Central Operations. Keon's 911 call came in just before one in the morning. Hunter allowed two hours either side of that mark and contacted the Valley Bureau's Traffic Division, asking them for whatever footage they might have from any road cameras surrounding the area from 11:00 p.m. to 3:00 a.m. They were still waiting on it.

'OK,' Garcia said, hitting the 'print' button on his computer. Hunter was at his desk, studying the photographs from the alleyway. He put them down and looked across his desk at his partner.

'Sodium hydroxide, or caustic soda, can be bought in four main formats,' Garcia explained. 'Pallets, pearls, flakes or liquid. Because one of its main uses is as a cleaning agent, it can be easily found and purchased over the counter and Internet in a range of grades and pack sizes. Many vendors

will sell it to pretty much anyone, no ID check necessary.'
Garcia got up and walked over to the printer in the corner
of the room. 'Actually, you can even find bottles of caustic
soda in supermarkets. It's also present in many cleaning
products, including drain unblockers and floor and oven
cleaners.' He handed the printout to Hunter. 'This thing is
way too easy to obtain. This is a dead path.'

As Hunter took the sheet, the phone on his desk rang.

'Detective Hunter, Homicide Special,' he answered it and
listened for a few seconds. 'On our way.' He put the phone
down and nodded at Garcia. 'Let's go.'

'Where?'

'The morgue. Doctor Hove is done with the autopsy.'

Fourteen

The drive to the Los Angeles County Department of Coroner in North Mission Road took them less than twenty minutes. Hunter and Garcia made their way up the lavish steps that led to the main entrance of the architecturally impressive building and approached the reception counter. The attendant, a large, kind-faced black woman of about fifty, gave them the same sympathetic smile she reserved for everyone who came through the doors of the old hospital turned morgue.

'Good afternoon, Detectives,' she said in a voice that seemed to have been trained in a library.

'How are you doing, Sandra?' Hunter smiled back.

'I'm well, thank you.' The question wasn't returned. Sandra had learned a long time ago never to ask anyone entering a morgue how *they* were doing. 'Doctor Hove is waiting for you in Autopsy Theater One.' With a subtle head gesture she indicated the swinging double doors to the right of the reception.

Hunter and Garcia pushed through them and carried on down the long, squeaky-clean white corridor. At the end of it they turned left into a shorter hallway, where an orderly wheeling a body on a gurney covered by a white sheet was coming their way. One of the two fluorescent ceiling lights was malfunctioning, flickering on and off at odd intervals. The scene reminded Hunter of some B-rated horror movie.

Hunter pinched his nose as if he was about to sneeze. The smell of the place got to him every time. It was like a hospital's, but with a different punch to it. Something that seemed to claw at the back of his throat and slowly burn the inside of his nostrils like acid. But today the overpowering smell of disinfectant and cleaning products was churning his stomach even more. It was like he could smell the sodium hydroxide in them. Garcia seemed to have picked that up too, judging by the look on his face.

Another left turn and they were at the door to Autopsy Theater One.

Hunter pressed the intercom button on the wall and heard static crackle from the tiny speaker. 'Doctor Hove?' he called.

The heavy door buzzed and unlocked with a hiss like a pressure seal. Hunter pushed it open and he and Garcia stepped inside the large and winter-cold room. Its walls were tiled in brilliant white. Its floor was done in shiny vinyl. Three stainless-steel autopsy tables sprang out of a long counter with oversized sinks that ran along the east wall. On the ceiling, above each table, was a circular island of surgical lights. Metal crypts took up two walls and looked like large filing cabinets with bulky handles. The Chief Medical Examiner for the Los Angeles County Department of Coroner was standing at the far end of the room.

Doctor Carolyn Hove was tall and slim with penetrating green eyes and long chestnut hair that she usually kept in a ponytail, but today it was rolled up into a simple bun. Her surgical mask hung loosely around her neck, revealing full

lips with just a touch of pink lipstick, prominent cheekbones and a petite, delicate nose. Her hands were tucked
into the pockets of her white lab coverall.

'Robert, Carlos,' she greeted each detective with a nod.
Her voice was velvety but firm, the kind that was always in
control.

Both detectives returned the gesture in silence.

'Mike told me the whole story,' Doctor Hove said. 'So the
killer called your office and made you watch?' She moved
toward the autopsy table closest to her. The other two were
mercifully empty.

Hunter and Garcia followed.

'Made us choose how the victim would die first,' Garcia
replied.

'Any idea why?'

'We're working on it.'

'Mike also told me that the killer created some sort of . . .
torture chamber?'

'Something like that,' Hunter answered.

'You can watch the footage if you like, Doc,' Garcia said.
'Maybe you can pick up something that we missed.'

She gave them a hesitant nod. 'Sure, if you send it to me,
I'll have a look.'

There was a moment of silence before their attention
moved to the corpse on the steel table. The skinless and
faceless victim lay there like an androgynous creature.
Nothing more than a distorted lump of flesh. The infamous
Y incision, decorated by thick, black stitches, now added
one more layer of grotesqueness to the body.

Doctor Hove put on a new pair of latex gloves, switched
on the lights on the island overhead and looked down at the
victim. 'All these years as a forensics doctor and I still don't

understand it. How can a person do this to another human being?'

'Some people are capable of worse, Doc,' Garcia replied.

'As far as pain goes, there isn't anything worse, Carlos.' Her tone sent a chill up Garcia's spine. 'Sodium hydroxide is a strong base substance,' she explained. 'It sits right at the opposite end of the pH scale from strong acids like sulfuric and hydrochloric. Everyone knows what sort of damage strong acids can do if they came in direct contact with human skin, right? But what few people are aware of is that strong bases, like sodium hydroxide, are over forty times more painful and destructive to the human body than strong acids.'

Garcia's eyes widened. 'Forty?'

Doctor Hove nodded. 'Sulfuric acid feels like lukewarm water when compared to sodium hydroxide. What this killer has done was create an alkali bath with the victim in it.' Her eyes returned to the body on the table. 'For him, it was like he was being burned alive, but his brain would've carried on working for longer ... a lot longer, so he felt every single burning pain that happened to his body. The solution ate through the two first layers of his skin in absolutely no time.'

'And then the real pain started,' Hunter said in a subdued voice.

'That's right,' Doctor Hove agreed.

Garcia looked a little doubtful.

'The main reason why sodium hydroxide is used in so many industrial cleaning products,' the doctor explained, 'is because of its incredible ability to dissolve grease, oils, fats and protein. The third layer of the human skin, the subcutaneous, is made mostly of fat. When that's gone, you get muscle tissue, which is made mostly of protein. Are you starting to get the picture now?'

Garcia cringed.

'Add to that the fact that the alkalosis in the solution would've kept overexciting the nerves, causing them to become terribly inflamed, and you have every single nerve in his body screaming in agony. The pain causes all the major muscles to spasm, lock and cramp. If he weren't tied down in a sitting position, he would've probably broken his spinal cord from contorting. And his brain was still working, registering everything as his body literally dissolved, layer by layer.'

'I think I get the picture now, Doc, thanks,' Garcia said, looking green.

'Luckily for him,' the doctor said. 'His heart gave up the fight early.'

'Not early enough,' Hunter said. 'He was in that alkali bath for eleven minutes before he died.'

Doctor Hove agreed, tilting her head to one side. 'Still, his heart gave in faster than it should have. Have you identified him yet?'

'We're still working on that,' Hunter said.

'So this might help.' She retrieved a document from the counter behind her and handed it to Hunter. 'The reason his heart failed earlier than a healthier one would have was because he suffered from mitral stenosis, which is a narrowing of the mitral valve in the heart. This forces the heart to work harder to pump blood from the left atrium into the left ventricle. With the immense pain he was put through, his heart would've had to speed up to supply his body with more blood. Because of his condition, his heart was fatally overworked sooner.'

'How much sooner?' Garcia asked.

'I'd say about forty to fifty percent.'

'He could've lasted double what he did?'

The doctor nodded. 'A healthier person like you probably would.'

Garcia shook away the chilling sensation that trickled down the back of his neck.

'A person with his condition would, most probably, be checking in with a cardiologist every few months just for precaution,' Doctor Hove said.

'Thanks, Doc,' Hunter said. 'We'll start checking right away.'

'Unfortunately the body is a forensics black hole,' the doctor concluded. 'If there were anything to be found, the sodium hydroxide ate it away. Not even bacteria would've survived.' She coughed to clear her throat. 'If you are considering looking at this from a drug angle, I can tell that he wasn't a drug user, or if he was it was purely recreational and he hasn't touched anything in at least a week.'

Hunter knew that would be the case, but he sensed a flicker of hesitation in the doctor's demeanor. 'Is there something else, Doc?'

'I'm confused about something,' she said. 'Even though the victim went into cardiac arrest quicker than a person with a healthier heart would have, the sodium hydroxide solution should've carried on eating away at the tissues and dissolving his body until there was nothing left. It didn't. It stopped just as it was reaching muscle tissue.'

'Just as he died,' Hunter said.

'I would say so, yes. Which suggests the killer emptied the torture tank and got the victim out of there as soon as he passed away.'

'That's probably what he did,' Hunter agreed.

'But why? And why dump the body in an alleyway? If the killer had left the victim in the tank it would've dissolved the body. Evidence problem solved. Why give the police something to work with?'

'Because the killer wants to make sure we take him seriously,' Hunter replied. 'Without a body, we have no proof that what we saw over the Internet wasn't just a graphics trick.'

'Or someone acting it out,' Garcia added. 'The water inside the tank went bloody really quick, Doc. All we could see was the victim's face, nothing else. We assumed he was in tremendous pain, that his body was dissolving, but it could've been somebody acting it out, playing a big "you-got-punked" hoax on the LAPD.'

'The intention was also for the body to be found fast,' Hunter said. 'Hence the location where it was dumped – a back alleyway used by several shops. Garbage collection was today, early morning. I'm sure the killer knew that.'

'So he gives you the body to prove that the whole thing wasn't staged,' Doctor Hove said.

'That's the idea,' Hunter confirmed. 'Because now we know he's for real.'

Fifteen

Christina Stevenson opened the door to her single-story house in Santa Monica and switched on the lights. The brightness that flooded her living room made her wince, and she quickly used the dimmer to bring the intensity down. Her headache had started in the middle of the afternoon, and after several long hours in front of her computer screen it had now reached torturing phase.

She placed her bag on the floor by the door and rubbed her tired blue eyes for a moment. It felt as if her brain was melting inside her skull. Headache pills had had no effect. What she needed was a long shower, a large glass of wine and a lot of rest.

'*Actually,*' she thought better of it, '*champagne would be much more appropriate.*' After all, all the effort she'd put into her work in the past few weeks had finally paid off.

In the now dim light of her living room, her eyes found the portrait of her mother on the shiny black console by the window, and she gave a smile full of sadness.

Christina had never met her father, and she never wanted to. She had been conceived in the men's restroom of a nightclub in West Hollywood. Her mother was drunk. The guy she had sex with was high on drugs. They had met that night. He was good-looking and charming. She was lonely. After they left the restroom, she never saw him again.

When Christina was old enough to understand, her mother told her the whole story. She also told her that she couldn't even remember his name. But her mother wasn't a bad person. Against all her friends' advice, she decided not to have an abortion. She had her baby daughter, and she brought her up on her own, in the best way she could. She saved every spare cent, and when Christina graduated from high school her mother had enough put away in a savings account to send her daughter to university. When, four years later, Christina received her diploma, there was no one prouder in that graduation ceremony than her mother.

That same night, her mother died in her sleep from a brain aneurysm. That had been seven years ago. Christina still missed her like crazy.

Christina walked into her open-plan kitchen and checked the fridge. She had a bottle of Dom Ruinart 1998 she'd been keeping for a special occasion. Well, this sure as hell was one. She pouted her lips, pondering.

'*Should I open it or not?*'

It seemed a shame that she had no one to share it with.

Christina wasn't married, and though she'd had plenty of affairs and flings, she wasn't seeing anyone at the moment. She thought about it for a second longer and decided that right now there was no one she would've wanted to share that bottle of champagne with anyway. She reached for it, undid the wire seal and popped the bottle open.

Christina had been told plenty of times that good wines needed to breathe. She had no idea if the same applied to champagne, but she didn't care either. She poured herself a glass and had a large sip – heaven. Her headache was already starting to fade.

Kicking off her shoes, Christina crossed the living room and took the corridor that led deeper into the house, and to her bedroom at the end. Her room was large and a lot more girly than she would like most people to know. Pale peach walls were complemented by a light pink ceiling skirting. Long floral curtains covered the glass sliding doors that led to her backyard and swimming pool. A pink dresser, complete with a mirror and dressing room-style lights, sat in the corner of the room. Her king-size bed, pushed up against the north wall, was overflowing with cushions and stuffed toys.

Christina placed her glass and the champagne bottle on the bedside table, attached her MP3 player to the portable stereo on the dresser and started dancing to the sound of Lady Gaga while undressing. Off came the shirt, followed by her jeans. She returned to her champagne and poured herself another glass, drinking half of it down before pausing in front of the mirrored wardrobe doors. The champagne was starting to have the desired effect, and she began dancing again while undoing her bra and slipping off her purple panties. Naked, she ran her hands over her breasts, pulled a sexy pose and blew herself a kiss in the mirror before bursting into laughter.

She unclipped the clasp on her diamond Tag Heuer watch, a present from an old lover, and as she pulled it off her wrist it dropped to the floor, hit her foot and slid under her bed.

'Damn, that hurt,' she said, bending over to massage her right foot. Without looking, she quickly swept a hand under the bed. Her fingers found nothing. 'Shit.'

Christina got down on her hands and knees and brought her face about an inch from the floor.

'There you are.'

The watch had slid toward the wall against the head-board. To reach it, she had to slide halfway under the bed. As she did, for no reason at all, her gaze wandered across the floor to the other side, and all the way to the glass sliding doors and the bottom edge of her long floral curtains. And that was when she saw them.

A black pair of male shoes with their heels pushed tight against the glass door.

Shock and fear caused her eyes to slowly glide up the curtains, and she noticed that at that exact spot the folds didn't sit right. For Christina, the next few seconds passed in slow motion. Her gaze moved up a little more before stopping dead.

From inside her room, through the break in the curtains, someone was staring straight back at her.

Sixteen

After managing four and a half consecutive hours of sleep, fantastic by his standards, Hunter got to his office at 8:10 a.m. Garcia was already at his desk reading through all the overnight emails – nothing interesting.

Hunter had taken off his jacket and powered up his computer when the phone on his desk rang.

'Detective Hunter, Homicide Special.'

'Robert, it's Mike Brindle. I've got the result from that partial tire print we got in the alleyway.'

'Anything good?'

'Well, we've got a match.'

'I'm listening.'

'The print came from a Goodyear Wrangler ATS tire. Specifically, a P265/70R17.'

'And that means . . .?'

'That we've got a common pickup truck tire,' Brindle explained. 'The ATS range is used by several truck manu-facturers as the original equipment tire on new vehicles. The one in question has been used by Ford for their F-150 and F-250 trucks for the past four years, and by Chevrolet for their Silverado for the past three.'

'Damn!'

'Yep, I've asked someone to check. Even with the

recession, in the whole of the USA Ford sold about 120,000 F-150 and F-250 trucks in the past year alone. Chevrolet sold around 140,000 Silverados. What percentage of those is dark in color, or has been purchased in California, is something you and your team will have to find out.'

'We'll get on to it,' Hunter said. 'I'm guessing that those tires aren't very hard to come by either.'

'That's problem number two,' Brindle told him. 'They're readily available, which means that anybody with an older or even a different brand of truck could drive into a shop and equip their trucks with those specific tires. But they're an expensive option, so chances are most people would go for a cheaper make if they are buying new tires for an older truck.'

Hunter nodded in silence.

'Now, as you will remember, the back alley was a black-top,' Brindle carried on. 'Which makes finding things like footprints a lot harder, but with the help of some special lighting we managed to find a few. They belong to at least eight different people.'

'*Not surprising*,' Hunter thought, given that that alley-way serviced several different shops.

'But a couple of them were very interesting.'

'In what way?' Hunter asked.

'They were found just by the space between the third and fourth dumpster, where the body was found. The prints came from a size eleven shoe. Keon Lewis, the only other person we know who had walked around that same area, is a size thirteen. The left shoeprint seems to be more promi-nent than the right shoe one. That could indicate that the person walked with a slight abnormality, like a limp, depos-iting more of his weight onto his left leg.'

'Or that he was carrying something heavy,' Hunter said.

'That's what I was thinking.'

'Probably over his left shoulder. Not in his arms.'

'Precisely,' Brindle agreed. 'He gets the body out of the car, throws it over his left shoulder and carries it to the space between the dumpsters.' Brindle breathed out. 'Now, the victim was quite a large man.'

'216 pounds,' Hunter said.

'Well, carrying 216 pounds over one of your shoulders isn't for just anyone, Robert,' Brindle said. 'The guy you're looking for is big and strong.'

Hunter said nothing.

'In the alleyway he was also very careful,' Brindle continued. 'Though we found footprints, we got nothing from the sole. No kind of imprint whatsoever.'

'He covered his shoe,' Hunter concluded.

'Yep. Probably with a plastic bag. I've also got toxicology for you.'

'Wow, that was fast.'

'Nothing but the best, my friend.'

'Was the victim drugged?'

'Anesthetized,' Brindle said. 'Traces of an intravenous anesthetic – phenoperidine – were found. It's a strong opioid, and with a little research you would find several illegal drugstores willing to sell it to you over the Internet.'

'*The wonders of the modern age,*' Hunter thought. 'You said traces?' he queried.

'Yep, almost negligible. If I had to guess, I'd say the killer used it only to subdue the victim for a short period of time. Probably during the abduction process. After the killer had the victim in a safe location, the anesthetic wasn't re-administered.'

He scribbled something down on a notepad.

'We've also got the results from the voice analysis done on your telephone conversation with the killer,' Brindle said, moving on. 'It seems that he was filtering and refiltering his voice several times over, only slightly altering the pitch each time. Sometimes higher, sometimes lower. That's why, even with the electronic variation, the voice still sounds so normal, so human, but nevertheless unrecognizable if you were to unknowingly have a conversation with him out on the streets.'

Hunter said nothing in reply. From the corner of his eye Hunter saw Garcia's face light up as he read something on his computer screen.

'Anyway, I'm emailing you all the results we've got so far,' Brindle said. 'If anything more comes up from the fibers and hairs, I'll let you know.'

'Thanks, Mike.' Hunter put the phone down.

Garcia hit the 'print' button.

'What's up, Carlos?'

Garcia collected the printout and showed it to Hunter. It was a black and white portrait of a white male in his mid to late twenties. His light brown hair was short and messy. His face was round with chubby cheeks, a prominent forehead and thin eyebrows. His eyes were dark and almond shaped. On the portrait he had a bit of a spaced-out look on his face.

Hunter's eyes widened. He would've recognized that face anywhere. He'd stared at it for hours on end. He watched him die again and again. There was no doubt in his mind. He was staring at a photograph of their victim.

Seventeen

Hunter finally blinked.

'Where did you get this?'

Garcia had handed the printout to Hunter and was already back at his computer, reading the email he'd just received.

'Missing Persons. They just sent it over.'

Hunter's eyes returned to the photograph.

'He was reported missing on Wednesday,' Garcia said. 'It took the Missing Persons' face recognition program until this morning to partially match that picture to the snapshot we sent them.'

'Who was he?'

'His name was Kevin Lee Parker, twenty-eight years old, from Stanton, in Orange County. He was currently residing in Jefferson Park with his wife, Anita Lee Parker. She was the one who reported him missing. He worked as a manager in a videogames shop in Hyde Park.'

'How long was he missing for?'

Garcia scrolled down on the attached file that had come with the email. 'Since Monday. That was the last time his wife saw him. Monday morning, when he left for work. He didn't go back home that evening.'

'But she only reported him missing on Wednesday,' Hunter said. 'Two days ago.'

Garcia nodded. 'That's what it says here.'

'Do we know if he turned up for work on Monday?'

A little more scrolling. 'According to his wife, yes. She called the shop on Tuesday morning and they said that he did turn up for work the day before.'

'But not on Tuesday?'

'No.'

'Does he have a cellphone?'

'Yes. Ms. Lee Parker has been calling it since Monday evening. No answer.'

Hunter checked his watch. 'OK, let's get the research team to run a check on Mr. Lee Parker's name. Usual stuff: all the background they can get.'

'They're already on it,' Garcia said.

'Great,' Hunter said, reaching for his jacket. 'Let's go talk to Mrs. Lee Parker.'

Eighteen

Jefferson Park, with its single-story homes and low-rise apartment buildings, was a small district in southwestern Los Angeles. It had begun as one of the city's wealthiest areas at the turn of the twentieth century. As the city grew, and newer, more modern neighborhoods were created, wealth started to abandon the area. A century on and Jefferson Park had become just one of many lower-middle-class neighborhoods in a city that never seemed to stop growing.

At that time in the morning the traffic on Harbor Freeway was a bumper-to-bumper snail procession, and what should've been a ten to fifteen-minute drive took the best part of forty-five minutes.

Kevin Lee Parker's street looked like a suburban post-card. Set back, single-story houses lined both sides of a road where tall trees shadowed the sidewalks. His house was white with blue windows, a blue door and a two-way pitched terracotta roof. The white picket-style fence that surrounded the property looked like it had received a new coat of paint recently. The front lawn, though, could've done with a trim. Two young kids were riding their bicycles up and down the street, incessantly ringing their handlebar bells. As he stepped out of the car, Hunter noticed a neighbor from the next house along studying them over her pristine hedge.

The short walkway from the wooden gate to the front door of Kevin Lee Parker's house was old and paved with cement-colored blocks. Several of them were cracked. Some were missing one or two corners.

They got to the porch and Garcia knocked three times – nothing for a long moment. He was about to knock again when the door was finally opened by a plump woman in her early twenties. Her disheveled hair was dark and short, her face round and meaty. She had a baby propped on her hip. She looked exhausted, and her eyes had the gritty red tint of someone who'd been crying, or had had very little sleep, or both. She just looked at the two detectives without saying a word.

'Ms. Lee Parker?' Hunter asked.

She nodded.

'My name is Robert Hunter. I'm with the LAPD. We spoke earlier on the phone.'

Anita Lee Parker nodded again.

'This is my partner, Detective Carlos Garcia.' They both showed her their credentials.

The baby girl in her arms smiled at them and moved her right hand, as if wanting to greet both detectives. Looking at the tiny baby, Hunter smiled back, but inside him his heart sank.

'You find Kevin?' Anita asked in an anxious voice. She had a strong Puerto Rican accent.

'Could we maybe talk inside, Ms. Lee Parker?' Hunter suggested.

For a moment she seemed confused, as if she hadn't understood him. Then she took a step to her left and showed them inside.

The front door led them straight into a small living room. On one corner, a portable fan stirred the air, which was heavy with the smell of baby stuff. A three-seat sofa and two armchairs were draped with multicolored sheets that looked like patchwork quilts straight out of the Deep South. A large picture of Jesus decorated one of the walls, and family portraits were scattered around the room. Anita was so nervous she didn't offer anyone a seat.

'You find Kevin?' she asked again. Her voice almost faltering. 'Where is he? Why he no call me?'

Anita already seemed on the verge of a breakdown. Hunter had been in that situation too many times before to know that he needed to extract whatever information he could out of her before she went hysterical.

The baby in her arms was starting to sense her mother's anxiety. She had gone from smiling to frowning, on the verge of crying.

'Anita,' Hunter said warmly, indicating the sofa. 'Why don't we all have a seat?'

Again, she looked at him as if confused. 'Don't want no seat. Where's Kevin?'

The baby girl started kicking her legs and flapping her arms. Hunter smiled at her again. 'What's her name?'

Anita looked down at her daughter with tender eyes and started rocking her. 'Lilia.'

Another smile. 'That's a beautiful name. And she's a beautiful baby, but because you're upset she's getting upset, see? Babies can sense these things better than anyone, especially from their mothers. If you have a seat, it will help Lilia feel more comfortable. And so will you.'

Anita hesitated.

'Please.' Hunter indicated the sofa again. 'Just try it. You'll see.'

Anita placed Lilia's dummy in her mouth. '*No llores, mi amor. Todo va a estar bien.*' The baby took the dummy and Anita finally took a seat. Hunter and Garcia took the armchairs.

Lilia settled into a comfortable position in her mother's arms and closed her eyes.

Hunter took that opportunity to fire a question before Anita could fire hers again.

'You said that the last time you saw Kevin was on Monday, is that right?'

Anita nodded. 'In the morning. He ate breakfast and left for work, like every morning.'

'And he didn't come home that night?'

'No. That was not so strange before, but since Lilia was born he no play late no more.'

'Play late?' Garcia asked.

Anita chuckled nervously. 'Kevin is a big *niño*. He works in games shop because he love games. He always playing games like a child. Before Lilia was born, many nights he stay in shop after work, playing games on Internet until morning with work friends. But he always called me to say he be playing. But now that we have Lilia, he doesn't play late no more. He's a good father.'

Garcia nodded his understanding.

'He didn't call you on Monday night?' Hunter asked.

'No.'

'Did you call him?'

'Yes, but he no answer phone. Message said phone not 'vailable.'

'What time was that, can you remember? What time did you call your husband?'

Anita didn't have to think about it. 'Not late. Around eight thirty. Kevin is never late home. He is usually back from work by eight o'clock.'

Hunter wrote that down.

'Did you talk to any of his work colleagues from the shop? Was he at work on Monday?'

'Yes. I call the shop Monday night. After I tried calling Kevin. No answer. Nobody there. I call the *policia* at eleven, but they didn't care. A cop came by at around one in the morning, but he just said I had to wait. Maybe Kevin would be back home in the morning. Morning came and Kevin not home. Then I call shop again. Talk to Emilio. Emilio is a good friend. Old friend. He said Kevin worked on Monday, but no stay after work to play Internet games. He said they closed the shop at seven and Kevin left. I called police again, but they still didn't care. They say Kevin was not a child. They had to wait one or two days before they could do anything.'

Hunter and Garcia knew that to be true. In America, any adult has the right to go missing if he or she wants to. Maybe they don't want to see their wife or husband for a day or two. Maybe they just need a break from everything. It was their prerogative. California's Missing Persons' protocol dictated that they should wait between twenty-four and forty-eight hours before filing a missing persons' complaint for anyone over the age of eighteen.

Hunter took some more notes. 'Does Kevin drive to work?'

'No, he takes bus.'

'Did you, as a family, have any financial problems?' Garcia asked.

'Financial?'

'Money problems,' Garcia clarified.

Anita shook her head vigorously. 'No. We pay everything on time. We don't owe nobody no money.'

'Did Kevin?' Garcia pursued it. 'Did he gamble?' He noticed her confused look and clarified again before she could ask. 'Bet ... *apuesta*. Did he bet ... on horses, or Internet poker or anything?'

The face Anita pulled was as if Garcia had bad-mouthed her entire family. 'No. Kevin is a good man. A good father. He's a good husband. We go to church every Sunday.' She indicated the portrait of Jesus on the wall. 'Kevin likes videogames, like boom, boom, boom, shoot monsters.' She used her thumb and index finger to create an imaginary gun. 'Shoot soldiers in war, you know? But he's no betting *chico*. *Él no apuesta*. Just like to play. We save all the money we can – for Lilia.' She looked down at her daughter, who was still happily sucking on her dummy. 'His heart is not so good, you know? He takes medicine. Doctor said he has to be careful. He is scared he won't see Lilia grow up, so he saves for her future.' Anita's eyes started to fill with tears. 'Something is wrong. I know it. Kevin always call. There was no bus accident. I checked. This neighborhood very dangerous. This city very dangerous. People think LA is all about Hollywood and big life, you know? It's not.' A tear ran down her cheek. 'I'm scared. Kevin and Lilia is all I have. My family is in Puerto Rico. You have to find Kevin for me. You have to.'

Hunter's heart sank for the second time, and he felt something tighten inside his chest because he knew there was nothing he could do. It was time to tell Anita the truth.

Nineteen

Hunter and Garcia sat in silence inside Garcia's car for a long moment. Having to break the news to somebody as vulnerable as Anita that her husband had been taken by a psychopath, that his body had been almost dissolved in an alkali bath, and that baby Lilia would never see her father again had a way of rattling even the most experienced of detectives.

At first Anita just stared at them, as if not a single word they'd said had registered. Then she started laughing. Loud, hysterical laughs, as if she'd heard the world's funniest joke. Tears streamed down her face, but the laughter carried on. Then she told them that they had to leave because her husband was due home at any minute. She had things to do before he got back. She wanted to prepare him his favorite meal, and then he would sit and play with his daughter like he did every night. Anita was shaking as if feverish when she closed the door on them.

Hunter left without saying another word. In his career he had seen the most diverse grief reactions: a mother who sincerely believed her son had been abducted by aliens rather than accept the fact that he'd been stabbed thirty-three times simply for walking down a neighborhood wearing the wrong colors; a new doctor, fresh out of med school, who lost all memory of his young wife rather than recall the night their house was broken into by four men, who tied him up and made him watch as they showed her absolutely no mercy. When reality becomes too senseless to make sense, the human mind will sometimes create its own.

Hunter would immediately request that a city psychologist got in touch with Anita. She would need all the help she could get.

Someone from the forensics office would also visit Anita in the next day or so. They would need a mouth swab, or a hair sample from her baby daughter. Hunter and Garcia were certain the victim was Kevin Lee Parker, but protocol required positive identification. With the body's grotesque disfigurement, Anita would never be able to identify it down at the County Coroner's. Positive identification would have to be made by DNA analyses.

'Shit!' Garcia said, resting his head against the steering wheel. 'We're looking for another I-don't-care-who-the-fuck-I-kill murderer.'

Hunter just looked at him.

'You just saw the victim's house. There's no wealth. You met his wife and daughter – simple everyday people. OK, we have to wait for whatever the research team can dig out on Kevin Lee Parker, but does any of what we know or have seen about his life so far strike you as anything other than ordinary?'

Hunter said nothing.

'I'll be surprised if the team finds even a parking ticket on him. He was just a young family man trying to get by, trying to build some sort of a future for his wife and daughter before his faulty heart gave up.' Garcia shook his head. 'I don't think Kevin Lee Parker became a victim because of money, or debt, or drugs, or revenge, or anything. He was just picked at random out of the general public by a sadistic maniac. It could've been anyone, Robert. He was at the wrong place at the wrong time.'

'You know we can't be sure of that at this point, Carlos.'

'Well, that's my gut feeling, Robert. This isn't about the victim. It's about the killer showing off on a God power trip. Why build that torture chamber? Why call us and stream the execution live over the Internet for us to watch, as if it were a goddamn killing show? You said so yourself, the whole setup behind this is too bold, too complex – a phone call that bounces all around LA, not the world or even America, just LA, but an Internet transmission that seemed to have originated in Taiwan?'

Hunter had no reply.

'This guy just wants to kill. Period. Who he kills makes no fucking difference to him.'

Hunter still said nothing.

'You were right in your assessment,' Garcia continued. 'If we don't stop this guy soon, Kevin Lee Parker won't be the only victim we're going to find. He's just going to pick someone else at random off the streets, put him in that torture chamber and start the nightmare again. Maybe Baxter is right. Maybe this psycho is playing a game. Showing off how sick and creative he can be at the same time. You're the psychologist here, what do you think? I must say that when he was talking to you on the phone, I had never heard anyone sound so cold and without emotion. The victim's life meant absolutely nothing to him.'

Garcia had picked up the exact same apathy in the caller's voice as Hunter had. There was no anger, no revenge tone, no satisfaction, no amusement, nothing. The caller had dealt with taking a life in the same way a person would deal with opening a tap and filling a glass with water. Hunter and Garcia both knew that that was the worst type of killer any detective could be faced with. The one to whom it seemed that nothing mattered. Killing was just a game.

Twenty

Hunter and Garcia drove straight to the Next-Gen Games Shop in Hyde Park where Kevin Lee Parker used to work. According to Anita, Kevin's best friend was another employee of the same store – Emilio Mendoza.

The videogames shop occupied a double corner unit in a small shopping mall in Crenshaw Boulevard. At that time in the morning business was slow, with only a handful of kids browsing the shelves.

'Excuse me,' Hunter said, grabbing the attention of a shop assistant who was reorganizing a couple of displays at the front of the shop. 'Could you tell me if Emilio is working today?'

The man's stare slowly zigzagged between both detectives for a brief moment.

'I'm Emilio,' he said, placing one last game on the shelf and offering them a cheesy smile. 'How can I help you today?' His Puerto Rican accent was subtle, charming.

Emilio looked to be in his early thirties, with a heavy and oddly shaped body – round and bulbous around the shoulders and stomach, a little like a child's party balloon that had been squeezed into shape. He had short dark hair and a thin, perfectly groomed mustache.

'We're with the LAPD,' Hunter said, displaying his credentials. Garcia did the same. 'Is there a place where we could talk with a little more privacy?'

Emilio shifted on his feet uncomfortably. His quizzical gaze started bouncing between both detectives again.

'It's about Kevin Lee Parker,' Hunter clarified, but Emilio seemed to become even more confused.

'Is Kev OK?'

Hunter's eyes circled the shop before returning to Emilio. 'Maybe we should talk back at the parking lot?' he suggested, jerking his head to one side.

'Yeah, sure.' Emilio nodded and turned to address the tall and skinny assistant behind the counter. 'Frank, I've gotta take a ten-minute break. Will you be OK?'

Frank's eyes lingered on the two men with Emilio for a quick moment. 'Yeah, I'll be fine.' He nodded. 'Is everything all right?'

'Yeah, we're all good. I'll be back in ten.'

Emilio followed Hunter and Garcia back to the parking lot. 'Kevin isn't OK, is he?' he asked once they reached Garcia's car. Hunter detected real fear in his voice.

'When was the last time you saw Kevin?' Garcia asked.

'Monday,' Emilio replied. 'He was working Monday. He was supposed to be working every day this week, but he didn't turn up on Tuesday morning, or any day after that. Anita, his wife, called me on Tuesday morning. Kev didn't go home on Monday night. She said that she had called the police, but they didn't pay her much attention.'

'What time did he leave work on Monday, do you know?' Hunter asked.

'Yes, same time as always,' Emilio said. 'He closed the shop at around 7:00 p.m., as he does daily. We usually walk up to the bus stop on Hyde Park Boulevard and 10th Avenue together, but on Monday evening I decided to grab dinner at Chico's, just around the corner.' Emilio pointed east. 'I asked Kev if he wanted to come along, but he said that he just wanted to go home and play with his daughter.'

'Do you know if he made it to the bus stop?'

'I don't.' Emilio's response was followed by a headshake.

'On Monday, did Kevin look or sound different in any way?' Garcia asked. 'Nervous, anxious, agitated, worried, scared . . . anything?'

Emilio pulled a face as if that was the strangest question in the world.

'No. Kev was . . . ' He shrugged. 'Kev. Always smiling. Always happy. Nothing different about him at all.'

'Was he a gambler of some sort?'

Emilio's eyes widened and he chuckled nervously. 'Kevin, a gambler? No way. He was into videogames and online gaming, more specifically "Call of Duty – Modern Warfare, Black Ops 2" and "Ghost Recon", but that was it. No casino games. Kev wouldn't throw money away like that.'

'How long have you known each other?' Hunter asked.

Emilio gave them an uncertain headshake. 'A long time. Over fifteen years. We met in lower school back in Gardena. Kev is the one who got me this job two years ago, after he became shop manager. I was struggling, you know? I was laid off a few years back and couldn't get a job nowhere. Kev is a real friend . . . my best friend.'

'So you don't think that he was in any sort of trouble?' Garcia asked.

'I don't think so. Look, if Kev is in any kind of trouble . . . anything, really, he would've told me, I'm sure of it; if not,

I would've picked it up anyway. He isn't very good at hiding things. He's a very average guy, quite shy sometimes. He loves his family, and he loves his job. There really isn't that much more to him. Something must've happened. And I mean something bad, you know what I'm saying? I'm telling you, he wouldn't just take off. He has no reason to. He's not a heavy drinker or anything, and I know he doesn't sleep around.' Emilio paused and looked back at both detectives, now visibly shaken. 'Something did happen to Kevin, didn't it? That's why you're here. You're not from Missing Persons.'

'No, I'm afraid we're not,' Garcia replied.

Twenty-One

It was twenty-eight minutes past five in the afternoon when Hunter finished going through the road camera footage he was sent by the Valley Bureau's Traffic Division. The closest, constant recording traffic camera to the alleyway in Mission Hills, where the victim's body had been found, was just shy of a mile away, on the intersection of two major freeways – San Diego and Ronald Reagan – an escaping man's dream. The problem was the killer didn't have to take any of those freeways at that junction. He didn't have to take a freeway at all. He could've easily gone from one side of LA to the other via city streets, where the largest majority of traffic cameras were activated only if you broke the speed limit or drove through a red light. He could've dropped the body in that back alley and driven all the way across town without a single camera ever picking him up.

Nevertheless, Hunter sped through four hours of traffic footage, spotting thirty-seven pickup trucks joining one of the two freeways at that junction. Twenty-one of them were dark in color, but none of them seemed to have a dented back fender. Hunter passed the license plate number of all thirty-seven vehicles to his team, just in case Keon had been wrong. He didn't want to leave anything to chance.

'I told you we wouldn't get anything out of the ordinary,' Garcia said, walking back into the office. He had a file in his hands. 'Kevin Lee Parker was your everyday John Doe. A simple guy, with a simple life. He's never been arrested. Always paid his taxes on time. He's not a homeowner; he rents. We contacted his landlord. Only once, about two years ago, Kevin wasn't able to pay his rent on time. It was just after his wedding and he was a little low on his finances. Anyway, he was only late by a couple of weeks. The landlord said that he was an upstanding guy.'

Hunter nodded and leaned back in his chair.

'Kevin grew up in Westlake, where he went to school. His school records were average. Not the best of students, but not the worst either. He never went to university. Kevin had a series of odd jobs all over the place – waiter, supermarket attendant, warehouse clerk . . . ' Garcia made a hand gesture indicating that the list went on and on. 'He started working for Next-Gen Games Shop in Hyde Park five years ago, and took the manager's position three years later. He married Anita around the same time. They'd been going out together for five years then. His daughter, Lilia, was born six months ago.'

Garcia had to clear his throat as the memory of the smiling baby in her mother's arms came back to him.

'It sounds like he was a very careful person too.' He moved on. 'As we found out, he had a heart condition – mitral stenosis. He was conscientious enough never to abuse it. No strenuous exercise, never smoked, apparently no drugs either. He was part of a healthcare plan, but it doesn't look like it was a great one. He still had to cough up a little more money every time he saw a doctor. And that's why in the last five years he'd been to see a cardiologist only twice

– Doctor Mel Gooding. His practice is in South Robertson. We can drop by tomorrow morning.'

Hunter nodded.

'As Emilio told us earlier today, Kevin didn't have a vast circle of friends. His life was centered around his family and his job; that was it. Emilio was his best friend.' Garcia flipped a page on the report before carrying on. 'We should have a statement on his latest bank transactions by tomorrow morning. Nothing yet from his cellphone or web provider, but hopefully we'll get something in a day or two.'

'Any news on the bus?' Hunter asked.

Garcia nodded. 'Kevin used to take a bus on route 207 back home. It goes from Athens to Hollywood. There were six drivers driving that route for the LA Metro on Monday evening. I've got all their names here. Four are working tonight. The other two will be in tomorrow morning.' He quickly consulted his watch and handed the report to Hunter. 'It's your call. But we can be at the depot in an hour or so and check with the four drivers working tonight if any of them remember seeing Kevin on their bus on Monday evening.'

Hunter was already out of his chair. 'Let's go.'

Before he got to the office door, his cellphone rang in his pocket. He checked the caller display window – unknown number.

'Detective Hunter, Homicide Special,' he answered it.

'Hello, Detective Hunter,' the caller said in the same raspy voice and calm tone as two days ago.

The way Hunter looked at Garcia suppressed the need for any words.

'No way,' Garcia said, hurrying back to his desk. Within seconds he was on the phone to Operations. 'I need you guys to try to trace a phone call that's being made to Detective Robert Hunter's cellphone, right now.' He gave them the number.

'How did you get this number?' Hunter asked and pressed the loudspeaker button on his phone so Garcia could hear it as well.

The caller laughed. 'Information, information, Detective Hunter. It's all out there. You just have to know how to grab it. But guess what?' There was a hint of amusement in his voice.

'You called me to give me your name and address?' Hunter said.

The caller laughed more animatedly this time. 'Not quite, but I do have something for you.'

Hunter waited.

'Your favorite website is back online.'

Twenty-Two

Hunter's eyes immediately sought the phone on his desk. He knew that Dennis Baxter at the LAPD Computer Crimes Unit was still tracking that infamous IP address. If the website was back online, he should've picked it up. There were no lights flashing on his desk phone. No calls.

Hunter moved purposefully toward the computer on his desk and brought up his browser application. He still remembered the IP address. He typed it into the address bar and hit 'enter'.

ERROR 404 – PAGE CANNOT BE FOUND.

Hunter frowned.

'This time I decided to do things a little differently, Detective,' the caller said. 'You were no fun the first time around, refusing to choose until I picked *fire*. And even then you tried to trick me. I didn't like that very much. So I've been thinking. You don't get to choose anymore. I decided to expand.' A short, tense pause. 'Have you seen any of those reality TV shows where the public get to vote for which artist they like best?'

Hunter felt adrenaline rushing through his body.

'Detective?' the caller insisted.

'No, I haven't watched any of them.'

'But you are aware that such shows exist, right? C'mon, Detective, I thought you were supposed to be an informed man.'

Hunter said nothing.

'Well, I decided that it would be real fun if I turned this into a web show.'

Hunter looked at Garcia, who had just typed the old IP address into his address bar and gotten the error page too.

'Are you at your office?' the caller asked.

'Yes.'

'OK. I want you to check this website out. Are you ready for it?'

Silence.

'www.pickadeath.com.' He chuckled. 'Isn't that a great name?'

Hunter and Garcia both quickly typed the address into their address bars and hit the 'enter' key.

The screen flashed once. The website loaded in three seconds flat.

There was nothing on the screen. It was completely dark. Hunter checked the web address again to see if he had mistyped it. He hadn't.

Garcia looked up from his screen, lifted both of his palms up in frustration and shook his head. His screen was also dark.

'Do you have it?' the caller asked.

'I've got nothing but a dark screen,' Hunter replied.

'Patience, Detective Hunter. You have the right page.'

Suddenly, in the top left-hand corner of the screen, three small white letters appeared – SSV.

'What the hell?' Garcia sighed.

Hunter squinted at the letters, as his brain searched for a meaning. He looked at Garcia and shook his head. 'I don't think it's a chemical formula this time,' he whispered.

Then, in the top right-hand corner, three small white numbers appeared – 678.

'Do you see it now?' the caller asked.

'I see it,' Hunter said calmly. 'What does it mean?'

The caller chuckled. 'You'll have to figure that out for yourself, Detective. But that is secondary. Here's the main attraction.'

All of a sudden, darkness dissipated from the screen. The familiar green tint of images being broadcast through night-vision lenses took over.

Hunter and Garcia were expecting to see the same reinforced glass structure they saw just a couple of days ago. They were expecting to see a new victim tied down to a metal chair and stripped of his clothes. They were expecting the caller to play the same sadistic game he did the first time around – a choice between drowning and burning the victim alive.

That was not what they saw.

What they saw chilled them even further to the bone.

Twenty-Three

Michelle Kelly, the head of the FBI Cybercrime Division in Los Angeles, sat behind her computer screen, typing frantically on her keyboard. Standing behind her, reading every word she typed, was Harry Mills, a Cybercrime Division agent and engineering genius. He'd joined the FBI CCD three years ago, after obtaining his PhD with honors in Electrical Engineering and Computer Science from the Massachusetts Institute of Technology in Cambridge.

Michelle and Harry had been involved in a sting operation for seven months now. They'd been tracking a serial pedophile, who'd been grooming ten to thirteen-year-olds via Internet chat rooms for years. The guy was a real scumbag. He knew how to identify the lonely kids. The ones who felt they didn't fit in. The outcasts. The vulnerable. He was very patient. He would chat with them for months, gaining their trust. At first he would tell them he was thirteen, but as their virtual relationship strengthened, he would reveal he was in his early twenties and that he was a university student. The truth was, he was in his late thirties.

He was always charming, understanding, supportive and very flattering, and to any teenage girl who felt she was misunderstood by everyone, including her parents, that was a very powerful wall breaker. It worked every time, and soon they'd be infatuated with someone they'd never met. After that, it was almost impossible for them to say no to a meeting.

To the FBI's knowledge, he'd seduced and had sex with six girls so far. Two of them were only ten.

But this predator was far from dumb. He was also very good with computers. He was always mobile. He used a laptop, and he only chatted from free Wi-Fi spots, like cafés, bars and hotel lobbies. He never purchased a Wi-Fi connection password, either hijacking them from other users or hacking the system. Most free Wi-Fi spots aren't best known for their unbreachable Internet security.

He also kept on jumping from chat room to chat room, sometimes even creating his own. He used different aliases, and he never chatted for more than ten to fifteen minutes at a time.

Four months ago, almost by chance, Michelle found him chatting out of a chat room set up in Guatemala. The FBI CCD had run hundreds of these operations. They all knew that the easiest way to reel these types of sickos in was to fool them into believing they were chatting with a potential victim. Michelle jumped at the chance, and in a blink of an eye she became 'Lucy', a thirteen-year-old girl from Culver City. He bought it, and they'd been chatting almost every day since. He'd been using the alias 'Bobby'.

'Bobby' was indeed very charming and supportive. It was very easy for Michelle to see how any teenage girl with low self-esteem would be completely swept off her feet by 'Bobby'.

'Lucy' and 'Bobby' had been talking about a meeting for weeks now, and yesterday morning 'Lucy' finally gave in. She told him that she could skip school on Monday. She'd done it before. They could meet somewhere not too far, and spend the day together, but they had to be careful. If her parents found out, she would be in a lot of trouble. 'Bobby' promised her that they would never find out.

Right now, they'd been chatting for seven minutes, making the final arrangements for where and when they'd meet on Monday.

'*We could meet in Venice Beach,*' Michelle typed. '*Do u know it?*'

'*Yes, of course I know it [smiley face],*' 'Bobby' replied.

Venice Beach was just a bus ride away from Culver City. It was a wide-open space where the FBI could easily set up long-distance cameras with powerful lenses, and pack the entire area with undercover agents and dogs.

'*[Smiley face] I can meet u there at 10,*' Michelle typed. '*Do you know where the sk8 park is?*'

'*I do. By the sk8 park sounds great. Can't w8.*'

'*[Smiley face with a tongue out] But I have to b back home b4 3, or else I'll b in BIG trouble.*'

'*Don't worry, Lucy,*' 'Bobby' replied. '*No one will know. It will be our little secret [face with a zipped-up lip].*'

'*K. LOL. Bye, Bobby. C U Monday.*'

'*[Four smiley faces] C U Monday, Lucy xxx.*'

They disconnected.

'Urghhhh,' Michelle said, rolling her chair back from her desk and shaking her arms in the air as if having a seizure. She always did that when she disconnected from a chat with 'Bobby'. 'What a fucking creep.'

Harry smiled. 'Are you OK, though?'

She nodded. 'I'm fine. I'm glad that this one is coming to an end.'

'You can say that again.'

'I want to be there on Monday. I want to look straight into his eyes when they cuff this sack o' shit,' Michelle said.

'You and me both.'

'I want to see the look on his face when he finds out I'm "Lucy".'

'Um, Boss, can you come and have a look at this?' Another CCD agent, who'd been monitoring some of their web crawlers, called from his desk.

'What is it, Jamie?' Michelle replied.

'I'm not sure, but I'm pretty certain you're going to want to see it.'

Twenty-Four

The woman looked to be in her early thirties, with long, straight, dyed blonde hair, which looked damp, probably from sweat. Her oval-shaped face was accented by plump lips and deep-set blue eyes that had undoubtedly been crying. There was a small black mole just below her bottom lip, at the right-hand corner of her mouth. She was average size and had nothing on except for a pair of purple panties and a matching bra.

Garcia felt his heartbeat pick up speed.

The woman looked absolutely petrified. Her eyes were open as wide as they would go, moving constantly, as if searching for something. She kept on turning her head from side to side, clearly trying to understand where she was, or what was happening to her. Her lips were trembling and it looked like she was having trouble breathing. She seemed to be lying down, but her movements were limited, not because she was tied up, but because she was locked inside a confined enclosure. Some sort of transparent box made out of glass, or Perspex, or a similar material. But it was much smaller than the one the killer had used for the first victim. The woman only had about five inches of space on each side, and maybe three inches above her head.

'Is she in a glass coffin?' Garcia looked at Hunter, who gave him an almost imperceptible shrug.

Hunter quickly opened the screen recording application he had asked IT to install on his computer and started recording the broadcast.

If the glass coffin was lying flat on the floor, the camera streaming the images seemed to be directly above it, positioned at a slight diagonal angle. But they could only see down to her waist. Her legs didn't make the shot.

Panic erupted inside the woman and she started to frantically hammer her fists and seemingly kick her feet against the glass walls, but they were way too thick for her feeble efforts to make any impression. She was screaming as loud as she could. The veins on her neck looked like they were about to pop, but neither Hunter nor Garcia could hear a sound.

'What is this?' Hunter asked, pointing at his screen.

Only then Garcia noticed the end of what looked like a large dark tube, about five inches in diameter, attached to one of the sides of the glass box.

Garcia squinted at his screen. 'I don't know,' he finally said. 'Ventilation, maybe?'

'OK,' the caller said, his voice booming out of the speakerphone and filling the room with even more tension. 'What do you say we get this little show started, Detective? But this time the rules have changed. Keep your eyes on the screen.'

Suddenly the word GUILTY appeared in capital letters, centralized at the bottom of the image. A second later, about halfway down the right-hand edge of the screen, the word BURIED appeared, followed by the number zero and a green button. Directly underneath it, the word EATEN appeared, also followed by the number zero and a second green button. At the top of the screen, the letters SSV and the number sequence 678 flickered twice like a warning before disappearing.

'What the hell is going on?' Garcia asked.

Hunter almost stopped breathing. 'It's a vote.'

'What?'

The caller laughed. He could hear them talking to each other. 'Wow, you're very quick on the uptake, Detective Hunter. Your reputation is well deserved. It *is* a vote. Because this time we are live over the internet.'

Garcia ran an anxious hand through his long hair.

'I gave it some thought,' the caller carried on. 'And decided that this would be much more fun if we allowed others to participate, don't you think? So today, anyone watching out there can vote. All they have to do is click a button.' He paused for effect. 'And this is how it's going to work, Detective: the first of the two death methods to reach a thousand votes wins. That sounds like fun, doesn't it?'

'Why are you doing this?' Hunter asked.

'I just told you. Because it sounds like fun, don't you agree? But I'll tell you what, Detective Hunter: to make this even more fun, I'll give her a chance to live. Let's make this into a race against the clock, what do you say? If I don't get a thousand votes for one method in ... let's say ... ten minutes ... I give you my word that I will set her free, unharmed. How does that sound?'

Hunter breathed out.

'I think that sounds like a pretty fair deal, don't you?'

'Please don't do this,' Hunter pleaded, but the caller simply ignored him.

'Would you like to be the first one to vote, Detective Hunter?' The caller laughed, not waiting for an answer. 'I didn't think so. But there's hope for her yet. The site has just gone online. Maybe no one will see it, or even if they do, maybe no one will vote. Who knows? But at least we're about to have ourselves ten very exciting minutes.'

In the bottom left-hand corner of the screen a blue digital clock appeared and began counting down – 10:00, 9:59, 9:58 . . .

Suddenly the zero under the word BURIED changed to 1, and then very quickly to 2.

The caller laughed loudly. 'Oops, that wasn't me. I promise you. I'm not cheating. I guess the race is on.'

The line went dead.

Twenty-Five

Hunter immediately reached for the phone on his desk and called Dennis Baxter at the LAPD Computer Crimes Unit. He answered it after the second ring.

'Dennis, it's Robert Hunter in Homicide Special. The website is back online.'

'What?'

Hunter heard a hurried shuffle followed by keyboard clicks.

'No, it's not,' Baxter replied.

'He's not using the same IP address. He's got a web domain this time.'

'You're kidding.'

'www.pickadeath.com.'

More keyboard clicks. Hunter heard Baxter breathe out heavily.

'Sonofabitch.' Baxter paused a beat. 'What the hell is all that on the screen?'

As quickly as he could, Hunter explained what he knew.

'So if he gets a thousand votes in ten minutes she's either going to be BURIED alive or EATEN alive?'

'That's what I gathered,' Hunter replied.

'Eaten by what?'

The number besides the word BURIED reached 22. EATEN was at 19.

'Don't think about that right now,' Hunter replied. 'Click whatever buttons you need to click. Do whatever you need to do. Trace this transmission or find a way to interrupt it so people can't vote. Call your buddies at the FBI Cybercrime Division, I don't care what you do, but get me something.'

'I'll do all I can.'

The countdown clock on the bottom left-hand side of the screen read 8:42, 8:41, 8:40 . . .

BURIED – 47.

EATEN – 49.

'This is just fucked up,' Garcia said, running both hands through his hair.

The woman in the box was sobbing so heavily it looked like she was running out of air. She had stopped hammering the glass walls with her fists and feet, and had started clawing at them like a crazed animal. Blood smears started to color the glass.

A moment later she gave up and brought her bleeding and trembling hands to her face. Her lips started moving, and though Hunter could lip-read, everyone watching could easily understand what she was saying.

'HELP ME. HELP ME.'

'C'mon,' Hunter said through gritted teeth. 'Hang in there.' Both of his hands had locked into tight fists.

CLOCK – 7:05, 7:04, 7:03 . . .

BURIED – 189.

EATEN – 201.

'How is this happening?' Garcia asked, shaking his hands in the air. 'How are people coming across this website so fast?'

Hunter just shook his head. His eyes were glued to his screen, his expression grave.

Without knocking, Captain Blake opened Hunter and Garcia's office door and stepped inside. 'Did you guys get . . .' She paused mid-sentence as she saw the way they were both staring at their computer screens. 'What's going on?' She started moving toward Hunter's desk.

No one answered.

Her gaze moved to the computer screen and her breath caught in her throat. 'Oh my God. He's back?'

Garcia nodded and quickly explained what was going on.

'Computer Crimes Unit is trying to do what they can,' Hunter said. 'I told Baxter to get in touch with the FBI Cybercrime Division and see if they can help.' He didn't glance over to see the captain scowl at him. He didn't have to. He could feel it. 'Right now, I'll take any help I can get to stop this.' He pointed at his computer screen.

CLOCK – 5:37, 5:36, 5:35 . . .

BURIED – 326.

EATEN – 398.

The woman inside the glass coffin gave up on all her efforts. All she could do now was cry. Suddenly her lips started moving again, and for a split second everyone held their breath. Captain Blake was about to ask Hunter to translate what she was saying, but she didn't have to. Everyone realized the woman was praying.

Twenty-Six

The phone on Hunter's desk rang, catching everyone by surprise like an electric shock. The light flashing on the phone's face indicated an internal call.

Hunter immediately snatched the receiver off its cradle. It was Dennis Baxter.

'Robert, you're not going to believe this, but the FBI CCD had already picked up the website. They were trying to figure out what it was when I called them.'

'Can they help?'

'I'm on the line with Michelle Kelly. She's the head of the department. Can you make this into a conference call?'

'Sure.' Hunter pressed the necessary buttons. 'Go ahead.' He had also put the call on loudspeakers.

'I'll make the formal introductions later,' Baxter said. 'For now – Homicide Special Detective Robert Hunter meet Special Agent and Head of the FBI Cybercrime Division, Michelle Kelly.'

'Ms. Kelly,' Hunter said in a hurried voice. 'I trust Dennis has explained what we are faced with here. Is there any way you can help?'

'We're trying, but so far we've only managed to hit brick walls.' Her voice was feminine but strong. Someone who was definitely used to leading. 'Whoever is doing this has this thing wrapped up pretty tight.'

'Ms. Kelly, this is LAPD Robbery Homicide Division Captain Barbara Blake. What do you mean – *wrapped up pretty tight*?'

'Well, one of the tricks in our arsenal is that we can shut down any web transmission inside US territory.'

'So shut this thing down.'

A nervous chuckle. 'We tried. It just pops up again.'

'What? How?'

'I'm not sure how much you understand about web technology, and I don't want to just throw tech language at you, but the site's IP address changes constantly.'

'Like bouncing a call?' the captain asked.

'That's right. Each new IP address is an exploited server that runs a mirror image of the real one. It's like looking at someone's reflection inside a room packed with mirrors. You see hundreds of identical images, but you can never tell exactly where the real image is coming from. Are you with me so far?'

'Yes.'

'OK. The server also uses an extremely low TTL – *time-to-live* – which is what dictates how long it will be until your computer refreshes its DNS-related information.'

'Sorry . . .?'

'It just means that your computer is constantly asking the server for the website's address, and every time it does, the server points your computer to a different mirror. So even if we managed to shut one down, it would make no difference, because the server would just show your computer the same website via a different mirror. It's technically complicated, but that means that whoever is behind this is a damn fine *coder*, a programmer with a fantastic knowledge of cyberspace.'

CLOCK – 3:21, 3:20, 3:19 . . .

BURIED – 644.

EATEN – 710.

'The name register and the domain servers are all in Taiwan,' Michelle added. 'Which adds another level of complication to the equation. As you probably know, since the island nation was claimed by the mainland People's Republic of China, Taiwan is not recognized as an independent country by the US, meaning we have no diplomatic relations with the Taiwanese.'

'How are so many people finding this website so fast?' Garcia asked. 'Pickadeath.com isn't exactly the kind of address people will type in by chance.'

'We've already checked it,' Michelle said. 'He used social networks. He hijacked other people's accounts and placed a message on some very popular Twitter and Facebook pages. Those pages get several hundred thousand hits a day. People see the message and curiosity takes over; consequently, they go check it out. Now the reason why people are voting might be because they don't think this is real. They might think this is a hoax site, or some new type of "click-and-explore" game.' Michelle paused for breath. 'There's also the fact that there are a hell of a lot of sadistic people out there. Some of them would happily eat popcorn and swig at a beer while watching American citizens being tortured to death. And if they are allowed to participate, even better.'

'Is there anything stopping people from voting more than once?' Garcia asked.

'Yes,' Michelle replied. 'Once you click one of the two buttons, both of them get deactivated. No one can vote twice.'

'How do you know?' It was Captain Blake this time.

'Because we tried it.'

'You *voted* on a death method?'

'Unfortunately, yes,' Michelle explained, but she wasn't being apologetic. 'We came across the website before we got the call from Dennis. We didn't know what we were dealing with. We were trying to figure it out.'

The woman on the screen removed her hands from her face. Blood and tears had created strange designs on her cheeks, but fear had shocked her into an almost tranquil state. Her eyes weren't searching anymore; instead they were now coated with immense sadness. Hunter had seen that look before, and he felt as if his stomach was being sucked into a large black hole. Just like the first victim, as if aided by a sixth sense, she had realized that no one would come for her, that she would never get out of that box alive.

A feeling of total helplessness hit everybody at the same time, because everyone had their eyes on their screens.

CLOCK – 1:58, 1:57, 1:56 . . .

BURIED – 923.

EATEN – 999.

Twenty-Seven

It took only a split second, but it felt like an eternity. BURIED changed first, three numbers in quick succession – 924, 925, 926.

Inside Hunter's office everyone held their breath.

And then it happened.

EATEN – 1000.

As soon as the number changed it started flashing on the screen, announcing to everyone that they had a winner.

No one moved. No one blinked.

On the phone, Michelle Kelly and Dennis Baxter had also gone quiet.

On the screen the woman was still crying. Her hands were still shaking and bleeding.

The seconds ticked away.

Everyone waited.

Suddenly, from the black tube attached to the glass coffin Hunter had noticed earlier, something small and dark shot out and flew across the woman's body.

'What the hell was that?' Captain Blake asked, her gaze ping-ponging between Hunter and Garcia. 'Did you all see that?'

'I saw it,' Garcia replied. 'But I have no idea what it was.'

Hunter was concentrating on the screen.

Then it happened again. Something shot out of the black tube with tremendous speed.

The woman twitched as if someone had abruptly shaken her awake from a trance. She looked down along the coffin toward her feet. It was obvious she couldn't see anything, but whatever it was that was now inside the glass enclosure with her had brought her panic back, and then multiplied it by ten. She twitched again, this time a lot more desperately. She ran her hands against her body, almost slapping it, as if frantically trying to brush something off of her.

Three, four, five more entered the glass coffin via the attached tube.

'Are those some sort of flying insects?' the captain asked.

'I'm not sure,' Hunter said. 'Maybe.'

'Can insects eat someone alive?'

'Some would be able to, yes,' Hunter answered. 'Certain ants and termite species can feed on flesh, but you would need several thousands of them in there, and none of them moves that fast or looks that big.'

The woman's face contorted into a look of agonizing pain. Her eyes squeezed tight and her mouth kicked open to let out a scream that no one could hear, only imagine.

'Oh my God,' Captain Blake said. Both of her hands moved toward her mouth. 'Whatever those things are, they *are* eating her alive. This can't be happening.'

The woman lost control as terror took over. She was desperately kicking her legs and, despite the cramped space, doing what she could to wave her hands across her body and face.

At once, at least fifty new flying insects were dumped into the coffin via the attached tube.

'Oh Jesus Christ.' They all heard Michelle say over the phone.

The camera zoomed in on one of the flying insects, and everyone froze.

It was about two inches long, with a blue-black body and raven-black wings. Its serrated, thin legs were just as long as its body. A pair of black antennas protruded from its head.

'Oh, fuck!' Garcia said, feeling a cold shiver travel down his spine. He took an awkward step back, as if he'd seen something no one else had. All of a sudden he looked like he was about to be sick.

Twenty-Eight

For an instant Hunter and Captain Blake's eyes left the screen and homed in on Garcia.

'Carlos, what's wrong?' the captain asked.

Garcia took a deep breath and swallowed hard before regaining his focus and pointing at the screen. 'That insect,' he said, still sounding rattled. 'That's a tarantula hawk.'

'That's a what?'

'A tarantula hawk,' Hunter said. He'd also recognized the species. 'A spider wasp.'

'That huge thing is a fucking wasp?' The captain coughed the words.

Garcia nodded. 'They're called tarantula hawks because they kill tarantula spiders for food and to lay their eggs.'

'Oh, for the love of God. Are you telling me that those are flesh-eating wasps?'

'No,' Garcia said. 'No wasp feeds on human flesh.'

Confusion set in on Captain Blake's face.

'But their sting,' Garcia clarified, 'is one of the most painful insect stings in the world. It's almost like someone sticking a three-inch, three-hundred-volt electric needle into your flesh. Trust me, their stings are so painful it does feel like chunks of flesh are being ripped from your body.'

Hunter didn't need to ask; his facial expression posed the question.

Garcia explained. 'In Brazil there's a very common species of tarantula hawk called Marimbondo. You find them everywhere. I was stung by four at once when I was a kid, and it put me in hospital. I almost died. The pain lasts only a few minutes but is totally sickening. It can make you delirious. I don't know that much about them, but I know that they aren't aggressive by nature, only if provoked.' He pointed to the screen. 'Her panic, the way she's waving her hands about: that would be more than enough provocation. Her best chance would be to lie still.'

Hunter and everyone else knew that would be impossible. They couldn't hear it, but they all knew that the buzzing sound of *one* two-inch-long wasp flying around inside a closed casket would be enough to fill most people with terrifying horror. By now, the woman had almost a hundred in there with her.

'I also know that tarantula hawks can't eat anyone alive,' Garcia added. 'But the venom from a single sting is enough to paralyze a tarantula spider. If a person is attacked by a whole nest . . .' He pointed at the screen again and shook his head. 'You tell me.'

On the screen the woman had stopped moving, paralyzed by the intense pain of the stings. Large red lumps now covered most of her torso. Inside the glass coffin there must've been over a hundred and fifty tarantula hawks buzzing around her, and still more were being released into the enclosure.

Her face had also been stung tens of times. Both of her eyes had swelled up so severely they were almost shut. Her lips had puffed up to twice their size, and her cheeks were totally disfigured, but she wasn't dead. Not yet. She was still breathing. With her mouth semi-open, she was taking short, staccato breaths in between body tremors.

'How long can this go on for?' the captain asked, nervously pacing before Hunter's computer.

Nobody answered.

The camera zoomed in on the woman's face just as three tarantula hawks landed on her lips, stung them again and then slowly moved onto her tongue before disappearing into her mouth.

Captain Blake just couldn't watch it any more. She looked away just as something began pirouetting inside her stomach. She struggled not to be sick right there and then.

A few seconds later a tarantula hawk climbed out through the woman's left nostril.

No one said anything.

The woman finally stopped breathing.

Moments later the website went offline.

Twenty-Nine

The disturbing silence that took over the room came from a mixture of sadness, helplessness and pure anger. Despite the website being offline, Hunter, Garcia and Captain Blake's eyes were still fixed on Hunter's computer screen.

Michelle Kelly and Dennis Baxter were still on the phone. Michelle spoke first.

'Detective Hunter, we've been monitoring the site's traffic from the beginning. In the few minutes it was online, it received over fifteen thousand hits.'

'Over fifteen thousand people watched this poor woman die?' Captain Blake asked with a tone of disbelief.

'It looks that way,' Michelle replied.

'Ms. Kelly,' Hunter took over. 'Can we meet? If necessary I'll put in an official request for a joint effort between the LAPD and the FBI, but I'd like to start on it as soon as possible.'

'Absolutely. Even with no official request, I want in. This goes way beyond department politics. My entire team and I will do all we can to help. I'll be in our office until late tonight, if you'd like to come by.'

'I will, thanks, and thanks for your help today.'

They disconnected.

'Over fifteen thousand people?' Captain Blake repeated it, still half shocked. 'This thing is already out there, Robert.

There's no way we can contain it. We better get ready for the mother of all shitstorms.'

Hunter's cellphone rang. The caller display window showed unknown number.

'That might already be the bloodsucking reporters,' the captain said.

'Detective Hunter, Homicide Special,' he said into the mouthpiece.

'I told you it would be fun,' the caller said in a serene voice.

Hunter had to take a deep breath before pressing the loudspeaker button.

'And with almost two whole minutes to spare.' The caller chuckled. 'Oh boy. That was something else, wasn't it? OK, OK, she wasn't actually *eaten* alive, but, believe me, those stings are so painful it feels like your body is being ripped apart by sharp teeth.'

Captain Blake looked at Garcia. 'Is that the sick fuck?' she whispered.

Garcia nodded.

The captain's nostrils flared. She was ready to let go of a barrage of abuse.

Hunter saw it first and lifted his hand, signaling her to stay calm.

'Do you know how many people watched that online, Detective?' The caller sounded amused. 'Over fifteen thousand. Isn't society sick?' He paused and snorted. 'Of course you know society is sick. You chase sickos for a living, don't you, Detective Hunter? Sickos just like me.'

Hunter said nothing.

'The problem is,' the caller continued. 'When is somebody considered a sicko, Detective Hunter? How about all the people who watched? How about all the people who voted? Are they sickos? Regular, everyday people, Detective: social workers, teachers, students, cab drivers, waitresses, doctors, nurses, even police officers. They all wanted to see her die.' He rethought his words. 'No ... worse. They didn't only want to see her die. They wanted to *help* kill her. They wanted to press the button. They wanted to choose how she would die.' He paused, allowing the gravity of his words to resonate. 'Does that make them all accessory to murder, or does it all fall under "human morbid curiosity"? You should know, Detective Hunter. You're both a cop and a criminal behavior psychologist, aren't you?'

Hunter didn't reply.

'Are you still there, Detective?'

'You know I'm going to catch you, don't you?' The conviction in Hunter's words was absolute.

The caller laughed. 'Is that so?'

'Yes. I will find you. And you will pay.'

'I do like your attitude, Detective.'

'It's not attitude. It's a fact. Your days are numbered.'

The caller hesitated for a fraction of a second. 'I guess we'll see about that. But since you're so confident in your abilities, Detective, I'll make a trade with you.'

Hunter said nothing.

'I had no doubt ten minutes was more than enough time for me to get at least a thousand votes on one of the two death methods. I had no doubt, because society is too predictable. You know that, don't you?'

Silence.

'But I also knew that EATEN would come out on top.'

A long pause.

'So this is the trade, Detective Hunter,' the caller carried on. 'You tell me how I knew they would pick EATEN over BURIED, and you'll find her body soon enough. You don't.

Her body vanishes. Since you're so confident in your abilities, let's see how good you are.'

Hunter's stare settled on Captain Blake.

'Tell him something,' she urged. 'We need that body.'

'C'mon, Detective,' the caller urged him. 'It's simple psychology. You should get this easy.'

Several seconds went by before Hunter spoke.

'Because EATEN appealed to "human curiosity", BURIED didn't.' His voice was calm and collected.

The captain frowned.

'I like it,' the caller said. 'Please explain.'

Hunter scratched his forehead. He knew that, for now, he had to play the caller's game.

'Everyone knows what to expect from BURIED. EATEN is the unknown. What would you use? How would it be done? What could possibly eat a human being alive? Natural human curiosity would tip the scale toward the unknown.'

A pause was followed by a loud laugh and then hand-claps. 'Very good, Detective. As I said, society as a whole is quite predictable, isn't it? It was a done deal from the start.'

Hunter said nothing.

'It must eat you up inside, mustn't it, Detective?'

'What must?'

'The knowledge that the vast majority of people who watched that online show enjoyed it. They probably even cheered every sting. They loved watching her die.'

No reply.

'And you know what? I bet that they are dying with anticipation for the next show.'

Captain Blake shivered with anger.

'Well, I must bid you all farewell. I've got things to do.'

The line disconnected.

Thirty

The next show.

Those words seemed to echo inside Hunter's office forever. They all knew exactly what that meant, and it filled everyone with dread.

The first thing Hunter did was to ask his research team to come up with a list of possible meanings for SSV, the three letters that had appeared in the top left-hand corner of the screen at the beginning of the broadcast. He had also asked them to prepare a report on tarantula hawks. Was the species found in California? Can anyone breed them in their back garden, or do they require special environment, conditions, etc.?

Garcia contacted the Missing Persons Unit again and emailed them a snapshot of the woman's face. They needed to identify her as soon as possible.

Operations called Hunter as soon as he had disconnected from the call with the killer. This time he hadn't bounced the call all over Los Angeles. He had used a prepaid cellphone. No GPS. But the call didn't last long enough for them to be able to accurately triangulate it. The call had originated from somewhere in Studio City.

The broadcast and Hunter's telephone conversation with the killer had left everyone shaken, but Hunter knew he had to keep his focus. He and Garcia left the PAB and drove to the bus depot in Athens, south Los Angeles. They needed to determine if Kevin Lee Parker, the first victim, had boarded any bus on route 207 on that Monday evening. With that, they could establish if the victim had been abducted in the stretch between the bus stop and his house in Jefferson Park or during the short walk from the Next-Gen Games Shop and the bus stop in Hyde Park.

Four out of the six drivers who had driven route 207 on Monday evening were on duty tonight. Hunter and Garcia struck it lucky with the third driver they interviewed. After showing him a portrait photograph of Kevin Lee Parker, the tall and skinny man nodded and told both detectives that he remembered Kevin because he was a regular – always took the bus from the stop at Hyde Park Boulevard and 10th Avenue, and usually around 7:00 p.m. The driver said that Kevin was a polite man, always said 'hello' as he boarded the bus. He couldn't one hundred percent remember if Kevin was alone or not, but he believed he was. The driver also couldn't remember if Kevin had gotten off at the stop at Crenshaw and West Jefferson Boulevard, his usual stop.

After leaving the bus depot, Hunter and Garcia drove to the intersection between Crenshaw and West Jefferson Boulevard. Kevin Lee Parker's house was a ten-minute walk from the bus stop there. They parked the car and walked the route twice. If Kevin had stuck to West Jefferson Boulevard, and then turned right into South Victoria Avenue, the whole trajectory from the bus stop to his house would've taken him down well-lit and busy roads, but cost him an extra three minutes. The fastest route would've been to cut through the West Angeles Church's car park, just past the Chevron Gas Station on the corner of Crenshaw and West Jefferson, and then carry on through the back alleys, behind South Victoria Avenue.

The West Angeles Church had no security cameras outside, and its car park was located at the back of the building, well hidden from any roads. According to the schedule posted at the front of the church, there were no services on Monday evenings. The car park would've been empty and concealed in the shadows of three not-so-bright lampposts. Snatching Kevin from there, or any of the back alleys on the way to his house, would've been child's play: no one would've witnessed it at all.

Thirty-One

The Los Angeles FBI headquarters in Wilshire Boulevard was a seventeen-story-high concrete and glass box-structure that looked more like a prison than a federal law-enforcement building. With small, one-way, special dark glass windows pigeonholed between long and thin cement pillars, all that was missing were thick metal bars and guard towers around the perimeter. In short, it looked like every FBI building around the country – nondescript and enigmatic.

It was coming up to eight in the evening when Garcia parked his car in the parking lot directly behind the FBI building. The lot was far from empty. Garcia picked a spot next to a shiny black Cadillac with tinted windows and chromed wheels.

'Wow,' he said as he turned off his engine. 'I'm surprised his license plate isn't "IMFBI".'

Before getting to the main entrance doors, both detectives had to go up a set of concrete stairs, across an open-roof green garden and down a CCTV-monitored corridor. They pushed open the heavy, thick glass doors and stepped into a well-lit and pleasantly air-conditioned reception lobby.

Two attractive and conservatively dressed receptionists, who were sitting behind a black-granite reception counter, smiled as they entered the building. Only one stood up.

Hunter and Garcia identified themselves, handing her their credentials. The receptionist quickly typed something into her computer terminal and waited for the application to reply. It did so in less than five seconds, confirming their names and ranks with the LAPD. It also displayed an identifying photograph of each detective. Satisfied, the receptionist returned their identifications to them together with two blue and white visitors' badges.

'An agent will escort you inside,' she said.

A minute later a tall man in a dark suit approached them. 'LAPD Detectives Hunter and Garcia.' He nodded his greeting. No handshakes. 'Please follow me.'

They were escorted through two sets of security doors, down a long hallway, then through a third set of security doors and into an elevator, which descended one floor to the FBI Cybercrime Division. The elevator opened onto a shiny, hardwood corridor, where hanging brass fixtures with several portraits in gilded frames lined the walls. Neither Hunter nor Garcia recognized any of the people in the photographs.

The glass double doors at the end of the hallway were pulled open before they got to them.

'I'll take it from here, thanks,' the woman said.

The escort nodded at her, then at Hunter and Garcia again, before turning on the balls of his feet and heading back toward the elevator.

Both detectives recognized Michelle Kelly's voice from the conference call earlier, but she was nothing like either of them had pictured her.

Michelle Kelly looked to be around twenty-eight years old. She was five foot eight, with long, raven-black dyed hair. Her fringe was spiked, falling over her forehead in a skate-punk way. Her deep green eyes were heavily framed by black eyeliner and pale green eye shadow. Her full lips were delicately accented by red lipstick. She had a thin, silver-loop nose-ring through her left nostril, and a second loop ring through the right edge of her bottom lip. She was wearing black Doc Martens over tight black jeans. Her T-shirt was black and red, with a flying skull design. It read 'Avenged Sevenfold'.

'Detective Hunter,' she said, offering her hand. Both of her arms were completely covered in tattoos, all the way to her wrists, which in turn were lined with different bracelets. Her fingernails were manicured and done in black nail varnish. She looked completely at ease and entirely self-confident.

The first thought that crossed Hunter's mind was that Michelle Kelly hadn't become an FBI agent out of choice. Hunter had been to the FBI Academy in Quantico, Virginia, more than once. He had dealt with agents and their section chiefs. He had read their rulebook. The Federal Bureau of Investigation was still run under a classical approach – old school. Dress codes, hairstyles and rules of conduct were strictly enforced, especially when inside an official building. Facial piercings and clearly visible tattoos were simply not allowed. Of course, exceptions were made for deep-cover agents who had to infiltrate gangs, cults, criminal organizations, etc., but a regular person applying for a place at the academy with his or her arms covered in ink would've been turned away at the gates. Hunter's conclusion was that Michelle Kelly probably owed the federal government a debt. Maybe she had been a master hacker in her former life. Someone with cyber skills the FBI didn't have and couldn't ignore. They had finally caught up with her, and a deal was placed on the table – a very long spell inside or a position with the Cybercrime Division. She took the job.

Hunter took her hand. 'Ms. Kelly, thanks for seeing us.' She had soft hands but a very firm grip. 'This is my partner, Detective Carlos Garcia.'

They shook hands.

'Please call me Michelle,' she said, showing them inside a large room that was chilled to a few degrees below comfortable.

Unlike the LAPD Computer Crimes Unit, which resembled a large open-plan high-tech newsroom, the FBI Cybercrime Division looked to be in a league of its own. First impressions were that the inside of the room looked like the bridge of the starship *Enterprise*. Lights were blinking on and off just about everywhere they looked. The east wall was taken by six massive monitors, each one showing maps, images or lines of data neither Hunter nor Garcia understood. Sixteen spacious desks, covered with monitors and high-tech computer equipment, were scattered around the room. There was no separate enclosure. No office. No visible hierarchy. Inside that room, everyone was equal.

Michelle guided them to the desk closest to the north wall. 'Dennis Baxter gave me very few details. He said that it would be better if you ran me through the whole story.' She dragged two chairs from the nearby desks and positioned them in front of her own.

A man in his mid twenties approached them. He had wavy, rust-colored hair, thin lips, longish eyebrows and large and round, almost black eyes. He looked like a pensive owl – the spitting image of what most people imagine a geek would look like, without the thick glasses.

'This is Harry Mills,' Michelle said, making the necessary introductions. 'He's part of our unit, and a computer genius, with the diplomas to prove it.'

More handshakes.

Harry took a seat and Hunter ran them through everything that had happened so far. Michelle and Harry listened without interrupting.

'And you managed to record most of the broadcast from the first murder?' Michelle asked when Hunter was done.

He retrieved a pen drive from his pocket and handed it to her. 'It's all in there.'

She quickly connected it to a USB port on the computer on her desk, and for the next seventeen minutes no one said a word.

Thirty-Two

When the footage ended, Michelle pressed the 'esc' key on her keyboard. Hunter noticed her hands were not as steady as they were before.

Harry let go of a breath that seemed to have been stuck in his throat for the past seventeen minutes.

'Jesus!' he said. 'Until late this afternoon I had never seen anyone die. I've seen pictures of dead bodies ... I was present during an autopsy, but never actually seen anyone die, never mind being tortured and murdered. Now I've seen two.'

Hunter explained the details of his first telephone conversation with the killer, and how the alkali bath came to be.

'And you believe he tricked you?' Michelle asked.

Hunter nodded. 'He knew beforehand that I would choose water. It was all part of the show.'

Michelle finally blinked. 'Can I get you guys some coffee or something? *I* certainly need a drink. My throat feels like the Nevada desert.'

'Coffee would be great, thanks,' Hunter said.

'Yeah, for me too,' Garcia added.

'I'll get it,' Harry said, already getting up.

'You said that he used an IP address for this transmission, not a web address like the one today?' Michelle asked.

'That's right,' Hunter said. 'According to Dennis, it was probably a hijacked IP address.'

Michelle nodded. 'It wouldn't surprise me at all, but that's strange.'

'What is?' Hunter asked.

Harry came back with four coffees, a small jug of milk, a container with cubes of brown and white sugar and sachets of sweetener.

'The fact that the first murder was practically a *for-your-eyes-only* broadcast,' Michelle explained, 'but the second one was let loose over the World Wide Web.'

Hunter tilted his head to one side. 'Well, according to the caller, the reason why he made the second broadcast a more public affair was because I was no fun the first time around. I didn't play his game the way he wanted me to.'

'But you don't believe that,' Harry said, handing both detectives a cup of coffee.

Hunter shook his head. 'He was too well prepared.'

'He was,' Michelle agreed. 'And that's exactly why it's strange he didn't go for a public broadcast the first time around. He already had everything in place. We've checked. The domain www.pickadeath.com was registered twenty-nine days ago with a server in Taiwan. I don't think he did that just in case. He knew he would go public, and that gives us a second huge problem.'

'Which is?' Garcia asked.

'Today's broadcast was live for exactly twenty-one minutes and eighteen seconds. It received over fifteen thousand hits while it was online. But we're now living in the social network era. Everyone shares everything.'

'The footage was cloned,' Hunter said, anticipating what Michelle was leading to.

'It was,' Michelle admitted. 'Two minutes after the transmission ended, snippets of it were uploaded to several video and social network sites such as YouTube, Dailymotion and Facebook.'

Hunter and Garcia said nothing.

'Unfortunately that was inevitable,' Harry added. 'Once something this weird hits the World Wide Web, it has the potential to go viral. Luckily for us, that potential didn't materialize. The video has spread a little over the net, but nothing close to going viral. Because we were able to go to work as soon as the transmission ended, we were also able to limit its spread.'

'We monitor thousands of video and social network websites around the world,' Michelle explained. 'As soon as a snippet springs up in one of those, we ask the site webmasters to take it down. So far, they are all cooperating.'

'The killer knew very well this would happen,' Garcia said. 'I mean, snippets, or even the entire original broadcast, spreading over the Internet. I'm sure he was counting on it. He's having fun torturing and killing his victims. And the more people who watch it, the better.'

No one said anything.

Michelle clicked a few icons on her computer and the image of the woman lying inside the glass coffin filled the large monitor to her right. The first victim, sitting inside the glass tank, was on the monitor to her left.

'We automatically record any Internet transmission that we deem suspicious,' she said. 'We obviously started recording this as soon as we came across it. I think we managed to get it all the way from the beginning.' She hit the 'play' button.

Hunter nodded, looking at the images. 'You did.'

'Judging by the devices he created,' Harry said, pointing to the glass tank and the see-through coffin on Michelle's screens, 'this guy is a pretty good handyman, with a decent understanding of engineering.'

'I have no doubt,' Garcia agreed.

'Any luck tracing his call?' Harry asked.

Garcia shook his head and explained that the first time around the killer had bounced his call to the LAPD all over Los Angeles.

'But not the second time?'

'No. This time he used a prepaid cellphone. No GPS. The call originated from Studio City, but it didn't last long enough for it to be properly triangulated.'

Harry looked pensive for a moment.

'Do you have an ID for her yet?' Michelle asked, indicating the woman victim.

'We're working on it,' Garcia replied.

'How about the first victim?'

Garcia nodded and gave her a very quick résumé of Kevin Lee Parker.

Michelle's attention returned to the images playing on the monitor to her right – the woman lying inside the glass coffin. 'These were only on the screen for exactly sixty seconds.' She pointed to the letters and numbers in the top left- and right-hand corners of the picture – SSV and 678. 'Do you know what they mean?'

'Not yet.'

'Clues to who the victim might be?' Harry suggested.

Garcia shrugged. 'So that's not a technical acronym? Something computer related?'

'Nothing that I can see having any relevance in this context,' Michelle replied, looking at Harry.

He agreed with a head gesture. 'From the top of my head – Storage Server, Systems Software Verification, Static Signature Verification, Smart Security Vector . . . None of that makes any sense here.' He paused and looked at the monitor to Michelle's left – Kevin Lee Parker bound and gagged inside the glass tank. 'Did the same happen during the first broadcast? I can see you didn't start recording the footage from the beginning. Did the same, or a different combination of letters and numbers, appear?'

'No, nothing,' Hunter replied. 'The only letters that appeared were the ones that formed the chemical formula for sodium hydroxide.'

'So "SSV 678" must be something directly related to the woman,' Harry concluded.

'Possibly,' Hunter said. 'We'll know more when we identify her.'

'Can you leave this with us?' Michelle asked, referring to the footage of the first victim. 'I'd like to analyze it better. Compare it to today's broadcast.'

'No problem.'

Michelle watched the images on both monitors play for a few more seconds before pausing them. The look on her face was a combination of anger, frustration and disgust. Her lips started to part as if she was about to say something, but she hesitated, weighing her words for a moment.

'Whoever this guy is,' she finally said. 'He's a gifted programmer with great knowledge of cyberspace. He covered every angle – TTL, exploited servers, hideware, registering the site in Taiwan, bouncing his telephone calls around and so on. When the broadcast was over, his website vanished, as if it were never there. No trace. He's expertly hiding under several electronic layers of protection. For us to get to him, we need to peel them back, one by one. There's no circumventing it. The problem is, each layer also works as an intruder's alert ... a warning to him. As soon as we manage to peel one back, he'll know, giving him more than enough time to react, to create more layers if necessary.'

Hunter took a deep breath. It was very clear that their investigation would have to concentrate on computer programmers with great knowledge of cyberspace, but in Los Angeles they were everywhere: public and private organizations, schools, universities, their own garages ... Just about everywhere you looked, you were bound to find someone with Internet expertise. They needed something more to guide them.

Michelle looked Hunter in the eye. 'The reason why this killer is so confident is because he knows that as far as cyberspace is concerned, he's untraceable. He's a cyber ghost. As long as he stays there, we can't get to him.'

Thirty-Three

Early the next morning Captain Blake was standing in front of the large pictures board set up against the south wall inside Hunter's office when he arrived. Garcia was standing just behind her.

New snapshots of the second victim lying inside the glass coffin had already been pinned to the board. Some showed her terrified face in varied stages of desperation. Some showed tarantula hawks freeze-framed as they entered the coffin, and then again as they covered her entire body, stinging almost every inch of it.

Garcia had already run Captain Blake through what had happened in their meeting with Michelle Kelly and Harry Mills at the FBI CCD the night before.

'Nothing from Missing Persons yet,' Garcia announced as Hunter took off his jacket and powered up his computer. 'This time the killer didn't gag the victim, so their facial recognition software should have no problems matching key points, but I was on the phone to them just moments ago. No matches so far.'

Hunter nodded.

'The research team delivered the report on tarantula hawks last night,' Garcia said, walking back to his desk.

Hunter and Captain Blake turned to face him.

He reached for the blue folder by his keyboard and flipped it open. 'As we suspected, this killer knew exactly what he was doing, and how to deliver incredible pain. Unlike bees, that can sting their victims only once, wasps can sting theirs multiple times, delivering the same amount of venom and ferocity with every single sting. And like I'd said, their sting *is* ferocious. In the Schmidt Sting Pain Index the tarantula hawk sits right at the top.'

'The what?' The captain interrupted him.

'It's a pain scale, Captain,' Hunter clarified. 'It rates the pain caused by the sting of large insects.'

'That's correct,' Garcia said with a nod. 'The scale ranges from zero to four, four being the most painful. Only two insects rate at four – the tarantula hawk and the bullet ant.'

'How common are they?' Captain Blake asked.

'In America, fairly.' Garcia flipped a page on the report and pulled a face. 'Actually, the tarantula hawk is the official state insect of New Mexico.'

The captain looked at him blankly. 'Do American states have official insects?'

'Apparently.'

'What's the official insect of California, then?'

Garcia shrugged.

'The dog-face butterfly,' Hunter said, and with a hand movement urged Garcia to continue.

He did.

'In California only a small number of species can be found, mainly around the Mojave Desert area and parts of southern California. Among those species, according to the entomologist we've spoken with, is one of the most intriguing ones – the *Pepsis menechma*.' He pointed to the pictures board. 'The one used by the killer.'

'What's so intriguing about them?' Hunter asked.

Garcia closed the folder and returned it to his desk. 'In essence, tarantula hawks are *lone* wasps,' he explained. 'They don't live in nests, or hives, or any sort of community. They don't move in groups either.' His shoulders moved up and down ever so slightly, in a *what-do-you-know* kind of shrug. 'With the exception of a handful of species.'

'The one the killer used is one of them,' the captain concluded. She didn't even attempt to use the scientific name Garcia had read out moments earlier.

'Exactly,' Garcia confirmed. 'That particular species is very similar to the Brazilian one that put me in hospital when I was a kid. They live in large hives, they hunt and attack in groups and they have one of the most powerful, painful and venomous stings out of all tarantula hawks. They are also diurnal creatures, which means that they don't like darkness very much. If they are forced to move around in it, they get very angry. And that's when things get ugly in a hurry.'

Everyone's eyes moved back to the pictures board. At the center of it was a large, zoomed-in photograph of a tarantula hawk in mid-flight.

'So there's no way we can know where he got them.'

'According to the entomologist,' Garcia explained, 'if we find her body before it decomposes, we might be able to trace their location of origin by chemically analyzing the venom they left in her bloodstream. How much help that can prove to be, no one knows.'

Thirty-Four

Garcia gave everyone a moment for his words to sink in, before reaching for two copies of a new printout that was on his desk.

'As far as the media is concerned, we've been a little lucky,' he said, handing the printouts to Hunter and Captain Blake. 'Nothing was actually picked up by the major press, but there's been a little speculation on the Internet. As you know, the broadcast was cloned and uploaded to several video network sites.'

The printout was of a current affairs web page. In the bottom left-hand corner there was a small snapshot of the woman lying inside the glass coffin. Tarantula hawks were all over her. The caption underneath the picture read: *"Reality or Hoax?"*

'It's a small article,' Garcia continued. 'It just talks about the on-screen voting process, and summarizes what happened next.' He gave Hunter and Captain Blake a brief smile. 'In this particular case, Hollywood came to our rescue.'

'How so?' the captain asked.

'At the moment everyone's best guess is that that broadcast was part of a publicity stunt for a new horror/reality-style movie. It's been done before. The trick is to start a buzz by trying to make the public believe it's a real documentary rather than a Hollywood production.'

The captain returned the printout to Garcia. 'That suits us just fine. Let them believe the Hollywood bullshit.' She turned and faced the pictures board again. 'But they do have a point. This *does* look like the storyboard for a horror movie. Stung to death by giant wasps, almost dissolved in a caustic soda solution. What the hell?'

'Most feared deaths,' Hunter said.

'What?'

'The options this killer gave us,' Hunter followed up. 'With the first victim – burned to death or drowned. With the second one – buried alive or eaten alive. Why these particular methods?' He walked up to his computer, brought up his browser and called a web page. 'Well, I found out that those particular methods are among the ten worst ways to die as voted by the public.'

Garcia and Captain Blake repositioned themselves behind Hunter's desk. The list on his screen started at number ten and counted down to number one. The death methods mentioned and used by the killer were all there. Drowning was at number six. Burned alive was at two. Eaten alive (by insects or animals) sat at number five, while buried alive held the third position. Voted number one most feared and painful death was being dumped into an alkali bath.

Captain Blake felt her core temperature drop a few degrees.

'I found several lists,' Hunter explained. 'Most of them are just a variation of that one. Different positions but most of the same death methods.'

'You think that's what he's doing?' the captain asked. 'Running through a crazy list of deaths he found on the Internet?'

'I'm not sure what he's doing, Captain. But he could've easily come up with that list by himself.'

Captain Blake glared at Hunter.

'If I hadn't showed you this list and just asked you to write down the worst ten death methods you could think of, I'm sure you'd have at least six or seven of those in there.'

Captain Blake thought about it for an instant.

'Buried alive, burned alive, eaten alive, drowning . . . all of those are universally feared deaths,' Hunter added.

'OK, so maybe he created his own list of fucked-up deaths,' the captain agreed. 'My question still stands. Do you think that's what he's doing? Going through a crazy list just for the fun of it?'

'It's possible,' Hunter admitted after an awkward pause.

'Sonofabitch. And what about this?' Captain Blake pointed to one of the printouts on the board, referring to the word centered at the bottom of the screen during the broadcast. 'GUILTY. He was obviously telling us that in his sick mind, he considered that woman guilty of something.'

'Possible,' Garcia said. 'But the problem is that if this guy really is a psychopath, then she could've been guilty of just about anything, Captain. She didn't even need to know him. She could've stepped on his toe inside a crammed subway train, or rejected his advances inside a bar, or maybe he simply didn't like the way she styled her hair, or looked at him. To a psychopath, any reason is a reason.'

Garcia was right. Psychopaths had a very distorted vision of reality. Their emotions were usually so detached that the simplest of things could affect them in the most unpredict-able ways, and just about anything could trigger an extremely violent reaction. They usually considered themselves superior to anyone else around them. More intelligent. More attractive. More talented. More every-thing. They didn't cope well with rejection, no matter how small, considering it an aggression against their superiority. They were very easily offended, and they often felt disgusted by the mundanity of other people's lives. In general, psycho-paths were usually impulsive, had little self-control, and their crimes tended to be spur-of-the-moment affairs, but some were very capable of more elaborate planning. Some were even capable of keeping the monster inside them on a leash until it was time to let him loose.

'Or he could just be playing on the gullibility of people,' Hunter finally said.

Captain Blake shot him a *what-the-hell-is-that-supposed-to-mean* look.

'Opinion manipulation or, in simplest terms, rumor,' Hunter said, stabbing his index finger over the word GUILTY on one of the printouts on the board. 'That's all some people need to make up their minds about a subject, or a person, Captain. It's a psychological trick. A way to steer someone's opinion one way or another. It's the press and the media's most powerful weapon. They use it every day.'

'Opinion manipulation?' the captain asked.

'That's right. It happens to all of us, whether we under-stand it or not. That's why it's such a powerful trick. If you see someone's picture in the paper, or on TV, with the word *guilty* in large letters at the bottom of it, subconsciously your brain starts to lean toward a preconceived, force-fed opinion about that person. "If it's written, then it must be true." You don't need to read the article. You don't need to know the person's name. You don't even need to know what he or she is supposed to have done. It's the power of rumor. And that power is strong.'

'And today's society thrives on voting on the outcome of other people's lives,' Garcia said.

Captain Blake turned to face him.

He cracked his knuckles and explained. 'Just turn on the TV, Captain, and you'll be inundated with reality shows of people in a house, in a jungle, on an island, on a boat, on stage, you name it. The public is asked to vote on every-thing, from what and if they'll eat, to where they'll sleep, who they are coupled with, silly tasks, if they should stay or go, the list is endless. This killer just stepped it up a notch.'

'But he did it in a very clever way.' Hunter took over. 'He never asked the public to vote on whether she would live or die. That was already decided. Psychologically that's enough to clear most people's conscience.'

Captain Blake thought about this for a beat.

'Meaning . . . why would people feel guilty?' she said, staring at a printout of the woman lying inside the glass coffin. 'It's not their fault she's inside that coffin. They didn't put her there. She was going to die anyway. They just played along and picked how.'

Hunter agreed. 'The problem is the reason why reality TV shows are so successful, and why there are so many of them, is because they're designed to give people the false impression of power. Power to control what happens in a given situation. Power to decide other people's fate, so to speak. And that power is one of the most addictive feelings there is. That's why they keep coming back for more.'

Thirty-Five

Sitting around, waiting for the Missing Persons facial recognition program to hit a match, wasn't something either Hunter or Garcia was prepared to do.

Earlier in the morning Hunter had checked with the city psychologist who had been assigned to help Anita Lee Parker, the first victim's widow, cope with her grieving. According to Doctor Greene, Anita was dealing with it in the worst way possible. She was still in denial. Her brain refused to understand what had happened to her husband. She'd spent the last two days sitting in her living room, waiting for Kevin to come home. Deep depression was starting to set in. The saddest thing was that as a consequence, Lilia, her baby daughter, was starting to be neglected. Doctor Greene had given Anita a prescription for antidepressants, but if she didn't start to get better soon mental health and child welfare organizations would have to get involved.

Hunter's primary intention was to show Anita a snapshot of the second victim. Check if she recognized the woman at all. Maybe Kevin knew her. Maybe she was a friend of the family. If they could establish that both victims knew each other, on any sort of level, it would at least steer the investigation onto steadier ground. The randomness with which they believed the killer picked his victims wouldn't look so random. But right now Anita Lee Parker wouldn't be able to answer any of their questions. Her subconscious was blocking out anything that forced her to deal with the tragedy of her husband's death. She probably wouldn't even recognize Hunter and Garcia. It would be no surprise if the entire memory of when they met, only two days ago, had been completely erased.

With Anita still in shock, their best bet was Kevin's best friend and work colleague, Emilio.

Saturday was Next-Gen's busiest day, and at 12:28 in the afternoon the shop was full of people browsing and having a go at the latest releases. Emilio was helping a customer choose between two titles when Hunter and Garcia entered the shop. As Emilio saw them, his entire demeanor changed.

'Can we have a quick chat, Emilio?' Hunter said, approaching him when he was done with the customer.

Emilio nodded nervously. He guided them through a door behind the cashier's counter and into the staff's break room at the back of the shop.

Emilio looked tired and nervous. There was no disguising the dark circles under his eyes.

No one took a seat. Emilio stood beside an old Formica table at the center of the room, and Hunter and Garcia by the door.

'Everything OK?' Garcia asked, referring to Emilio's noticeable trepidation, something that hadn't been there the first time they met.

Two quick nods. 'Yes, sure.' He wasn't meeting anyone's eyes.

'Did you remember something about Kevin that we should know?'

'No. Nothing. I told you everything already.'

'Well, something happened,' Garcia said. 'Because truthfully, your poker face sucks.'

Emilio finally met Garcia's stare.

'Whatever it is, we're going to find out one way or another, so you might as well tell us and save everyone some time.'

Emilio took a deep breath and looked down at the floor. Hunter and Garcia waited.

'I was offered the manager's position here at the shop. Kevin's old job.'

'OK . . .?' Garcia was still waiting for something else.

'That's it,' Emilio said, running a nervous hand over his mustache.

'And what is the problem?'

An uneasy chuckle. 'I know how it goes, man. If I take the job you'll start thinking that I had something to do with what happened to Kevin. It's a motive, isn't it? Me taking over his old job. But believe me, I had no idea they would ask me to be the manager. I'm not even the most senior employee here. They should ask Tom. He would be a good manager.' His voice almost croaked. 'Kevin was my best friend. He was like my brother . . .'

Garcia gave Emilio a sympathetic smile and lifted his hand, stopping him. 'Emilio, let me cut you off there. You've been watching way too many *CSIs*, or *Criminal Intent*, or whatever it is that you watch.'

Emilio looked back at both detectives.

Hunter nodded. 'He's right. Unfortunately for us, things aren't as simple as that. You taking the manager's job isn't going to send your name to the top of the suspects' list, Emilio.'

'Really?' It was like a heavy load was suddenly lifted from Emilio's shoulders.

'Really,' Garcia reassured him. 'The reason we're here is because we would like you to have a look at something for us.'

They showed him a printout of the woman lying inside the glass coffin. The snapshot had been taken right at the beginning of the broadcast; the word GUILTY hadn't appeared at the bottom of the image yet, and neither had the voting buttons. But the letters SSV and the number sequence 678 were clearly visible in the top left- and right-hand corners of the image.

Emilio stared at it for a long moment while scratching his chin. 'I'm . . . not sure,' he finally said. 'But there's something familiar about her face.'

Both detectives kept their excitement in check.

'You think you've seen her before? With Kevin, maybe?'

He stared at the printout for a few more seconds before shaking his head. 'No, I don't think it was with Kevin. Kevin really didn't have that many friends. He was always at home with Anita, here at work or playing online games after we shut the shop. He didn't hang out in bars or night-clubs or anything like that. He didn't meet a lot of people.'

'Maybe she was a customer,' Garcia pushed. 'Maybe you saw her in the shop.'

Emilio considered it for a moment. 'It's possible. Can I show this to the other guys in the shop? If she's a customer, maybe one of them might remember her better.'

'Please do,' Garcia said. 'But let me ask you one more thing. These letters and numbers at the top here.' He indicated on the printout. 'Do they mean anything to you? SSV and 678?'

Emilio thought about it for a beat. 'The only SSV I can think of is the SSV *Normandy*.'

'The what?'

'The SSV *Normandy*. It's a starship that appears in a game called Mass Effect 2.'

'A starship?'

'That's right. The game is a few years old now. It was first released in . . . 2010, I think. I completed it. It's quite a good game.'

'Did Kevin play it? Online with others, I mean?'

Emilio shook his head. 'Mass Effect 2 doesn't have a multiplayer option. It's a solo game. You play against the computer.'

Garcia nodded. 'How about the numbers? A game score, maybe?'

'Not for Mass Effect 2,' Emilio said. 'There's no scoring in the game. You simply finish a level and then move onto the next one until they're all completed.'

Garcia looked at Hunter and they both shook their heads at the same time. Neither of them believed that SSV or 678 had anything to do with a videogame.

They returned to the shop's main floor, and Emilio showed the printout to the three other employees on duty. Hunter and Garcia saw them one by one stare at the woman's picture, frown, pouch, scratch their noses and then slowly shake their heads. If she had been a customer in that shop, no one seemed to remember her.

'I still think there's something familiar about her face,' Emilio said, still staring at the printout.

Hunter and Garcia gave him a few more minutes.

Nothing.

Both detectives knew that forcing it was pointless.

'It's OK, Emilio,' Garcia said, handing him one of his cards. 'Why don't you keep that picture? Give it a little break and then go back to it a few more times throughout the day. Memory works better that way. If you remember anything, no matter how small, give me a call, anytime. All my numbers are on the card.'

Thirty-Six

Despite being only seven days since their investigation had started, Hunter and Garcia had been on a fifteen-day stretch with no break. Captain Blake ordered both of them to take Sunday off.

They did.

Garcia finished drinking the rest of his coffee, and from across their small breakfast table he feebly smiled at his wife, Anna. They'd been together since their senior year in high school, and Garcia was certain she was some sort of angel, because he knew no human being could understand and put up with him the way she did.

Anna had been by his side from the beginning. From way before he decided to become a cop. She'd seen how hard he'd worked for it and how dedicated he was. But most important of all, she understood the commitment and the sacrifices that came with his job, and she'd accepted them, no complaints and no angry recriminations. She also understood that Garcia would never offer anything about his job or any of the investigations he was working on. She would never ask about them either. She knew that he just didn't want to bring any of the madness of his professional life back home with him, and she admired him for that. But despite all her strength, Anna feared that the things Garcia saw on a day-to-day basis were changing him inside. She could feel they were.

'So what would you like to do on your day off?' she asked him, returning his smile. Anna had an unusual but enthralling kind of beauty. A delicate, heart-shaped face perfectly complemented by striking hazel eyes, short black hair and a smile that could melt a man. Her skin was creamy smooth, and she had the firm figure of a professional dancer.

'Whatever you want to do,' Garcia replied. 'Do you have anything planned?'

'I was thinking about going for a run after breakfast.'

'Down at the park?'

'Uh-huh.'

'That sounds great. Mind if I come along?'

Anna pulled a face at Garcia. He knew exactly what it meant.

In school, Garcia had been a great track and field athlete, especially at long-distance events. Since leaving school and becoming a cop, his fitness had actually improved. He'd run the Boston and the New York marathons three times each, always completing them in less than two hours and forty minutes.

'I'll run at your pace, I promise,' he said. 'If I get in front of you even once, you have my permission to trip me from behind and then kick me while I'm down.'

Montebello City Park was just a couple of blocks away from their apartment. A subtle breeze blew from the west, and not a single cloud spoiled the bright blue sky. The park was full of people jogging, cycling, rollerblading, walking their dogs or simply lying around lazily, enjoying the sun.

Despite never being an athlete, Anna was no pushover. Her running pace was strong and steady. Garcia kept to his word, always alongside or just a step behind his wife. They had just completed two out of their three intended laps of the park when Garcia heard a clattering noise just behind them. He quickly turned around and saw a man, who looked to be in his mid fifties, collapsed on the ground. His bicycle was carelessly dumped onto the jogging path a few feet in front of him. He wasn't moving.

'Anna, hold on,' Garcia called.

Anna stopped and turned. Her eyes went straight to the man on the ground. 'Oh my God. What happened?'

'Not sure.' Garcia was already rushing toward the man.

Another cyclist, younger, had slowed to a halt about six feet from where the man had fallen.

'What happened?' Garcia asked, kneeling down by the man's side.

'I don't know,' the cyclist replied. 'He was just riding in front of me, when all of a sudden he started wavering all over the place and then, boom, dropped off his bike and hit the ground face first.'

More people were starting to gather around.

'Do you know him?' Garcia asked.

The cyclist shook his head. 'I have no idea who he is, but he must be local. I've seen him cycling around the park a few times before.'

Garcia quickly turned the man over so he was lying on his back. His chest wasn't moving. He had stopped breathing, a given sign that he had gone into cardiac arrest.

'He's having a heart attack,' he said, looking at Anna.

'Oh my God.' Anna brought a shaking hand to her mouth. 'What can I do to help?'

'Call for an ambulance, now.'

'My phone is at home.'

Garcia quickly reached into his pocket for his cellphone and handed it to Anna.

A crowd of curious people had formed around the scene. Everyone was just standing there, looking on, wide-eyed. No one else offered to help.

In the past seven days Garcia had watched two people die before his eyes without being able to lift a finger to help them. Today there was no way on earth he would stand still like all those people. There was no way on earth he wouldn't do all he could to help that man.

Garcia immediately began pumping the man's chest with both hands, trying to artificially pump blood out of his heart and around his body.

'What happened?' a man dressed in running clothes with sweat dripping down his face called as he approached the group of onlookers.

'Heart attack, I think,' a woman replied.

'Let me through,' the man cried out. 'I'm a doctor.'

A path cleared straightaway.

The man kneeled down next to Garcia. 'How long has he been in cardiac arrest?'

'Less than a minute.' Garcia looked up, searching for the younger cyclist for confirmation. He was gone.

'Ambulance should be here in five minutes or less,' Anna announced, her voice a little shaky.

'OK, I'm going to need your help,' the doctor said, addressing Garcia. 'We need to continue with CPR until the ambulance gets here.'

Garcia nodded.

'You carry on with the chest compressions, while I'll give him artificial respiration. Aim for a rate of around a hundred compressions a minute. I'll count you on. Give me ten now before I start.'

Garcia started pressing down firmly and rhythmically, and with each press his memory spat out a new random image from the Internet victims as they died before his eyes.

'. . . and ten,' the doctor said, snapping Garcia out of his horror trance. He pinched the man's nostrils shut with two fingers to prevent air leakage, took a deep breath and sealed his mouth over the man's mouth, before breathing into it for about two seconds. His eyes were fixed on the man's chest, which rose slightly, indicating enough air was being blown in. He repeated the procedure twice.

The man still wasn't breathing on his own.

'I need thirty compressions this time,' the doctor said.

Sirens were heard in the distance.

'They're about two and a half minutes away,' Garcia said, pumping the man's chest again.

The doctor looked at him curiously.

'I'm a cop, I can tell.'

When Garcia reached thirty chest compressions, the doctor performed two more artificial respirations.

Still no self-sufficient breathing from the man.

They repeated the process two more times before they heard a loud commotion as the ambulance drove onto the grass and around some trees to reach them.

'We'll take it from here,' a paramedic said, kneeling down by the man's head.

Garcia let go of the man's chest. His hands were shaking, and despite being a naturally calm person he was visibly distressed.

'You did well,' the doctor said. 'We did all we could, and

everything possible given the circumstances. No one could've done any better.'

Garcia kept his gaze on the man as the paramedics took over, strapping a resuscitator mask onto his face.

'We need to shock him,' one of the paramedics said. 'We're losing him.'

Tears welled up in Anna's eyes. 'Oh God.'

Garcia hugged her, while the paramedics brought out a portable defibrillator.

'Clear,' a paramedic called out, before delivering a controlled, two-hundred-joule electric shock to the man's chest.

Nothing.

The paramedic increased the energy to three hundred joules and delivered a new shock.

Still nothing.

Three hundred and sixty joules.

No movement from the man.

Both paramedics looked at each other. There was nothing else they could do. Everyone's efforts had been in vain.

Anna buried her face into Garcia's chest and began crying, while Garcia struggled with the enormous guilt that took over him.

Thirty-Seven

'Everything OK?' Hunter asked Garcia as soon as he got to his office the next morning, immediately picking up that something was bothering his partner.

Garcia told him about what had happened in the park the day before.

'I'm sorry Anna had to see that,' Hunter said.

'It's like death has been following me around lately,' Garcia replied. 'And there's nothing I can do to help any of these people.'

'From what you told me, you did all you could yesterday, Carlos. And you know that we are doing all we can in this investigation.' Hunter leaned against the edge of his desk. 'That's exactly what this killer wants. If we allow frustration to get the better of us, that's when we start making mistakes and not seeing things.'

Garcia took a deep breath and nodded. 'Yeah, I know. I'm just still a little rattled about the whole thing yesterday. I thought I could save him, I really did. And I wished Anna hadn't seen him die.' He stood up and looked around himself as if searching for something.

'I'm going to go to the machine downstairs,' he said, checking how much change he had in his pocket. 'I need some sort of energy drink. Would you like one?'

Hunter shook his head. 'I'm OK.'

Garcia nodded back, returned his change to his pocket and exited the office.

Twenty minutes later Hunter and Garcia received two reports. The first was a trace on all calls made to and from Kevin Lee Parker's cellphone in the past two weeks. There was nothing out of the ordinary there. All the calls made or received had either been to or from his wife, or to or from Emilio. As Emilio had said, it didn't look like Kevin had much of a social life.

The second report was on possible meanings for SSV, the three letters that had appeared in the top left-hand corner of the screen during the second broadcast. It was divided into five categories: Information Technology (twenty-six entries), Military and Government (twenty-two entries), Science and Medicine (thirty-two entries), Organizations, Schools and Others (twenty-four entries), Business and Finance (eighteen entries).

They spent a long while going over everything.

'Any of this mean anything to you?' Garcia finally asked.

Hunter slowly shook his head while reading the entire list of abbreviations for the zillionth time. Not a single one seemed to have any relevance to their case.

'Symphony Silicon Valley, Society for the Suppression of Vice?' Garcia frowned as he read the two first entries from the Organizations, Schools and Others category. He flipped the page and looked at the Military and Government entries. 'Soldier Survivability, Space Shuttle Vehicle? This is totally nuts.'

An observation at the end of the report stated that no meanings had been found for SSV678 or 678SSV. They had tried everything, even entering the numbers as map coordinates. 6,78 had returned a spot southwest of Sri Lanka, in the Laccadive Sea. 67,8 had also hit water, several miles west of Norway in the Norwegian Sea.

Hunter put the report down and rubbed his eyes. So far, nothing was making sense. Just like Michelle Kelly had said, everything came back a dead end. Missing Persons still hadn't found a match for the woman either.

Hunter's stare wandered over to the pictures board and settled on the printout of a snapshot taken during the early stages of the broadcast. The woman's fate hadn't been decided by then. She was just lying inside that glass coffin, petrified, confused and praying for a miracle. Her face still showed hope. On the printout, BURIED was at 325 and EATEN at 388.

Garcia had finally abandoned the acronyms report and placed it back on his desk when his phone rang.

'Detective Garcia, Homicide Special,' he answered.

'Detective, it's Emilio Mendoza.' A short pause. 'The woman on that picture you gave me . . . I know where I saw her before. I'm looking at her now.'

Thirty-Eight

Michelle Kelly and Harry Mills had gone over every step of their sting operation plan to catch 'Bobby', the Internet pedophile, a hundred times. Still, they knew that there were a million chances that something could go wrong. They just prayed that nothing did.

Michelle was also very keen to bring this FBI investigation to an end. The two Internet murders were now beginning to haunt her every moment. The killer's arrogance more than bothered her. She wanted to move all her efforts onto the LAPD case.

'Lucy', the young schoolgirl Michelle had pretended to be over the Internet, was sitting on a bench in Venice Beach facing the skate park when 'Bobby' came up behind her.

'Lucy?' he asked tentatively, but he already knew the answer. He'd been observing her from a distance for the past twenty minutes.

Lucy turned and looked back at Bobby for a moment. Confusion colored her face.

'It's me, Bobby.'

In reality, Lucy was Sophie Brook, a twenty-one-year-old professional actress from east LA, whom the FBI had used on three previous occasions. She was an excellent actress, but her real gift, as far as the FBI was concerned, was that she had the looks, the body, the voice and the skin of a teenager. Dressed in the right clothes, she had no problem passing as a thirteen-year-old schoolgirl. And that had been exactly the picture Michelle Kelly had sent Bobby over the Internet. A sweet and naive-looking Sophie dressed up as Lucy, the chat-room schoolgirl, and Bobby bought it.

This morning, though, they didn't have to concern themselves with making Sophie look thirteen, because any thirteen-year-old girl trying to impress an older 'boy' would go for a more mature look. They dressed her up in a blue jeans skirt, flat ballerina-style shoes, a trendy white top and a cropped jeans jacket. Her blond hair was loose, falling past her shoulders, and she had applied a little makeup, in tune with a younger girl trying to look older.

Sophie had been coached for this job for weeks, even going through an intensive self-defense course with an FBI instructor. In her right jacket pocket she was also carrying a mini canister of pepper-spray, just in case.

The FBI had spotted Bobby the second he started walking down East Market Street in the direction of the skate park. He was wearing a dark blue hooded jacket with the hood up, blue jeans, white Nike sneakers and a red backpack. Funny – she dressed older, he dressed younger.

Every movement Bobby made was being filmed by a camera set up at a strategic point at the top of one of the skate ramps. Every word he uttered was being recorded by the wire Lucy was wearing under her top. At the beach an undercover agent and his dog were pretending to play with a ball, while watching Bobby from a safe distance.

The surprise on Lucy's face was all pretend. Michelle had run her through the scenario dozens of times.

'Remember, you believe he's twenty-one. When you see him for the first time, be shocked. Be hurt that he has lied to you. Be angry that he has abused your trust.'

'Wow,' Bobby said with a big smile, taking down his hood. 'You're even prettier in person. Look at you, you look amazing.'

'What a scumbag,' Harry said from his observation point at the top of East Market Street.

Lucy's eyes moistened. 'Is this a joke?'

'No, it's me, Bobby.'

Bobby was in his mid-thirties, with short fair hair, a squared jaw, masculine lips, a strong nose and inviting light blue eyes. He wasn't exactly a bad-looking man. He probably had no problems getting female attention. The problem was that he preferred young girls.

Bobby sat down.

Lucy recoiled a few inches.

'The bird is in the nest,' Harry said into his microphone. 'We can take him down.'

'Not yet,' Michelle replied. She was standing just a few yards from Lucy and Bobby, pretending to listen to her iPod while watching the skate kids do their stuff. 'Let them talk for a minute.'

'You're not twenty-one,' Lucy said in a trembling voice.

'Oh, please don't be upset,' Bobby said, giving her his best sad-puppy face. 'Give me a chance to explain, Lucy. It's still me, the Bobby you know. The Bobby you've been chatting to for four months. The Bobby you said you were falling in love with. I just . . . didn't know how to tell you in the chat room.'

A tear rolled down Lucy's cheek.

'Damn, she's good,' Harry whispered to himself.

'Forget the age thing,' Bobby said in a tender voice. 'That shouldn't be important. Remember how we connected? How we chatted? How we got to know and understand each other so well? Nothing has changed. I'm the same person inside. C'mon, Lucy, don't you believe that when two people connect as strongly as the way we did, when they find their soul mate, nothing else matters? I know you're mature enough to know that.'

No reply.

'I think you're an incredible and beautiful person,' Bobby continued. 'I'm in love with you, Lucy. I don't get why age has to change that.'

'Are you getting this crock of shit?' Harry said into his microphone.

'Yep, every word,' Michelle replied. 'He's one sick slimeball.'

Lucy said nothing. She just sat there, looking hurt.

'Could we go for a walk and talk some more?' Bobby said. 'I've been looking forward to seeing you so much.'

'OK, that's it,' Michelle said, checking her watch. 'I'm ending this shit right now.'

Out of the six young girls the FBI knew Bobby had had sex with, only one had agreed to cooperate. She was twelve. But one was all they needed. All she had to do was pick him out from a lineup, and they had him. Michelle also knew that once they had Bobby in custody, and one of the victims had cooperated, the others would also come forth and point their fingers.

Michelle pulled her earbuds out of her ears, strolled up to where Lucy and Bobby were sitting and simply stood in front of Bobby for a moment, sizing him up.

Bobby looked at her and frowned. 'Can I help you?'

Michelle smiled. 'Can *you* help *me*? No.' She asked and answered, gesticulating at the same time. 'Can *I* help *you*? No. Can *you* help *yourself*? No. Are you a sick scumbag who deserves to rot in prison? Positively yes.' She pulled out her credentials. 'FBI, you sack o' shit. We need to talk to you about some of your online chat-room activity.'

For a second everyone remained still, then, in a flash, Bobby came alive. He jumped up and slammed the top of his head into Michelle's chin. The brutal impact sent her head flying back as if she had been shot. Her jaw slammed against her skull with such force that her vision instantly blurred. Blood flew up in the air from the fresh cut on her lip. She stumbled backward awkwardly, her body half limp, her legs too jellified to keep her up. She hit the ground like a puppet on severed strings.

Bobby jumped over the bench and made a run for it in the direction of Oceanfront Walk.

Thirty-Nine

'What?' Garcia said into his phone. Emilio's words had caught him completely by surprise. 'Wait a second, Emilio. Let me put you on speakerphone.' Garcia clicked a button and returned the receiver to its cradle. 'Go ahead, say that again.'

Hunter looked at Garcia.

'The woman in that picture you gave me on Saturday when you came by the shop. I now know where I saw her before. I'm actually looking at her right now.'

It was Hunter's turn to look baffled. 'What? Emilio, this is Detective Hunter. What do you mean, *you are looking at her right now*? Where are you?'

'I'm at home. And what I mean is, I'm looking at another picture of her right now.'

'Another picture?' Garcia asked.

'That's right. A picture in yesterday's newspaper.'

Garcia frowned. 'The press caught up with the video?' he asked Hunter.

'Not that I'm aware of. Captain Blake would've been going apeshit if the press was onto this.'

'You saw her in yesterday's paper?' Garcia returned his attention to the phone. 'Which one?'

'The *LA Times*,' Emilio answered.

Instinctively Hunter and Garcia's gaze shot to the only window in their office. The *LA Times* headquarters was literally across the road from the Police Administration Building. It was the first edifice they saw when they looked out of their window.

'But she isn't part of the news,' Emilio said. 'The story isn't about her.'

A moment of confused looks.

'She's the reporter.'

'What?'

'That's why she looked so familiar to me. My girlfriend loves to read the entertainment supplement of the *LA Times* on Sundays, mainly the celebrity gossip part. She's into that kind of stuff, you know? Sometimes I flip through it myself. Anyway, that woman writes a column in the entertainment supplement. There's always a small picture of her at the top of whatever article she wrote that week. And that's why she looked so familiar. I'd seen her picture before several times.'

Garcia was writing something down on a notepad.

'I didn't look at the paper yesterday. I was working,' Emilio explained. 'I'm off today. I was just having a quick look through yesterday's paper before I threw it away, and there she was.'

'What's her name?' Hunter asked.

'Christina, Christina Stevenson.'

Hunter typed her name into an Internet search engine. Within a few seconds he had her picture on his screen. Emilio was right. There was no doubt Christina Stevenson was their second victim, unless she had an identical twin or a clone working for the *LA Times*.

'Great job, Emilio,' Garcia said. 'We'll be in touch.' He disconnected.

Hunter was scanning through the information on one of the pages he had on his screen.

'What have you got?' Garcia asked.

'Not much. Christina Stevenson, twenty-nine years old. She'd been with the *LA Times* for six years. The last two of those she spent with the entertainment desk, which is called by many *the gossip pit*. That's all the personal information I have here.'

'She was a gossip reporter?' Garcia asked.

'It looks that way.'

'Damn, no one makes more enemies than they do, not even us.'

Garcia was right. In a city like LA, where to so many being in the public eye was as important as breathing air, gossip reporters could make or break anyone's career. They could destroy a person's relationship, break their family homes, expose dirty secrets, do almost anything they liked. And the worst of all was that it didn't even have to be true. In LA the smallest of rumors could completely change someone's life, for better or worse. Gossip reporters were known for having false friends, and real enemies.

Hunter hesitated for a second, pondering a few things over.

Garcia knew exactly what Hunter was debating in his head. If they started asking questions inside the headquarters of the *LA Times*, there was no hiding this story anymore. A story that, so far, no newspaper or TV news channel had picked up on. It was like taking raw meat to a pack of hungry wolves, even if the raw meat was one of their own. No information would be forthcoming, because reporters love to obtain it, but they hate giving it away.

'So what do you want to do?' Garcia asked. 'Start asking questions at the *Times*?'

'We'll have to. If the victim was a reporter there, there's no escaping it, but not just yet.' Hunter reached for the phone on his desk and called the research team. He asked them to find out everything they could on Christina Stevenson, but more important he needed her home address ASAP. They could start there.

A minute later his phone rang.

'Do we have an address already?' Hunter said into the phone.

'Um . . . Detective Robert Hunter?' a male voice asked.

Hunter paused. 'Yes. This is Detective Robert Hunter. Who is this?'

'This is Detective Martin Sanchez with the Santa Monica Police Department.'

'How can I help you, Detective Sanchez?'

'Well, earlier this morning one of our patrol cars, answering a 911 call, found a female body at a private parking lot near Marine Park in Santa Monica.' Sanchez paused to clear his throat. 'Somebody left a note with the body. Your name is on it.'

Forty

It took several seconds for the blurriness to dissipate from Michelle's vision, and even then bright spots of light seemed to be exploding everywhere. Her entire head hurt as if it was being gradually squeezed in a vise. She could feel her bottom lip pulsating from the blood pressure so ferociously she thought it would blow up like an air balloon.

'Are you OK?' Sophie asked. She was kneeling next to Michelle, holding her head in her hands. Everything had happened so fast she'd had no time to react.

Michelle looked at her with dopey eyes. No recognition. Her brain still wasn't registering much.

'Michelle, are you OK?' Harry's voice came through her earbuds dangling from her neck. Harry was already running down East Market Street in the direction of the skate park. All bets were off.

'Michelle?' Sophie called again.

Suddenly, just like being woken up by a bucket of cold water to the face, her brain re-engaged. Her eyes refocused on Sophie's face, and everything came back to her in a flash. Her hand shot to her lip and she winced as her fingertips touched it. She pulled her hand away and looked at it.

Blood.

Confusion was immediately replaced by anger.

'Oh no, he didn't,' she said to herself, quickly returning her earbuds to her ears.

'Bird is trying to fly,' she heard Harry say.

'Like hell he is,' Michelle replied.

'Michelle, are you all right?' Harry asked, sounding a little relieved and out of breath at the same time.

'I'll live,' she replied in an angry voice.

'That was one hell of a headbutt.'

'Stop worrying about me, goddammit,' she blurted into her microphone. 'Somebody pin Bobby's bitch-ass down.'

'We're already on it.'

As soon as Bobby had headbutted Michelle and run for it, the undercover agent at the beach had kneeled down by his German shepherd and pointed at Bobby, running away in the distance. 'Take him down, boy. Take him down.'

The dog had taken off like a rocket.

Bobby was fast, but not fast enough. The dog was able to get to him in just a couple of seconds.

The *takedown* command instructed the dog to simply use its body weight to drop a fleeing subject to the ground. A fully developed German shepherd with running momentum produced an impact force equivalent to being hit by a motorbike at 25mph.

Bobby was catapulted forward and onto the ground, hitting the deck hard.

Fifteen minutes later Bobby was sitting in the backseat of a tinted, unmarked SUV, parked in a back alley around Venice Beach. His hands were cuffed behind his back. An FBI agent was sitting to his left. Michelle Kelly and Harry Mills were sitting directly in front of him.

Bobby kept his head low. His eyes on his knees.

'You sucker-punch sonofabitch,' Michelle said, touching her swollen lip again.

Bobby didn't look up.

'But it's all good,' Michelle carried on. 'Because guess what? We've got your sorry ass. And you're not going anywhere for a very long time.'

Bobby said nothing.

Michelle picked up Bobby's backpack, unzipped it and dumped all its contents on the floor between them. There wasn't much: several different chocolate bars, various packs of gum, three bottles of soda, a small, squared gift box with a red ribbon, a map of the area and a key on a keychain. No wallet. No driver's license. No identification of any kind. Bobby had already been searched. He had nothing on him.

'So what do we have here?' Michelle said, rummaging through everything.

Bobby's eyes followed her hands. 'Don't you need a warrant for that? That's private proper . . . urgh.'

The agent's elbow connected with Bobby's ribcage.

'If I were you,' the agent said. 'I'd limit myself to answering the questions you're asked, or else this thing can get very ugly, very quickly . . . For you, that is.'

Michelle picked up the chocolate bars, together with the packs of gum and the bottles of soda, and passed them over to Harry. 'Let's get these to the lab ASAP,' she said, before looking back at Bobby. 'I'm willing to bet your freedom that at least some of those are drugged.'

No answer. Bobby's eyes went back to his knees.

Michelle smiled. 'And what is this?' She reached for the gift box. The tag on it said *To Lucy, with love.* She undid the ribbon and pulled the lid open.

Harry's jaw dropped. 'You're kidding me.'

Michelle stared at the gift inside with angry eyes. 'Red lacy underwear?' she finally said. 'You thought Lucy was thirteen years old, and you bought her lacy panties?' She looked at Harry. 'Somebody give me a gun and I'll shoot this barf-bag in the face, right now.'

Bobby shifted nervously in his seat.

'You know, it doesn't really matter that you don't want to talk right now, or give us your real name, or anything. Because we've got this.' Michelle held up the key and keychain that was inside Bobby's backpack. The key ring simply said *103*. 'We now know that you got yourself a shitty hotel room somewhere not very far from here. It might take us a few hours, but we'll find the hotel, and whatever else you left behind in that room. I bet we'll find a wallet and an identity.' She paused for a moment. 'Actually, I bet we'll find a laptop or a smartphone.' Michelle leaned forward, her face just inches away from Bobby's. She could smell his cheap cologne. His minty breath. She smiled at him. 'You can't even begin to imagine what we can extract out of a laptop or a smartphone's hard drive. You see, Bobby, all those months in the chat rooms, and you had no idea you were chatting to *me*. I'm your Lucy.' Michelle allowed the weight of those words to crash down on Bobby for a moment. 'This is checkmate, buddy. Whichever way you play it, the game is over.'

Forty-One

The address they were given revealed a small, squared, two-story office building in Dewey Street, just behind Marine Park in Santa Monica. It took Hunter and Garcia forty-seven minutes to make the journey from the PAB. The outside of the old building was littered with *For Sale* and *For Lease* signs.

Hunter wondered who in their sane mind would want to buy or rent any office space in a building that looked to have been so terribly neglected in the past few years – tired and discolored bricks, ill-fitted windows and dark rainwater marks coming down from the roof like some sort of muddy icing on a cake.

The parking lot was hidden behind the property, away from the main street. Weeds were sprouting up through a web of cracks. Of the eight car spaces, only one was taken – a red Ford Fusion. Several wooden crates were pushed up against the wall, just a few yards from the car. The entrance to the parking lot had been sealed off by the Santa Monica Police Department with yellow crime-scene tape. A crowd had formed outside the perimeter, and though nothing could be seen from where they were standing, no one looked prepared to move an inch. Some were actually drinking coffee out of a thermos while they waited.

Hunter and Garcia parked in front of the building, next to the three police cars and the forensics van, before slowly weaving their way through the crowd.

As they reached the crime-scene tape and Hunter quickly chatted to the two officers guarding the entrance to the lot, a tall, lean and spare man dressed in a black hooded sweatshirt and dark blue jeans caught Garcia's eyes. He was standing at the back of the crowd, hands tucked deep into his pockets. But contrary to everyone else's tense and apprehensive body language, his was calm and relaxed. He looked up and his eyes met Garcia's for a brief moment, before darting away.

'Detective Sanchez is over there,' the older of the officers said, indicating a short and round man, who was chatting to one of the forensics agents. The man was about five foot six, and had his hands clasped behind his back like an undertaker overseeing a funeral. There was something funereal about the way the man looked as well – a black suit with an inch of crisp white cuff protruding from each sleeve, polished black shoes and a black tie. He had dark brown hair, which had been combed back and plastered with hair gel, Dracula-style. His bushy mustache curved around his top lip like a horseshoe.

'Detective Hunter?' Sanchez said, as he noticed the two new arrivals.

Hunter shook hands and introduced Garcia.

'This is Thomas Webb,' Sanchez said, nodding at the forensics agent he'd been chatting to. Webb was a few inches taller than Sanchez, and several pounds lighter. The forensics team were already packing up, ready to leave.

Sanchez didn't look like a man who would waste time, shooting the breeze. Introductions over, he readily reached into his inside pocket for his notebook. 'OK, let me tell you what we've got,' he addressed Hunter and Garcia. 'At 8:52 a.m. dispatch received a call from a Mr. Andrews.' He indicated the red Ford Fusion. 'The owner of that car. He's an accountant, and he has an office on the second floor of this building. The place is almost completely empty, as you can probably deduce from the number of real estate signs up front. An insurance company used to occupy the entire first floor, but they went under six months ago. The only other business in the building is a sole trader's quantity surveying firm, also on the second floor. We haven't established contact with him yet.'

Sanchez paused, maybe waiting for some sort of comment from Hunter or Garcia. He got none. 'Anyway, a black and white was dispatched to this address. When they got here, they found the body of a white female on the ground over there, right by those crates.' He indicated the location. 'She could've been anywhere between early twenties and late thirties. No one could tell.'

'The body was taken to the state coroners about an hour ago,' the forensics agent offered, checking his watch. 'Unfortunately, as far as studying the scene with the body *in situ* goes, you'll have to do with pictures.' He looked around himself for an instant. 'But this isn't a crime scene. It's a disposal area. If this really is a homicide case, she sure as hell wasn't murdered here.'

Sanchez observed Hunter and Garcia for a moment before moving on. 'Anyway, Mr. Andrews parked his car in his usual space, and as he got out he noticed the body on the ground. From where he was, his first thought was that it was probably some homeless soul, but according to him he never saw a homeless person sleeping out here before.

He moved a little closer to check, and that's when he freaked out. He called for help straightaway. He swears he didn't touch a thing.'

'Where is he?' Hunter asked.

'Up in his office. There's an officer with him. You can interview him again if you like.'

'The entire body was severely deformed by hundreds of different-sized lumps,' the forensics agent explained. 'They were inflammations and swellings, probably caused by wasp stings, more specifically tarantula hawks.'

Hunter and Garcia said nothing.

'We recovered three wasps from inside her mouth,' the agent continued, producing a small, tubular, plastic container with three dead tarantula hawks inside. 'One was lodged in her throat.'

'Was she dressed?' Garcia asked.

'Not completely. Underwear only. Purple in color, lacy in type.'

'Any belongings found?'

'Nothing. We've already checked the dumpster. It's empty. As Detective Sanchez said, the building is virtually unoccupied.'

'If you were able to identify lumps all over her body,' Hunter said, 'I'm assuming the body wasn't bloated.'

Hunter knew that in the early stages after death, especially the first three days, if the body is kept in relatively normal environment conditions, cellular metabolism slows as the internal systems begin to break down. Lack of oxygen in the tissues triggers an explosive growth of bacteria, which feed on the body's proteins, carbohydrates and fats, producing gases that cause the body to smell. That chemical reaction also causes the body to start to bloat and swell considerably, while secreting fluids from the mouth, nose, eyes, ears and lower body cavities. It had been exactly three days since they watched that woman die inside that glass coffin.

The forensics agent shook his head. 'No. No bloating of the body, whatsoever. Actually the body was just entering rigor mortis. My guess is that she died sometime yesterday or overnight.'

Garcia looked at Hunter, but his gaze gave nothing away.

'You'll have to wait for the autopsy results for a more accurate time frame,' the agent concluded.

'Was the body sent to the coroners in North Mission Road?' Hunter asked.

'That's right.'

'Now, the *really* fucked-up thing is,' Sanchez said, retrieving a clear plastic evidence bag from his pocket, 'together with the wasps, they found this stuffed in her mouth.' He handed the envelope to Hunter. Inside it was a yellow, square sticky note. Written in black ink, from what looked to have been a felt-tip pen, were the words *Enjoy, Detective Hunter. I know I did.*

Forty-Two

Hunter and Garcia read the note, and without saying a word returned it to the forensics agent. He would take it back to the lab for analysis.

'I'm assuming that this case will now be transferred to the Homicide Special Section?' the agent asked, as his stare flip-flopped between Hunter, Garcia and Sanchez.

Before Hunter or Garcia could answer, Sanchez lifted both of his hands, palms forward. 'It's all yours. Whoever did this asked for you by name, so, please, be my guest.'

'As soon as we have any results from anything,' the agent said, addressing Hunter and Garcia, 'you'll be the first to know.' He turned and rejoined the rest of his team.

'What the hell is going on?' Sanchez asked, once Webb was out of earshot. 'I've been observing the two of you since you got here. Checking your reactions while Webb revealed everything his team found so far, while he showed you the wasps they retrieved from inside the woman's mouth, while you read that note and all ... Nothing. No anger. No surprise. No disgust. Not even a wince. Fair enough, you didn't get to see the state of that poor woman's body up close, but even if you had I don't think it would've surprised you.' He was still studying both detectives' faces. 'I know you're Homicide Special, and you're supposed to have seen some pretty messed-up crap, but in my view, no matter how much experience you have, or how well trained you are, in a case like this something's gotta give.'

Neither Hunter nor Garcia replied.

'Don't fucking tell me that you've seen something like this before. It looks like that woman was killed by hundreds of big-ass wasps. The biggest I've ever seen. That's already nuts in itself. But from that note, one can only conclude she was murdered. I might not be Homicide Special, but I've been to plenty of crime scenes, and I've seen plenty of dead bodies. Twenty-two years' worth of it. God knows I've seen some shit that would make anyone puke. But I'll tell you now, I've never seen shit like this. When forensics pulled the first wasp from that woman's mouth, my blood sugar hit the floor. I'm allergic to those things. When they pulled out that note, my balls shrunk.' He paused and used the palm of his hand to wipe the sweat from his forehead and the nape of his neck. 'What kind of psycho kills someone using wasps?'

Still silence from Hunter and Garcia.

'But even after being told that hundreds of wasp stings deformed her entire body ... even as you read that note, neither of you showed the slightest of reactions. So, you both are either the coldest motherfuckers I've ever met, or you were expecting this. So let me ask you again. What the hell is going on? Has this happened before?'

A tense moment passed.

'Not exactly like this,' Hunter finally replied. 'But yes, it has happened before, and, yes, we were expecting it.'

Sanchez was clearly debating something in his head. He wasn't sure he wanted to know any more details. The circumstances dictated that the case wouldn't end up on his desk anymore, and truthfully he was glad. He ran his thumb and index finger over his mustache while staring back at the location where the body was found.

'Do you know what?' he said. 'I can't wait for retirement. I can't wait to get the hell away from this city. Last week we arrested a father, who threw his own baby daughter out the window of his tenth-floor apartment just because she was crying too much. When, just seconds later, his girlfriend realized what had happened and started freaking out, he threw her as well. When we kicked his door down, he was sitting in his living room, watching a baseball game and eating cornflakes. The daughter died. The girlfriend is a vegetable in a hospital bed. Her brain is gone. She has no insurance, so they're already talking about turning off the machines. The guy couldn't give a damn either way.'

Sanchez straightened his white cuffs under his suit jacket, and then his tie. 'This city has no conscience. It has no mercy. I wouldn't be surprised if in the end you find out that whoever did this did it just for the fun of it.'

Forty-Three

California oaks shaded the road as Hunter turned into Loma Vista Drive from West 8th Street in Long Beach. The house they were looking for was almost at the end of the drive. Sat back from the street, it had a pale yellow front that contrasted nicely against the white door and window frames. A low wrought-iron fence surrounded the house. Behind it, a neatly mowed front lawn. The narrow driveway on the left led to the one-car garage at the back of the house. The driveway gates were open. A metallic-blue Toyota Matrix was parked just outside the garage. The license plate number matched the one they had for Christina Stevenson's car.

According to the research team, Christina had left the *LA Times* headquarters on Thursday evening. She had taken Friday and Saturday off, but they were expecting to see her back on Sunday. She never turned up, but that wasn't surprising. Reporters had a tendency of disappearing for days, depending on the story they were working on.

Hunter parked on the street, directly in front of the house. On a Monday afternoon the road was quiet. No kids playing. No one tending to their gardens or lawns. No one sitting out on their porches, enjoying the day.

They entered the property grounds via the driveway gates. Hunter knocked, and then tried the front door

– locked. Both front windows were also locked, with their curtains drawn shut.

Garcia had carried on down the driveway in the direction of the blue Toyota. He gloved up and checked the car doors first, before moving onto the garage – all locked.

'Everything up front is locked,' Hunter said, joining Garcia. 'Curtains are all shut.'

'Same on this side of the house,' Garcia replied. 'Car and garage are locked too. But she obviously came back home on Thursday evening after she left the paper.'

They both made their way around toward the back of the house. The fence to the right of the garage wasn't just for decoration like the one up front. This one was solid wood and about eight feet high, with a sturdy-looking door. Hunter tried the door handle. The door clicked open.

'That's not a good sign,' Garcia said.

They walked through to the house's ample patio, where a rectangular swimming pool was its main feature. Four sun loungers were arranged on one side of the pool. A small shelter at the north end of the patio housed a barbecue grill. The house was to their right, where the entire back façade was completely made of glass. There were two sliding doors leading back into the house. One led back into the living room, the other back into a bedroom. The one closer to them, leading back into the bedroom, was wide open. They started moving toward it, and at that exact moment a strong gust of wind blew east, in the direction of the house. The floral curtain behind the open door flew back just enough for them to catch a glimpse of the inside of the room. It was enough to make both detectives stop and look at each other.

'I'll call forensics,' Garcia said, reaching for his phone.

Forty-Four

Christina Stevenson's house was spacious, bigger than most in that part of town, but for the moment Mike Brindle and his forensics team were concentrating all their efforts in processing her bedroom.

The room was large and comfortable, overflowing with girly touches – from the pink dresser to the stuffed toys – but it looked like it had been hit by a hurricane. The toys, the bed pillows and several colorful cushions were scattered all over the floor. The bed covers had been partially pulled off, as if someone had grabbed at them with both hands while being forcefully dragged away from the bed. The bed itself was twisted out of position, and that had knocked the bedside table on its side. The bedside lamp had hit the floor and shattered into tens of tiny pieces. A bottle of Dom Ruinart 1998 champagne was tipped over, lying next to the bedside table. Most of the bubbly liquid had spilled out onto the floor. Some of it had seeped through the wooden floorboards; the rest had pretty much evaporated, leaving just a tiny pool by the bottle's neck. A smashed champagne flute was lying just inches away from the bottle.

The pink dresser looked as if somebody had kicked it in a fit of rage. Perfume flasks and hair product bottles had been knocked over, and most of them were now on the floor, together with an MP3 speaker docking system, a hair dryer and various makeup items. The dresser mirror was cracked. Though they hadn't found any blood anywhere yet, the entire room screamed one word at everyone – *struggle*.

But to a forensics team, a crime scene marked by a struggle was almost like hitting the jackpot. A struggle meant that the victim resisted, fought back in some way. Even if the assailant was prepared for it, with rivers of adrenaline rushing through the victim's veins no one could predict how long or how intense that struggle would be. A struggle would always cause more evidence to be left behind – more clothes fibers lost, maybe a hair follicle, or an eyelash. A bump against the sharp corner of a bedside table or a dresser could cause a micro cut, invisible to the naked eye, but nevertheless leaving behind traces of blood and skin, and consequently DNA. Ironic as it might sound, forensically speaking a struggle was a great thing.

A forensics agent in white Tyvek hooded coveralls was dusting the glass door that Hunter and Garcia had found wide open. A second agent was slowly moving about the place, tagging and photographing every item in the room. Mike Brindle was working the bed and the area immediately around it.

Hunter and Garcia had also suited up in hooded coveralls, and were now checking the living room. The space was pleasantly decorated. The furniture was elegant and expensive-looking. A well-equipped open-plan kitchen was located at the south end of the room. To the right of the front door, three portraits were arranged next to a bowl of fake fruit on top of a stylish black sideboard.

The living room and the kitchen were in perfect order. Nothing seemed out of place. The struggle had happened only inside the bedroom.

They had found Christina Stevenson's bag on the floor by the sideboard. Her wallet was in there, together with her driver's license, her credit cards, her car keys and her cell-phone, which had run out of battery.

Garcia was looking around the kitchen when his smart-phone beeped.

'We've got a file on Ms. Stevenson,' he announced, checking his email application.

Hunter was studying the three pictures on the sideboard. One was of Christina sitting on a beach somewhere. In the second one, a kind-faced woman with vivid blue eyes and full lips was smiling. Christina had definitely inherited her mother's eyes, strong nose, high cheekbones and the small mole under her bottom lip. The woman on the picture had an almost identical one. The last picture showed Christina in a black and gray cocktail dress, holding a glass of champagne and talking to an elegantly dressed group of people.

'What do we have?' Hunter asked, turning to face Garcia.

'OK, I'll skip what we already know,' Garcia said. 'Christina Stevenson was born right here in LA. She grew up in Northridge, where she lived with her mother, Andrea. No brothers or sisters. Her father is unknown, and according to this, Christina never had a legal stepfather. Her mother never married. She went to Granada Hills High School, and it looks like she was a good enough student – good grades, never in trouble. She was part of the cheer-leaders' team from her sophomore to her senior year.' Garcia scrolled down on his phone application. 'Her mother died of a brain aneurysm seven years ago, on the exact same day Christina received her degree in journalism from UCLA.'

Reflexively Hunter's gaze returned to the portrait of the smiling woman on the sideboard.

'It looks like her mother's death knocked the life out of her,' Garcia moved on. 'Because we've got nothing for a whole year here. After that, she managed to land an intern's job with the *LA Times* and has been with the paper ever since.'

'Was she always with the entertainment desk?' Hunter asked.

'Nope. She spent four years jumping from desk to desk – city, international, politics, economy, current affairs, crime, even sports. She only settled into her own when she joined the entertainment desk two years ago. Never married. No kids. There's no mention of any boyfriends here either. No records of drug use. They're still checking her financial records, but the mortgage on this house is almost paid off. She earned a very decent salary from the paper.' Garcia scrolled down a little more. 'She had a big story published yesterday, in the Sunday edition of the *LA Times*. Probably the story Emilio was talking about.'

'What was the story?'

More scrolling followed by a surprised look from Garcia.

'Listen to this. It was a scoop on a Hollywood celebrity who'd been fooling around with her kid's teacher while her husband, who is also a celebrity, was away, recording the latest episodes for the TV series he stars in. The story made the front cover of the entertainment supplement, with a sizable "call" on the paper's front page.' Garcia put his smartphone away. 'Correct me if I'm wrong, but that's the kind of story that can get you a whole bunch of new enemies. The kind that can break up marriages and destroy lives.'

'Who was the celebrity?' Hunter asked.

Before Garcia could answer, Mike Brindle poked his head through the living-room door. 'Robert, Carlos, you better come have a look at this.'

Forty-Five

The atmosphere inside the FBI Cybercrime Division was one of triumph. Smiles and congratulations were going around the room like a carousel. Even the FBI director in charge of the Los Angeles field office had called Michelle Kelly to express his satisfaction. He had two small daughters of his own and he couldn't even begin to imagine what he would do if either of them ever fell victim to an Internet pedophile.

Sitting at her computer, Michelle brought up Bobby's case file. On its front page she right-clicked on the empty square in the top right-hand corner that said "photo file", and selected 'add' from the pop-up menu. Harry Mills had already transferred a series of mugshots taken after Bobby's arrest into the FBI's mainframe computer. Michelle selected one, and clicked 'add'.

She then placed the cursor over the 'Name' field and typed in Bobby's real name – *Gregory Burke*.

Bobby was no longer a faceless, nameless threat to young kids anymore.

Michelle moved the cursor over to the *Investigation Status* field, deleted the word 'open', and as she typed in 'closed – subject arrested', she felt enormous satisfaction run through her. But she knew that that feeling wouldn't last long.

Unfortunately there were way too many 'Bobbys' out there, stalking social network sites, chat rooms, games websites or wherever kids would gather to socialize in cyberspace. Michelle and the FBI CCD were doing the best they could, but the simple truth was that they were hugely outnumbered, and the ratio grew the wrong way year after year. She knew that putting Bobby away was only a small victory in a war they'd been losing since the early days of the Internet, but even so it was days like today that made the fight worthwhile.

'You OK?' Harry asked, coming up behind her.

'I'm great.' She clicked the 'save' button.

'How's the lip?'

Michelle brought her fingertips to her swollen bottom lip. 'It hurts a little, but I'll live. A small price to pay for sending one more scumbag to prison.'

'And I hope he rots in there.'

Michelle chuckled, more out of relief than amusement. 'With what we have on him, I'm sure he will.'

It had taken the FBI less than two hours to discover the small hotel Bobby had booked for the day. It was only three blocks away from Venice Beach, where he was arrested. Inside the room they had found personal documents, credit cards, money, sex paraphernalia, pills, alcohol and a small, medicine-sized bottle containing some clear liquid. The bottle was already with the FBI forensics lab, and everyone had their money on the liquid testing positive for some sort of homemade date-rape drug, like gamma-hydroxybutyric acid. But the real finding came from a small black case by the bed. Inside it they'd found Bobby's personal laptop computer with hundreds of images and video clips, together with a digital video camera.

To Michelle's delight, Bobby hadn't had a chance to transfer the contents of the camera's memory card to his laptop – an unedited, twelve-minute video clip filmed only two days ago. The clip clearly showed Bobby with a girl who looked no older than eleven.

'So,' Harry said. 'You're coming out to celebrate, right? We're all going to Baja for a few drinks, and maybe some food.'

Baja was a Mexican grill-restaurant and bar just two blocks away from the FBI building.

Michelle glanced at her watch. 'Sure, but why don't you guys go ahead and I'll meet you there in about forty minutes or so. I just want to have another look at that crazy footage we recorded on Friday. You know, that woman inside that glass coffin . . . that whole voting thing.'

Harry gave her a feeble smile. He knew they had thrown everything they had at that transmission while the stream was live, but they'd gotten nowhere. Every path had led to a dead end. The FBI CCD was rarely blocked out of an Internet transmission so professionally, and their "failure" to find a way in had pissed Michelle off in a way Harry had only seen once before. She simply didn't know how to accept defeat.

'What are you hoping to find, Michelle?'

'I don't know. Maybe nothing.' She avoided eye contact. 'Maybe the killer is *that* much cleverer than we are.'

'It's not a competition, you know?'

'Yes, it is, Harry.' She finally looked at him with something burning in her eyes. 'Because if he's better than we are . . . if he wins and we lose, people die . . . in a very grotesque way.'

Harry lifted both hands in a surrender gesture, but he knew Michelle wasn't angry with him. 'Would you like some help?'

Michelle smiled. 'I'll be OK. You know me. Go celebrate with everyone, and I'll be down in a little while. And don't get too drunk before I get there.'

'Oh, I can't promise you that.' He started moving toward the door.

'Harry,' she called. 'Order me a Caipirinha, will you? Extra lime.'

'You bet.'

'I won't be long.'

Harry turned away from Michelle and smiled at himself. 'Yeah, I bet you won't,' he muttered.

Forty-Six

After everyone had left, Michelle dimmed the lights around her desk, poured herself a large cup of coffee and started going over the footage they had recorded from the Internet three days ago. She had never forgotten those images, but watching that woman locked inside that glass coffin again, while a nest of tarantula hawks slowly stung the life out of her, made every hair on Michelle's neck stand on end. Her swollen bottom lip started throbbing again, as her heartbeat accelerated. For an instant, right at the end of the footage, when one of the large black wasps exited through the woman's nasal cavity, Michelle had to fight the urge to be sick, a sensation, she remembered, not that much different from the day four FBI agents blasted through her door in the early hours of the morning to arrest her.

From a very early age, Michelle had always been great with computers, something that not even she could explain. It was like her brain was wired differently, patched up to make even the most complicated lines of machine code read like a nursery rhyme.

Michelle Kelly was born in Doyle, northern California. Her father passed away when she was only fourteen years old. A smoker since his early teens and with a weak immune system, he had contracted pneumonia while he struggled to get over a very bad cold. Her mother, a timid and submissive woman, who had always dreaded being alone, remarried a year later.

Michelle's stepfather was a violent drunk, who very soon transformed her low-self-esteem mother into a drug-taking, alcohol-drinking zombie. Despite trying hard, Michelle was powerless to stop her mother from becoming a wreck.

Late one night, six months after her stepfather moved in, he carefully pushed open the door to Michelle's bedroom and stepped inside. Her mother was passed out in the living room, after consuming three-quarters of a bottle of vodka.

Michelle jerked awake as her stepfather threw his large, sweaty and naked body on top of her, her heart racing in her chest, her breath rasping in her throat, confusion and terror lighting her eyes. He cupped his meaty hand over her mouth, pushed her head hard into the pillow and whispered in her ear, 'Shhhh, don't fight it, babe. You gonna like this. I promise you. I'm gonna school you on what a real man feels like. And very soon you'll be begging me for more.'

He had managed to partially rip her clothes off, and as he prepared to enter her he relaxed his grip over her lips. Michelle opened her mouth wide, but instead of screaming, she bit down hard with all the strength she had in her. Her young teeth cut through flesh and bone as if she was biting into a slab of butter, severing his pinky finger clean off. She spat it back into his face while he screamed in agony, blood cascading down his hand and arm. Before running out of the house and into the night, she grabbed a baseball bat and swung it right between his opened legs so hard and with such precision that it made him vomit. She never went back.

Three days later, after hitching four different rides, Michelle arrived in Los Angeles. She lived on the streets for several days, eating out of trashcans, sleeping under cardboard boxes and using the shower and facilities at Santa Monica Beach.

It was at that same beach that she met Trixxy and her boyfriend, two heavily tattooed surfers who told her that she could crash at their house if she wanted to. 'A lot of people do,' they explained.

It was true. Their house was always full of people coming and going.

Michelle soon found out that Trixxy and her boyfriend weren't only surf lovers. They were part of one of the first generations of Internet hackers. Back then the Internet was still taking its initial baby steps into the commercial world. Everything was new, and security was flawed.

It didn't take Trixxy and her boyfriend long to find out that Michelle was a natural with computers. No, 'natural' wasn't really the right word. Michelle was an absolute genius. She was able, in minutes, to work out and write the correct code procedures to overcome problems that would take Trixxy and her boyfriend hours to do, if not days. In no time she was hacking into all sorts of web servers and online databases – universities, hospitals, public and private organizations, financial institutions, federal agencies, international enterprises . . . Nothing was off limits. The more secure they were supposed to be, the bigger the challenge, and the better Michelle became. She even broke into the FBI and the NSA databanks twice in the same week.

Like every hacker in cyberspace, Michelle gave herself an alias – Thrasos, the Greek mythological spirit of boldness. Very becoming, she thought.

In cyberspace the possibilities were endless, and Michelle was just starting to have fun. That was when she found out that her mother had passed away after ingesting half a box of sleeping pills and washing them down with a bottle of bourbon.

Michelle cried for three whole days, a combination of sadness and anger. She soon learned that only a few months before, her stepfather had convinced her mother to make a will, leaving the house that they lived in, which had been bought by her real father, and everything of any value she still had to him. With that, Michelle's anger mutated. Her stepfather had transformed her mother into a drunken junkie, and then stolen everything she had. When Michelle checked, she found out that he had already put the house up for sale. That was when the angry monster inside her started screaming – REVENGE.

Within a week her stepfather's life had taken a turn for the very worst. Through the Internet, Michelle started wrecking his life. All the money in his bank account went mysteriously missing, seemingly due to some internal computer error that no one could track down. She ran up absurd gambling debts in his name, maxed out his credit cards, suspended his driver's license, and modified his internal revenue tax declaration in such a way that it would be only a matter of time before the IRS came asking questions. She left him broke, unemployed, homeless and alone.

Three months later he stepped in front of a train.

Michelle never lost a second of sleep over what she did.

It was an ex-boyfriend, after being arrested for possession of drugs with intent to distribute, who, in exchange for a deal, tipped the cops about Michelle. The cops, in turn, escalated the tip to the FBI Cybercrime Division, who'd already been looking for Thrasos for some time. With the information the ex-boyfriend had given them, it took the

FBI less than a week to set up a monitoring operation. The arrest came a few days later. Four agents blasted through her front door, just as Michelle had broken into the WSCC database – the interconnected power grid that distributes electric energy to the entire west coast of the United States. She had just restructured their rates system, giving every-one, from Montana down to New Mexico and across to California, electric energy at dirt-cheap prices.

By then, cybercrime and cyber terrorism had already become a major threat to America and its way of life. The government of the United States understood that someone with the kind of expertise Michelle Kelly possessed had the potential to become a tremendous asset and an ally in their new fight, rather than an enemy. With that in mind, the FBI offered her a deal – carry on hacking, but on this side of the law, or a very, very long stint in prison.

Michelle took the deal.

She soon realized that she didn't really miss her old life. She wasn't a hacker because she liked to break the law, or for monetary gain. She was a hacker because she enjoyed the challenge and the thrill, and she was brilliant at it. The deal she was offered took none of that away; it just made it all legal.

Not surprisingly, the FBI played its cards perfectly. Knowing that the reason why Michelle had run away from home had been her abusive stepfather, they acclimatized her to her new role by making sure that every case she dealt with throughout her first year with the Bureau involved a cyber-sex crime – more precisely, pedophilia. Michelle's anger and disgust toward such offenders were so intense, she buried herself in work, making every case a personal issue.

She was so good at what she did that within four years she was heading the Los Angeles FBI Cybercrime Division.

Michelle shook the memory out of her head now before turning her attention back to the footage of the woman locked inside the glass coffin again. She watched the recording one more time from the beginning, her eyes searching for any sort of missed detail, but once again she failed to pick up anything.

'What the hell are you looking for, Michelle? There's nothing here,' she said to herself, while rubbing the palm of her hand against her forehead.

She took a bathroom break, refilled her coffee cup and returned to her desk. She wasn't ready to give up just yet.

Her next step was to slow the footage down 2.5 times, and, with the help of a 'color and contrast' application, to enhance the images using a color saturation method. The over-saturation tended to heighten small details, things people wouldn't pick up on otherwise.

Michelle sat forward on her chair, placed her elbows on her desk, rested her chin on her knuckles and started from the top again.

The reduced speed made watching the footage almost mind numbing. The color and contrast saturation tired the eyes faster, straining the ocular globes. Michelle found herself taking short breaks every three to four minutes. To relax her eyes, she would refocus them on something at the opposite end of the room for a moment, while massaging her temples, but she could already feel a headache gaining momentum right behind her eyeballs.

'Maybe I should've accepted Harry's help,' she murmured to herself. 'Or better yet, maybe I should've just gone with them, because right about now I sure as hell could do with a drink.'

She had another sip of her coffee before letting the footage play again, and checked the time counter in the bottom right-hand corner of the screen. She had just over a minute to go.

As her eyes returned to the screen, Michelle swore she saw something flash past.

Not a tarantula hawk.

'What the hell?'

She paused the recording, rewound the images back just a couple of seconds and hit 'play'.

Zoom.

She saw it go past again.

Adrenaline rushed through her body.

Once more Michelle rewound the images, but this time she zoomed in on a specific section of the screen and shut down the color and contrast saturation program. Instead of allowing the footage to play, she manually advanced it frame by frame.

And there it was.

Forty-Seven

Hunter and Garcia followed Brindle down the short corridor that led deeper into the house and back into Christina Stevenson's bedroom.

'We ran a UV test against the bed sheets, the bed covers and the pillowcases,' Brindle announced, guiding both detectives toward the bed. 'No traces of semen anywhere, but there are tiny bloodstains, mainly on this corner of the bed covers. The lab will tell us if the blood belongs to the victim or not.' He indicated the location before turning the UV light back on. 'Have a look.'

One simple and quick way to detect bloodstains on dark or red surfaces was to use an ultraviolet light. It provides enough contrast between the background and the stain to allow the stain to be visualized.

As soon as the UV light came on, four small, smeared bloodstains became clearly noticeable on the dark blue bed cover. But they were minimal, and totally inconclusive. A small razor nick from shaving her legs in the shower could've produced them.

Brindle knew that too, but he wasn't finished yet. He turned off the UV light and handed Hunter and Garcia a small clear plastic evidence bag. Inside it was a woman's diamond Tag Heuer watch.

'I found that under the bed, near the wall.'

Still neither detective looked impressed. The room was an absolute mess. Objects of all shapes and sizes had been knocked over and kicked across the floor in all directions. The watch could have been on the dresser to start with, but ended up under the bed.

'That's not all,' Brindle said, noticing the skepticism on both detectives' faces. He showed them a second clear plastic evidence bag. It contained three tiny items. 'I also found these under the bed. Here, use this.' He handed them an illuminated magnifying glass.

Hunter and Garcia studied the items in the bag for several seconds.

'Fingernail chips,' Hunter said.

'Torn fingernail chips,' Brindle clarified. 'They were stuck to the floorboard grooves.' He paused, giving Hunter and Garcia a chance to digest what he was saying. 'It looks like the victim was hiding under the bed. The perpetrator found her, and I'd say he pulled her out by the legs. The dislodged dust from under the bed created a smeared pattern, which is consistent with something heavy . . . like a person, being dragged from under it.'

Instinctively Hunter and Garcia took a step back and tilted their heads to one side, as if trying to look under the bed.

'With nothing to hold on to,' Brindle carried on with his theory, 'it looks like she clawed at the floor, trying to resist the drag – that was when her fingernails chipped and broke off. Once he got her out from under the bed, she frantically reached out for whatever she could grab.' Brindle paused and looked at the bed covers again. 'And that's how I think the blood got onto them.'

Everyone's attention returned to the bed covers.

'You see,' Brindle explained. 'An extracted nail will cause the nail bed to bleed as much as a cut to the finger, but a chipped and broken nail will cause bleeding only if it manages to nick the tip, or the sides of the nail bed. And even if it does, there might be no bleeding at all. If there is any, it should be minimal. Just like what we've got here.'

Hunter and Garcia considered it for a moment.

'I also found these stuck to the underside of the bed's box spring.' He showed them one last evidence bag. Inside this one, four blond hair strands. 'Her head most certainly bumped against it while she was being dragged from under the bed.' He let out a concerned breath. 'Looking at the state of the room, I'd say she fought as hard as she could, kicking and hitting all the way, until she was completely subdued.'

Thoughtful silence.

Garcia spoke first.

'That all makes sense except for hiding under the bed. That implies that she knew someone was coming for her.' He looked at the glass sliding doors and then back at the bed. 'Why hide under here when she could've escaped from the house through the patio doors?'

As if on cue, Dylan, the forensics agent who was dusting the glass sliding doors, announced, 'I've got prints here.'

Everyone turned and faced him.

'The lab will confirm it, but by just looking at them I can tell you that the patterns are all the same. I have no doubt they all come from the same person. Small fingers. Delicate hands. Definitely a woman's.'

When it came to fingerprints, Dylan was as good as it got.

'How about the lock?' Brindle asked.

'The lock isn't broken,' Dylan said. 'We'll have to remove it and take it for analysis, but this is a standard pin tumbler lock. Not very secure. If the perpetrator entered the house through this door, he could've easily bumped it. No sweat.'

Lock bumping was a lock picking technique for opening pin tumbler locks where a specially crafted bump key was used. A single bump key would work for all locks of the same type. There were several videos over the Internet that could teach anyone how to bump a lock.

Hunter was still looking at the three evidence bags Brindle had handed him. He agreed with Garcia. Hiding under the bed made no sense under the circumstances.

'Mike, where exactly did you find this watch?' he asked.

Brindle showed him.

Hunter lay down on the floor and looked under the bed, his eyes studying the location where the watch had been found, his mind rushing through possibilities. Still nothing made sense.

Garcia walked across the other side of the bed and positioned himself just in front of the floral curtains, at the opposite end from where Dylan had dusted the glass door and lock. That distracted Hunter, and for a second his attention refocused on Garcia's black shoes and socks that he could see from under the bed.

Hunter's body tensed. His thought process went from A to Z in just one second. 'No way,' he whispered, his gaze locked on his partner's shoes.

'What?' Garcia asked.

Hunter got up. All his attention had now moved to the curtains just behind Garcia.

'Robert, what did you see?' Garcia asked again.

'Your shoes.'

'What?'

'I saw your shoes across the floor from under the bed.'

Confusion all round.

'OK, and . . .?'

Hunter lifted a finger, indicating that he needed a moment, before walking in a straight line over to the curtains and slowly pulling them open. He kneeled down and carefully studied the floor for a little while.

'I'll be damned!' The words oozed out of his lips.

'What?' Brindle asked, moving closer. Garcia was just behind him.

'I think we've got dust-shift,' Hunter said and indicated with his index finger. 'Probably created by a footprint.'

Brindle kneeled down next to him, his eyes scrutinizing the floor area. 'Holy shit,' he said a moment later. 'I think you might be right.'

'That's what I think Christina saw,' Hunter said, looking at Garcia. 'Her killer's shoes. I don't think she was hiding under the bed. I think she probably got under it to retrieve her watch, but while she was under there she saw him. She saw her killer. *He* was the one who was hiding.'

The room went silent for a moment.

'OK, let's get a photograph of this,' Brindle finally said, addressing Dylan. 'I also need some lift film. Let's see how much of a print we can obtain here.'

Hunter stood up and slowly allowed his eyes to move along the panoramic glass wall in front of him.

'Actually we better dust just about everything here,' he said. 'The killer might've been hiding and waiting for a while.' He leaned forward a few inches, his nose almost touching the glass wall, as if searching for a smudge mark. 'Maybe he leaned against the glass. Maybe he left someth—'

Hunter froze. The word dying in his throat.

'What?' Garcia asked, pausing just behind his partner and trying to look over his shoulder, but he had no idea what he was looking at. He thought Hunter had seen something through the window, out back.

Hunter blew another warm breath against the glass, this time a long, purposeful one, moving his head around to deliver the breath against a wider area. The glass misted for just a few seconds.

That was when Garcia finally saw it.

'You have *got* to be joking.'

Forty-Eight

The vast open-plan office floor inside the *LA Times* headquarters building on West 1st Street sounded like a schoolyard at lunch break. The place was bustling with phone chatter, keyboard clacks, loud conversations and the shuffling of hurried feet, as every reporter rushed to meet the day's deadline.

Pamela Hays sat at her corner desk, undistracted by the noise and oblivious to the chaos of movement around her. She was the *LA Times'* entertainment desk editor, and she too was rushing, reviewing all the articles that would make the final cut of the supplement for tomorrow's paper.

Entertainment Pam, as everyone always called her, had been working for the *LA Times* for only seven years, since she graduated from university at the age of twenty-four. Her first year with the paper had been a struggle. Fresh out of college, and with no experience working for a high-circulation newspaper, she was made to prove her worth by writing an infinite number of second-rate articles on stories she was sure only she and her mother read. Many of them never even made it into print. But Pamela knew she was a good reporter, and an expert researcher. It didn't take long for others to start realizing that too.

Bruce Kosinski, a larger-than-life man in more than one way, and at that time the city editor at the entertainment desk, was the first to give Pamela a shot at trying her hand at a 'real' story. She did well. Very well, in fact. Her research had been second to none, and the story made the front page of the paper. Two years ago, Bruce Kosinski was appointed as chief editor for the *LA Times*. His old job was offered to Pamela Hays, who gladly accepted.

It's true that Pamela did sleep with Bruce, but she knew that that wasn't the reason why she was offered the enter-tainment desk's editor's position. The way she saw it, she had more than earned it.

Pamela finished editing another article on her list, rolled her chair back from her desk and stretched her stiff neck.

'Where the hell is Marco?' she asked out loud to no one in particular. She got no answer.

Unlike most of the other section editors at the *LA Times*, Pamela didn't have an office. She didn't much care for one either, preferring to sit among her reporters and the hustle and bustle of the main room.

She checked the clock on the wall.

'Goddamn it, he's got less than twenty minutes to get his article to me. If he's late again, I'm firing his ass. I've had it with his crap.'

'What the hell?' Pedro, the reporter whose desk was just opposite Pamela's, said, frowning at his computer screen. 'Pam, is Christina doing extra work as an actress?' he asked.

Pamela looked at him as if he'd lost his mind. 'What the hell are you *hablando* about, *muchacho*?' As a joke between the two of them, she had gotten into the habit of speaking Spanglish with Pedro.

'Come have a look at this,' Pedro called. There was no play in his voice.

Pamela got up and made her way around to Pedro's desk.

'I was just checking a few things on the net,' Pedro said, 'when I came across this article.' He pointed to his screen.

It was a short article named 'Reality or Hoax?' The title didn't catch Pamela's attention, but the small picture under the headline did – a woman lying inside some sort of glass enclosure with hundreds of very scary black insects swarming around her body. Despite the bad quality of the picture, her face was clearly visible, including the small black mole just below her bottom lip.

Pamela felt her blood almost freeze inside her veins. As she read the article, the color drained from her already naturally pale face.

There was no doubt in her mind. The woman in that picture was Christina Stevenson.

And whatever that was, it was no hoax.

Forty-Nine

Hunter woke up at 5:15 a.m. with a headache that could've raised the dead. He sat in bed, in the darkness of his bedroom, catatonically staring at the blank wall in front of him, as if he stared long and hard enough it would magically start answering all the questions choking his brain.

It didn't.

He forced himself to stop thinking before his brain went into complete meltdown. He got ready and made his way to the twenty-four-hour gym just three blocks from where he lived. A heavy workout always had a way of clearing his head.

Almost two hours later, after a hot shower, he headed out to the PAB.

Garcia had just arrived when Hunter got to his office. Captain Blake followed just seconds later.

'Brace yourselves,' she said, allowing the door to close behind her with a *bang*. ''Cos the delayed storm is finally here.'

'Storm?' Garcia frowned.

'The shitstorm,' she replied, slapping this morning's copy of the *LA Times* on his desk. The top half of the front page was taken by a series of six small photographs of Christina Stevenson lying inside the glass coffin. They were arranged sequentially. The first three showed her terrified and confused face at different stages of the voting process – EATEN at 211, then at 745, and finally at 1000. The next two showed her sharing the glass coffin with the tarantula hawks. Her face in both pictures was twisted and contorted in agonizing pain.

The last picture showed her with a still, cold stare, her body all covered in red-raw lumps and black wasps, her lips swollen and bleeding.

The life had been stung out of her.

The headline at the top of the pictures read DEATHNET. KILLER BROADCASTS BARBARIC EXECUTION LIVE ONLINE.

Garcia started skimming over the article. It confirmed that the broadcast appeared to have been real, not a hoax. It described what had happened, but not in great detail. There was also no mention of Christina's body being found.

Hunter leaned back against his desk. He didn't seem interested in what the paper had to say.

'I thought the FBI had told you that this video was off the net,' Captain Blake said. 'How the *hell* did they get this?'

'Not completely off the net,' Hunter replied. 'Just out of most people's reach. But once something goes on the net, then it's always on the net. Even if most people can't find it. The *LA Times* has enough resources and people on their payroll to be able to track the video down.'

The room was starting to feel stuffy. Captain Blake walked over to the only window in the room and pushed it open.

'So far, that's the only paper carrying the story,' she said irritably. 'But our press office already received a battery of calls – from local, to nationwide and international newspapers. The avalanche of crap is just about to start.'

Hunter and Garcia knew she was referring to all the jack-asses that would no doubt start calling in or sending in anonymous letters with all sorts of bogus tips and information, most of which would have to be checked out because it was protocol. Adding to that, there were always the obligatory phone calls from psychics and tarot card readers with visions, or messages received from beyond the grave that could help break the case. They were all used to it. It happened every time the news of a new high-profile killer broke.

'The mayor was on the phone this morning,' Captain Blake added. 'He called me at my home. As soon as I put the phone down, I got a call from the governor of California. Everybody wants to know what the hell is going on, and my home phone seemed to have become this case's information hot line.' She grabbed the paper back from Garcia's desk and hastily threw it into the wastebasket, knocking it over and spilling its contents.

'What did you tell them?' Hunter asked, calmly returning the wastebasket to its place.

Captain Blake looked back at Hunter. Her makeup was as impeccable as always, but she was wearing a darker shade of eye shadow than she usually did, and that made the angry look in her eyes appear deadly. Still, Hunter didn't shy away from it.

'Enough to assure them we're doing everything we can,' she replied. 'But I gave them nothing they didn't need to know. No one knows the killer contacted you first, and that we were already investigating this case way before it hit the papers. No one knows that this killer has already claimed at least one victim prior to Christina Stevenson. I want to keep all that under wraps. As far as everyone is concerned, we're starting our investigation into these online murders today.'

'Suits us fine,' Hunter said.

'I refused the request for a press conference this early in the investigation,' the captain continued, still annoyed. 'But we won't be able to escape it, as you both well know it. There will eventually be a press conference. And guess what?' She didn't wait for a reply. 'The two of you are the ones who will be facing that execution squad.'

There were few things in life Hunter hated more than press conferences. He breathed out and pinched the bridge of his nose. His headache was still eating away at his brain, despite the grueling workout.

'Did you read the Sunday edition of the *LA Times*?' Captain Blake asked. 'Did you read Christina Stevenson's story?'

Both detectives nodded.

'Well, she burst that "celebrity" affair wide open,' the captain said. 'I don't care for tabloids or gossip publications, but since yesterday I've had to become intimately acquainted with them. They are all saying that the cheated husband will probably file for divorce.' She paused, but there was no reaction from Hunter or Garcia. She moved on. 'Whatever happens, that relationship is now severely dented. The wife's actions will also probably put an end to her not-very-successful acting career. Though I won't be surprised if she gets a book deal out of this. My point is, we've all seen and worked on cases where people were murdered for a lot less than something like that. Are you looking into this celebrity couple as suspects?'

'We did a preliminary check,' Garcia said. 'The husband had been filming in Sacramento since the beginning of the week. He obviously had no idea about the affair, or that the story was coming out. He returned to Los Angeles on Sunday evening. The wife and her lover both have solid alibis for Friday night, the night Christina Stevenson died. And no, they aren't each other's alibis, Captain. We're looking into other aspects of this, but the big head-scratcher is – how do we link Kevin Lee Parker, our first victim, to Christina's celebrity affair story? We know for sure that the same person is behind both murders.'

'Well, that's your job, isn't it?' Captain Blake retorted. 'Finding a connection, if there is any.'

'And as I said, we're looking into it,' Garcia replied firmly. 'The possibility that Ms. Stevenson was murdered because she was a reporter is very real, and we know that. We have a team working on collecting every article she wrote for the *Times* in the past two years.'

'Get them to work faster,' the captain said, turning to face the pictures board on the south wall. She immediately noticed two new sets of photographs. The first one had been taken at the car park in Dewey Street, Santa Monica, where Christina Stevenson's body had been found yesterday morning. When her stare found the pictures of the body itself, the captain held her breath for an instant.

With the wasps gone, the deformation caused by their stings was absolutely shocking. Christina's body was an unrecognizable mass. The tarantula hawks had shown no mercy. Even her eyes and tongue had been stung several times.

'Jesus!' The word unintentionally escaped the captain's lips. 'Good thing the paper didn't get hold of this picture.'

The second new set of photographs came from Christina's bedroom.

Captain Blake scanned the pictures slowly, and Hunter and Garcia saw her body go rigid when she came to the last photo on the set.

'What the hell is that?'

Fifty

After Hunter's discovery inside Christina Stevenson's bedroom, the forensics team used a fluorescent orange fingerprint powder on the glass wall to enhance what was found. Though fluorescent powders were usually used against multicolored surfaces, they were often used to dust large areas, due to how easy it was to photograph the results under a UV light.

'The killer left us that,' Hunter said.

'What?' Captain Blake stepped closer to have a better look.

'He left that on the glass wall behind the curtains,' Hunter clarified. 'We think he hid there while waiting for his victim to come home.'

'How did he do this?'

'The same way kids do. He misted the glass with a warm breath, and then wrote on it.'

Forensics had used a handheld steamer to properly steam the desired section on the glass. The fluorescent orange powder attached itself to the water particles created by the steam that surrounded whatever the killer had drawn onto the glass, making the whole thing look like a large, fluorescent orange stencil.

At the center of it the killer had written three words: THE DEVIL INSIDE.

'What the hell does this mean?' the captain asked, spinning around to face her detectives. 'Inside what ... or who ...? His head ...? Her ...? That glass coffin ...?'

'We don't know what it means yet, Captain,' Hunter said.

'That's why I got here early,' Garcia joined in. 'The only reference I could find was to a horror film released in January 2012. It's called *The Devil Inside*.'

'A horror film?' Captain Blake's left eyebrow arched in a peculiar way.

Garcia nodded, while reading out of his computer screen. 'It's a documentary-style horror film about a woman who becomes involved in a series of exorcisms, while trying to figure out what happened to her mother.'

A moment of stunned silence.

Up went the second eyebrow. 'Did you just say exorcisms?'

Garcia breathed out, sharing the captain's frustration. 'That's right. According to the movie blurb, her mother had murdered three people while possessed by a demon. The daughter wants to find out if that's true or not.'

The captain's gaze went from Garcia, to Hunter, to the pictures board and then back to Garcia. 'I can't believe I'm about to ask this question.' She shook her head. 'In the film, how does this girl's mother murder these three people?'

'I haven't watched it yet,' Garcia answered. 'That's what I wanted to do before you guys got here.' He nodded at his computer screen.

Captain Blake took a step back and scratched her forehead with her manicured pale pink nails. 'Oh, give me a fucking break. Do either of you two really believe that any of this—' she indicated the pictures board '—has anything to do with a supernatural horror film about exorcisms?'

'I didn't know a movie with that title existed until Carlos mentioned it just now,' Hunter said. 'But now that we know, we might as well check it out.' He shrugged, while tilting his head to one side. 'Murderers replicating crimes that have appeared in films or books, true or fictional, is nothing new, Captain. You know that.'

She *did* know that. Only two years ago the RHD was involved in a case where a twenty-one-year-old kid murdered four people in as many weeks. When he was finally apprehended, it transpired that he was obsessed with an obscure crime novel published a few years earlier. He identified with the killer's character so much that he actually believed he and the fictional serial killer were the same person. He followed the crimes in the novel exactly as they'd been described.

'Maybe it's just a coincidence that there's a movie with those exact same words for a title, Captain,' Hunter continued. 'As you've just said, the killer could be speaking figuratively, referring to *the devil inside* him ... or her ... or something else.'

'And that would mean what?' the captain shot back.

'Depends,' Hunter said. 'If those words are a reference to the devil inside *himself*, then he could be talking about something he can't control. An overwhelming desire to kill. A monster inside. Maybe dormant most of the time, but when he awakes—' Hunter indicated the pictures board '— that's the result.'

Captain Blake's thoughtful and frustrated look intensified.

'In a different light,' Hunter moved on. 'The killer could be talking about the devil inside us all, referring to how pathetic he considers other people's lives to be.' Hunter pointed to a picture on the board. 'Kevin Lee Parker led a normal and unambitious life. He liked his job at the videogames shop, and he was very content with his family life. He didn't want or need any more than that. The killer might have seen his lack of ambition as a waste of life, and that pissed him off. Christina Stevenson's life, on the other hand, was completely dedicated to her job. A job that was highly dependent on gossip and rumor. A job that intruded on other people's lives, with very little regard for anything else. To many, a despicable job. Maybe the killer thinks he's ridding the world of mundanity, a kill at a time.'

'And then there's also the obvious more religious connotation,' Garcia said, taking over.

The captain faced him.

'The killer might believe that his victims are possessed by demons or something, and he's saving their souls by killing them. The torture targets the evil being inside, not the person.'

Captain Blake might've wanted to laugh, but she knew from first-hand experience that people's insanity was no joke, and it had no limits. As absurd as they might sound, any of those theories could be true. No one, maybe not even the killer, knew what was going on inside his head.

'Or it could be none of the above,' Garcia continued. 'As Robert said before, this killer might be so detached from everything that those words—' he guided the captain's attention back to the fluorescent orange powder photograph '—could be just him killing time, while he waited for his victim to come home.'

'Is there any connection between the two victims?' Captain Blake asked.

'We're checking,' Garcia replied.

The silence that followed was ruptured by the ringing of Hunter's phone.

'Detective Hunter, Homicide Special,' Hunter answered it.

'Detective, it's Michelle Kelly at the FBI Cybercrime Division. I reanalyzed the footage we had from the broadcast on Friday. And I think there's something you need to see.'

Fifty-One

This time Garcia drove, but during the short trip to the FBI building in Wilshire Boulevard, neither detective said a word. It had been ten days since they'd been catapulted into this investigation, and in those ten days this case had had so many twists it was starting to look like a bowl of spaghetti. And both detectives could sense there was more to come.

At the FBI building's reception desk, they went through the same security checks as the first time, before being escorted down to the Cybercrime Division by the same black-suited FBI agent.

'Dude, we're inside an elevator going underground,' Garcia said to the agent. 'You can take those shades off.'

The agent didn't move. Didn't reply.

Garcia smiled. 'I'm only messing with you. I know you have to keep those on at all times so no one knows what your eyes are focusing on, right?'

Still nothing from the agent.

'Ah, screw it,' Garcia said, reaching into his pocket for his sunglasses and putting them on. 'It's a good look. I think we should all wear them, regardless.'

Hunter stifled a smile.

The elevator doors opened again. Harry Mills was waiting for them by the glass double doors at the end of the hallway.

'Nice talking to you,' Garcia said to the agent, who kept an expressionless face as he turned and walked away.

Harry guided both detectives into the uncomfortably chilled Cybercrime Division quarters.

Michelle was sitting at her desk with a phone wedged between her right shoulder and ear, while her fingers danced frantically over her keyboard. She looked at Hunter and Garcia and bobbed her eyebrows up and down once in a silent 'hello'. Five seconds later she was done with the call.

'Wow,' Garcia said, staring at her still-swollen bottom lip. 'You either picked a fight with the wrong guy or that Botox thing isn't working well for you.'

Harry smiled.

'Funny man,' Michelle said.

Garcia shrugged. 'I do OK.'

'I actually picked a fight with the right guy, who will now be in prison for a very long time. Have a seat.' Michelle indicated the two empty chairs by her desk.

Hunter and Garcia took them.

Michelle was wearing a skintight black top with synchronized small rips down both sides. At the front of the top, in pink letters, were the words 'Rock Bitch'. The low-cut top also revealed a wall of colored tattoos on her chest.

'Last night I finally got some time to go over the footage of both murders,' she explained. 'I had no idea what I was looking for or what I was hoping to find. I was trying things out. One of the things I tried was a color and contrast saturation trick, together with slowing the images down.' She paused and typed something on her keyboard. The familiar images of Christina Stevenson lying inside the glass coffin loaded onto the left monitor on her desk. 'And I came across something I didn't expect to be there. I don't think anyone did. Not even the killer.'

Both Hunter and Garcia kept their attention on Michelle for a while longer before simultaneously allowing their eyes to shift toward the monitor.

Hunter had also watched both footages several times. He too had slowed them down, but he hadn't picked up anything new.

'Let me show you,' Michelle said, pulling her chair closer to her desk.

She first forwarded the footage to a late stage – 16.15 minutes out of the total 17:03 – and paused it. Christina Stevenson's torso was completely covered by tarantula hawks. She'd already been stung hundreds of times.

'Without the color and contrast saturation trick,' Michelle explained, 'I would've never seen it. Look at this.' She clicked and dragged her mouse over a portion of the image – somewhere just above where Christina's belly button would've been, creating a small, dotted-lined square over it. She typed a command and the dotted-lined square zoomed in to fill the entire screen.

Hunter and Garcia scooted to the edge of their seats.

'As you know,' Michelle continued. 'The killer was using a night-vision camera, so lighting was almost none. The camera was static, positioned above the coffin at an angle. We calculated it to be somewhere between thirty-eight to forty degrees.'

Hunter and Garcia nodded.

'Remember when I told you that this killer seemed to have everything covered,' Michelle said, moving on. 'Well, I think there was one thing he forgot to bring into his equation.'

Hunter and Garcia were still staring at the image on the screen. There was nothing there but a bunch of zoomed-into wasps.

'Those wasps are alive and moving all the time,' Michelle clarified. 'At this particular spot, by pure chance, a small group of them moved at the same time, in exactly the same direction, and over another bunch of wasps. The camera was just panning right toward the woman's face. The combination of all that movement, for a fraction of a second, produced a different light angle. Are you still with me?'

Both detectives nodded again.

'Now, the wasps' bodies are black, and any dark background behind plain glass can create a mirror effect if the light angle is right.'

Michelle typed another command and the image sharpened considerably, before advancing a single second and pausing.

Silence.

Squinting.

Head tilting.

And then Hunter and Garcia finally saw it.

Fifty-Two

Due to the new light angle created by the position the tarantula hawks had moved into, in combination with the camera just starting to pan right, something was suddenly reflected on the coffin's glass lid.

'It's only there for 0.2 seconds,' Harry said. 'But when we break it down into frames, we've got eight frames of it.'

Hunter and Garcia were still squinting at the screen and tilting their heads from side to side, trying to better understand what they were looking at. Whatever it was, it was only being partially reflected. An object high off the ground, maybe five or six feet, set back from the coffin, and placed against what looked like a nondescript brick wall. They could only see what they guessed was the top quarter of the object, and not very well. It was a thin structure that looked like a T. Probably made out of metal. The ends of the horizontal bar at the top of the T curved around themselves, creating two small loops, one at each end, like two hooks. Something looked to be hanging from the loop on the right-hand side, but the reflection showed only a tiny sliver of it.

'What the hell is that?' Garcia spoke first. 'Some sort of coat hanger?'

Hunter stared at it for a couple more seconds, and then shook his head. 'No. It's an IV drip stand.'

Garcia frowned. 'What?'

'That's exactly what we think it is,' Harry agreed. 'We've been comparing images on the internet for a while now.'

Michelle handed Hunter and Garcia two large color printouts.

Hunter didn't need to look at them. He knew he was right. He'd lived with one of those inside his house for several months when he was seven, while cancer ate away at his mother. He helped his father change her IV drip every day. When her pain convulsions caused her to violently jerk her arms in the air, tugging at the drip and throwing the whole stand to the ground, Hunter was always the one who picked it up. When he was twenty-three, after his father was shot in the chest, Hunter spent twelve weeks sitting in a hospital room with him while he lay in a coma before dying. For twelve weeks he stared at the IV stands, the drips and all the machinery inside that hospital room. No, he certainly didn't need to look at the printouts. Some memories and images would never leave his mind, no matter how much time had elapsed.

'An IV drip stand?' Garcia asked, his eyes moving back and forth between the printouts and the computer screen.

Hunter nodded.

'And as you can see—' Michelle took over again, pointing back at the screen and at the right loop '—something is definitely hanging from it.' She clicked her mouse and the picture magnified thirty times, but even then no one could be one hundred percent sure of what they were looking at. 'This is the best we could do,' she continued, shrugging. 'Our best guess ... that's some sort of an IV bag.'

Hunter and Garcia kept their eyes on the image.

'If it is,' Harry said, 'then you're mainly looking at two possible scenarios. One: that stand and drip are there for the killer.'

Neither detective commented back, but they both knew that it was possible.

In truth, they knew nothing concrete about this killer. All they had were assumptions based on the killer's actions so far. Even Mike Brindle from forensics believed that they were after someone big and strong. Strong enough to carry a 216-pound person over his left shoulder. But that assumption was based on the shoeprints retrieved from the alleyway in Mission Hills, where the first victim's body had been found. The prints they believed had been left by the killer. Brindle had told them that the left shoeprint seemed to be more prominent than the right one. He said that that could indicate that the killer walked with a slight abnormality, like a limp, depositing more of his weight onto his left leg. They assumed the abnormality was caused because the person was carrying a heavy load over his left shoulder – the victim's body. But what if they'd assumed wrong? What if this killer had some sort of physical impairment? What if this killer *was* in some sort of constant pain and in need of daily medication?

'Scenario two,' Harry said, moving on, 'and the most probable, is that the IV is meant for the victims. Maybe the killer sedates his victims for some reason.'

Again, no comment from Hunter or Garcia, but neither of them believed that the killer had sedated his victims.

IV sedation, also known as Twilight Sleep, worked on the brain like amnesia, producing either partial or full memory loss. The person went in and out of slumber, totally relaxed, and could still hear what goes on around him or her, but nothing really registered. IV sedation usually didn't work as an anesthetic, so the person would still feel pain, but that would depend entirely on the type of drip used.

Christina Stevenson was alert and totally terrified while locked inside that glass coffin. Not relaxed. And in no way drifting in and out of slumber. The same could be said for Kevin Lee Parker. No, if the IV drip stand was there for the victims, Hunter was sure its purpose was not sedation, and that thought was what filled him with dread. The killer could've used some sort of feeling-enhancing drug. Something not so easily picked up by a blood toxicology test. Something that boosted their nervous system and ultra-sensitized it. To this killer, the violence had a purpose. He wanted his victims as sober as possible. He wanted them to feel every bit of pain, but he also wanted their fear. He wanted them to know that death was coming to them. And there was nothing anyone could do to save them.

Fifty-Three

As Hunter and Garcia left the FBI building, they received a phone call from Doctor Hove. She was done with Christina Stevenson's autopsy.

In bumper-to-bumper traffic, it took them just over an hour to reach the Department of Coroner in North Mission Road. Doctor Hove was waiting for them in Autopsy Theater One, the same autopsy theater used for Kevin Lee Parker's postmortem.

The room felt even colder than before. The stale, intrusive, sweet disinfectant smell seemed stronger, chokingly so. Hunter pinched his nose a couple of times before folding his arms over his chest. Goosebumps pricked the skin around his triceps.

Doctor Hove led them deep into the room toward the last of the three autopsy tables that sprang from the east wall.

Since they'd missed it at the parking lot in Santa Monica yesterday morning, this was the first time either of the two detectives had seen Christina Stevenson's body live and up close. Her disfigurement was even more disturbing than what the pictures had shown. Her skin, which had once been silky smooth, judging by the photographs they'd found in her house, now looked rubbery and porous. The lumps that covered most of her body came in all different sizes, but all of them grotesque, nonetheless. The unimaginable pain she'd been through was still there, etched on her distorted face like a horror mask.

'A different approach,' Doctor Hove said, slipping a brand-new pair of latex gloves on. 'But just as sadistic as the first murder, if you ask me.' She had already watched the recorded footage.

Hunter and Garcia positioned themselves on the left side of the stainless-steel examination table.

'Because wasps do not leave their stinger behind,' Doctor Hove began, 'allowing them to sting multiple times, it's impossible to tell how many times she was actually stung. As an educated guess, I'd say close to a thousand times.'

Garcia's throat knotted as beads of cold sweat broke out on his forehead. Only four stings had sent him into hospital when he was a kid. He could still remember the pain, and how sick he felt. His brain couldn't even begin to contemplate what a thousand stings would've been like.

'As she was lying on her back during the attack,' Doctor Hove continued, 'the wasps concentrated their efforts on the front and sides of her body. The least-stung areas are these small sections of her breasts.' She indicated with her index finger. 'And this area around her groin and hips. As you know, the reason for that is because she was wearing a bra and panties. The lab is already analyzing them. Any findings, you'll be the first to know.' She paused to clear her throat. 'Safe of those areas, as you can see, she was stung pretty much everywhere else, including the inside of her mouth, the back of her throat, her tongue, her eyes and the inside of her nostrils.' Doctor Hove glanced at the chart on the west wall that itemized the weights of the deceased's internal organs. 'I retrieved dead wasps from deep inside her aural cavity, her esophagus and her stomach.'

Garcia closed his eyes and swallowed dry. He was starting to feel unwell.

'Stomach analysis showed that it was practically empty,' Doctor Hove said.

Hunter knew that that wasn't unusual in a kidnap/murder case where the murder was committed only a day or two after the kidnapping. Even if the perpetrator had tried to feed his victim, the sheer fear, anxiety and uncertainty that come with being held in captivity would've undoubtedly acted as a very powerful appetite suppressant, even for the most steady of individuals.

'She died from cardiac arrest, *probably* caused by anaphylactic shock.'

From what Hunter and Garcia had witnessed with the broadcast, they were sure the victim hadn't been allergic to wasps' venom. If she had, her body would've started shutting itself down immediately after the first sting. Without help, death would've come too fast. A lot faster than the almost eighteen minutes it took her to die.

The doctor looked up and noticed that Garcia had taken a step back. He didn't look too good. 'You OK, Carlos?'

He nodded, avoiding eye contact. 'Yep. Fine. Just carry on, please.'

'You probably already know this,' she continued. 'But for an anaphylactic reaction to occur, one must have been exposed, in the past, to the substance that causes the reaction, called the antigen. In this case, the wasps' venom. This process is called *sensitization*. The problem is, even if she wasn't already allergic to the antigen, in the case of a prolonged attack, like the one she suffered, the sheer volume of venom injected directly into her bloodstream could've easily caused one of two extreme reactions – either force an exceptionally quick sensitization or skip the process all together, forcing the body straight into anaphylaxis – extreme allergic reaction.'

Garcia used the sleeve of his white coverall to wipe the sweat from his forehead.

'But I did say that the cardiac arrest was *probably* caused by anaphylactic shock.' Doctor Hove opened a red folder that was resting on the stainless-steel counter to her right. 'But there's another possibility. The main characteristic of the tarantula hawk's venom is that it paralyzes its prey. Now you have to remember that its main prey is the tarantula spider, which can be twice, maybe three times larger than the wasp itself.'

'Very strong venom,' Hunter said.

'For its natural prey, fatal,' Doctor Hove agreed. 'But its paralyzing ability shouldn't affect humans, unless a very high quantity of it is injected into the bloodstream. In that case, there's a very high possibility that the venom could induce a human heart into paralysis.'

Everyone's gaze came back to the body on the table for a long, silent moment.

'I read Mike Brindle's report,' Doctor Hove said, grabbing their attention again. 'And I also looked through his inventory list from the abduction scene . . . her own home, right?'

Hunter nodded.

'The broken nails he found . . . they match.' She indicated the body's hands.

Hunter and Garcia moved a little closer to examine them. The nails of the index and middle fingers on the right hand had been torn. The same had happened to the nail of the index finger on the left hand.

'Anything under the remaining nails?' Hunter asked.

Doctor Hove pulled a face. 'Well, there should have been, right? Brindle's report describes a typical struggle scene.'

'That's right,' Hunter confirmed.

'So if she fought her aggressor, chances are that something would've lodged itself under a nail – fabric fiber, skin, hair, dust . . . something.'

'There was nothing?' Garcia this time.

'She was cleaned up,' the doctor said. 'Her nails have been scrubbed with bleach. They're as clean as a newborn baby's. This killer is taking no chances.'

Doctor Hove allowed them to study the body's hands for a few more seconds before she spoke again.

'Now, here's a surprising fact,' she said. 'The killer preserved the body after she died, by cooling it down.'

Hunter wasn't so surprised. He had had his suspicions.

'We all know that she died five days ago, on Friday evening,' the doctor explained, 'but her body was only discovered on Monday morning, that's almost seventy-two hours later. The average temperature in Los Angeles in the past week was around eighty-three degrees. After three days, the body should've been bloated and discharging fluids from just about everywhere. The inflamed lumps from the wasps' stings should've subsided considerably, large blisters substituting them, caused by body gases. Rigor mortis should've come and gone two days ago. The body was still in the late stages of it by last night. The perp preserved the body.'

Refrigeration slowed decomposition in the same way it delayed cold cuts from spoiling, and preserved fruits and vegetables from going bad too quickly.

Both Hunter and Garcia knew that in most cases, when the perpetrator preserved the *whole* body after the murder, a very strong emotion was involved. The three most common ones were hate, love and lust.

In the case of love, the perp generally avoided disfiguring the victim, keeping the body as close to its original state as possible, for as long as possible. Disposing of the body wasn't something the perp was prepared to do so easily.

In the case of hate, the perp kept physically punishing the victim over and over again, to soothe the anger inside. Disfigurement was inevitable.

And in the case of lust, the victim was usually raped several times prior to the murder. After death, necrophilia was also often committed.

'Was she raped?' Hunter asked. 'Prior to or after the murder?'

'No, she wasn't.' The doctor shook her head. 'As I've said before, because she was wearing a pair of panties, her groin area wasn't as exposed to the wasps' stings as the rest of her body. I found no indication of forced penetration. No abrasions to the skin surrounding her vagina. No semen left inside her, or on her skin. No lubricant residue in her vaginal walls either, which could indicate that the perp did rape her but used a prophylactic. The lab will tell us if they find any semen on her underwear, but I don't think they will. I don't think this killer was after sex. I don't think he was in love with her either. Which theoretically leaves you with two alternatives.'

'Hate, or pure homicidal mania,' Hunter said.

Doctor Hove agreed.

'Maybe he was unable to dispose of the body straightaway and didn't want it to start rotting and smelling up the place,' Garcia suggested.

'The killer probably used a medium-sized chest freezer to preserve the body,' she said. 'From skin folds and blood pooling marks, I can tell you that she was most certainly preserved in a fetus position.'

Doctor Hove waited a few seconds before pulling a white sheet over the body. 'Unfortunately there isn't much else I can tell you. Her death wasn't a mystery. We all saw what happened to her. Toxicology will be a few days.'

Hunter and Garcia nodded and made for the door as if they were schoolkids who'd heard the final bell before summer vacation.

'Keep us posted if anything new comes out of any of the tests, will you, Doc?' Hunter said.

'Always do.'

They were both already halfway down the corridor by the time she looked up.

Fifty-Four

Dennis Baxter had managed to break through the simple four-digit security password in the smartphone Hunter had handed him last night – Christina Stevenson's cellphone. With the phone active, he had no problems accessing all the information on the SIM card.

Baxter quickly found out that the phone's battery had died sometime on Sunday morning, two days after the killer's broadcast. In between Thursday night, the night Christina was abducted, and Sunday morning, the smartphone's voicemail picked up twenty-six messages. There were also forty-two new text messages. A quick check through the smartphone's applications and memory revealed several photo albums, a few videos, four voice memos and sixteen pages of notes. It didn't look like Christina had ever used her cellphone's calendar application, but she sure as hell used her email one. Adding up the contents of her inbox, sent and deleted folders, there were literally hundreds, maybe thousands of emails.

When Hunter and Garcia got back to the PAB, Baxter quickly gave them a summary of everything he'd found, and handed over the phone. He was certainly glad it wasn't his job to read through that mountain of emails.

Hunter and Garcia began by listening to Christina Stevenson's cellphone's voicemails, checking her memos, reading her text messages and notes, and looking through all the photo albums and videos she had saved in the phone's memory and SIM card. It took them almost two hours to get through everything.

Most of the voicemail messages were left on Sunday morning. They came mainly from other reporters and press-related people – all congratulating her on her article. Some even sounded a little jealous. But one person, who had called three times since Sunday and sent Christina two text messages, sounded more like a friend. Her name was Pamela Hays. Hunter found out that Pamela was actually Christina's editor at the *LA Times'* entertainment desk.

It took Hunter just over half an hour to map every caller who had left Christina a message to an entry in her smart-phone's address book, and that meant that every caller was known to her. No strangers.

None of the voicemail, text messages, notes or voice memos were interesting enough to raise any suspicions, but what Christina's phone had given them was a long list of people they could talk to. Kevin Lee Parker's name wasn't in her address book.

'Now that this story is out there,' Hunter said, pushing himself away from his desk. 'I'd like to take a trip down to the *LA Times* building and have a chat with this Pamela Hays woman, Christina Stevenson's editor.'

Garcia rubbed his eyes. 'OK, I'll get started on these emails.' He pointed to Christina's phone on the desk. 'I'll call Dennis and see if there's a way we can connect the phone to a computer monitor or something. Reading all these emails on a 3.5-inch screen is just not an option.'

Hunter agreed with a head gesture. 'I'm sure Dennis will be able to sort something out. But it might be an idea to ask him if he can batch-copy or download all the emails to a hard drive. What you have there is a live connection to her inbox at the *LA Times*. If their IT department cancels her password, or shuts her account down, we're locked out.'

'Yeah, I thought of that too.' Garcia got up to stretch his body. 'And I would still like to have a look at that film, *The Devil Inside*, just to scratch that itch, you know what I mean? I can watch it on my computer, here. I don't want to do it at home in front of Anna.'

Another nod from Hunter. 'I haven't forgotten about that.' He checked his watch and reached for his jacket. 'Let me know if you come across anything.'

'You too.'

Fifty-Five

Hunter didn't call the *LA Times* to request an appointment with Pamela Hays. He much preferred turning up unannounced. He'd dealt with too many reporters in the past to know that they loved asking questions but hated answering them.

Hunter didn't know how much of a friend Pamela Hays was to Christina Stevenson. Maybe Hunter had misinterpreted her concerned tone in the voicemail messages she'd left Christina. If that had been the case, Hunter knew that if he called in advance to try to arrange an appointment, chances were that Pamela Hays would've given him some sort of lame excuse, like being in a meeting all day. Turning up unexpectedly put the element of surprise on Hunter's side, catching the person being interviewed unprepared. In Hunter's experience, that was always an advantage.

The *LA Times* headquarters was an odd complex of four different constructions grouped together to form one massive building. From one side it looked like a courthouse, from another like a multistory car park, and if you approached it from West 2nd Street, you'd be forgiven for thinking you were walking into a branch of some European bank.

The tall, tinted-glass double doors set deep inside the plush brown-granite entrance led to a wide, pleasantly lit and comfortably air-conditioned lobby. The place was active with people. Some coming and going. Some sitting patiently in the waiting area to the right. Some waiting not so patiently. The entire floor was tiled in marble, which amplified the sound of every footstep, making the whole entrance area sound like a beehive.

Hunter was making his way up to the large reception counter at the back when a slim woman of about five foot five caught his eye as she walked across the busy lobby. She was walking slowly, her head low, her demeanor sad and drained. He immediately recognized her from a picture on the *LA Times* website – Pamela Hays.

Hunter caught up with her just as she was approaching one of the four elevator doors in the empty corridor to the left and past the reception counter.

Pamela pressed the button, took a step back and waited. Her head still low.

'Ms. Hays?' Hunter said.

It took her a moment to look up. Her eyes moved to Hunter's face, but they lacked focus. She was wearing a well-fitted dark suit that almost made her fade into the black and gray granite walls around her.

Hunter waited a couple of seconds, and as her stare intensified he saw the moment her absent mind reentered reality. Her eyes were steel blue, her hair caramel blonde, worn just off her shoulders. There was an angular quality to her jaw, cheekbones and nose that made her look as though she was concentrating very hard. Pamela smiled for an instant, but it did nothing to soften her.

'Ms. Hays,' Hunter said again, this time displaying his credentials. 'I'm Detective Robert Hunter with the LAPD

Homicide Division. I was wondering if you could spare a few minutes of your time?'

Pamela Hays didn't reply. Things were still slotting into place inside her head.

'Ms. Hays, I could really use your help . . . and so could Christina Stevenson.'

Fifty-Six

Pamela guided Hunter back out onto West 1st Street and around the corner to The Edison Lounge, just across the road from the Police Administration Building. She didn't feel like sitting in a conference room, or anywhere else inside the *LA Times* headquarters at the moment.

The Edison was an elegant and sophisticated bar located in the basement of the famous Higgins Building in downtown LA. At the beginning of the twentieth century, that same basement housed the city's first privately owned power plant. As homage to the plant's place in history, The Edison retained many of its original architectural and mechanical artifacts.

In an area to the left of the main bar, they found two high-backed leather armchairs, arranged around a knee-high, varnished, marble-effect coffee table. The dim lights and soft 1930s music, together with the period features and detailed decoration, created such a nostalgic atmosphere that could almost take you back in time.

Hunter waited for Pamela to have a seat before he took his.

She gave him another weak smile, acknowledging the gesture.

'Before you start asking questions,' Pamela said. 'Please answer me this: has Christina's body been found?'

It wasn't hard for Hunter to read Pamela's thoughts. Right at that moment she wasn't being a reporter. She wasn't asking questions because she wanted information for a possible story. Right at that moment she was still holding onto a sliver of hope that all of what she'd seen had been some crazy hoax – some big misunderstanding.

Hunter had been in this position countless times. And it only got harder.

His stomach tightened.

'Yes.'

He saw a light turn off inside her eyes. Something he'd seen many times before. Not like a parent who'd just lost a son or a daughter, but like someone who'd not just lost a close friend, but now also realizes that danger and evil are closer than what they had once believed. If it had happened to someone like Christina, it could happen to her. It could happen to her family. It could happen to anyone.

Pamela took a deep breath as tears welled up in her eyes.

'When?'

'Yesterday.'

'Where?'

'Not far from her house.'

A waitress, who could easily have run for Miss California, approached them.

'Hello, and welcome to The Edison,' she said with the same smile Hunter was sure she gave every guest. 'Would you like to see our cocktail menu?'

'Um . . . no, that's OK,' Pamela said, shaking her head. 'Can I just have a vodka martini, please?'

'Absolutely.' The waitress looked at Hunter, ready for his order.

'I'll just have a black coffee, please.'

'Coming right up.' The waitress turned and walked away.

'Who is capable of something like that?' Pamela asked. Her voice had gone dry, as if she had something stuck in her throat. She took a moment and swallowed down her tears. 'We were able to find some snippets of the original Internet broadcast. Did you see it?'

Hunter held her gaze for an instant before nodding once.

'What the hell was that she was in? A handmade glass coffin?'

Hunter didn't reply.

'And those buttons on the Internet. People were voting on how Christina was going to die?'

Still no reply.

'They did, didn't they?' Pamela looked disgusted. 'People actually *voted*. Why? They didn't even know who she was. Did they think it was funny? Did they think it was some kind of game? Or did they simply believe that because the word GUILTY was written at the bottom of the screen, she was actually guilty of something?'

This time the intensity in Pamela's eyes demanded an answer.

'I can't tell you what people were thinking when they clicked one of those two buttons, Ms. Hays,' Hunter said, his voice even. 'But all the reasons you've just put forward are valid. People could've believed that it was some sort of game, that it wasn't real ... or maybe they believed the GUILTY headline.'

Hunter's words made Pamela pause, holding her breath. She quickly read between the lines. Headlines were what she used on a daily basis ... what the press used to catch people's attention. She knew that the more sensational the headline, the more attention it would grab, so to maximize the impact of what was said, words were chosen very carefully. Sometimes a single word was all that was needed. She also knew very well that, psychologically, headlines served different purposes. Sometimes they were geared toward grabbing people's attention, while at the same time attempting to stamp a preconceived opinion onto one's subconscious. And its power was much greater than what people gave it credit for. It worked. She knew it did.

'*The killer used Christina's trade trick against her,*' Pamela thought, and that made her shiver.

The waitress came back with their drinks. She handed Pamela her martini, and even before she had placed Hunter's coffee on the table Pamela knocked her drink back, emptying the glass in three large gulps.

The waitress looked at her, trying her best to hide her surprise.

'Could I have another one, please,' Pamela said, handing the glass back to the waitress.

'Um . . . of course.' The waitress moved back toward the bar.

'Is it OK if I ask you a few questions now, Ms. Hays?'

The drink had settled her nerves a little. Her attention refocused on Hunter and she nodded. 'Yes, and stop calling me Ms. Hays. It makes me feel like I'm back in Catholic school again, and I hated that place. Call me Pamela, or Pam. Everybody does.'

Hunter began with simple questions, just to establish what sort of relationship Pamela and Christina had. It was soon clear that Pamela wasn't just Christina's boss, but that over the years they had also become very good friends. She told him that as far as she knew Christina wasn't seeing anyone. Her last relationship, if anyone could've called it that, ended about four months ago. It had lasted only a few weeks. Pamela told Hunter that it had been doomed from the start. The guy was a lot younger than Christina, a total womanizer, and a drummer in an up-and-coming rock band called *Screaming Toyz*.

Hunter's eyebrows arched. He had seen *Screaming Toyz* play at the House of Blues not too long ago.

The waitress returned with the new martini, and this time Pamela sipped it instead of gulping it.

Hunter asked her about the three letters – SSV – and the number sequence – 678. Pamela thought about it for a long moment, but said that they meant nothing to her, and that she couldn't think of how they could relate to Christina Stevenson either.

Hunter thought about asking Pamela if she'd heard the name Kevin Lee Parker before, but decided not to. Chances were she hadn't, and there was no escaping the fact that she was still a reporter. Hunter was sure she would check the name later, and consequently find out that he'd also been murdered just a few days ago. Armed with that information, a sensational headline about a new serial killer who liked to broadcast his own killing show would be across the front page of the *LA Times* in no time at all. One dramatic murder headline across the front page of the papers created shock and got people talking, but the news of a new serial killer loose in LA would create city-wide panic. He'd seen it happen before. And right now Hunter and the investigation could do without it.

'Did she mention anything about any threats?' he asked. 'Any letters, emails, phone calls? Anything that was worrying her at all? People who disliked her?'

Pamela chuckled nervously. 'We're reporters for the fourth-highest-circulating newspaper in the whole of the

USA, Detective. Due to the nature of what we do, everyone dislikes us, no matter how friendly they seem. For example, you and all your cop friends across the road do.'

Hunter said nothing. But she was right. He was yet to meet a cop who liked journalists.

'On people's "scum scale", we rank right up there with corrupt politicians and lawyers.' Pamela paused and had another sip of her martini. Despite her aggressive words, she knew full well what Hunter meant.

He waited for the moment to subside.

Pamela went back to the question. 'The fact is, as reporters, we have all written articles that have upset some people. We have all received threatening letters and emails and phone calls. We still do every so often, but it's all just bravado, really. People get angry when we expose the *truth*, because a lot of the time the truth doesn't suit them.'

There was no denying that Pamela Hays was very passionate about her job.

'Has Ms. Stevenson ever mentioned any of these letters, or emails, or phone calls to you? Something that she believed to be more than just bravado?'

Pamela started shaking her head, but paused halfway through the movement. Her stare became more purposeful, and if her Botoxed forehead could crease, it would have.

'What did she say?' Hunter asked, trying to seize the moment.

Pamela sat back on her chair. Her hand came up to her chin, and she partially extended her index finger so it was touching both of her lips. Her eyes moved down to her lap.

Behavioral psychology read the finger-over-mouth gesture as a tell sign – someone who was about to say something, or wanted to say something, but wasn't sure if he or she

should. In certain situations, the gesture was a clear giveaway that a lie was about to be told.

Hunter watched Pamela. Her reporter's mind was clearly
considering something, wondering if she should share whatever information she had, or hold it back. There could be a
story there.

The problem for Pamela was that she wasn't a crime
reporter. The information would have to be passed over to
someone at the crime desk. And she hated those pricks.
Always looking down at everyone else, specially the entertainment desk, or as they called it *the gossip pit*.

Hunter sensed her hesitation and urged her again.
'Pamela, even the tiniest piece of information could help us
catch whoever took Christina. Was she frightened of something, or someone?'

Her gaze returned to Hunter's face, and in his eyes she
picked up the sort of determination and sincerity she didn't
see very often. Her features relaxed a little.

'About four months ago, Christina wrote an article on a
guy called Thomas Paulsen.'

'The software millionaire?'

'The one and only,' Pamela replied, a little surprised that
Hunter had heard of him. 'What happened was, she was
contacted by a former employee of Mr. Paulsen with a
potentially big story. Christina came to me, and I gave her
the go-ahead to investigate it. She spent two months working on it, and she unearthed a truckload of dirt on the scumbag. The story went to print, and Mr. Paulsen's business and
personal life were affected.'

'What was the story about?'

Pamela had one more sip of her drink. 'He liked to take
his secretaries, PAs or whoever he fancied inside his

company to bed, then intimidate them, using whatever means he saw fit, into keeping their mouths shut. He's married with a daughter. When the exposé was printed, it was revealed that he'd been doing it for years. He allegedly bedded over thirty-five employees.' She paused, measuring her words. 'I know that to many that might not sound too devastating, but this is the USA, a country full of false morals and where being religious, faithful and a true family man counts for more than you would know. And this is LA, a city where the tiniest of affairs can end someone's career overnight. The article affected Mr. Paulsen's life pretty badly.'

Hunter wrote something down on his notebook. 'And did he threaten Ms. Stevenson?'

Pamela pulled a dubious face. 'Right after the article came out, she started getting these phone calls ... something about pain, making her suffer and dying slowly. Christina had been through stuff like that before, and she wasn't the type who would spook easy, but I know that something about those calls did really frighten her. We tried tracing the calls, but whoever was calling her was too smart. The calls were being redirected all over the place.'

'Was she still receiving them recently?'

'I'm not sure. She hadn't mentioned anything for a while.'

Hunter took some more notes.

'But we're talking about articles she wrote while with the entertainment desk,' Pamela offered. 'Before I brought her over to entertainment, Christina was with the crime desk for nine months. And before that she'd spent time with just about every other desk in the paper. If what happened to her was because of an article she wrote, you're looking at a very long list.'

'Yeah, we know,' Hunter said. 'Is there a way I could get an archive of all the articles Ms. Stevenson wrote while with the entertainment desk? I'd like to start there.'

Though Pamela looked surprised, her eyebrows didn't move. 'We're talking two years' worth of articles here.'

'Yes, I know. We have a team working on gathering them, but your help can really speed things up.'

She held his stare for a couple of seconds. 'OK. I'm sure I can gather everything together and get a compressed archive to you by tomorrow.'

Fifty-Seven

The driver had started his day before the break of dawn. He had patiently sat behind the wheel, quietly observing the entrance to the apartment block across the road from where he was parked. Most people would consider the task boring, but he didn't mind it at all. He actually enjoyed the stakeout process. All that waiting gave him time to think. To organize his thoughts. To work things out. Plus, he loved watching people. One could learn so much just by observing from afar.

For example, at 6:45 a.m., a balding, heavyset man, wearing an old and ill-fitting gray suit, exited the building and crossed the road. He walked slowly, defeated, with hunched shoulders and his head down, as if his thoughts were too heavy for him. His entire demeanor screamed one thing – sadness. Just getting through each day was a terrible struggle. The driver could tell that the man hated his job, whatever it was that he did. The thick, golden ring strangling his chubby finger on his left hand indicated that he was married, but it also indicated that he had put on a lot of weight since that ring first graced his hand. It was safe to assume that his marriage had long lost the fire that it might have once had.

The driver looked up at the building. On the first floor a woman with short dirty-blond hair, and clearly carrying a little more weight than she would like to, was staring out the window at the heavyset man. Her eyes followed him until he disappeared down another street. When he was gone, she faded back into the apartment, but three minutes later she was at the window again. This time, her anxious gaze concentrated at the opposite end of the road. The driver also noticed something different about the woman. Her hair had been brushed and the unflattering nightgown she was wearing was gone, replaced by something sexier.

Five minutes elapsed and nothing else happened. Then the woman's lips spread into a smile. The driver followed her stare all the way to another man who had turned the corner and was now hurriedly walking toward the apartment block. He was at least forty pounds lighter than her husband, and about ten years younger. The woman's lips broke into a wide smile.

The driver chuckled. *Yeah, the things you can learn just by observing.*

But he wasn't there to catch anyone's extramarital affair. His task was much more important than that.

At 7:15 a.m., another man exited the building. This one was tall with an athletic build. He walked with purpose. His eyes showed strong resolve and determination. Reflexively, the driver slid down on his seat, making himself even more unnoticeable, while at the same time attentively observing the man as he jumped into his own car and drove away.

The driver smiled. Everything was going to plan.

Twenty minutes later, his mark finally stepped out of the building. He sat forward and watched her walk to her car. She was attractive, with a charming aura around her, and a body he knew would be the envy of all her friends.

He took a deep breath and allowed the excitement to avalanche down his spine. Adrenaline rushed through him as he checked his broadcasting equipment and started his engine.

He'd spent the entire day tagging her, waiting for the right moment to strike. He knew that his success depended on choosing the perfect moment. Anything less than perfect and things could turn around very quickly.

After so many hours, that moment had finally arrived.

His show was about to go online again.

Fifty-Eight

When Hunter got back to the PAB, Garcia was rubbing his eyes vigorously.

'Everything OK?' Hunter asked.

Garcia looked up and let out a deep breath. 'I just finished watching that film – *The Devil Inside.*'

'Anything?' Hunter asked, taking a seat behind his desk.

Garcia got up and massaged his neck. 'I don't think the note the killer left in Ms. Stevenson's bedroom refers to the film.'

Hunter paused and looked at him.

'As I said before, the plot revolves around a young woman whose mother had murdered three people while supposedly possessed by a demon. I was mainly interested in finding out about those murders. Specifically, the method used.'

'And . . .?'

'No resemblance at all to our case. It was a frenzied knife attack. All three victims were slaughtered inside the same house, in the same night, and in the space of minutes. The film then focuses on the woman's daughter attending several exorcism sessions to try to figure out if her mother was really possessed by the devil when she did it. No one is locked inside any sort of enclosure, glass or not. No wasps or any other insect appear. No one is left inside an alkali or acid bath, nothing is broadcast over the Internet, and there's no voting or choosing between death methods. If there really is a meaning behind the message the killer left in Ms. Stevenson's bedroom, that film isn't it.'

Hunter's focus moved to the pictures board and the fluorescent orange fingerprint powder photograph. He scratched his head. '*The devil inside. What the hell does that mean?*'

'How about Ms. Stevenson's emails?' he asked. 'Any developments at all?'

Dennis Baxter, from the Computer Crimes Unit, had batch-downloaded all of Christina Stevenson's emails into an external hard drive, now connected to Garcia's computer. No more going over them on a 3.5-inch screen, and no more risk of being locked out of her account.

'Nothing so far that I'd call suspicious,' Garcia replied, returning to his desk. 'There are a lot of quick-fire internal emails between Ms. Stevenson and other *LA Times* reporters – jokes, gossip, discussions about articles . . . things like that. I've filtered all her emails, searching for everything that didn't come from a @latimes.com address. I'm hoping that will give us some sort of separation between her personal and work emails. Nothing has flagged up yet, but I still have a long way to go here. How about you?'

Hunter ran over his meeting with Pamela Hays.

'Whoa, wait,' Garcia said, lifting his right hand and pausing Hunter when he told him about the phone threats Christina had been getting. 'Who's this guy?'

'His name is Thomas Paulsen,' Hunter explained. 'He's a software millionaire, based right here in LA.'

'Software?' A muscle flexed on Garcia's jaw. He was already typing Paulsen's name into a search engine.

'That's right. His company was one of the first to create enterprise Internet database systems.'

Garcia looked up from his screen. 'When did you get time to research him?'

'I didn't,' Hunter replied. 'I read a lot. I read the piece in *Forbes* magazine a while ago.'

'Did you read the article Christina Stevenson wrote on him?'

'Not yet.'

Garcia clicked on the topmost result link on the page returned by his search. It took him to PaulsenSystems' website. He quickly skimmed through the information on the 'About Us' page. According to it, Hunter had been right about everything. Paulsen's company had been among the very first ones to develop enterprise Internet database systems, and it was now one of the world leaders. Its systems were used by companies all over the world.

'Are we talking to him?' Garcia asked. 'He sure sounds like someone who knows his way around cyberspace.'

'We probably will be, but not just yet. First I want to find out how badly Christina Stevenson's article affected him. But even then we would still need to link Paulsen to Kevin Lee Parker. Maybe he had a beef with Ms. Stevenson because of the article she wrote, but how would our first victim fit into his payback plan?'

Garcia said nothing.

Hunter's desk phone rang, sucking his attention away from the board.

'Detective Hunter, Homicide Special Section.'

There was a click on the line.

'Hello . . .?'

'Detective Hunter,' the caller finally said. His tone was cold and unrushed, like a doctor greeting a patient. 'I'm glad you are at your desk.'

In hearing his voice, Hunter felt an emptiness form in his stomach, a kind of vacuum sensation, that was instantly replaced by a rush of anxiety. Hunter clenched his jaw and locked eyes with Garcia.

'Are you online?' the caller asked, his voice now filled with mocking amusement. 'Because I'm about to show you something I am certain you and your partner will enjoy watching.'

Fifty-Nine

Despite the temperature inside their office being around a hundred degrees Fahrenheit, Hunter felt cold sweat break out on the nape of his neck and trickle down his back.

'Are you ready, Detective Hunter?' the caller asked rhetorically. 'Because your favorite website just went back online. You don't need me to give you the web address again, do you?'

Hunter was already typing it into his browser's address bar.

The web page loaded in less than three seconds. But what Hunter saw forced him to do a double take. This time the picture wasn't dominated by the green tint of a night-vision lens. Neither was it being broadcast from a dingy, dark dungeon-looking room somewhere. The caller was broadcasting in broad daylight from a busy city street. And this time the camera wasn't static either. It was moving with the crowd, walking along leisurely, as if handheld by a tourist filming his LA vacation.

Hunter's eyes narrowed.

There were people all around. Men and women dressed in a variety of different attires, from casual jeans, T-shirts, shorts and dresses to business suits. Some seemed in a hurry, with their cellphones glued to their ears. Some were casually walking around, maybe window-shopping. It was hard to tell, as the camera lens angle was straight and narrow, like tunnel vision. Hunter could see people coming toward the camera and walking past it, but the peripheral vision was blurred.

Hunter quickly used the palm of his hand to cover the phone's mouthpiece. 'Call Michelle at the FBI Cybercrime Division,' he whispered to Garcia. 'The website is back online.'

Garcia's desk was probably the best-organized desk inside the entire PAB. Everything had its designated place, and always seemed to be symmetrically positioned. Michelle Kelly's card was the first of three arranged side by side to the right of his telephone. He dialed the number, and Michelle answered within two rings.

'Michelle, it's Carlos.'

Instantly Michelle picked up on Garcia's serious tone.

'Hey, Carlos. What's wrong?'

Garcia typed into his browser's address bar as he spoke. 'He's back online. The website is back online.'

'What?'

'He's on the phone to us right now.'

He heard frantic keyboard clicks from the other end.

The page loaded on Garcia's screen and he cocked his head back, frowning at the street images before looking at Hunter. 'What the hell?'

Hunter gave him a subtle headshake.

'What do you mean – the website is back online, Carlos?' Michelle said over the phone. 'I've got nothing here.'

'What?'

'I'm looking at an Error 404 page. *File not found.*'

'Recheck the web address you typed,' Garcia replied, instinctively rereading the one on his address bar. 'The images are playing live on my screen. I'm looking at them right now.'

'I've already rechecked it. You sure it's the same address?'

'Positive.'

More keyboard clicks.

'Damn, he's blocking us out,' she ultimately said.

'He's what . . .? How can he block you out, but not us?'

'There are a few methods, but I'm not going to get technical with you right now.'

Garcia shook his head at Hunter. 'They can't see it,' he whispered. 'Somehow he's blocking them out, but not us.'

Hunter wrinkled his nose at the information, but he knew he didn't have time for an explanation. He switched the call to loudspeaker.

'Are you watching?' the caller asked.

'We're watching,' Hunter replied, his voice calm but firm.

'Where the hell is that?' Garcia mouthed the words at Hunter, pointing at his computer screen. 'Rodeo Drive?'

Hunter shook his head. 'It doesn't look like it.'

Rodeo Drive was Los Angeles' best-known shopping district, situated in Beverly Hills, famous for its designer labels and haute couture fashion. It attracted a multitude of people every day. But Hunter was right. What they were looking at didn't look like Rodeo Drive. Right now, those images could be coming from any regular shopping street – in a city with thousands of them.

'Nice day for a walk, isn't it?' the caller commented. There was a distinct lilt in his tone.

'Indeed,' Hunter agreed. 'In fact, if you tell me where you are, I'll come and walk with you.'

The caller laughed. 'Appreciated, but I think I've got enough company for the moment. Can't you see?'

People were walking by in all directions.

Hunter and Garcia were glued to their computer monitors, looking for something, anything that could give them some sort of clue to where the caller was broadcasting from. So far they'd seen nothing.

'Isn't it great that we live in a city so full of people?' the caller carried on. 'So vibrant and full of life?'

Hunter said nothing.

'The downside is that Los Angeles is also a very busy city, where people are always rushing somewhere, too busy with their own thoughts, their own problems, their own obsessions. Too busy to notice others.' The caller laughed, as if what he'd just said amused him immensely. 'I could be wearing a Batman outfit out here, and no one would look at me twice.'

The caller carried on walking as he talked, but still neither Hunter nor Garcia had seen anything they'd recognized yet.

Suddenly the caller had to quickly shuffle left to avoid colliding with a man whose eyes were locked on his cellphone's screen while typing a text message. As the man whizzed past the caller, missing bumping into him by an inch, the caller turned around, his camera following the man's walk. A few yards ahead, the man slammed into a dark-haired woman who was going in the opposite direction. The man never stopped. His eyes didn't even leave his cellphone's screen.

'Wow, did you see that?' the caller asked. 'That guy just shouldered that woman to one side without giving a shit. No "I'm sorry", no apologetic smile . . . He didn't even miss a step. People out here just don't care, Detective.' Another laugh. This one with a hint of contempt. 'No one cares for anyone else but themselves.' A short pause. 'The good old American way, huh? Always look out for number one. The rest can go fuck themselves.'

Despite his harsh words, there was no anger in his voice.

Garcia was through with this one-sided conversation. 'You've got something against the American way?'

Hunter's eyes moved to him.

'Ah, Detective Carlos Garcia, I presume,' the caller said. 'Delighted to make your acquaintance. No, I've got nothing against the American way. On the contrary. But your question strikes me as a little odd, coming from a person who wasn't actually born here.' He paused again. 'Brazil, isn't that right?'

Carlos Garcia *was* born in Brazil. São Paulo, in fact. The son of a Brazilian federal agent and an American history teacher, he moved with his mother to Los Angeles when Garcia was only ten years old, after his parents' marriage collapsed.

'How the hell . . .' Garcia began, but Hunter gave him the most subtle of headshakes, suggesting that he didn't engage in a verbal confrontation with the caller.

A laugh came through the phone. 'Information is easy to obtain when you know how to get it, Detective Garcia.'

Garcia took Hunter's advice and bit his lip.

The caller took the silence as a cue and moved on. 'There are so many people out here, walking around, just getting on with their own lives. You know, being out here makes me feel like a kid in a candy shop. So many choices. Anyone could become my next guest, if you know what I mean.'

Unconsciously, Hunter held his breath. Was this the reason for this call? The killer had shown them how he tortured and killed people. He had shown them how he chose the death method. Was he now showing them his selection process?

'But I think I already have someone in mind,' the caller said before Hunter could say anything back. 'Can you guess who it is?'

Hunter and Garcia craned their necks, moving closer to their monitors, but the camera didn't zoom in to anyone in particular.

Just ahead and a little to the left, a blond woman had stopped. She was searching for something inside her handbag. Was she the one the caller had chosen?

An odd-looking man with thin lips and a pointy nose, separated by a thick mustache that looked designed to offset both, was walking slowly, coming straight toward the camera. Maybe the caller had picked him.

The truth was anyone walking down that street could be the next victim. Hunter and Garcia had no way of knowing.

The man with the thick mustache moved right, stepping out of the way.

Inside Hunter's office, the world stopped moving.

Standing in a direct line with the camera, about ten feet away, Hunter and Garcia finally saw who the killer was talking about.

Sixty

There were two of them walking together. Two friends enjoying a day out, window-shopping somewhere in Los Angeles, completely unaware of the evil that'd been following them. Their backs were toward the camera, but the one on the left didn't need to turn around for Garcia to recognize her.

'Jesus Christ!' Garcia's voice croaked.

'Anna,' Hunter whispered, also recognizing Garcia's wife. His gaze shot toward his partner as a thousand butterflies came alive inside his stomach.

For a moment Garcia seemed unable to move, to speak, to blink. And then he exploded.

'You motherfucker . . . I swear to God . . . if you touch her . . . if you come close to her, I'm going to find you, and I'm going to *kill* you. You hear me? I'm going to *kill* you. Screw the badge. Screw being a cop. I will bring hell and all its demons to your doorstep, no matter what.'

Garcia was now shaking. Adrenaline fueling every inch of his body.

The caller laughed once again. 'She's beautiful, isn't she?'

'Fuck you, you sick freak. You have no idea what I will do to you if . . .' Garcia reached for his cellphone.

'Let me tell you how this is going to work, Detective,' the caller cut in, predicting Garcia's next move. 'If you call her now to ask her where she is. If I see her reaching for her phone and turning around to look at me, I promise you you'll never see her alive again. The two previous victims will look like Christmas morning compared to what I'll do to her. And you know I mean it. Trust me. You can't get here fast enough.'

Garcia's desperate stare moved from his phone to the monitor on his desk and then to Hunter.

Hunter lifted his right hand, signaling Garcia not to dial. 'Do you know where she is?' he mouthed the words. 'Did Anna tell you where she was going today?'

Garcia shook his head. 'I didn't even know she was going out,' he mouthed back.

'Do you know what intrigues me?' the caller proceeded. 'Both of you keep saying that you'll find me. That you will catch me. Detective Hunter said that last time we talked. Do you remember it?'

No reply.

'Do you remember it, Detective Hunter?'

'Yes.'

'But the truth is that you aren't even close to getting to me, are you?'

Silence.

'Meanwhile, as you can see, *I* can get to people close to you, and if I so see fit, take them away from your lives. It's my choice, not yours, or theirs. I can even get to you if I want to. I can be anywhere, and everywhere. But all you have are empty threats.'

'It's not a threat, you sack o' shit.' Garcia's voice was still trembling with rage. 'It's a *promise*. If you touch her, nothing else matters. Not even the law will matter. There isn't a hole under a rock on this earth that will be safe for you to hide in. Do you understand what I'm saying?'

'I do,' the caller said, as calm as a priest in a confessionary. 'Would it make a difference if I took your wife's friend instead?'

Hunter and Garcia tensed once again.

The caller didn't wait for an answer. 'But of course it would. Then it wouldn't be personal, and your reaction wouldn't have been the same, isn't that right, Detective Garcia? As you said, when it's someone close to us, nothing else matters. We will even forget who we are. Maybe even become a monster in the process.' The caller let out a heavy breath, and for the first time his voice got a little harsher. 'You know, most people believe that we, as humans, always have a choice, no matter what situation we find ourselves in. Well, I'd like to contest that theory. I'd like to suggest that we don't *always* have a choice. Sometimes choices are made for us by others, and there's nothing we, *as humans*, can do about it, except react. For example, if I decide to take your wife from you right now, Detective Garcia, *my choice*, not yours, will change *your* life forever.'

Garcia didn't know what to say.

'But anger and emotional pain are good things,' the caller moved on after a silent moment. 'They show that we're still alive. That we still care. That other people still matter to us. Is my psychology correct, Detective Hunter?'

Hunter looked deep in thought for a split second. 'Yes,' he replied.

'You should be proud, Detective Garcia, you did well. I like your reaction. A reaction of a man who cares.' The caller chuckled. 'Well, I guess my work here is done. But we'll be talking again soon – *that* is a promise.'

The line went dead.

The images disappeared from their computer screens.

The website went offline.

Sixty-One

Silence ruled the room for only a couple of seconds before Hunter turned to Garcia.

'Call Anna,' he said. 'Find out where she is. Tell her to find a busy place, like a coffee shop, and stay there until we get there.'

Garcia looked at Hunter as if he were from outer space. 'Are you kidding? You heard what he said, right? If he saw Anna reaching for her phone . . .' He wasn't able to finish the sentence.

'He's not going to do anything, Carlos,' Hunter said. 'It was a bluff. He wanted to get a reaction.'

'What?'

'It was a bluff. Trust me. There were signs all throughout his telephone conversation with you. I'll explain in the car. Right now you need to get Anna on the phone and find out where she is so we can get to her.' Hunter had already grabbed his jacket. 'Let's move.' He dashed for the door. 'Call her.'

'Woah, hold the fuck on, Robert,' Garcia said in an unsteady voice, lifting his hands. 'We've been partners for over five years. There's no one alive I trust more than you, you know that, but we're talking about the sickest, most sadistic and psychopathic killer this department has ever faced, and at this precise moment he's following my *wife*. As he said, we can't get there in time, even if we knew where she was. If I make this call and you're wrong, he'll take her, you know he will.'

Hunter paused by the door and faced his partner. 'I'm not wrong, Carlos. He will *not* take Anna.' Hunter's conviction was absolute, Garcia could see that, but still he didn't move.

Hunter checked his watch. He wanted to gain time, but right now they were doing exactly the opposite. 'Carlos, whatever agenda this killer has, Anna just doesn't fit in.'

'How so?'

'OK, one possibility we're facing is that the killer picks his victims at random from the general public, right? Well, if that really is the case, Anna isn't a random pick. She's your wife, and he knows it. There's no random factor there, which, in that case, would be a detachment from his MO. If he's after his victims for some other reason, like revenge or something else, again, I can't see how Anna would fit.'

Garcia scratched his chin.

'He went after Anna for one reason, and one reason only.'

'Because she's my wife.'

'Exactly. He did it to get under our skin. To prove a point. Not to satisfy whatever agenda he has.'

'And what point would that be? That he can get to anyone he wants? That he can hurt us?'

'That too,' Hunter agreed. 'And to stamp his superiority. To remind us who is in control of this game. *He is*, not us, and he can change the rules anytime he wants, just like he did with the Internet broadcasting and the online voting. But there were other things he said that hinted at something else.'

Garcia frowned. 'Like what?'

'He talked about how personal your reaction was. He wanted you to lose control. He wanted you to allow your emotions to take over, and for you to feed on them. He wanted you to forget who you are, who you've always been . . . and you did just that.'

Garcia knew Hunter wasn't being critical of his actions. 'I wasn't bullshitting, Robert. If he touches Anna, I will find him, I will make him suffer, and then I will kill him. I don't care what happens to me.'

'I understand. And I don't blame you. But when you told him that if he ever harmed Anna, nothing else would matter, not even the law, not even the fact that you were a cop. When you told him that you would hunt him down until you find him, and that you would kill him, no matter what, no matter how long it took . . . it didn't scare him. It *pleased* him.'

'What?'

'It pleased him,' Hunter repeated. 'He even congratulated you, remember? His words were – *You did well, Detective Garcia. I like your reaction. A reaction of a man who cares.* But you didn't do anything other than threaten him with death. So what was he so pleased about, and why?'

'Because he's a fucking psycho?' Garcia was still feeding on his emotions.

'No. It was because you gave him his little victory.'

'Victory? What the hell are you talking about, Robert?'

Hunter's eyes peeked at his watch again. 'As I said, he had no real interest in Anna. He only went after her to get under our skin and to prove a point. And he knew he could do that without the need to touch her. Your reaction told him that he'd more than accomplished his task. You gave him more than a small victory, Carlos. You equated yourself

with him when you told him that you would act just like
him.'

'What?'

Hunter shook his head. 'I don't remember his exact
words. We can play the recording back later, but he said
that when a threat or harm comes to someone close to us,
nothing else matters. *We* will even forget who we are. We
may even act like monsters. We'll do anything to protect
those we love. Your reaction proved that . . . And it pleased
him.'

Garcia said nothing.

'One of the last things he said before disconnecting,'
Hunter continued. 'Was that his work there was done . . . as
in *finished*, nothing left to do. He got what he wanted. Anna
is of no interest to him anymore.'

Garcia still remained silent.

'He also talked about people not always having a choice,'
Hunter said.

Garcia nodded. 'I remember that. He said that sometimes
choices are made for us by others, and there's nothing we
can do about it. He gave Anna as an example.'

'No, not nothing,' Hunter countered. 'He said that we
can *react*. That's what you did. And I think that's exactly
what he's doing.'

Things started to frantically move around in Garcia's
head, searching for the right place to slot in. 'You think
something happened to someone close to him? That's why
he's going around torturing and killing people? He's
reacting?'

'I'm not sure,' Hunter replied. 'Right now we can only
speculate. But in the past, every time he called us, he was
always   calm,   never   excited,   never   angry,   never

remorseful . . . never nothing. His tone of voice never gave anything away . . . no emotion. But not today.'

Garcia had been too angry and scared for Anna's life to notice.

'Today, for the first time, anger crept into his tone when he talked about people not always having a choice. He said that anger and emotional pain were good things. It proved that we, as humans, are still alive inside. That we still care for something. He used Anna and your love for her to prove that.'

Silence.

'He wasn't talking about me and my anger,' Garcia finally said. 'Or my reaction to what I would do if Anna was ever harmed. He was talking about him and his anger. He was talking about his reaction.'

Hunter nodded and looked at his watch for the third time. 'Carlos, look, I understand that I'm asking you to trust me with your wife's life, and that is asking a hell of a lot, but if you still don't want to trust me, trust yourself. Forget about everything I think I picked up throughout your conversation with the killer. Take a step back and do what *you* know how to do – analyze the whole scenario. Analyze the facts. Right now Anna is walking down a busy street, and she isn't alone, which means that as long as she stays on that busy street, the killer can't approach her without grabbing her friend's attention as well. That means that he can't drag Anna away from that street without either neutralizing her friend or taking her with them. Abducting one adult from a busy street without alerting anyone else is already a very hard task. Abducting two without causing a commotion is almost impossible. Even if he wanted to take them both, which I'm sure he doesn't, he would still have to wait for the right moment to do it, and that moment won't come while they're out in the open, in the middle of a crowd, or in a busy place, like a café. This killer is bold, but he isn't stupid. Now you've got two options, Carlos. You either make that call and we get a move on, or you don't, and we sit here, imagining the worst and wondering how long we should wait until you eventually call her to find out if the killer kept his word or not. It's your *choice*.'

Sixty-Two

'So . . .' Patricia said matter-of-factly. A devilish smile curving the edge of her lips. 'When are you going to properly introduce me to that detective, you know, Carlos' partner?'

Anna stopped walking and looked at Patricia over the rim of her sunglasses.

'What?' Patricia said. The smile was still there, just a little bit more pronounced now. 'Everyone knows he's hot. And I know he isn't hitched 'cos you told me.'

Patricia had met Hunter only once before, two months ago, during Anna's birthday party. Hunter hadn't stayed long. But after he left, Patricia had been one of three friends who'd asked Anna who the quiet good-looking guy was.

Someone riding a black and red Harley-Davidson motorbike turned the corner and decided to park it just a few yards ahead of them. For a moment no one could hear anything over the double-barrel exhaust noise.

When he finally switched his engine off, Anna faced Patricia again. 'I thought you were seeing someone.'

They began walking again.

'I was, but not anymore. Hence the request.' She smiled again.

Anna gave her *the look*.

'He was just a fling. It lasted a few weeks, that's all. Don't worry about him.' Patricia gave Anna a dismissive wave.

They both stepped onto the street to avoid zigzagging through the many tables set outside a bustling Italian pizzeria. Anna caught the smell of freshly baked pepperoni pizza coming from one of the tables, and her stomach rumbled. She quickly pushed her pace to avoid giving in to temptation.

Patricia followed.

'Now,' she said, catching Anna's attention again. 'Carlos' partner, Robert, isn't it?'

'Are we still talking about this?'

'Yes, we are. He's not seeing anyone, is he?'

'No, I don't think so.'

A renewed, suggestive smile from Patricia.

'I can introduce you to him if you want,' Anna finally said. 'But don't get your hopes up.'

Patricia looked hurt.

'Oh no, it's not you. Nothing to do with you. I know you could charm any man alive. I've seen it.'

The hurt look softened.

'But Robert is just—' Anna's eyes wandered, searching for the right words '—unique, and a complete enigma. He's a loner by choice, not because he's a difficult person to get along with, far from it. He's probably the easiest-going person I know. But he shies away from relationships as if they were a curse.'

'Bad past experience?' Patricia asked.

'No one knows.' Anna shrugged. 'I'm telling you, he's an enigma. He'll talk to you about anything but his job or his personal life. I do think he had someone important in his life once, years ago, but he just won't talk about it.'

'So he doesn't date?'

'I never said that. I said that he doesn't do *relationships*. He dates plenty.'

Patricia smiled. 'There you go, then.' A hip-hop swagger found its way onto her words. 'Hook me up, sista.' She smiled, but it didn't sound like she was joking.

'You want me to try to hook you up for a *one-night stand* with my husband's work partner?'

'Are you kidding? With that man I'll take meaningless sex any day of the week, and twice on Sundays, thank you very much.'

Anna knew that Patricia was serious.

'You are incorrigible.'

'I know, but that's what makes life fun.'

As Anna heard the ringtone of her cellphone come from inside her handbag, Patricia started eyeing a skimpy black dress with white details in the window of the trendy shop to their right.

Anna riffled through the contents of her bag. She found the phone and brought it to her ear.

The man standing just a few feet behind Anna and Patricia smiled.

Sixty-Three

'Hey, hun!' Anna said into her cellphone. 'This is a surprise.'

Garcia kept his voice as calm as he could manage. 'Anna, listen. Where in town are you right now?'

'What?'

'I know you're out shopping with your friend, but where exactly are you now?'

Anna looked at Patricia and pulled a face. 'How do you know I'm out shopping with a friend?'

'Anna, please . . . I don't have time to explain everything. What I need is for you to tell me exactly where you are, OK?'

'Um . . . I'm in Tujunga Village . . . Carlos, what's going on?'

Located near bustling Ventura Boulevard, in Studio City, but seemingly a world away from everything, Tujunga Village was nestled between the Colfax Meadows neighborhood and Woodbridge Park. The heart of the Village was the block-long stretch of Tujunga Avenue, between Moorpark and Woodbridge, where boutiques, restaurants, cafés and miscellaneous stores catered for even the most discerning of visitors.

'Baby, I told you, I don't have a lot of time to explain,' Garcia said. 'But I need you to trust me right now, OK?'

Anna nervously tucked a loose strand of her short black hair behind her left ear. 'Carlos, you're scaring me.'

'I'm sorry. There's no need for you to be scared. I just need you to trust me right now. Can you do that?'

'Yes, of course.'

'OK. Who's with you?'

'Um ... Pat, my friend from yoga. You remember her, right?'

'Yeah. She came to your birthday drinks, right?'

'That's right.'

'OK. Listen, I need you to find a busy place – like a café, or a pizzeria, or a burger joint, whatever, and go sit in there with Pat and wait for me. I'm on my way to you now. Do not engage in a conversation with anyone. *No one at all.* And do not leave the place, under any circumstances, until I get to you. Do you understand that, baby?'

'Yeah ... but ...'

'Call me as soon as you find a place, OK?'

Anna knew Garcia too well to be fooled by his calm tone. He'd never questioned her about her whereabouts, or who she was out with, or anything else for that matter. They had always trusted each other, pure and simple. That was the foundation their relationship was built on. And he had never before told her what to do, unless she had asked for his advice first. Something was definitely off.

'Carlos, what's this about?' Anna's voice weakened a notch. 'Did something happen? Are my parents OK?'

Patricia was standing next to Anna with a concerned look on her face.

'No, baby,' Garcia replied. 'Nothing has happened to anyone, I promise you. Look, I'll be there in twenty-five minutes, half an hour tops. I'll explain everything then. Just trust me. Find a place and sit tight.'

Anna took a deep breath. 'OK. Look, I already know where we're going to go. We'll be inside Aroma Café. It's halfway up Tujunga Village. We're just coming up to it now.'

'Great, baby. Get in there, grab a coffee and I'll be with you in a few minutes.'

Garcia disconnected.

Sixty-Four

Garcia saw Anna even before Hunter finished parking right in front of the Aroma Café. She and Patricia were sitting at a small table toward the front of the glass-fronted store.

Anna had sat there deliberately, her nervous eyes wandering up and down Tujunga Avenue, as if following a tense, invisible tennis match. As she saw Garcia and Hunter step out of the car, she got up and dashed outside. Patricia followed her.

Garcia met her by the door, and instinctively threw his arms around her as if he hadn't seen her for years, kissing her hair as she buried her face into his chest.

'You OK?' he asked, relief taking over him.

Anna looked up at her husband, and the tension of the moment filled her eyes with tears. 'I'm OK. What's going on, Carlos?'

'I'll explain in a moment. Did you drive here?'

Anna shook her head.

'We took the bus,' Patricia said. She was standing next to Hunter, wide-eyed and confused, watching the scene between Anna and Garcia.

Hunter's eyes were scanning the street, searching for anyone who looked to have taken any sort of interest in their group. No one seemed to care. People on both sides of

Tujunga Avenue were just getting on with their lives. Some
window-shopping, some entering or exiting one of the many
cafés or restaurants on the busy road, and others just enjoying a leisurely walk at the end of a nice Californian autumn
day. No one inside the café seemed interested in them either.

Hunter had also already surveyed the street for CCTV
cameras. There weren't any. Unlike many cities in Europe,
some with as many as one camera for every fourteen people,
Los Angeles wasn't a surveillance-crazy city. There wasn't a
single government or law-enforcement CCTV camera in
the entire Tujunga Village stretch.

'Oh, I'm sorry,' Anna said. 'Robert, this is my friend
Patricia.'

Hunter shook her hand. 'Pleasure to meet you.'

Patricia was a little over five foot five, though black high-
heeled boots added a couple of inches to her height.

'The pleasure is mine,' she replied, sending him a sincere
smile.

Hunter handed the car keys back to Garcia. 'Carlos, you
take the car and take Anna and Patricia home,' he said. 'I
can make my way back to the PAB from here. Though I
might stay and look around for a little while.'

'Look around for what?' Anna asked. Her eyes settled on
Hunter, as she knew her husband wouldn't offer an
explanation.

Hunter's gaze rested on his partner for only a split second
before moving to his wife. 'Nothing in particular, Anna.'

Anna's stare remained hard. 'That's bullshit.'

'Look,' Hunter said. 'Trust us on this. Carlos will explain
everything to you later.'

'I promise I will,' Garcia said, squeezing her hand. 'But
right now, we need to go.'

Sixty-Five

As soon as Garcia dropped Patricia off in front of her apartment block in Monterey Park, Anna turned and faced him.

'OK, I'm not waiting until we get home so we can talk about this, Carlos. What the hell is going on?' Anna still sounded rattled. 'I could see there was nothing happening in Tujunga Village – no squad cars, no one being arrested, no emergency, nothing out of the ordinary to speak of.'

Garcia shifted a gear and joined North Mednick Avenue, going south.

'This has got something to do with whatever you're investigating at the moment, hasn't it?' Anna asked rhetorically. 'I know because Robert was surveying the street like a man on a mission. Who are you guys looking for? How did you know that I was out shopping with a friend? Why are you scaring me like this?' Tears welled up in her eyes.

Garcia took a deep breath.

'Talk to me, Carlos, please.'

'I have to ask you for something,' Garcia finally said, his voice steady.

Anna leaned back against the passenger's door, wiped the tears from her eyes and stared at her husband.

'I need you to stay at your parents' for a few hours. I'll come and pick you up later.'

Anna took two whole seconds to digest the request before her nerves took over again. 'What? You said that nothing had happened to my parents. Are they OK?'

'Yes, yes, they're fine, baby. Nothing happened to them. I just need you to stay there for a few hours. I need to go back to the PAB and sort a few things out. I'll come and get you in a short while.'

Anna waited.

Garcia said nothing else.

'And that's all you're going to say?' she challenged.

One of the reasons why Garcia and Anna's relationship worked so well was because they both knew they could always talk to each other, no matter what. And they always did. There was never any recrimination, jealousy or judgment. They were both great listeners, and they supported and understood each other better than they understood themselves.

Anna could see Garcia was struggling with it.

'Carlos,' she said, placing a hand on his knee. 'You know I trust you. I always have, and I always will. If you want me to go stay with my parents for a few hours, I can do that, it's not a problem, but I have the right to know the reason why. Why don't you want me to go home? What is going on?'

Garcia knew Anna was right. He also knew that there was no way he could give her the real reason without frightening her, but he had no other alternative. If he lied, she would see right through him. She always did.

He took another deep breath and told her what had happened earlier in the day.

Anna listened without interrupting. When he was done, tears had returned to her eyes, and Garcia felt his heart tighten inside his chest.

'He was right behind us?' Anna asked. 'Filming us?'

Garcia nodded.

'And he was broadcasting it live over the Internet?'

'Over the Internet, yes,' Garcia said. 'But not open to everyone, just to Robert and me. No one else could see it.'

Anna didn't want or need to know the technical details.

'Please, Anna, just stay with your parents for a few hours. I need to get a few things in motion, and I want to check our apartment.'

Anna coughed. 'You think he's been in our *home*?'

'No, I don't,' Garcia said with conviction. 'But I have to be absolutely sure, because the paranoid cop in me won't rest until I am. You know that.'

At that moment Anna couldn't be sure if the emotion in Garcia's voice was anger or fear.

'So this is the same person who abducted and killed that *LA Times* reporter who was on the paper this morning,' she finally said. 'He broadcast it over the Internet, didn't he? Just like he did with Pat and me.'

Garcia didn't need to reply. Anna knew she was right.

He kept his eyes on the road and tightened his grip on the steering wheel, bottling all he could inside. What he really wanted to ask Anna was for her to leave Los Angeles until they had this psycho behind bars. But she would never agree to it, even if her life *were* in danger. Anna was a determined, very stubborn and totally committed woman. She worked with deprived elderly people, people who needed and depended on her on a daily basis. Even if she could, she wouldn't just get up and leave them overnight. And Garcia had no way of knowing how long this hunt would take.

Garcia had agreed with Hunter that *today*, this killer had no real intention of harming Anna. But he took it as a warning, an eye-opener. The killer could very well change his mind tomorrow, or the day after, or the day after that . . . and Garcia knew there was very little he could do about it. What the killer had broadcast this afternoon had filled him with real fear, and highlighted a frightening truth. The truth that despite who he was, despite how much he wanted to, he couldn't truly protect Anna twenty-four hours a day. The killer knew that. And today he made sure Garcia and Hunter knew it too.

Sixty-Six

With the old-fashioned, closet-sized elevator stuck somewhere at the top of the building, Ethan Walsh took the steps up to his fourth-floor apartment in a hurry, and two at a time. The problem was that physical exercise wasn't even part of his vocabulary, never mind his daily routine. By the time he hit the second floor, he was out of breath, red-faced and sweating like a sumo wrestler in a sauna about to have a heart attack. Though Ethan had gained a little extra weight in the past few months, he wasn't exactly fat, but he sure was unfit.

Usually he would've taken his time conquering the eight flights of stairs that led up to his flat, cursing as he reached the top of each one, but tonight he was already ten minutes late for his half-hour, face-to-face call with his four-year-old daughter, Alicia.

When Alicia was born, Ethan's life seemed to be on a plain-sailing course to success. Ethan was an independent videogames programmer, and a very good one at that. He had developed several online games by himself, and for three consecutive years he'd won the prestigious Mochis Flash Games Award for Best Strategy and Puzzle Game of the Year. But with the advent of direct online stores for major platforms like Microsoft's X-Box 360 and Sony's PlayStation 3, a whole new world had been presented to independent videogames developers. And there was a hell of a lot of money to be made.

Ethan had discussed the idea of creating a game for the X-Box 360 with Brad Nelson, a brilliant Canadian games programmer he had met several years back. Brad said that he had also been playing around with the same idea, but doing it alone was a mountainous task. After a few more talks, they decided to do it together, and that was how Ethan and Brad created AssKicker Games just six months before Ethan's baby girl was born.

Brad was very well connected, and on the strength of Ethan's games awards he managed to secure a couple of very healthy investments, which enabled both of them to quit their day jobs and concentrate solely on developing their first major console game.

Within seven months they had a short playable demo that went viral on the X-Box 360 store. An incredible buzz started about the game and their company, but Ethan was a perfectionist, and he kept on stripping and redoing enormous chunks of the game, which severely hindered its progress. Arguments started breaking out between Ethan and Brad on a daily basis. The completion date for the game just kept on being put back further and further, and two years later it was still under development. No one knew for sure when it would be finished. The buzz about the game and their company had died down. The investments dried up. Ethan ended up remortgaging his house and putting everything he had into the company.

The pressure and frustration Ethan was under at work started seeping through into his relationship with his wife, Stephanie, and they started rowing practically every night. Their daughter was almost three then. Ethan was obsessed, depressed and becoming a nervous wreck. That was when Brad Nelson decided to pull the plug on the company. He'd had enough. The arguments had gotten out of hand. He was out of patience and out of money, but not as in debt as Ethan.

The partnership ended badly. Brad refused to sign the papers that would transfer his share of the company to Ethan, and that meant that Ethan could not carry on developing the game on his own. Fifty percent of the game's intellectual property belonged to Brad, and he declined to let it go. Ethan had no money to hire a lawyer and try to fight Brad in a court of law. If he were to develop a game for the X-Box 360, he would have to forget everything he'd done so far and start a new one from scratch. He didn't have the means or the mental stamina for that.

Ethan was left completely broke, including his spirit. He didn't know what to do, but the experience had left him bitter, and he didn't want to program anymore. He was in so much debt that his only way out was to declare bankruptcy. He lost his house to the bank, and with that the arguments at home intensified. Stephanie moved out and filed for divorce six months ago. She'd taken their daughter with her, and was now living in Seattle with someone she'd met while still married to Ethan.

Ethan missed his daughter like crazy. In the past six months he had seen her only once. His only comfort at the moment was that twice a week he would speak to her on a thirty-minute Internet, face-to-face call, as stipulated by a family court judge.

When Ethan got to the door of his apartment, his breathing was so heavy he sounded like a malfunctioning vacuum cleaner. He fumbled for his keys, opened the door and stepped inside the small, dark and claustrophobic flat.

'Shit!' he murmured, checking his watch. It had taken him three minutes to climb up to the fourth floor. His hand found the light switch on the wall, and the old yellow bulb in the center of the ceiling flickered twice before bathing the room in such a weak light it made almost no difference at all. He rushed over to the laptop on the Formica table pushed up against one of the walls, and quickly turned it on.

'C'mon, c'mon, boot up, you prehistoric brick,' he urged it, waving both hands at the old computer. When it finally did, he brought up his face-to-face call application and clicked the "call" button. His daughter's account was already programmed in.

His ex-wife answered it at the other end.

'You are unbelievable,' she said, her tone angry. 'Fifteen minutes late . . .?'

'Don't even start, Steph,' Ethan cut her short. 'I left work on time, but the bus had a flat. We all had to get out and cram into the next one . . . Anyway, who cares? Why am I wasting my time talking to you? Where's Alicia?'

'You're a jerk,' Stephanie said. 'And you look like shit. You could've at least combed your hair.'

'Thank you for the kind words.' Ethan ran a hand through his fair hair to try to smooth it into place, before using the sleeve of his shirt to wipe the sweat from his forehead. A second later Alicia's smiley face appeared on his screen.

Alicia was a stunning little girl. Her rosy cheeks and curly blond hair made her look like a cartoon character. Her eyes were deep blue, and their shape gave the impression that she was always smiling, which incidentally she usually was. And it was a smile that could disarm any grown-up.

'Hi, Daddy,' Alicia said, waving her hand vigorously at the camera.

'Hi, sweetheart, how are you?'

'I'm very well, Daddy.' She brought her little hand to her mouth and started giggling. 'You look funny.'

'Do I? How funny?'

More giggles. 'Your face looks all red like a big strawberry, and your hair is sticking up like a pineapple.'

'Well,' Ethan said. 'You can call me "fruit salad Daddy" today, then.'

Alicia laughed one of those contagious laughs that people couldn't help but join in.

Ethan laughed with her.

They talked for another twelve minutes. Ethan felt a knot grow tight in his throat, as he knew he would soon have to say goodbye to Alicia. It would be four days before their next Internet chat.

'Daddy . . .?' Alicia said, frowning, her eyes displaying a little confusion.

'Yes, honey. What is it?'

'Who is . . .?'

Ethan's cellphone rang inside his shirt pocket. He always switched it off when he talked to Alicia, but because today he was in a hurry, he'd forgot ten.

'Just a second, honey,' he said, reaching for the phone. He didn't even check the caller display. He simply turned it off and placed it back in his pocket. 'Sorry, sweetheart. Who is what?'

For some reason Alicia looked scared.

'Darling, what is it?'

She lifted her little arm and pointed at the camera. 'Who is that man standing behind you, Daddy?'

Sixty-Seven

Garcia dropped Anna off at her parents' house in Manhattan Beach and headed straight back to his apartment. As he told Anna, the paranoid cop inside of him was screaming 'check and recheck', but logic told him that the killer hadn't been inside their home.

Garcia and Anna lived on the top floor of a six-story building in Montebello, southwest Los Angeles. They had no balcony or back alley fire escape. The only way in was through the front door. Garcia had worked too many house burglaries as a uniformed cop to know better. He had installed an anti-snap, high-security, ten-lever lock on his door. The lock was extremely resistant against picking and drilling attacks, even from someone with special tools. If somebody had breached that lock, there would be signs everywhere. There were none.

Satisfied, he called Hunter and found out that he was on his way to the FBI headquarters to talk with Michelle. Garcia told him he would meet him there.

Hunter had been waiting for less than five minutes when Garcia pulled into the parking lot behind the FBI building in Wilshire Boulevard.

'How's Anna?' Hunter asked as his partner stepped out of his car. He knew Garcia would have told her the truth.

'She's rattled, but you know Anna, she's putting on a brave face. I left her with her parents until I get back. How did you get on?'

Garcia didn't have to tell Hunter that no matter what he'd told Anna, she wouldn't simply pack up and leave Los Angeles. Hunter also knew how determined and committed to her job she was, and though he believed that the killer had targeted Anna solely to prove a point, neither he nor Garcia was prepared to take any chances. They had agreed earlier that since they couldn't keep an eye on her twenty-four hours a day, somebody would.

'The paperwork is all done,' Hunter said. 'And it's already been approved by the captain. Anna will have a police escort with her 24/7, until we call it off. A squad car has just been dispatched to your place.'

Garcia nodded but made no comment. The look in his eyes was distant and pensive.

'Why don't you go home, Carlos?' Hunter said. 'Go pick Anna up and stay with her. She needs you by her side . . . and you need her.'

'I know I do. And that's why I'm here. Me being with Anna . . . The best surveillance in the world . . . None of it will make any difference while this psycho is still out there. He proved that today.' Garcia paused and looked at Hunter. 'Even the tiniest glimpse into how the mind of a perpetrator works can turn out to be a huge step toward capturing him . . . You taught me that, remember?'

Hunter accepted it with a head gesture.

'So one way to get closer to him is to know all we can about how he does what he does, and Michelle and Harry are the only people who can help us understand how he does it.' He took a deep breath to steady himself. 'I'll pick Anna up straight after I leave here, but right now this is me doing the best I can do to protect her.' Garcia started walking toward the building.

Sixty-Eight

Harry Mills had come up from the Cybercrime Division's underground floor to greet Hunter and Garcia at the entrance lobby of the FBI building. He guided them past the reception desk, through the security doors, down the hallway and finally into the elevator, but this time he pressed the button to sublevel three instead of sublevel one.

'Michelle is at the underground shooting range on the third sublevel,' Harry explained. 'It's how she lets off steam – Metal music and shooting the hell out of a paper target.' The elevator doors seemed to take forever to close, and Harry repeatedly stabbed his finger at the button.

'Everything OK?' Hunter asked.

Harry shrugged. 'We just got some bad news. A victim in one of the pedophile cases we're investigating committed suicide about an hour ago. She was twelve.'

The silence that followed was only broken by the mechanical female voice announcing they'd arrived at underground level three.

The elevator doors slid open, and Harry escorted them down another concrete corridor. Light came from fluorescent tubes that ran down the center of the ceiling. They turned left, then right, and arrived at a set of thick, dark glass double doors. Harry swiped his FBI ID card through the electronic keypad on the wall, typed in a six-digit code and the doors buzzed open.

As they stepped inside a small anteroom, the very familiar sound of target practicing filled their ears. A weapons master sat alone inside a separate room, visible through a large security glass window on the east wall. Harry signed both detectives in.

'She's in the usual booth,' the weapons master said, jerking his head to one side.

Another short hallway finally led them into the target practice range, where the noise level shot up five-fold. Twelve individual shooting booths were lined side by side facing a large westward target forum. The first four booths were taken by FBI agents in crisp black suits, yellow-tinted shooting glasses and clunky earmuffs. None of them acknowledged the new arrivals.

The next seven booths were empty. Michelle Kelly was occupying the very last one. She was wearing a black T-shirt, black jeans and black boots. Her long hair had been twisted around and thrown forward over her right shoulder in a casual manner. Instead of the usual large earmuffs, she had white earphones stuck deep into her ears. As they approached her booth, they all saw her fire six quick shots with a semi-automatic handgun at a male torso painted onto a paper target twenty-two yards away.

Michelle removed her earphones and thumbed the safety on before placing the gun on the booth ledge in front of her. She pressed the button that controlled the target slide, and the male torso came flying toward her like Superman.

Six body shots – four around the heart area, one to the left shoulder and one at the stomach/chest borderline.

'Great shooting,' Hunter said.

She looked at him with fire in her eyes. 'If you think you can do better, grab a gun, hotshot.'

Garcia and Hunter cocked their heads back in surprise.

'I didn't say that,' Hunter said. 'And I wasn't being sarcastic. That was actually very good shooting.'

'For a woman, you mean?'

Hunter looked at Garcia, then Harry, then back at Michelle. 'I didn't say or imply that either.'

Garcia sleekly took a step back, sensing trouble. He didn't want to get caught in whatever it was that was happening.

'Why don't you grab a gun?' Michelle forced the issue. 'Let's do this. FBI against LAPD. Guy against girl. Whatever you want to call it. Let's see how well you can shoot.'

Hunter held her burning stare for a second. She definitely hadn't let off enough steam yet.

'I can save you the hassle,' he said. 'I'm not that accurate.' He nodded at the paper target as she unclipped it from the slide and put a brand-new one in place. 'And we don't have a lot of time to spare, Michelle.'

'That's a bullshit excuse. And this won't take more than a few seconds,' she replied, slotting a new ammo clip into her gun. '9mm pistol OK for you?' she asked, but answered it herself. 'But of course it is. Harry, could you, please?' She nodded toward the weapons room.

Hunter and Garcia knew full well that arguing with a woman when she was in that frame of mind was a futile exercise. Especially one with a gun.

A minute later Harry was back with a pair of protective earmuffs, a pair of yellow-tinted anti-haze glasses and a 9mm Glock 19 compact pistol – the same type Michelle was using.

Hunter said no to the glasses.

'Standard six shots practice,' Michelle said, even though the Glock 19 ammo clip holds fifteen bullets. She indicated the empty booth to her left. 'Kill shots *only*, and don't hold back. I'll know if you do.'

Garcia peeked at Hunter but said nothing.

Hunter took booth number ten, leaving an empty one sandwiched between him and Michelle. She returned her earphones to her ear, cranked up the volume on her MP3 player and gave Hunter a head signal. Still, he waited for Michelle to fire first.

The shots came out fast and furious. Twelve shots in eight seconds.

When the noise died down, they both removed their ear protection and reached for the target slide buttons.

Michelle's target showed three heart-shots, two head-shots – left cheek and forehead – and one throat-shot. She smiled as she unclipped the paper target.

Hunter had placed one shot on the target's left shoulder; the other five were spread around its chest area. Only two could be considered lethal shots to the heart.

Michelle looked at Hunter's targets. 'That's not very reassuring, taking into account that you're trained to protect and serve.'

'What do you mean?' Garcia said, checking Hunter's target. 'Any of those shots would've halted any perpetrator.'

'That's true,' Michelle accepted. 'But I did say kill shots *only*, didn't I?' She glared at Hunter. 'Want to go again?'

Hunter thumbed the safety on and returned the pistol to Harry. 'There's no point. I *was* going for kill shots,' he admitted, locking eyes with his partner.

Garcia avoided Michelle's gaze, afraid she would've read him like a book. Time and time again, down at the LAPD's practice range, he'd seen Hunter empty entire clips on a *moving* target's forehead, *thirty* yards away. Fifteen shots, clustered together in an area never larger than the diameter of a tennis ball. Garcia was a good shot himself, but he'd never seen anyone as accurate as Hunter with a handgun. On a standing target twenty-two yards away, he was sure Hunter could've drawn eyes and a smile on the target's face.

Hunter looked at Michelle. 'I did mean it when I said that was great shooting earlier.'

Awkward feet shuffling.

'I'm sorry for taking a stab at you, and for forcing you to shoot,' Michelle finally said, ejecting the ammo clip from her gun. 'It hasn't been the best of days.'

'You can say that again,' Garcia agreed.

Hunter simply nodded.

Both detectives understood that refusing to shoot, or achieving a better score with the target, had the potential to unconsciously aggravate Michelle's already upset state of mind. Playing along, and coming second best without being too obvious, had had a comforting and soothing psychological effect for Michelle. The effect was immediate. Though she was still visibly upset, the hostility she showed just moments ago was now under control.

'Can you explain how come we could see the Internet broadcast earlier today, but you couldn't?' Garcia asked, not wanting to waste any more time.

'Sure,' Michelle said. 'But let's get away from this noise first.'

Sixty-Nine

'There are several ways to block a viewer from watching a live online broadcast,' Michelle said as they boarded the elevator back up to the Cybercrime Division's floor. 'The easiest one is by identifying the viewer's computer IP address.'

Garcia looked at Michelle blankly.

The elevator doors opened and they made their way down the corridor.

'Remember when I said that a computer's IP address is like a license plate or a telephone number?' Michelle asked. 'Every computer has a unique identifying one.'

'Um-huh.'

Harry swiped the security door before typing in the code and allowing everyone back into the cold, starship *Enterprise*-looking office.

'OK,' Michelle continued. 'So just like a cellphone, if a person calls out, but doesn't activate *caller ID secrecy*, the cellphone receiving the call can easily see the number that's calling in, right? It appears on the caller display.'

'Yes.'

'Same with computers. The difference is, unless you're an expert with some clever gadgets, you can't hide your computer's IP address. There's no *caller ID secrecy* feature for people to activate on their computers.'

'In fact,' Harry jumped in, 'every time you connect to any website on the World Wide Web, the host computer records your IP address. It's their first line of defense against fraud. With an IP address, it makes identifying where the connection came from a lot easier.'

Garcia thought about it for a second. 'So if you're a computer programmer, and you know the computer's IP address in question, you could write some code to block it, whenever it tries to connect to the site.'

'Or in our case, the opposite,' Hunter said. 'The killer could've written some code that allowed only one IP address to connect – ours – blocking everyone else's. That's why we could see the broadcast but no one else could.'

'Exactly,' Michelle and Harry said in unison.

'But that means he has to know the specific IP address to the computers in our office,' Garcia said. 'How easy is it to obtain them?'

'Depends on how clever you are,' Harry replied. 'And this guy is *very*.'

'When we couldn't connect to the broadcast after you called us,' Michelle explained. 'We started trying to figure out how he managed to block us out. We came to that same conclusion. In order for him to do so, he needed to know the specific IP addresses for the computers in your office.' She shrugged. 'But how did he get them?'

'The first-ever broadcast,' Hunter said, thinking back.

'Bingo.' Michelle smiled.

Garcia looked at Hunter. 'The first-ever broadcast?'

'It wasn't open to the public,' Hunter said. 'Only to us, remember? He called us, gave us an IP address and asked us to type it into the address bar. We were the only ones watching that broadcast. No one else.'

'So if you were the only ones,' Michelle said, 'and the killer knew you were the only ones connecting to his server, the IP address, or addresses, the host computer recorded that day must belong to you.'

'Sonofabitch,' Garcia whispered.

'Dead simple,' Harry said. 'And dead clever. Without you guys suspecting a thing, he singled your IP addresses out right then. It seems he's been playing you from the start.'

Seventy

When Hunter got to the Police Administration Building the next morning, Garcia was already at his desk, reading over the last of Christina Stevenson's emails. Despite the freshly ironed shirt, the clean-shaven face and the hair pulled back into a tidy ponytail, he looked tired. Hunter doubted he'd had more than a couple of hours' sleep.

'How's Anna?' Hunter asked.

'She barely slept last night,' Garcia said, pushing himself away from his desk for a moment. 'And the few hours she did were punctured by nightmares.'

Despite sensing the hidden anger in Garcia's words, Hunter knew there was nothing he could say that would make any sort of difference. He stayed silent.

'I can see you didn't sleep much either,' Garcia said, moving the subject along.

'Well, no surprise there,' Hunter replied. 'Still nothing interesting from the emails?'

Garcia shook his head and shrugged. 'I've got through all of them now. Not a damn thing, but we did get an email from forensics this morning. Just like they expected, the lock on the glass door to Christina Stevenson's bedroom *was* bumped. That was how the killer got access to the house. The exam on the fibers found in her room has, so far, proved inconclusive. They could've come from any garment inside her wardrobe, but they'll carry on testing.'

Hunter nodded, fired up his computer, and while it booted up he poured himself a strong cup of coffee – the third one this morning, and it wasn't even 8:30 a.m. yet. As soon as he sat down, there was a knock at the door.

'Come in,' Hunter called out.

A young uniformed police officer pushed the door open and stepped inside. 'Detective Hunter?'

'Right here,' Hunter said, lifting his coffee cup as if toasting something.

'This just came for you. It was delivered by someone from the *LA Times*.' As the officer handed Hunter a small, sealed envelope, his gaze wandered past the detective's shoulder toward the pictures board on the south wall. His body tensed, and his eyes lit up with a mixture of curiosity and shock.

'Is there anything else?' Hunter quickly said, gently stepping to his left to obstruct the officer's view.

'Um . . . no, sir.'

Hunter thanked the young officer and escorted him back to the door.

Inside the envelope he found a USB pen drive and an *LA Times* complimentary slip with a handwritten note.

Here are the files you asked for. I hope they help. Pamela Hays.

'What's that?' Garcia asked.

'About two years' worth of articles by Christina Stevenson.' Hunter connected the pen drive to his computer.

Garcia walked over to check it out.

As the contents loaded onto Hunter's screen, he let out a frustrated breath. 'Damn!'

'*Phew*,' Garcia whistled. 'Six hundred and sixty-nine files?' He half chuckled, half coughed. 'Good luck with those. I hope they're at least more interesting than her emails.' He gestured back toward his computer.

'I wouldn't bet on it.'

The immediate problem Hunter faced was that the files weren't searchable text files. Every document in that USB pen drive was actually a scanned image of the newspaper page with the published article. No file titles, just published dates. He would have to read through them all.

Hunter sat back and took a deep breath. The first thing he wanted to do was to find the article Christina Stevenson had written about Thomas Paulsen, the software million-aire. Pamela Hays had told him that Christina had written the article about four months ago, so that's where he started, opening and quickly scanning through every file where its publishing date was within that time bracket. It didn't take him long. He hit the jackpot on the twelfth file he opened.

The article had been a two-page spread. Christina Stevenson had spent two months gathering information and interviewing past and present employees from PaulsenSystems. The result had been an open book on sexual harassment, bribery and intimidation. Christina Stevenson made the fifty-one-year-old software magnate look and sound like a sexual predator.

The article began by telling the story of how a young Thomas Paulsen, only twenty-one at the time and a compu-ter enthusiast, saw an opening in the market and a golden opportunity to start a software company. He then borrowed whatever he could from family and friends and started PaulsenSystems from his parents' garage in Pasadena. He made his first million a year and a half later.

The article also carried three photographs of Paulsen. One was a professional portrait, also found on the company's website, but the other two were more personal, taken inside a nightclub – hidden-camera style. The first one showed Paulsen kissing the neck of a brunette woman who looked to be at least twenty years younger than him. The second photo showed him with his hand firmly planted on the woman's ass.

The story went on to reveal that the young woman was actually Thomas Paulsen's new secretary. She'd been with the company for six months. According to the paper, Paulsen would do his best to wine, dine and charm any employee he took a fancy to, take them to bed and then intimidate them into keeping their mouth shut, in whichever way necessary, including terrorizing them. The story ended by saying that the accurate number of women Thomas Paulsen had taken advantage of was unknown, but he'd been doing it for over twenty years.

Hunter had no doubt that a story like that one, with a front-page call on a high-circulating national newspaper like the *LA Times*, would've seriously rocked Paulsen's personal life and public image.

Hunter spent the next hour or so searching the net for aftermath and spin-off articles. He wanted to find out what sort of snowball Christina's piece had started. He found several. And the snowball had been big and damaging.

A very interesting article he came across had also come from the entertainment desk at the *LA Times*, published two and a half months ago, but it hadn't been written by Christina. The article talked about how Christina's report had stabbed at the heart of Paulsen's marriage. Gabriela, Paulsen's wife of twenty-seven years, had no idea of what her husband had been getting up to with some of his female employees. She had filed for divorce a month after the article was published. It was also reported that their twenty-five-year-old daughter had stopped talking to him.

Another hour and Hunter had found numerous articles referring to Paulsen's company. He had business contracts all over the country, and apparently, due to Christina's story and the moral issues it touched, several of them had been terminated. Financially, PaulsenSystems had taken a sizable hit.

As Hunter read each article, he passed it over to Garcia.

'Christina Stevenson's story cost Paulsen a hell of a lot,' Hunter said. 'In every aspect of his life. If anyone had a good reason to go after her, Thomas Paulsen did.'

'True,' Garcia agreed. 'But as far as we know, he had no reason to go after Kevin Lee Parker, our first victim.'

Hunter pulled a face. '*As far as we know.*'

Garcia smiled. He knew exactly what was going through his partner's mind.

'I'll get a team on it,' he said, reaching for the phone on his desk.

Before Garcia came off his phone, the one on Hunter's desk rang.

'Detective Hunter, Homicide Special,' he answered it while trying to massage his aching neck.

'Guess what, Detective,' the caller said with the same electrifying enthusiasm of a television hit show host. 'It's *show time* again.'

Seventy-One

Garcia was still on the phone to the research team when he noticed the look on Hunter's face. A look so cold it could've frozen the air inside their office. A look that could only mean one thing – *the killer was at work again.*

Immediately Garcia thought of Anna, and his heart almost exploded inside his chest. He cut his conversation mid-sentence, slammed the phone down and frantically reached for the keyboard on his desk.

Hunter switched the call into loudspeaker mode before also reaching for his keyboard.

'No, no, no, no . . .' Garcia whispered to himself as he typed the address into the address bar, his fingers unsteady.

The website loaded on both detectives' screens in just a couple of seconds.

Glaring.

Squinting.

Confusion.

'Shit!' Garcia finally breathed out, slumping back down onto his chair with a thud. His instinctive emotional response was relief. They were looking at a close-up shot of someone's face, but that someone wasn't Anna. He was a white male who looked to be in his mid thirties. He had an oval-shaped face, a round nose, plump cheeks, thin eyebrows and short darkish hair.

The images were shrouded by a green tint, indicating that the killer was once again using night-vision lenses. Just like with the first two victims, the pictures were being broadcast from a dark place.

The man's eyes were darting from side to side, scared . . . confused . . . pleading . . . searching for an answer. It was easy to tell that they were light in color, but the green tint made it impossible to be specific. A leather gag had been strapped so tight around the man's mouth it was cutting into his skin. Fear and sweat covered his entire face.

Silently Hunter signaled Garcia to call Michelle and Harry at the FBI Cybercrime Division. He knew that the call was already being recorded by Operations.

Garcia quickly used his cellphone, cupping a hand over his mouth to minimize the noise.

'The website is back online,' he whispered into the phone when Michelle answered.

'We know,' she replied, her voice tense. 'I was just about to call you. We're trying, but he's using mirror sites again, reflecting the broadcast from server to server. We can't track it.'

Garcia suspected that would be the case.

'Has he called you guys again?' she asked.

'He's on the line right now.' Garcia got up and placed his cellphone on Hunter's desk so Michelle could listen in.

Suddenly, just like with the broadcast of the second victim, the word GUILTY was displayed, centered at the bottom of the picture.

Then, on the top right-hand corner of the screen, a new number sequence was displayed – 0123. They waited for another letter sequence similar to 'SSV' to appear on the top left-hand corner of the screen, but it never came.

'The rules are the same as last time, Detective,' the caller said, almost laughing. 'But today I am feeling generous ... and dare I say it, a little confident, even. So instead of a thousand votes in ten minutes, let's make it ten thousand votes in ten minutes. What do you say, huh? That should give you a prayer.'

Hunter didn't reply.

About halfway down the right-hand edge of the screen, the word STRETCH appeared, followed by the number zero and a green button. A fraction of a second later, directly underneath it, the word CRUSH appeared, also followed by a zero and a button. Both buttons were deactivated for the time being.

Hunter and Garcia frowned at the screen at the same time, and as they did the camera started to slowly zoom out.

Little by little, the man's whole body started to come into view. He was wearing nothing but a pair of dark boxer shorts. He wasn't a slim man, but he certainly couldn't be called overweight either. He looked to be lying down on some sort of wide wooden table. His arms were extended high above his head in a V shape. His armpits had been shaved clean. His legs had been placed a little wider than shoulder length apart, and were also completely stretched out.

It took several long seconds for the zooming out to be completed. Only then Hunter and Garcia could see the man's hands and feet, and that was when they finally figured out what the sadistic voting process meant.

Seventy-Two

Thick leather cuffs had been firmly strapped around the man's wrists and ankles. Those cuffs were, in turn, attached to the ends of four sturdy-looking metal chains, which were then connected to mechanical rollers. The entire device looked just like an improvised but updated version of the rack, one of the most sadistic medieval torture apparatuses ever created, used to slowly stretch a person's limbs until they were ripped from the body.

Inside Hunter's office, they could hear a pin drop.

'From the silence I hear,' the caller's voice came blasting through the phone's loudspeakers, 'I assume you are starting to get the picture.' He laughed a cartoon dog laugh.

Again, no reply from either detective.

'But that picture isn't complete yet,' the caller continued. 'So let me remedy that for you.'

The camera started to slowly pan upward, toward the ceiling.

All of a sudden Hunter's office door was pushed open in a hurry and Captain Blake stepped inside. The look on her face was a cocktail of anger, disbelief and dread.

'Are you watching this . . .' she began, but Hunter lifted a hand, stopping her, and gesturing toward the speakerphone on his desk.

Too late.

'Well, well, well,' the caller said, amused. 'So who might we have joining us now . . .?' He didn't wait for an answer. 'By the angry tone of her voice, I'm guessing – the Robbery Homicide Division Captain herself. Barbara Blake, is the name correct?'

Captain Blake knew that the killer could've easily gotten her name from the LAPD's official website.

'Welcome to *pickadeath.com*, Captain. Glad you can join us today. The more the merrier.'

'Why are you doing this?' she said, her words swimming in anger.

Hunter glared at the captain. Rule number one of any negotiations with any sort of perpetrator – *one negotiator only, unless the offender has requested otherwise. Any more, and the negotiation could easily be exposed to confusion, which might in turn frustrate and anger the perpetrator, causing the entire process to collapse.*

'Why am I doing this?' the caller repeated derisively. 'Are you asking me to do your job for you, Captain Blake?'

Hunter gave her a subtle headshake.

The captain stayed quiet.

The camera carried on panning upward.

Hunter frowned at the screen again, intrigued by something. The first thing he realized was that the location was different from the one used for the broadcast of the two previous victims. There was no brick wall at the back, and the room seemed larger, much larger. Then something else caught his attention – the camera movement. It took him a few seconds to figure out why. He looked at Garcia and mouthed a few words.

Garcia failed to understand them, shook his head and moved closer.

'It's a remote-controlled camera.' Hunter whispered it this time.

'What?' Garcia and Captain Blake looked uncertain.

Hunter pressed the 'mute' button on his phone. 'The way the camera is zooming and panning around the place,' Hunter explained. 'It's too slow, too steady. You try doing that by hand, and there's no way you'll get such a smooth and constant movement.'

Garcia and Captain Blake looked back at the screen.

'He's controlling it remotely,' Hunter said. 'He might not even be there.'

'So?' Captain Blake shot back. 'What difference does it make?'

Hunter shrugged.

On the screen the camera's panning came to a stop, and everyone inside Hunter's office went rigid. Suspended several feet directly above the victim and the makeshift medieval torture device was a man-made concrete slab. It looked to be around one and a half foot thick, four foot wide and about six and a half foot long. The rock easily weighed over a ton. It was being held in place by very thick chains attached to ten metal hooks that had been built into the top surface of the slab. They couldn't see what the chains were connected to at the very top.

'I guess the picture is now complete,' the caller said with a chuckle. 'But the beauty of what I've created here is . . . I don't have to crush him all at once. I am able to slowly lower that concrete rock onto the table, gently compressing his body, like a giant vise, until every bone is crushed.'

Hunter knew there would be a twist. The rack was originally a medieval *torture* device, not an execution one. Its main purpose was to *slowly* stretch a person's limbs to obtain a confession or to extract information. The pain it caused was so severe that a confession would usually come very quickly, and the stretching would stop after only a few seconds. But if the rollers weren't stopped, the body would eventually be dismembered – usually the arms would be ripped from the person's torso. Death would soon follow from blood loss. But the victim would suffer tremendously before dying. Crushing someone to death with a huge concrete block, when compared to using a torture device like the rack, was relatively painless, and very, very fast. This killer simply wouldn't allow that to happen.

'You sonofabitch,' Captain Blake blasted out, not caring for protocol or rules anymore.

The caller's response was a laugh full of joy. 'I guess it's time we start the show. Enjoy.'

The line went dead.

On the screen both voting buttons were activated, and at the bottom left-hand corner a digital clock started its count-down – 10:00, 9:59, 9:58 . . .

Seventy-Three

Inside the Office of Operations on the first floor of the Police Administration Building, Desiree and Seth were glued to their computer monitors, watching the events unfold on *pickadeath.com*. They, together with everyone else on their floor, could barely believe their eyes.

'Sweet Lord and His Creation!' Desiree said, crossing herself and kissing the tiny golden crucifix on the chain around her neck. 'He wants people to vote if he should crush that poor man to death or rip his arms and legs from his body like an insect?'

'Ten thousand votes in ten minutes?' Seth replied. 'That's a lot of votes when you consider that not every vote will go to the same death method.'

'So you think that if time runs out,' Desiree came back, 'and he doesn't get ten thousand votes, this killer will keep his word and just let this guy go?'

Seth simply shrugged.

Watching the events unfold on their computer monitors wasn't the only thing Seth and Desiree were doing. They were also the ones in charge of recording and tracking the killer's call to Hunter's desk.

The first thing they found out was that the call was coming from a cellphone. Immediately they used an application to query the service provider for the phone's GPS coordinates.

Nothing.

No GPS.

The caller was either using an old phone or had deactivated the GPS chip.

Instantly Desiree and Seth moved onto cellphone triangulation, a much more cumbersome and laborious process that usually took several minutes and depended on two main factors. One, the phone must stay active during the whole process. If the caller came off the phone and switched it off, the triangulation procedure failed. Two, the phone must stay inside the same triangulation zone. If the caller was mobile and happened to move out of range of any one of the three triangulating towers, the process collapsed and it had to be started again from scratch.

But so far, so good.

The caller was still on the line, and it didn't look like he was moving anywhere. If he stayed on the phone for just a little while longer, they would probably have a location. But neither Desiree nor Seth showed a lot of excitement with that prospect. They had both worked on the two previous calls from this same perpetrator to Hunter. They had seen how he had expertly bounced the calls all over Los Angeles, laughing at the LAPD. If there was one thing this perpetrator was not it was 'stupid'. He knew full well that this call, just like the previous two, would be recorded and traced.

One of the two computers on Seth's desk beeped once, indicating that the triangulation process had come to an end. Seth and Desiree turned to face the monitor, without paying too much attention to the final coordinates. They were simply waiting for the triangulated location to quickly change, as the caller bounced it onto a different spot, in the same way he had done with the first call.

It didn't happen.

Ten, twenty, thirty seconds passed and the location stayed the same.

'You're joking,' Seth whispered, leaning over his keyboard. Only then he and Desiree checked the coordinates for the originating phone call.

'Oh my God.'

Seventy-Four

'Is this for real?' Captain Blake asked, her disbelieving eyes fixed on the computer monitor on Hunter's desk.

Less than sixty seconds had elapsed since the digital clock at the bottom left-hand corner of the screen started counting back from ten minutes.

CRUSH: 1011.

STRETCH: 1089.

'Not even a minute gone, and over two thousand people have voted?' Captain Blake finally looked at Hunter.

'He's probably placed links on several major social network sites again,' Hunter replied.

'*He has.*' The barely audible comment came from Garcia's cellphone on Hunter's desk. Michelle Kelly was still on the line.

Garcia quickly switched the call to loudspeaker mode. 'Can you repeat that, Michelle?'

'I said that he *has* placed links on several major social network sites. A minute gone and the site has received—' there was a quick pause punctuated by keyboard clicks '— nearly four thousand hits, and the ratio is increasing by the second.'

'That's just perfect,' Captain Blake said. 'Is there anything the FBI Cybercrime Division can do about this?'

'We're already doing all we can,' Michelle came back. 'But this guy looks to have anticipated every move we could make. Whichever way we turn, we hit a wall.'

'Are you and Harry recording this?' Hunter asked.

'Harry isn't here,' Michelle said. 'But yes, I'm recording every second of it.'

CLOCK: 7:48, 7:47, 7:46 . . .

CRUSH: 3339.

STRETCH: 3351.

Captain Blake's cellphone vibrated inside her suit jacket pocket. She reached for it and checked the caller display window – the mayor of Los Angeles. She knew exactly what that meant. She declined the call and returned the phone to her pocket. Right now, she had no time for a pointless argument. She would deal with the mayor in her own time.

Garcia took a step back from his desk and nervously rubbed his face before looking down at the floor and away from the screen. Hunter could almost read his thoughts. After what happened yesterday, Garcia's subconscious mind couldn't help but to put forward the worst imaginable scenario for him, swapping the man they could see on their screen for his wife, Anna.

Garcia quickly shook his head, trying to banish the thought. He took a moment or two to try to calm the rapid beating of his heart, waiting for the rate to settle slowly. When it did, his eyes returned to the screen.

Captain Blake was also getting fidgety. The helplessness of watching the voting process without being able to move a finger to stop it was polluting the air inside the room like a sarin gas attack.

'Over ten thousand hits.' They all heard Michelle say. 'It's going viral.'

CLOCK: 6:11, 6:10, 6:09 . . .

CRUSH: 5566.

STRETCH: 5601.

'This can't be happening,' Captain Blake said.

The phone on Hunter's desk rang again – internal call. He snapped the receiver off its cradle.

'Detective Hunter, this is Seth Reid from Operations. You're not going to believe this, but we've got a trace on the caller's location.'

Seth was wrong: right about now, Hunter would believe anything. He placed the call on speaker mode. 'You've got a fixed location for the originating call?'

'That's correct. The caller stayed on the line for long enough, and this time he didn't bounce the call all over the city.'

Hunter and Garcia frowned. This killer would not make that kind of mistake.

'I'll be damned,' Captain Blake said, reaching for the phone on Garcia's desk, ready to assemble the whole of the LAPD if necessary. 'So what *is* the location?'

'Well, that's the thing . . .' Seth said. 'He's on West 1st Street, somewhere around number 100.'

'What?' Hunter, Garcia and Captain Blake said at the same time, everyone turning to face the speakerphone on Hunter's desk.

'This building *is* number 100 West 1st Street,' Captain Blake said, putting Garcia's phone back down. 'Are you telling me he's calling from just outside the Police Administration Building?'

'Yes,' Seth replied. 'That's *exactly* what I am telling you.'

Seventy-Five

'Yo, Spinner, come have a look at this.' Tim called his best friend over while staring wide-eyed at his smartphone screen.

Tim was sixteen years old and Spinner seventeen. They were both students at Glendale High, and, just like they did every day after school, they were practicing their moves in the skate ramps in Verdugo Park.

Spinner kick-flipped his board before performing a 180-spin to face his friend. Tim was taking a break and sitting at the edge of the kidney pool they were riding.

'Damn, dude, you're on your phone again?' he called back, shaking his head. 'You need to skate more and Tweet less. You know what I'm saying? What is it anyway?'

'You have to come check it out, bro. This is sick – literally.'

Spinner paused and pulled a face at Jenny, another student from Glendale High who was hanging out in the park with them. She also loved skating, but she had a long way to go to get half as good as Tim and Spinner.

Both Spinner and Jenny kicked their boards up and approached Tim.

'Is it a new move?' Spinner asked.

'Nah, dude.' Tim shook his head. 'Remember I told you about that crazy website – pickadeath.com?'

'The one you said was a film stunt?' Jenny said.

'Yeah, but you guys saw the paper a couple of days ago, didn't you?' Tim replied. 'It was no stunt, bro. That shit was real. Some crazy fucker killed that woman live on the net.'

'Maybe the bitch deserved it,' Spinner commented.

Jenny punched him on the shoulder. 'Don't be a dick, Spinner. That's a horrible thing to say.'

Spinner shrugged. 'Just saying.'

'Anyway,' Tim waved a hand, cutting them short. 'I just got a Tweet from Mel. The site is back online, bro. Check this shit out.' Tim showed them his smartphone.

Spinner and Jenny both frowned at the screen at the same time.

'Damn, is this shit for real?' Spinner asked, his eyes glistening.

'Like I said,' Tim replied. 'Last time it was very real. So I think – yeah, bro, this shit is happening. Some dude is gonna die.'

Jenny pulled a disgusted face. 'You guys, this is sick. You gonna watch some poor dude get killed live over the Internet?'

'Hell yeah,' Spinner said. 'And I don't know what you're complaining about. You watch all those crap reality shows on TV.'

'That doesn't even compare, Spinner,' Jenny spat back.

'You bet your ass it doesn't. This beats them all hands down. They should call this *American Dead Idol*.'

'I like that,' Tim said.

'Well, I'm not watching it,' Jenny said, annoyed, jumping onto her board and riding back into the pool.

'Have you voted?' Spinner asked, not really concerned about Jenny.

'Not yet.'

'Well, give me a sec,' Spinner said, reaching into his pocket for his phone. 'OK, gimme the address, and let's get this sucker cooked.'

Seventy-Six

Even though the window in Hunter and Garcia's office looked out over South Spring Street on the west side of the Police Administration Building, everyone inside the room instinctively turned toward it.

'You've got to be shitting me,' Captain Blake said. 'How can that be possible when he's broadcasting all this right now?'

'Because he's controlling the camera and everything else remotely,' Hunter replied. 'That's how.'

The captain thought about it for a beat. 'Sonofabitch,' she mumbled. 'Is he in the park?' she asked Seth.

City Hall Park, or South Lawn, as it was called by many, is a 1.7-acre green park area shaded by a dense canopy of trees that fronted the famous Los Angeles City Hall building. It sits on West 1st Street directly across the road from the entrance to the PAB.

'He could be,' Seth admitted. 'We had to use triangulation,' he explained, 'which is not as accurate as if the phone he was using carried a GPS chip. But even then, because we're talking about downtown Los Angeles, the triangulation accuracy is much better than if he was calling from out of town somewhere – we narrowed it down to an area of only fifty to a hundred meters.'

'And that area is right outside the PAB?' Captain Blake asked again, still doubtful.

'That's correct,' Seth confirmed one more time.

'OK, thank you,' the captain said and hastily reached for the phone on Garcia's desk again.

'What are you going to do, Captain?' Hunter asked.

'Get everyone I can out there. What do you think?'

'And ask them to do what?' Garcia this time. 'Arrest every male carrying a cellphone?'

She paused, her eyes rolling from Garcia to Hunter. 'The psycho who is responsible for this is just outside our front door.' She pointed to the computer screen. 'You want me to sit here and do nothing?'

CLOCK: 4:41, 4:40, 4:39 . . .

CRUSH: 8155.

STRETCH: 8146.

'He probably *was* there during the call,' Garcia admitted. 'He's arrogant enough, and playing these kinds of games empowers him, but I'm sure he's long gone now, Captain. He knew we would be tracing the call. And the only reason we've got a hit is because he wanted us to. This is all planned.'

'Carlos is right, Captain,' Hunter agreed. 'He wanted us to know that he was calling from just outside the PAB, and I'm sure he knew exactly how long it would take us to triangulate his call.'

'It's been almost six minutes since he disconnected,' Garcia announced. 'He's probably miles away from here now.'

'I don't think he will be,' Hunter countered. 'I don't think he'll be far at all.'

Captain Blake just glared at him.

'As Carlos said,' he explained, 'he's too arrogant, and this game of cat and mouse excites him too much. He came all the way to our doorstep to tease us and to make his game a little more challenging and fun ... at least for him. He'll want to see how we react to his little joke. He'll be observing West 1st Street and the South Lawn from somewhere close ...' Hunter paused, considering something. The memory of the second victim's bedroom and what they found on the glass wall behind the curtains coming back to him. 'No, wait, I'm wrong,' he said. 'He won't be observing just to see how we react. He'll be observing to see if we find it.'

Captain Blake's forehead creased. 'Find what?'

'Some sort of clue,' Hunter said. 'Because that's how he likes to play.'

Captain Blake picked up the phone on Garcia's desk once again, dialed an internal extension and started barking commands down the line.

'Tell them to check out the park and the roads immediately surrounding the PAB, Captain,' Hunter said. 'Tell them to look everywhere – trashcans, park benches, flower-beds, street gutters, everything.'

CLOCK: 3:15, 3:14, 3:13 ...

CRUSH: 9199.

STRETCH: 9180.

On the screen the camera zoomed in on the man tied to the wooden table. The fear etched on his face had intensified ten-fold, as if he'd received some kind of warning or had simply sensed his time was about to run out.

It was a proven fact that if a human being is deprived of one of his/her senses, the remaining ones compensate by over-sensitizing. Maybe it was that, together with a super flow of adrenaline, that gave him a new surge of strength, and all of a sudden he sprang to life, fighting against his restraints once again, tugging, pulling, shaking and kicking as hard as he could. It was all for nothing. The leather straps were too well secured, the chains too strong. No one, no matter how physically fit or strong they were, would've been powerful enough to escape that torture table.

Just as suddenly as the man's new fight had begun, it ended. The little strength he had left had now been completely drained from his body. All his hopes and prayers had abandoned him.

No one was coming. There would be no last-minute miracle.

'Why the hell are people still voting?' Captain Blake spat the question out, truly dumbfounded. 'Everyone knows this isn't a game anymore, or a publicity stunt for a movie. This is real. The papers made sure everyone out there knows that.' She pointed to the screen. 'He's going to die. No fake. No tricks. They all know it, and they're still voting . . . Why?'

'Because this is the crazy reality we live in today, Captain,' Hunter said. 'No one cares. People upload their *happy slapping*, or gang fight videos to YouTube, and it gets hundreds of thousands of hits. The more violent the better. And people are begging for more. You give them real violence – not staged, no actors, no fake – and you will have people out there jumping for joy. You turn it into a "reality show" and give people the chance to participate by voting, and you will have millions tuning in, itching to click that button just for the hell of it. The killer knows that. He knows the psychology behind it. He knows the mad society we live in.

That's why he's so confident. It's a game he knows he can't lose – a winning formula we see every day on TV.'

The camera zoomed in on the man's face. His teary eyes saddened even further. There was nothing else in them. He knew it was over.

The captain's cellphone vibrated inside her pocket once again. This time she didn't even look at it, letting it ring out.

CLOCK: 2:04, 2:03, 2:02 . . .

CRUSH: 9969.

STRETCH: 9965.

Total silence.

CLOCK: 1:49, 1:48, 1:47 . . .

CRUSH: 9995.

STRETCH: 9995.

Everyone held their breath.

. . . 10,000.

Seventy-Seven

On their computer monitors, the entire picture faded to black, as if the broadcasting camera had been turned off. A second later the word STRETCH reappeared, larger, blood-red, blinking at the center of the dark screen, quickly followed by the number 10,000.

Everyone inside Hunter's office was transfixed.

As the blinking word and number faded out, the images of the man tied to the wooden table faded back in. This time there were no other distractions on the screen – no buttons, or words, or numbers – nothing.

The camera had zoomed out, once again enabling all viewers to see the man's entire stretched-out body, together with all four leather straps and a portion of the chains.

Captain Blake brought both hands to her face, cupping them over her nose and mouth, as if about to say a prayer, but no words left her lips.

Suddenly a metal grinding mechanical noise exploded through the computer speakers on both detectives' desks, sending a horror wave across the room. The rollers had been activated.

'What the hell?' the captain blurted out.

'He enabled the camera's microphone,' Hunter said,

feeling his heart rate pick up speed inside his chest. 'He wants us to hear him die.'

The tension in the room was pierced by the man's first agonizing scream, muffled only by the tight gag around his mouth. It sent shivers down everyone's spine.

'There are over a quarter of a million viewers watching this,' Michelle, who was still on the phone, announced. Her voice was cloaked by an angry sadness.

'Isn't there any way you can scramble this broadcast?' Captain Blake asked her.

'I wish there was,' a defeated Michelle replied.

The man screamed again, this time trying to form words, but the gag and the excruciating pain he was going through made whatever he was trying to say indecipherable. Spit and blood flew out of the corners of his mouth, producing a thin red mist, only to splash back down again onto his face, neck and chest.

Reflexively the man stretched his neck as far as it would go, as if that would give his arms and legs an extra centimeter or two and ease his agony, even if just for a brief moment. It didn't work. Pain had now reached every fiber of every muscle in his body. Soon those fibers would be stretched beyond human endurance, which would cause them to lose their ability to contract, rendering them completely ineffective. After that, the fibers would start to slowly tear, ripping his muscles in a multitude of ways and locations, and drowning his body in unimaginable pain.

The man's eyes rolled back into his head and his eyelids flickered like butterfly wings over them for a second or two. It looked like he was about to pass out, but instead he coughed violently a couple of times before throwing his head to one side and vomiting.

Captain Blake looked away.

Hunter clenched his fists.

The next noise the man made wasn't so much a scream but a guttural shriek that stabbed at everyone's eardrums.

Garcia anxiously brought a hand to his face, half rubbing his forehead, half shielding his eyes. His subconscious mind was once again playing with him.

POP! POP!

Two distinct popping noises followed in quick succession.

Hunter's jaw tightened and he softly closed his eyes for just an instant. He knew those popping noises were the sound of snapping cartilage, ligaments and maybe even tendons. Pretty soon they would hear the tormenting sound of bones fracturing.

The man's eyes came back from his head, but they had no more focus in them, wandering deliriously, as if he'd been drugged.

The leather straps were now cutting deep into the man's skin and flesh – blood was dripping from his wrists, drawing thin red veins on his forearms. His feet were also covered in blood from where the straps had dug into his ankles.

The next sound they heard were bone breaks.

'Oh my God! No.' They all heard Michelle plead through the phone.

The skin around the man's armpits was starting to rupture.

Captain Blake kept her eyes on the screen but placed her hands over her ears. She wasn't sure how much more she could take.

As the mechanical rollers started working harder to overcome the resistance posed by skin and muscle, their grinding sound became louder, more piercing, like an office shredder fighting to chew through too many sheets of paper.

The man made as if he was about to scream again, but he had no more strength left in him, no more air in his lungs, no more voice in his vocal cords . . . no more life to give. His head slumped to one side and his eyes disappeared back into his head a millisecond before his eyelids closed over them. His body convulsed a couple of times, and that was when blood really started dripping from his armpits, as the man-made rack finally started to rip his arms away from his body.

It would now be just a matter of seconds before the pressure applied by the rollers snapped the brachial artery, the major blood vessel in the upper arms, producing massive blood loss.

They all watched it happen.

Blood gushed out from the man's torso, where the arms had once been, with incredible speed and pressure.

The armless man writhed and twitched several times, but each one less erratic than the previous, until he lay motionless.

Three seconds later the website went offline.

Seventy-Eight

It had been almost an hour since *pickadeath.com* had gone offline. Captain Blake was back in her office. She had spent most of that time on the phone to the mayor of Los Angeles, the Chief of Police and the governor of California. Everybody wanted answers, but all she had were more questions.

Not surprisingly, the press was already bombarding the LAPD Media Relations Office with hundreds of questions and interview requests. Captain Blake was still refusing to schedule a press conference because she knew exactly what would happen. Questions and comments would be lobbed at them from all corners of the room – some defiant, some angry, but all of them derisive of what the LAPD and the Homicide Special Section had accomplished so far. The captain knew that they wouldn't be able to supply answers to anything, not yet, and that would simply fuel the press to criticize their efforts and sensationalize the story even more. No, for now, still no questions.

Instead, the LAPD Media Relations Office would issue a new statement to the press. The statement would reveal nothing at all about the progress of the investigation. The true purpose behind it was to ask the press and the media for their cooperation in launching an appeal for the identity of the latest victim. The statement would be accompanied by a portrait photograph of the victim, captured from the early part of the broadcast, asking every paper to print it out, and every TV station to broadcast it as soon as possible. Somebody out there had to know who he was.

Seventy-Nine

Immediately after the broadcast ended, Garcia called Anna at work. She was doing fine. She knew nothing about what had just happened, but he knew she would find out soon enough. There was nothing he could do about that. He just wanted to make sure she was OK. After he disconnected from the call to his wife, Garcia went to the bathroom, locked himself inside a cubicle and silently threw up.

Hunter sat at his desk, trying his best to gather his thoughts together while his gut fought waves of nausea and an almost incontrollable desire to be sick. He knew he needed to watch the entire broadcast recording again, probably several times over, but he just couldn't bring himself to do it quite yet. Right now, what he really needed was to get out of that office.

Two minutes later he and Garcia were downstairs talking to the senior sergeant in charge of searching City Hall Park and the streets immediately surrounding the PAB.

'So far, we've got trash,' the sergeant announced, clearly annoyed with the 'garbage hunt' task he was given. He'd been on front-desk duty all day and had no idea what had happened less than fifty minutes ago. 'Wrappers, all kinds of it,' he continued, his tone a step away from being sarcastic. 'Burgers, sandwiches, candy bars, Twinkies – you name it, we've got it. We also have truckloads of cans, bottles and paper coffee cups.'

Hunter was listening to the sergeant, but his eyes were roaming around the park, the streets and all the buildings surrounding it. He was positive the killer would still be nearby. This killer took too much pride in what he did to simply walk away without savoring the result to such an audacious trick, like making the call from just outside the Police Administration Building, and maybe, leaving something behind for the LAPD to find. Psychopath or not, it would appeal to his sense of satisfaction. It follows the same principle as when a person surprises someone else with a present that he/she spent a long time creating, or choosing. The real satisfaction comes from observing that someone's reaction as he/she unwraps the gift.

Yes, Hunter thought, *this killer will be observing. He'll be close by. No doubt about it. But where?*

Hunter's eyes kept searching, but rush hour had just begun. Crowds of people were leaving work and making their way back home. There were too many people on the streets and in the park, too many public buildings surrounding the area, too many places where someone could easily observe the park from, without looking suspicious or being noticed. In downtown Los Angeles the killer wouldn't have found a better place than City Hall Park for what he had in mind. It being located just across the road from the PAB was just the perfect bonus.

The sergeant pulled a handkerchief from his trouser pocket and dabbed it over his sweaty forehead. 'We're bagging every little piece of trash into evidence bags, and you know why?' He was in no mood to wait for an answer. 'Because no one told us what the hell we're supposed to be looking for out here, and if that one thing so happens to be a bubble gum wrapper and we miss it, it's *my* ass, and I'm not losing my retirement pension over this bullshit. You guys want it, you can sort through it in your own time. Good luck with it.'

The radio clipped to the belt around the sergeant's thick waistline crackled loudly before a thin voice came through.

'*Um . . . Sergeant, I think I've . . .*' HISS, HISS. '*. . . here.*'

The sergeant unclipped the radio from his belt, clicking the 'talk' button. 'That's a negative, officer. Ten-one. You gonna have to repeat that.'

Both detectives knew that 10-1 was police ten-code for 'poor reception'.

More radio crackles.

The sergeant moved around to the other side of Hunter and Garcia.

'*I said that I think I've got something here, Sergeant,*' the officer came back. This time the reception was much clearer.

Reflexively the sergeant looked back at both detectives to check if they'd heard the message.

They had.

'Well, I'll be damned,' the sergeant replied. 'What have you got?'

'*Not quite sure, Sergeant.*'

'OK, then. Where are you?'

'*Northeast corner of the park, by the trashcan.*'

Hunter, Garcia and the sergeant turned and looked in that general direction. They'd been standing by the Frank Putman water feature, right at the center of the park, not that far from the northeast corner. They could see a young officer standing by a trashcan waving at them. They quickly walked over.

The officer was in his early twenties and looked to be fresh out of the police academy. He had bright blue eyes, red, acne-riddled cheeks and a pencil-tip nose. He was wearing a pair of latex gloves and holding a compact, black camcorder in his hands. He greeted everyone with a single head nod.

'I found this in there, Sergeant.' He pointed to the trash-can to his left. 'It was inside a regular brown-paper sand-wich bag.' He handed the camera to his sergeant, who barely looked at it before passing it over to Hunter.

'This is your show,' he said, looking very uninterested.

Hunter gloved up and took the camera. The letters and numbers on one side of it read Sony Handycam CX250 HD. The camera was one of those with a flip-out screen on the side.

'I'm not really sure what we're looking for out here, sir,' the officer explained. 'But that's a brand-new digital camera, worth at least a few hundred bucks. It's got no business being in the trash.'

'Where's the sandwich bag the camera was in?' Hunter asked the officer, who promptly produced a clear plastic evidence bag.

'All bagged up and ready to go, sir,' he said. 'I figured somebody would want this separate from the rest of the garbage.'

Garcia acknowledged the officer's good work before quickly checking the sandwich bag.

Nothing. No marks, no stains, nothing written anywhere.

He and Hunter returned their attention to the camcorder.

'Did you try turning this on?' Hunter asked the officer.

He shook his head. 'Not my place, sir. I found it and called it in straightaway.'

Hunter nodded his agreement. For an instant he considered if he should take the camera straight to forensics, but the reality of the matter was that there was no clear evidence that that camcorder had indeed been left behind by the killer.

Hunter flipped open the viewer screen and froze. He didn't need to turn the camera on to know. Staring back at him was all the confirmation he needed.

Eighty

The man stood at the crowded bus stop by the northwest corner of City Hall Park, calmly observing the events unfold on the South Lawn. He had to admit that he was surprised.

He had considered using a thick blood-red marker pen to write Detective Robert Hunter – LAPD on the sandwich bag he'd left inside the trashcan at the northeast corner of the park less than an hour ago. By doing so, he would make sure that if anyone else came across the bag, like a garbage collector (homeless trashcan scavengers tended to stay away from the park due to its proximity to the Police Administration Building), chances were they'd drop it in at the PAB. But in the end the man had decided against it. He'd read a lot about Detective Robert Hunter in the past few months. Hunter was supposed to be 'a class above', according to some of the articles he'd read. Well, how good could he really be, if he wasn't even able to figure out that there was bound to be a hidden reason behind the fact that the LAPD was *allowed* to trace his last call? A reason other than the pure fun factor of being just outside their front door while tormenting them.

But the man had to admit that he was a little bit surprised because things had happened fast. Faster than what he had foreseen. Very shortly after the Internet voting had ended, a team of five uniformed officers exited the PAB and purpose-fully crossed the road in the direction of the park. One of them, an officer with red acned cheeks and a thin-tip nose, had almost bumped into him. The team was being coordi-nated by an overweight senior officer, probably a sergeant, now too old and too fat for any kind of more physically demanding job, the man concluded. The four young officers under his command had clearly been instructed to search the park, not to stop and interview people.

The man's lips stretched into a skewed, wry smile. *Maybe Detective Hunter's reputation is true after all.* The man was sure that the order to solely search the park, instead of wasting time interviewing passersby, had come from Detective Hunter's office. Which meant that he had very quickly made a connection between the triangulated loca-tion of the incoming call and the possibility of a clue or a teaser being left behind.

'Not bad, Detective Hunter,' the man said under his breath. 'Not bad at all.'

His smile widened a fraction as he saw Detective Hunter himself, followed by Detective Garcia, exit the PAB and make their way toward the park. The look on their faces told its own story, and it spoke of frustration, defeat, unre-lenting concern and maybe even fear. It was the same look the man had had etched on his face for many years. But not anymore.

The man's left leg started hurting again, and as he began rubbing his knee with the palm of his hand he saw the young officer who was searching the northeast corner of the park wave at both detectives and the sergeant.

The man's smile grew wider still, and he felt a wave of excitement surge inside him.

The officer had found it.

As the number 70 bus to El Monte pulled in at the bus stop, the man saw Detective Hunter flip open the camcorder's view screen. The look on his face made the man want to throw his head back and laugh loudly, but instead he quietly turned around, boarded the bus and took a seat toward the back.

It was almost time to finish this whole thing off.

Eighty-One

The sergeant and the pencil-tip-nosed officer both craned their necks awkwardly to have a better look at the camcorder's view screen before intense frowns simultaneously shadowed their faces.

They saw the same thing Hunter and Garcia did. They just didn't understand it.

'Sonofabitch,' Garcia murmured, his breath catching in his throat.

Hunter said nothing, but his eyes left the camcorder and quickly returned to searching the park. That was the event this killer wouldn't want to miss. What he had waited around for – the moment they came across his little gift. Hunter was sure this killer would want to be looking straight at them so he was able to see the surprise on their faces. To the killer, it would be the perfect punch line.

But with the rush hour picking up momentum, the streets and the park had gotten busier. People were cutting across it in a multitude of directions, all in a hurry to get somewhere fast. Hunter's eyes moved as quickly as they could. He understood that this killer needed only a second, maybe two, to completely savor the moment and laugh at their frustration. After that, satisfied, he would just fade back into anonymity. *Just another honest living person trying to*

make his way back home. There was no need for the killer
to allow his gaze to linger on their group for longer than a
brief instant and risk being spotted.

Maybe if Hunter had looked west first, he would've
noticed the man standing at the bus stop by the northwest
corner of the park, staring straight at them. The smirk on
his face was insolent, arrogant . . . proud, even. But Hunter
had instinctively looked up from the camcorder in his hands
and forward. He was facing east. By the time his gaze
reached the bus stop, the man had his back to them, waiting
patiently at the end of the line, ready to board the bus – *just
another commuter facing rush hour.*

Hunter missed him.

His attention returned to the camcorder.

Using what seemed like a special glass-writing marker
pen, the killer had written the word STRETCH across the
view screen.

'Stretch?' The sergeant wrinkled his nose. 'Does that
mean anything to you guys?'

Garcia nodded in silence and felt something tighten deep
down in his gut, as his subconscious mind started spitting
out random images of the broadcast.

Hunter's forefinger hovered over the 'on' button, for a
moment unsure and hesitant if he was ready for whatever
new surprise the killer had in store for them, but the doubt
vanished fast.

He pressed the switch.

Nothing happened.

He tried again.

Still nothing.

'Battery seems to be dead,' the pencil-tip-nosed officer
offered matter-of-factly.

Despite holding no real hopes for any sort of clue to come from it, Hunter asked the sergeant to get the sandwich bag the camcorder was found in to forensics ASAP. He and Garcia rushed back to the Police Administration Building and went straight down to the LAPD Computer Crimes Unit.

Eighty-Two

Dennis Baxter told them that he had watched the entire Internet broadcast from his desk, but he had no idea the killer's call had been traced. Hunter gave him a very quick run-through of the past few minutes.

'And he left this inside a trashcan out in the park?' Baxter asked, looking down at the compact camcorder Hunter had placed on his desk. The word STRETCH stared back at him from the flip-out view screen.

'That's right,' Garcia confirmed. 'It looks like he was controlling everything remotely.'

Baxter thought about that for a second.

'How difficult would that really be to accomplish?' Garcia asked.

'For an average person? Quite a bit. For someone with his knowledge of computer programming and electronics, not hard at all. All he had to do was develop an application that monitored the voting process and link it to a second program that controlled the mechanics of both death methods. As soon as one of them reached a specified number, in this case ten thousand, it would activate the machinery for that specific death method. It's the same engineering behind any regular timer, but instead of a specific time he used a count. The way the camera zoomed in and out during the broadcast could've easily be controlled from anywhere with a simple smartphone application.'

Someone's personal cellphone rang a few desks away, grabbing everyone's attention. The ringtone was the original theme tune to *Star Wars*.

Hunter was mulling over what Baxter had just said. The truth was that this killer could've done the exact same thing with all the previous broadcasts. He could've controlled them remotely if he wanted to. There was no real need for him to be there, and no real proof that he was.

Baxter finally retrieved a pair of latex gloves from his top drawer, slipped them on and cautiously picked the camera up from his desk.

'It looks like the battery is dead,' Garcia explained. 'Do you have a power supply that will fit it?'

Baxter nodded. 'I do.' But instead of looking for it, he turned the camera upside down and flipped open a very small hinged lid on the underside of it. He paused and chewed on his bottom lip for a second. 'But a power supply will make no difference here.'

'What do you mean?'

'This is a CX250 Handycam,' Baxter explained, pointing to the model number specified on the side of the camera. 'It's a fairly well-known camera, and the reason why it's smaller than some of the more expensive models is because it has no hard drive. It uses something called a memory stick duo. What that means is that this camera has no storage facility built into it. Everything it records gets saved into a removable memory stick, which goes in here.' He indicated the now opened hinged lid. The compartment was empty. 'In this model,' he added, 'even after unclipping the lid you would have to press down on the memory stick so it clicks in before popping up.' He made an 'eject up' movement with his index finger. 'It's a double safety mechanism, which means that the memory stick didn't fall out by mistake: it was removed.'

That caused both detectives to pause momentarily.

'I can get a power supply and plug it in if you want. It will turn the camera on, but that's all it will do. There will be no images in it for you to see, if that was what you were expecting.'

That was exactly what both detectives were expecting.

'So nothing can be retrieved from this camera?' Garcia asked.

'Image-wise, no,' Baxter replied. 'As I've said, the camera has no hard drive that can be explored. Without a memory stick, it's just like an old photographic camera without the film. It becomes nothing more than a box with a lens.'

'Let's do it anyway,' Hunter said after a short, uncomfortable silence. Right now he wasn't prepared to put anything past this killer.

'Give me a sec,' Baxter replied and disappeared into a back room. Moments later he came back carrying a power supply that was slightly larger than a regular cellphone charger. He plugged it in and switched the camcorder on.

There was nothing there.

The camera worked just as it should, but it recognized that it was missing the memory stick, disabling the *view and playback* menu.

'As I've said,' Baxter commented, 'no memory stick, no images or stills for us to see here.'

No one said anything for a long moment. Hunter had to admit that he *was* expecting the camera to contain some sort of footage. What exactly, he wasn't sure – maybe a short clip of one of the victims prior to being abducted, or pleading for mercy or something. Some new twist just to further torment their thoughts and their investigation.

Why leave us an 'empty' video camera?

If all the killer wanted to do was to prove that he had really been standing outside when making the call, he could've written his little dig at the police on absolutely anything – a piece of paper, a burger box, a sandwich wrapper, a paper cup . . . anything. He no doubt had anticipated that once the call had been traced, the LAPD would be emptying and bagging the contents of every trashcan in the park and around the PAB in a hurry. They would've eventually found his message, no matter what it had been written on.

No, Hunter thought. *Even a compact camcorder is way too big and clunky for such a simple task. There has to be another reason.*

His next consideration was that the camera could've belonged to the victim. Maybe he had it on him when he was first abducted. Maybe that was why the memory stick was missing. Maybe the victim had filmed the killer by accident – strolling down the street, buying a hot dog, at a gas station, or worse . . . something incriminating. Something that could've given away the killer's identity. Maybe that was why he had become the latest victim. They would have to wait for forensics to examine the camera, and hope that they could get something out of it.

Hunter couldn't remember an investigation where he felt more defeated or powerless. All he had was a long list of maybes, ifs and buts, and none of it made any real sense. Three victims tortured and murdered in the most brutal ways while he watched, unable to help. And that helpless feeling was spreading through him like strong poison. Even his thoughts were starting to fail him.

He was right. This game of cat and mouse excited the killer like a brand-new drug, but right now Hunter couldn't tell who was the cat and who was the mouse.

Eighty-Three

For Hunter, falling asleep that night was an almost impossible task. There were way too many thoughts and questions bouncing around inside his head for his brain to disconnect, and one thing he'd learned over the years was that battling insomnia with pills and stubbornness only made things worse. The best remedy was just to roll along with it. And rolling along was exactly what he intended to do, but he couldn't face doing it alone inside his claustrophobic one-bedroom apartment.

Hunter sat at a small table toward the back of the bar, staring at the glass tumbler in front of him. Inside it, a single dose of twelve-year-old Cardhu single-malt whisky with just a little water. Single malts were Hunter's biggest passion. Back in his apartment he had a small but impressive collection that would probably satisfy the palate of most connoisseurs. Hunter would never consider himself an expert, but he knew how to appreciate the flavor and robustness of single malts, instead of simply getting hammered on them. Though, sometimes, getting hammered worked just fine.

He brought the glass to his lips and had a small sip, letting the clean, crisp oak and sweet malt infuse his whole mouth for a moment before allowing the smooth liquid to travel down his throat.

Soothing, no question about it. A few more and he would probably start to relax. He closed his eyes and took a deep breath through his nose. Rock music blasted through the tiny speakers strategically positioned on the ceiling throughout the bar area, but the music didn't bother him. It actually helped him think.

'This killer has been playing you from the start.'

Harry Mills' words from yesterday still echoed in his ears like a loud scream. And Harry was right. Hunter remembered how, with his first victim, the killer had tricked him to pick water instead of fire, only to add a sadistic, chemical twist to it. With the second victim, the killer had used a small level of psychology to trick his viewers into picking *eaten alive*, a much more intriguing and painful death method than the alternative – *buried alive*.

Now with the third victim, it appeared that no trick had been used to influence the voting. It had been too close to call – CRUSH: 9997, STRETCH: 10,000. Instead, the killer had seemingly allowed the voting to play out unaided, not knowing himself the final outcome. Hunter was sure that that had excited him like a young child with a new toy.

What the killer had decided to do this time in order to demonstrate his cleverness over the police was to control everything remotely, but not just from anywhere – from literally outside the LAPD headquarters' front door. He had *allowed* the LAPD to trace his call and even waited until the voting was finally over before writing his message onto a camcorder's view screen and stashing it inside a trashcan in City Hall Park. And just to add insult to injury, the killer had timed everything perfectly to coincide with the rush hour. That way, he could stay within eyesight distance, but still remain anonymous among the high flux of people. So close, yet they couldn't touch him.

'*This killer has been playing you from the start.*' The words rang out in his head again.

What else had the killer thrown at them just for fun? The abbreviation – SSV? The two different number sequences – 678 and 0123? The words – *The Devil Inside*? The camcorder? Did any of it mean anything at all, or was it all just to keep the police guessing and running around in circles?

Well, if that was the intention, it sure was working.

Maybe even the IV stand reflected onto the glass coffin lid hadn't been a mistake. Maybe the killer did it on purpose. One more twist added to the tale.

Hunter brought both hands to his face and massaged his exhausted eyes with his palms. The more he thought about it, the more it made his head hurt. How could he come up with answers when he didn't even know what questions to ask anymore?

'Did you see that thing on the Internet today?' Hunter overheard the barman ask a brunette and a redheaded woman at the bar, while he poured them a couple of cocktails.

Hunter's gaze subtly moved to them.

'I did,' the redhead replied. 'Absolutely awful. And everyone is saying that was no hoax.'

'It isn't,' the brunette one agreed. 'It was in the papers. He broadcast the murder of an *LA Times* reporter just a few days ago.'

'Did you watch it today?' the redhead asked.

The brunette woman shook her head. 'Everyone in the office was glued to their screens, watching it. I just couldn't. It would make me sick. I can't believe something like this is now happening on the Internet.'

'You watched it?' the barman asked the redhead.

She nodded.

'Now the big question is – did you vote?' he asked.

She pushed her hair behind her ear and shook her head. 'No. Never. Did you?'

The barman's gaze flicked to the brunette and then back to the redhead. 'Um . . . no, I didn't. I watched it, though.'

Even from where Hunter was sitting, it was easy to pick up their tell signs. They were both lying.

His cellphone lit up and rattled against the tabletop before him. He frowned at the name displayed on the caller screen before answering it. 'Michelle?'

'Robert, I'm sorry to be calling you this late and out of office hours.'

Hunter checked his watch. 'It's not that late, and I haven't worked office hours since . . . ever.'

Michelle started saying something else, but stopped mid-word. 'Um . . . is that Black Stone Cherry playing in the background?'

Hunter paused and listened to the music for a moment. The song was called 'Blame it on the Boom Boom'. 'That's correct,' he said. 'Do you know the band?'

Michelle almost choked on the question. 'Do *I* know Black Stone Cherry? Are you kidding? I've seen them live five times. Where *are* you?'

'At the Rainbow Bar and Grill on Sunset Strip.'

'For real? That's one of my favorite bars in LA.' She hesitated for a beat. 'I'm not that far from Sunset. Do you mind if I join you?'

Hunter looked at his almost empty glass. 'Not at all. I'm just starting here.'

Eighty-Four

The Rainbow Bar and Grill was a famous old-school casual restaurant and dive bar located on Sunset Boulevard. The décor was simple but effective – big red-vinyl booths and dark wood. Every inch of wall space was crammed with rock star snapshots. Since the 1980s the Rainbow had been known as the hangout hot spot for rock musicians and fans alike, with one of the most laid-back atmospheres in the whole of West Hollywood. The food and their great selection of single-malt whiskies weren't bad either.

The place had gotten relatively busier by the time Michelle got there, twenty-five minutes after she came off the phone with Hunter. She was wearing skintight, stone-washed blue jeans with a natural wear-and-tear over her right knee, black boots and an old Motörhead vest under a thin black-leather jacket with silver details. Her hair was loose and tousled in a 'rock chick' style. Her smoky-eyed makeup added to the look perfectly, and as she crossed the bar floor to where Hunter was sitting it was hard not to notice a few heads turning.

Hunter stood up to greet her, and her lips cracked into something that he wasn't sure if it was a smile or not.

'I would've never guessed you drank here,' she said, taking off her jacket. Strangely, under the dim bar lights, the bright colors of the tattoos on her arms appeared more vivid.

'Sometimes,' Hunter replied, indicating the seat across the small table from him. 'I ordered you a Jack Daniel's and Diet Coke. I hope you don't mind.' The drink was already on the table.

Michelle half looked, half squinted at him. 'How did you know I drank JD and Diet Coke?'

Hunter shrugged. 'I guessed.'

More of a squint this time as she studied his face. 'No, you didn't. You knew. How did you know?'

Hunter took a seat and sipped his drink.

'How did you know I drink Jack Daniel's and Diet Coke?' Michelle's voice was more demanding this time, but not aggressively so.

Hunter put his drink down. 'Just simple observation.'

His answer didn't suffice.

Her stare didn't soften.

'You have a picture frame on your desk,' Hunter finally explained.

Michelle thought about it for a moment.

Almost hidden behind one of the computer monitors on her desk was a photograph of Michelle with the vocalist and the guitarist of an American rock band called Hinder. They were all smiling and raising their glasses toward the camera in a *toasting* gesture. The band members were clearly drinking whiskey shots, while Michelle's glass was filled with what look liked Coke, though the look in her eyes betrayed a sober state. The picture frame the photograph was in was a novelty Jack Daniel's bottle-shaped frame.

Michelle's smile was sincere. 'That's not bad,' she said. 'But how did you know I drank Diet Coke and not regular Coke, or Pepsi, or Tab, or something similar?'

'The wastebasket by your desk,' Hunter replied.

A new smile. Michelle knew that at any given time there would be at least one can of Diet Coke in her wastebasket or on her desk. She much preferred it to coffee, and drank several cans of it a day. 'That's not bad at all.' She reached for her drink and touched glasses with Hunter. 'Here's to observation and simple deduction. No wonder you're a detective. And yes, JD and Diet Coke *is* my favorite drink. Thank you.' She had a quick sip before her eyes darted over Hunter's left shoulder, lingering there for a few seconds.

'Everything OK?' Hunter asked without turning around.

'There was a guy sitting behind you at the bar, right at the very end by the entrance. He just left, but I think I know him from somewhere.'

'Short blond hair, nose ring, a two-day-old stubble, about one hundred and forty pounds ... Was wearing a jeans jacket over a black T-shirt and drinking beer with tequila chasers?' Hunter asked. Still he didn't turn around.

'That's him,' Michelle replied. 'Do you know him?'

Hunter shook his head. 'I saw him sitting there when I came in. Looked like he'd been there for a while.'

Michelle chuckled. 'You saw him when you came in, probably for a couple of seconds, and you remember all that about him?'

Hunter half nodded, half shrugged.

'You do that observation thing without even knowing that you're doing it anymore, don't you? A good detective is never off duty, always watchful, always prepared.'

Hunter said nothing.

Her eyes circled the bar area for a quick instant before she leaned forward and placed both elbows on the table.

'OK. Test. Group of four over your left shoulder by the bar counter, about halfway up. Hair color?'

Hunter sat back, having another sip of his Scotch, his eyes studying Michelle.

'C'mon, humor me, Robert. Hair color?'

'Both women are blonde,' Hunter finally said, without looking over his shoulder. 'Though neither of them is natural. One has shoulder-length hair; the other one's is slightly longer, pulled back into a ponytail. One of the men has light brown curly hair; the other guy has dyed black wavy hair with pronounced sideburns.'

'Age group?'

'All four in their early thirties.'

'Drinks?'

'The women are drinking white wine, the men are both having beer – curly hair is drinking Mexican with a lemon slice down the bottle's neck. Wavy hair is drinking Bud.'

'Anything else you can tell me?' Michelle asked.

'It's probably their first double date, because all four of them seem a little tense. Body language indicated that wavy hair and ponytail blonde will hit it on, probably tonight, but the other two, I'm not so sure. She doesn't look very impressed. She's probably there more to help her friend.'

Michelle looked at Hunter with a faint smile on her lips but said nothing for a moment or two, obviously weighing up something in her mind. 'You certainly are a very interesting and intriguing man, Robert.'

Hunter wasn't sure if that was a compliment or not.

Michelle had another sip of her drink and drew in a long, heavy breath. 'We came across a new piece of information today.' Her tone went serious. Playtime was definitely over.

'About this afternoon's broadcast?'

Hunter already knew that the video had gone viral. Snippets, snapshots and even the full nineteen minutes and thirty-four seconds of it had been uploaded to so many different Internet sites no one could keep track anymore. If there were someone out there who hadn't seen it yet, they would soon.

'Actually, we think it might have affected the previous one too, but there's no way we can be sure.'

It was Hunter's turn to lean forward and place his elbows on the table.

'I've told you this before,' Michelle proceeded. 'But we don't really come across offenders who can shield themselves so proficiently from a FBI Cybercrime Division counterattack. And though I'm sure that we would eventually find a way through his defense system, I'm aware that we just don't have the time, because every time he transmits, someone else gets tortured and murdered.' She paused and finished the rest of her drink in one large gulp, her hands just a little unsteady. It wasn't hard for Hunter to guess that images of the killer's third victim being dismembered on the rack were popping into her head as she spoke.

'During today's broadcast,' Michelle carried on, 'we again threw everything we had at it, and we got exactly the same result as before – nothing. Every time we got past one of his defense layers, there was a thicker one waiting for us just behind it.'

Hunter could see the frustration building up in her eyes.

'But this time we weren't the only ones who tried launching a counterattack.'

'What do you mean?'

'I had already contacted the head of the FBI Cybercrime Division in Washington. Their office deals mainly with cyber terrorism, which is great, because I knew they would approach the killer's transmission in a different way.' She tilted her head slightly to one side in an almost coy gesture. 'I had also got in touch with a very good friend of mine who lives in Michigan. Someone I knew before I joined the FBI. He's not part of any law-enforcement agency, but apart from Harry he's the best programmer and cyber hacker I know. I thought that maybe he could help, especially because I know he wouldn't look at the transmission from a law-enforcer's point of view.'

She paused, maybe waiting for some sort of disapproving look or words to come from Hunter for failing to consult him first. There were neither.

'OK,' he said. 'Did they have better luck than you?'

'That's the problem, Robert,' Michelle said. 'Neither could even see the site.'

'What? Why?'

'They were blocked out.'

Hunter's frown deepened.

'The killer used the same kind of "IP address exclusion" program that blocked us out from Carlos' wife's transmission yesterday.'

Hunter was trying to process this new piece of information in silence.

'As I told you before,' Michelle said, 'a computer's IP address works in the same way a telephone number does. It also has a prefix that identifies the country, the state and even the city where the computer is located.'

Hunter acknowledged it.

'Well, that's exactly how the killer did it. He blocked off every IP address from outside California.'

'The rest of the world too?'

Michelle nodded. 'California, that's it. No one else was allowed to watch it.'

Hunter breathed out slowly. The new question now banging a gong inside his head was: *why would the killer do such a thing?* Since day one, Hunter feared that all this killer wanted to do was to broadcast a morbid and brutal 'killing show'. Something that would mimic the hundreds of reality TV and cable programs fighting for viewing space inside people's homes. Hunter figured that maybe what the killer wanted was to prove how messed-up the world really was. How a celebrity- and 'reality contest'-obsessed society would take part and vote on absolutely *anything*, even murder, if dressed up and presented to them in the right way. And the *one* thing all these game shows fight for is audience. The more the better, the more successful the show. So why restrict it only to California, when through the Internet he could've broadcast to the world?

As if reading Hunter's thoughts, Michelle said, 'No, I can't come up with a single reason why he would do that either.'

They both went silent for a while.

'I haven't had the time to reanalyze the footage from this afternoon yet,' Michelle finally said. Paused. Looked down at her glass, and then back at Hunter. 'No. I'm lying. I haven't had the stomach to reanalyze it yet. And I'm dreading the fact that I will have to. I'm dreading the fact that we can't get to him, and sooner or later he'll broadcast again.'

For the first time Hunter saw a hint of fear creep into Michelle's eyes. The kind of fear that takes shape during the day and then re-forms much stronger in nightmares. Tonight, Michelle would do anything not to go to sleep.

Eighty-Five

Hunter and Michelle stayed at the Rainbow until closing time, but soon after Michelle's revelation that the killer had blocked out every IP address from outside California, it became clear that both of their brains needed a break from the case, even if only for a few hours. Hunter did his best to lighten the mood and distance the subject from their investigation.

Alcohol had started to relax them, and they talked about music, films, hobbies, drinks, food, even sports. Hunter found out that Michelle could ballroom-dance, and had once knocked an FBI instructor out with a kick to the groin after he tried to grope her during a hand-to-hand combat class. In turn, Michelle found out that Hunter had never been outside the USA, couldn't stand cauliflower, and when he was a kid he had taught himself how to play keyboards and joined a band just to impress a girl. It didn't work. She fell for the guitar player.

After the Rainbow shut for the night, Hunter put Michelle in a cab and took one himself.

Hunter must have nodded off sometime during the early hours of the morning, because, when he awakened, the day was just breaking outside his living-room window. His neck muscles were stiff, and every joint in his body ached with the irritation of falling asleep in an uncomfortable chair.

He had a quick shower and an even quicker breakfast before calling Garcia and telling him that he was through with the waiting game and had decided to pay Thomas Paulsen a visit that morning. True, he had nothing to really warrant an interview with the software millionaire other than the fact that Christina Stevenson, their second victim, had written a very damaging exposé on how he had sexually harassed many of his employees over a very long period of time. An exposé that had cost Paulsen millions, wrecked his twenty-seven-year marriage and severely damaged his relationship with his only daughter. Though Hunter also knew that they had nothing to link Paulsen to their first or third victim, experience had taught him that a face-to-face could reveal much more in a few minutes than days of research sitting behind a desk.

PaulsenSystems was located just off Ventura Freeway, in the very affluent San Fernando Valley neighborhood of Woodland Hills, in northwest Los Angeles. Hunter had called the company just to make sure Thomas Paulsen would be in that morning. His secretary said he would be. Hunter made no appointment.

The drive from the PAB took Hunter and Garcia just over an hour. Traffic was as heavy as any other weekday morning, and Hunter used the time to tell his partner the news Michelle had told him the night before. Garcia also couldn't make any sense of it. He too believed that this killer would've wanted as much exposure as he could get, so why restrict his viewers to California only?

The only conclusion they could draw was that whatever the reason behind it was, it had to be something very personal to the killer.

PaulsenSystems' headquarters was a grand L-shaped, mirrored-glass and dark granite-fronted building on the corner of Burbank and Topanga Canyon Boulevards. The main entrance was hidden away from the street, through the large private car park at the back. An elegant staircase, flanked by two colorful mini gardens, led up to the heavily air-conditioned and brightly lit entrance lobby. The air inside it was lightly perfumed with the subtle fragrance of sweet alyssum and a hint of wisteria.

'Nice,' Garcia said, as they stepped through the automatic sliding doors. 'Makes a difference from the stale sweat scent you get when you enter the PAB.'

A circular reception counter occupied the center of the spacious lobby like an island. Behind it, the petite, Asian receptionist with long and sleek black hair smiled at both detectives. Her dark eyes shone like two polished marbles.

'Welcome to PaulsenSystems,' she said. Her voice was velvety and warm. 'How can I help you today, gentlemen?'

'Hello,' Hunter replied. As much as he would like to, his smile didn't carry the same level of enthusiasm as hers. 'We were wondering if we could have a few moments of Mr. Paulsen's time.'

The receptionist glanced down at her computer, where she would no doubt have a list of Thomas Paulsen's appointments for the day, but Hunter quickly got her attention back to him.

'We do not have an appointment,' he clarified, displaying his credentials. 'Nevertheless, this matter carries a certain urgency, and we would really appreciate if Mr. Paulsen could give us a few minutes this morning.'

The receptionist smiled again and nodded once, reaching for the phone behind the counter. She spoke quickly and discreetly. Hunter could tell that she wasn't speaking directly with Thomas Paulsen but with a secretary or PA.

Seconds later, sitting behind his handcrafted oak desk, Thomas Paulsen answered the ringing phone and listened for a few seconds. A dry grin came to his lips, and he sat back, gently rocking in his high-backed leather chair for a moment.

'Do I have anything scheduled for now?' he asked.

'You are actually free for the next hour, Mr. Paulsen,' his PA confirmed. 'Your next appointment is at 12:45.'

'OK,' Paulsen said, considering his thoughts. 'You can tell the detectives that I'll be able to spare a few minutes, but make them wait. I'll see them when I'm good and ready. Oh, and Joanne . . .'

'Yes, Mr. Paulsen?'

'Let's make them wait downstairs in the lobby, not in my anteroom. They might smell the place up.'

'Of course, Mr. Paulsen.'

He put the phone down, stood up and walked over to the large panoramic window that faced the Santa Monica Mountains. He felt like laughing out loud, but instead he allowed himself only a proud smile.

About time they came talk to me.

Eighty-Six

And wait they did . . .

Even the petite receptionist had started to look embarrassed after the first ten minutes or so. She went over to where Hunter and Garcia were sitting several times and offered them water, coffee, cookies, juice . . . When they said no to all, she suggested that she could send someone out for some donuts if they preferred. That made both detectives laugh.

Twenty-nine long and frustrating minutes after they had arrived at PaulsenSystems, the receptionist was finally told to allow both detectives to go up. She apologized yet again, and told them to take the elevator to the top floor. Someone would meet them there.

The elevator doors rolled back on a new, very elegantly furnished lobby. Three sofas clad in black leather sat on antique Persian rugs, surrounded by several modern American sculpture pieces. The walls were adorned with an impressive collection of original paintings.

Waiting for them just outside the elevator doors, and standing beneath a halogen spotlight, was Joanne, Thomas Paulsen's PA. Her long red hair sparkled under the light. As Hunter and Garcia stepped out of the elevator, Joanne smiled.

'Good morning, gentlemen,' she said in the most professional of tones. 'I'm Joanne Saunders, Mr. Paulsen's personal
assistant.' She offered them her manicured hand. Both detectives shook it, introducing themselves. 'If you'd like to follow
me, please, Mr. Paulsen is waiting for you in his office.'

They crossed the anteroom and followed the PA down a
softly lit hallway that terminated in a highly polished wood
set of double doors. She knocked twice, paused for a second
and pushed the doors open, which led them into a sprawl-
ing and luxuriously decorated corner office.

'Mr. Paulsen,' Joanne announced. 'This is Detective
Robert Hunter and Detective Carlos Garcia from the Los
Angeles Police Department.'

Standing with his back toward them, facing the window,
Thomas Paulsen nodded at the view but didn't bother turning around. 'Thank you, Joanne.'

The PA swiftly stepped out of the room, soundlessly closing the doors behind her.

Hunter and Garcia stood by the entrance, quickly assess-
ing the office: more black leather and sumptuous rugs. Two
recessed bookcases containing books on computer programming languages, Internet security and finance shared the
north wall with even more expensive-looking works of art.
Hunter knew that the south wall was what was known as
the Ego Wall – a potpourri of framed photos showing
Thomas Paulsen grinning and shaking hands with well-
known and not-so-well-known celebrities, certificates
attesting that he was highly skilled and qualified, and a few
shiny plaques producing clear proof that he had been justly
recognized over the years.

'This is indeed a beautiful city, isn't it, gentlemen?'
Paulsen said, still facing the window. He was tall and

broad-shouldered with a physique that even under his elegant pin-striped suit was easy to tell was lean and strong. His voice was dry and authoritative, clearly belonging to someone who was used to giving orders and getting things done his way.

Neither Hunter nor Garcia replied.

Paulsen finally spun around and faced them. He had a thin and remarkably youthful face for a man who was in his early fifties. His short peppered hair was combed slickly back from his forehead, giving him a boyish charm. His light blue eyes seemed full of knowledge, like a university professor's, glowing with an intensity that was unsettling. There was no denying he was an attractive man, despite the crooked nose that had certainly been broken once or twice. He had a squared jaw, strong cheekbones and full lips. A small scar graced the tip of his chin. Everything about him suggested tremendous self-confidence, but his presence was almost menacing. He didn't so much as smile, but smirked at them.

'Would you please have a seat?' he asked, indicating the two armchairs in front of his desk.

Hunter took the one on the left, Garcia the one on the right. There were no handshakes. Paulsen remained as he was, standing by the window.

'We're very sorry for barging in unannounced like this, Mr. Paulsen. We do understand that you are a busy man . . .' Garcia said in his best, polite voice, but Paulsen interrupted him with a brisk hand gesture.

'You didn't barge in, Detective Garcia. If you had, especially without some sort of warrant, I'd have my lawyer here, you removed from the premises and a complaint made to your captain and the Chief of Police so fast you'd probably experience time travel.' None of it was delivered with anger, or even sarcasm. 'You're here because I've allowed you to be here. But as you've said, I am a very busy man, and I have an important meeting in a few minutes, so I suggest you use this time wisely.'

Garcia paused, surprised by the retort.

Paulsen sensed his hesitation and took the opportunity.

'Actually, there's no need for pleasantries, or even beating around the bush, so we can speed things up. I know why you're here, so let's just get on with it, shall we?'

Hunter could clearly see that Paulsen's tactics were to take control of their meeting. He had kept them waiting – not because he was busy, but because waiting time irritates and frustrates even the most calm of individuals. He had assumed the textbook interviewer's position of power – standing, while everyone else sat. There had been no physical contact, and Paulsen was keeping a reasonable distance between him and both detectives, making the meeting impersonal, as if he was interviewing someone for an entry-level job. Paulsen was also careful to keep his voice as calm as Garcia's, but just a notch louder and firmer, stamping authority. Thomas Paulsen was a very experienced man, and the kind who wouldn't be easily intimidated. Hunter was keen to allow Paulsen to play his game . . . for the time being.

'You already know why we're here?' Hunter asked, his voice calm, its decibel level deliberately not matching his host's.

'Detective Hunter, please. Look around you.' Paulsen lifted both of his hands, palms facing up. 'I didn't achieve all this by sheer luck, as I'm sure your file on me would've told you already. Sure, I could play dumb with you gentlemen and pretend that I don't know what this is all about.'

Paulsen looked bored as he adjusted the cuffs of his shirt under his suit jacket. 'Then act offended and insulted when the real reason finally transpires, but hey . . .' The smirk came back to his lips. 'I don't have that much time to throw away. And I'm sure you could use yours to run around in circles some more.'

Garcia's eyebrows arched, and his eyes stole a peek at Hunter, who had sat back and comfortably crossed his legs.

'Why do you think we're running around in circles?' Hunter asked.

Paulsen threw his head back and laughed a full-bodied laugh. 'Detective, please . . . This isn't a psychoanalysis session. Your "double-meaning" questions will get you nowhere, and—' he checked his watch '—tick-tock, tick-tock, time's a wasting . . . for you at least.'

Paulsen spoke and carried himself like a man with zero worries in life. He placed both hands inside his trouser pockets and walked around to the front of his desk. Before Hunter or Garcia could formulate the next question, he spoke again.

'But OK, let me indulge you, just this once. The reason why you're here is because of your investigation into this . . . shall I say . . . "Internet show murderer"? And because Christina Stevenson was one of the victims.' He allowed his eyes to move from Hunter's face, to Garcia's, and then back to Hunter's before nodding confidently. 'Yes, I watched the broadcast too. Superb, wasn't it?' He tagged the question with a chuckle.

No reply.

Paulsen moved on.

'And you're running around in circles because you're here, in my office. And the only reason why you're here is because you've got nothing . . . not a thing. I'm the only "person of interest" you've got on your list, isn't that what you cops call someone like me?' He smiled sarcastically. 'And the only reason I am a "person-of-interest" is because an article written by Miss Stevenson months ago has set off the most negligible of bleeps on your radar. If you had anyone else of more substance on your list, any other "person of interest", you would be talking to him, her or them, not me. *This* is a panic visit. You know it, and I know it.'

'And what makes you think that we haven't talked to others already?' Garcia asked.

Another laugh from Paulsen. 'The desperate look on your faces is a pretty good giveaway.' He paused. Checked his watch again. 'The evasive words in your press conference last night.' An unconcerned shrug. 'You look and sound defeated . . . out of options. Everyone can see it. And you're here now to try to assess me.' He adjusted his tie. 'So let me help you with that. Am I glad that Christina Stevenson is dead? Delighted. Do I feel bad because she was tortured before being murdered? Not even a little bit. Do I have the knowledge, the IQ, the means and the nerve to do something like that, and then vanish into cyberspace before you even knew what hit you? You bet your bottom dollar I do. Did I know yesterday's victim? Maybe, maybe not. What difference would it make? Could I be behind these murders? Possibly. Did I ever threaten Christina Stevenson after her article came out? Perhaps. Did I want to make her life hell, like she did mine? Absolutely. Did I succeed? Who cares? She's dead. Thank you very much.' He winked at them. 'Would that be all?'

'Not quite,' Garcia said.

Paulsen's egotism was setting Garcia's teeth on edge, and he had to take a moment to contain his anger.

'Could you tell us where you were yesterday in between five and six in the afternoon?'

'Ah!' Paulsen lifted a finger in the air. 'The all-important placement question at the time of the murder. And this is where it gets good, Detective.' He returned his hands to his pockets. 'I wasn't feeling too well, so I left the office early. At that specific time I was at home, alone, in front of my computer, logged into pickadeath.com, and watching the show, like so many others.' A new grin. 'And before you ask, *no*, I don't have an alibi. Would you like to arrest me?'

'What time did you leave the office?' Garcia asked.

'Early enough.' Another quick glance at his watch. 'Let me ask you this, if I may, Detective Hunter. If I am behind these Internet murders, and as I've said that's a possibility, what makes you think that you'd be able to catch me?'

Before Hunter could reply, the phone on Paulsen's desk rang.

'Oh,' he said in an apologetic tone. 'That will probably be my PA reminding me of my meeting. Excuse me for a second.' He answered the call, listening for a few moments. 'Thank you, Joanne. I'll be right out. We are pretty much done here.'

Paulsen put the phone back down and walked over to his office door.

Hunter and Garcia stood up.

Paulsen reached for the door handle, halted and looked back at both detectives. 'I must admit, these Internet killing shows are terribly entertaining, don't you think?' He opened the door. 'I wonder if we're going to get another one soon.'

Eighty-Seven

'What the hell just happened in there?' Garcia asked as soon as he and Hunter stepped outside PaulsenSystems. His anger now clearly getting the best of him.

'I'm not quite sure,' Hunter replied, looking back at the building. 'But he'd been expecting us. For some time, I'd say. That little show he put on was very well rehearsed.'

'What do you mean?'

'We barely asked a question, Carlos,' Hunter answered. 'Paulsen controlled the whole thing from the moment we entered the building, never mind his office. He kept us waiting for as long as he wanted to, and I'm sure it was just to check how desperate we really were, not because he was busy. In his office, he was very quick to stamp his authority, from body language to tone of voice. He asked and answered his own questions, and timed everything perfectly. I'm certain that he'd given his PA the exact time he wanted that "meeting reminder" call to be put through to his office. That's why he kept checking his watch. He wanted to get through his script in time. He gave us only what he wanted to give us. And despite the somewhat shocking and suggestive nature of what he said, his words were measured.'

'Measured?'

Hunter nodded. 'He knew exactly what he could and could not say. And nothing he did say is actionable on our part. Every incriminating question he asked himself was answered with either *maybe*, *perhaps* or *possibly*. He suggested a lot, but gave us nothing.'

'We should take him in on "probable cause" anyway, and let him sit in a cell for a while just to teach his arrogant ass a lesson,' Garcia said, unlocking his car.

'That was probably what he wanted us to do, Carlos.' Hunter got in and closed the door. 'In such a high-profile case, it would've been excellent publicity for him and his company. I'm sure he had his lawyers sitting around the phone, just waiting for the call. If we had taken him in, he would've been back in his office within the hour, but not before his PA had contacted every newspaper and TV station she could get hold of. His arrest would've been deemed as a desperate action from our part, embarrassing the department and earning us a severe ass chewing from high up, if not suspension.'

'Well,' Garcia said. 'I have a very bad feeling about this guy. I think that we should put him under surveillance.'

'He's too well prepared, Carlos. He knows that we can't do that. We don't have anything to justify the request and the expenditure, other than his arrogance.'

'And a hell of a gut feeling.' Garcia started his car and ran an anxious hand over his mouth. 'Isn't that what this killer has been doing all along, Robert – playing us from the start? He's always been a step ahead of us. Like a chess player. He hasn't made a move yet without first pondering what our response would be. And it looks like he's got it right every time.'

Hunter said nothing.

'Well, that's exactly what Paulsen did to us in there.'

'I know.'

Hunter's phone rang in his pocket.

'Detective Hunter, Homicide Special.'

He listened for a moment before disconnecting and looking at Garcia. 'They've found yesterday's victim's body.'

Garcia's eyes widened. 'Where?'

'Maywood.'

Eighty-Eight

The body had been found by a construction worker refurbishing a small, single-story, two-bedroom house near the Atlantic Bridge in Maywood. The killer had placed the dismembered arms inside a heavy-duty black-plastic bag, wrapped the body up in more of the same bags, and dumped everything inside the medium-sized construction dumpster that had been placed in the house's backyard.

The press was already out there in force, and as Hunter and Garcia stepped out of the car they were hit by a wall of shouted questions and a thunder of camera clicks. Neither detective so much as glanced in the direction of the ravenous pack of reporters.

'There isn't much to see here,' Mike Brindle, the same lead forensics agent from the previous two scenes, said as Hunter and Garcia reached the house's backyard. He looked ready to leave. 'At least not forensically. The killer never even entered the premises.'

'How come?' Garcia asked.

'Well, the body was all wrapped up like a postal package,' Brindle explained. 'And then dumped inside that construction dumpster over there.' He indicated the bright red dumpster at the end of the small yard. It looked to be about ten foot long, seven or eight wide and maybe five high. Two uniformed officers were standing to its right.

Hunter, Garcia and Brindle made their way toward it.

'As you can see,' Brindle continued, 'the dumpster is pushed back against the yard's back wall, which is only about a foot higher than the dumpster itself.'

'The killer drove up the back alley,' Hunter said, anticipating what Brindle was about to say.

'That's right,' Brindle confirmed. 'Nice and dark, easy to access, no one to bother him. He stops his vehicle directly behind the house, drags the body and the arms out of the car and quickly throws them over the wall and into the dumpster. Job done. Back into the car, and he's gone. The whole thing would've taken less than a minute.' Brindle pulled a cigarette out of his pocket, lit it up and took a long drag, letting the smoke escape as he spoke. 'This killer is a planner. He'd probably been driving around for a few days, scouting for a place to dump his next victim. This house is at the beginning of the road, easy to spot from both sides, front and back. Anyone driving by can see that it's empty and being refurbished. The bright red dumpster is also easily spotted from outside.'

'And because it's being refurbished,' Hunter added, 'the killer knew that if he dumped the body late at night, it would be found the next day by the working force.'

Brindle nodded and took another drag. 'We've checked the back alley already. There's nothing there. Solid asphalt, no tire marks or footprints. A few cigarette butts and gum wrappers, but none directly behind the house. I wouldn't hope for much.'

They looked inside the dumpster – plasterboards, wood pieces, red bricks, broken tiles, rags and empty cans of paint.

'The body?' Garcia asked.

'On its way to the coroner's. You've missed it by—' Brindle glanced at his watch '—twenty-five minutes. No point checking it here. The body was well wrapped up. If there are any forensics clues to be found, they'll be on the body itself, or on the inside of the plastic bags. Better to properly unwrap it under a controlled environment.'

'And you're sure it's our victim?'

'It's the victim, all right,' Brindle said, retrieving a digital camera from his bag. He turned it on, switched it to view mode and handed it to Hunter. 'I cut open enough of the plastic wrapper to expose the head.'

The first picture was a close-up of the man's face. His eyes had already started to sink into his skull, and the skin around his face and neck had taken a greenish-blue color, making him look like an alien, or a horror film prop, but there were still enough features there for Hunter and Garcia to recognize him. They slowly flipped through the rest of the photographs – a few more close-ups, followed by some wide-angle shots.

'I'll email these to you as soon as I get back to the lab,' Brindle said, checking his watch again.

'Who found the body?' Hunter asked, handing the camera back to the forensics agent.

'The builder who's refurbishing the house.' Brindle pointed with his right index finger. 'He's in the kitchen with an officer.'

Hunter nodded and turned to face Garcia. 'Do we have any of those printouts of the victim we handed the press yesterday?'

'We have a few in the car, yes.'

'Great, let's get some of the uniforms to go around this street and some of the neighboring ones too. Maybe the victim was a local. Maybe that's why the killer chose this house to dump the body.'

'I'll go get them,' Garcia said, already making his way outside again.

Eighty-Nine

The door-to-door gave them nothing. No neighbor or shop-keeper in the vicinity of the house could offer any informa-tion regarding the victim's identity. Many of them had already seen his picture in the morning paper or, worse, had watched the killer's broadcast the day before.

Garcia interviewed the construction worker who'd found the body. He was a strong man, in his early thirties with tattooed arms, a shaved head and a bushy blond mustache. He and his father owned the small refurbishing company he worked for, and he'd been doing the same job for over fifteen years. He'd been working on that house for only five days, and the job was expected to last no more than another four.

The house belonged to a small property developer, Akil Banerjee, who for the past four years had been investing in disused and repossessed properties, cheaply refurbishing them and selling them on for a small profit.

Both the property owner and the construction worker checked out. They also had solid alibis for their where-abouts overnight and at the time the killer was on the phone to Hunter yesterday. But as Hunter and Garcia got back into the car, Hunter received a new phone call. This time it was Homicide Detective Mario Perez.

'Robert, I think we've got an ID on your victim.'

'I'm listening.'

'Are you in your car?' Perez asked.

'No, in Detective Garcia's car.'

'OK, I'm emailing you a few pictures now.'

Hunter switched the call to loudspeaker and used the car's police computer to log into his email.

'With the press and the media appealing for people to come forward, we've been getting calls all day,' Perez clarified. 'As expected, most of them have been crackpots, attention seekers or people who couldn't be one hundred percent sure, you know how it goes – except one.'

'Go on.'

'A restaurant owner called Paolo Ghirardelli called a couple of hours back. He owns a pizzeria in Norwalk. I was the one who spoke to him. He was absolutely positive that the man in the picture that came out in the papers today was one of his waiters – Ethan Walsh. He hasn't turned up for work in two days. Hasn't answered his phone either. Mr. Ghirardelli is one of those proud Italians who has framed photographs of everyone who works for him, kitchen staff included, hanging on his restaurant wall. He emailed me Ethan Walsh's picture, and . . . you can see for yourself.'

Hunter opened the email and the first of its three attachments – a colored photograph of a man in his early thirties with an oval-shaped face, a round nose, plump cheeks, thin eyebrows and short darkish hair. He and Garcia stared at it in silence for a long moment, and reflexively, but not that they needed to, checked the snapshot printout they'd been showing around the streets for the past few hours. Neither one had any doubts.

'It's him,' Garcia said at last. 'Or an identical twin.'

'Ethan Walsh's got no brothers or sisters,' Perez confirmed. 'I've already done a preliminary check on him. That's the second attachment to the email. And it turns out that he used to be an expert computer programmer.'

'He was an expert computer programmer?' Garcia interjected.

'That's right.'

'What's an expert computer programmer doing working as a waiter in a pizzeria in Norwalk?'

'If you open the second attachment, you'll see our official details sheet on Ethan Walsh,' Perez replied as Hunter double clicked on it. 'The third attachment is a quick selection of a few Internet articles I found on him. That will give you a better idea of why he left games programming behind.'

'Great work, Mario,' Hunter said, quickly scanning the fact sheet. 'Could you carry on and dig out everything you can on this Ethan Walsh?'

'Already on it. By the time you guys get back here, I should have some more.'

'Thanks.' Hunter disconnected.

Ethan Walsh's registered address was as a tenant in an apartment block in Bellflower, the first neighborhood west of Norwalk. A footnote at the bottom of the email Detective Perez had sent Hunter said that just to be sure, Perez had already contacted the Bellflower police station and asked them to send a black and white unit to knock on Ethan Walsh's door. There had been no reply.

The fact sheet also carried the name, address and phone number for Ethan Walsh's landlord – Mr. Stanislaw Reuben. Hunter lost no time in calling him, and Mr. Reuben told Hunter that he could meet them at Ethan Walsh's address in an hour.

Ninety

Hunter and Garcia made it to Bellflower in south Los Angeles just as the sun was starting to set over Venice Beach. The apartment block Ethan Walsh used to live in was an old and dirty brick building in dire need of some repairs, located at the end of an unglamorous street.

Mr. Stanislaw Reuben, Ethan's landlord, met the detectives by the entrance to the building's lobby. The man had an undeniable seediness to him, with ill-fitting clothes, a pockmarked face and a lip marred by a scar. His throaty voice sounded like it had come straight out of a horror film.

'I thought that the man I saw in the paper this morning looked rather familiar,' Mr. Reuben said after Hunter and Garcia identified themselves. 'I suspected that he might've been one of my tenants, but it was hard to be sure. I have so many, and I only see them once or twice a year, really. Most of my tenants post me predated checks a few months in advance. I find it easier that way.'

'And that was how Mr. Walsh paid his rent?' Garcia queried.

'That was indeed.' Mr. Reuben smiled, showing badly cared-for teeth.

'How long has he been a tenant of yours?' Garcia followed up.

'Not long at all. Just over six months. Seemed like a nice tenant too. Quiet, no complaints . . .' Mr. Reuben pinched his left earlobe a couple of times. 'It's him, isn't it? The man who was killed on the Internet? That was my tenant, Mr. Walsh, wasn't it?' He sounded truly excited.

'We can't be certain at this time,' Garcia replied.

'Do you think I'll get interviewed by TV?' His excitement grew. 'I've never been on TV.'

'And that's not such a bad thing,' Garcia said, gesturing toward the building. 'Shall we?'

The landlord used his key to unlock the lobby door and ushered the detectives inside. The confined space smelled of cat piss with something else that carried an acid undertone.

Garcia wrinkled his nose while his eyes quickly searched the dusky lobby as if he was expecting to identify the source of the smell.

'I suggest we take the stairs up,' Mr. Reuben said. 'That elevator is very small, and I wouldn't really risk it, if you know what I mean.'

The stairs were dirty and dark, with graffiti decorating the walls all the way up. As they got to the fourth floor, Mr. Reuben led the way down a long and dimly lit corridor. The cat piss smell from the downstairs lobby was replicated there, but it now had a fetid, sickly quality to it that made both detectives grind their teeth.

It didn't seem to bother the landlord.

'Here we are,' he said as they reached a door three-quarters of the way down the hallway. The number on it read 4113. Mr. Reuben unlocked the door and pushed it open. With the windows shut and the curtains pulled to, the room before them was hidden in shadows, and the built-up heat made it feel like a prison cell even before they stepped inside.

Mr. Reuben hit the lights, revealing a small living area, with a tiny kitchen to the left. The room was sparsely decorated. There was an old wooden table, four wooden chairs, a small stereo, a sofa with a flowery cover thrown over it, a portable TV set and a chest of drawers, on which a few picture frames had been placed. There were no immediate signs of a disturbance. The walls were bare, save for a picture of Ethan Walsh with a little girl who looked to be around three years old.

'The bedroom and the bathroom are through there,' Mr. Reuben said, indicating a door across the room.

Hunter and Garcia gloved up.

'Do you mind waiting outside?' Garcia said to the landlord. 'We're not sure if there's any evidence here, but if there is I'd like to reduce the risk of contaminating it.'

Mr. Reuben looked disappointed as he took a step back. 'Of course. I understand. I'll be right out here if you need me.'

The first thing Hunter and Garcia noticed inside the narrow living room was Ethan Walsh's laptop computer on the wooden table. A webcam was clipped to the top of the screen.

Hunter retrieved two large evidence bags from his pocket, and placed the laptop, the web camera and all the computer cables inside them.

Garcia was looking through the photographs on top of the chest of drawers. There were four in total. All of them of Ethan Walsh with his baby daughter. The drawers revealed a few books and magazines, all on computer programming, and a vast number of comic books. The kitchen was a little untidy, but not any more than one would expect for a single man living on his own. The fridge had several microwavable dinners and a lot of beer.

Hunter left Garcia to look around the living room some more and moved onto the rest of the apartment. The bathroom was a sardine can, with a cracked shower enclosure, a toilet and not much else.

The bedroom didn't look much bigger either. A full bed was pushed up sideways against the far wall, directly under a small window, and even so it left very little space for one to maneuver around it. Besides the unmade bed, there was only a sliding-door wall wardrobe and a bed table with a reading lamp on it.

Hunter checked under the bed – two empty suitcases. The wardrobe had shirts, T-shirts, jeans, trousers, jackets, two pairs of sneakers, a pair of social shoes and two cardboard boxes full of videogames. Ethan's bedroom was untidy, but again within what would be expected. Once more, nothing suggested a disturbance.

Hunter returned to the living room, where Garcia was standing next to the uncomfortable-looking sofa, flipping through the pages of what looked like a notebook or a diary. As Hunter stepped back into the room, Garcia paused and frowned at the page he was reading.

Hunter recognized the look. 'What have you got?'

Garcia looked up and smiled.

'Our first link.'

Ninety-One

The man carrying his empty basket walked down the long fruit and vegetable aisle in the supermarket for the third time, still unable to decide what to get. He stopped by the oranges section once again, picked one up, brought it to his nose and breathed in its intense aroma. He really liked oranges, but still, not one made it into his basket. He moved a couple of steps further along and paused by the ample and diverse apples display. His favorites were Fireside apples, but they were hard to find in Los Angeles, being a lot more popular in the upper Midwest. It didn't much bother him though, because Pink Pearls were just as nice, and they were a product of northern California, abundantly found everywhere in LA. He held one in his hand for a long moment, resisting the temptation to bite into it right there and then. He put the apple back and moved along to yet another fruit display.

The indecisive man wore a dark blue suit jacket that didn't match his light-colored trousers. His shoes were battered, showing years of wear. His hair had been combed back loosely, but only by his fingers, and his two-day stubble made him look a little older than he really was.

The man moved past the blueberries display without stopping. He didn't like their grainy texture, and to him they were never sweet enough. Anyway, blueberries were way too expensive. He reconsidered buying some pears, peaches or nectarines, but in the end he moved on once again without making his mind up.

When he reached the end of the aisle, he paused and looked back at it, sighing with disappointment. He placed his hand inside his trouser pocket, closed his fingers around all the money he had, pulled it out and counted it again. He didn't have a lot, just enough to buy the few items he had placed on his mental list. Fruit was one of those items, if only he could decide which one. He returned the money to his pocket and slowly walked back to the top of the aisle again. An attractive woman, who looked to be in her late twenties, was carefully selecting oranges and placing them inside a small, clear plastic bag. The man paused by her side, and after a few seconds tentatively reached for one.

'These are great,' the woman said quite enthusiastically.

The man smiled shyly.

'I bought some the other day,' the woman continued. 'And they were the sweetest oranges I've had in a very long time.'

'Really?' the man replied, now intriguingly eyeing the orange in his hand.

'I'm telling you.' She paused and looked at him. He had kind eyes, she thought. 'It's like they've been infused with sugar or honey or something. You should try some.'

And just like that, a decision was made.

The man smiled and nodded happily. 'OK, I think I will, then.' He placed two oranges inside his shopping basket. Two were all he could afford.

A few minutes later the man had, at last, managed to buy all the items on his mental list. Happy with himself, he exited the supermarket, carrying everything inside a brown-paper bag. When he reached the semi-dark parking lot he paused, looking a little confused. He glanced left, then right, trying to decide which way to go. As he turned to go right, the brown-paper bag he was carrying ripped open at the bottom. The few groceries he had in it spilled to the ground, scattering around his feet. The two oranges he bought began rolling away in different directions.

'Shit!' he whispered, scrambling after the first of them like a cat after a tennis ball. He finally managed to pick it up, and quickly turned to look for the other one. He spotted it just as it was about to roll away under a parked SUV. All of a sudden, a foot came out of nowhere and stopped it.

The man looked up and saw the woman he'd met at the orange display. She bent over and collected the fruit from off the ground. 'This one is a runaway, huh?' She smiled.

The man looked at her, then at the ripped bag and the rest of his groceries on the ground.

'It's a bummer when that happens, isn't it?' she said. 'I can't believe this supermarket still uses paper bags. They're crap, and not very good for the environment either.'

The man was unsure of what to say, so he said nothing. Timidly, he started collecting his things.

'Here, let me help you,' she said, picking up half of the items, among them a jar of coffee. 'You're lucky this didn't break.'

The man nodded, thinking that he was also lucky that he hadn't chosen apples instead of oranges. They would've certainly bruised.

'Thank you,' he finally said, trying to collect the items she had picked up, but he didn't have enough hands.

'It's OK. I can help you with these,' she said. 'Do you have a car?'

The man nodded. 'Just over there.' He pointed to his car, which was further down the parking lot.

'Do you live around here?' she asked, as they started walking toward the man's car.

'Not very far, you?'

'A couple of blocks away.'

The man nodded. 'Oh!' he said after a few seconds, as if he'd just realized something. 'Would you like a ride home?'

She smiled again. 'Oh no, my car is parked just back there. The SUV that your orange almost rolled under. But thank you for the offer, anyway.'

When they got to the man's car, he unlocked it and opened the back doors. 'You can just put everything in the back seat, if you don't mind.'

'Sure,' the woman replied.

As she placed the groceries down, one of the oranges rolled away from her, off the seat and onto the floor. She moved quickly, thrusting her body forward, stretching her arm and managing to stop it just before it disappeared under the driver's seat.

'This one really *is* a runaway,' she thought.

Suddenly she felt a presence behind her. She twisted her body slightly, and looked over her right shoulder. The man was standing right behind her. The kind look in his eyes had changed to something much darker. He smiled in a way that scared her. When he spoke, his voice also sounded different – calm, but with a cold edge to it that sucked the air straight out of her lungs.

'Didn't anyone ever tell you not to talk to strangers?'

Ninety-Two

The next morning brought with it the first autumn downpour. The sky was dark with heavy clouds, and daylight seemed to be fighting a losing battle to break through. The bitter wind that blew from the north made Los Angeles feel like Winnipeg in November.

For Hunter, Garcia and Captain Blake, the day started with an update meeting, held in Hunter's office. None of them looked like they had managed much sleep overnight.

'OK,' Captain Blake said, using both hands to tuck her loose hair behind her ears. 'Before we talk about anything else, I need to know what's the deal with this Thomas Paulsen guy?' A pinch of irritation colored her voice.

No immediate answer, but the exact same questioning frown suddenly appeared on both detectives' faces.

'I got a call late last night from the Chief of Police,' Captain Blake explained, 'who, in turn, received two separate calls yesterday, one from the governor of California, and the other from the mayor of Los Angeles. Apparently the two of you have been harassing a Mr. Thomas Paulsen, software millionaire, who so happens to be a major *funds* contributor to both of their political campaigns.'

'Harassing?' Garcia chuckled.

'That was the word that was used,' the captain confirmed.

'We barely managed to get a word out, Captain.' Garcia was struggling to keep his calm. 'As soon as we entered his office yesterday, he launched onto this rehearsed speech of his. When he was done, he kicked us out. And that was all that happened. I don't think we even got to ask a single question.'

'And what else do you have on him other than him being the subject of an article written by Christina Stevenson, our second victim?'

A moment of hesitation.

'We are investigating the possibility that Thomas Paulsen had threatened Christina Stevenson after the article was published,' Garcia finally said.

'You are *investigating*,' the captain came back. 'As in *you have no proof yet.*'

'Not yet,' Garcia admitted. 'But if you were there you would understand, Captain. Everything about Thomas Paulsen stunk of crap. And he sure as hell fits the profile. He said so himself. He's intelligent enough. He's got the means and the cyberspace knowledge to pull it off. He's as arrogant and as bold as the killer is on the phone, if not more. And he admitted that he was very glad to see Christina Stevenson die the way she did. Doesn't that stink of psycho to you?'

'It doesn't matter if he stinks of psycho, dog shit or roses,' Captain Blake shot back irritably. 'We need probable cause. And you shouldn't need *me* to tell you that. Arrogant . . .? Of course he's arrogant. He's extremely rich. He's got politicians eating out of his hands, and he's the CEO of a very large, influential and successful company. That gives him power, and a lot of it. Everyone with that much power inevitably becomes arrogant and detached from what we, mere mortals, call the real world. And you shouldn't need *me* to tell you that either. This Paulsen guy has the power and the contacts to slam every investigation door right on our faces. He snaps a finger, and you two will be issuing traffic tickets for a very long time. He does it again, and I'll probably get transferred to "Shitkickers Creek" somewhere in North Dakota. Do you understand what I'm saying?'

Hunter and Garcia said nothing.

'Let me ask you this,' the captain said, moving on. 'Are you investigating anyone else who had also been the subject of any of Christina Stevenson's other articles? Don't tell me Thomas Paulsen is the only person she has ever pissed off.'

'No,' Hunter answered. 'At the moment we're not investigating anyone else.'

Garcia lifted a hand in a stop gesture. 'Wait a second, are we getting heat for doing our jobs, Captain?'

'No,' the captain spat out, her voice rising a notch. 'You're getting heat because I got heat, and I always pass it on. You're also getting heat because this Paulsen guy doesn't mind putting a large chunk of his money into politicians' campaigns, and that will buy him the fires of hell when it comes to how much heat he can bestow upon this department.'

'So?' Hunter said. 'Are the mayor and the governor saying that rich folks don't kill people?'

'No.' The captain glared at him. 'They are saying that you better have something very substantial in your bag before you go knocking on Thomas Paulsen's door again, because if you don't they'll lose a very important contributor to their political campaigns on the run-up to a new election, and we'll be slapped with a lawsuit that will make

Rodney King's seem like kindergarten stuff.' She paused, taking a moment to recompose herself, her voice going back to its normal pitch. 'Look, I know we're all just doing our jobs here. You know me enough to know that I don't give a flying fuck for who Thomas Paulsen is, or who he has in his pocket, but the truth of the matter is that with this guy we *will have* to play it by the book, because if we don't and we screw up even an inch, the chief has guaranteed me that the next job any of us will be doing will involve a brush, a toilet bowl and human excrement. Do you get the picture?'

'Yes,' Garcia replied. 'And the picture I'm getting smells like bullshit, Captain.'

'Well, that's the smell of power and politics, and you as well as I know that this department is drowning in it, and there's nothing any of us can do about it. So investigate the hell out of him if you like, but *play it by the book*. If you get anything else on him other than the article Christina Stevenson wrote about him, come to me with it first. That's all I'm asking.'

The captain dropped the subject and moved toward the pictures board. 'OK, let's move on. The third Internet victim: I was told his body has been found.' Her eyes searched the board, but found no new photographs.

'It has, yesterday,' Garcia confirmed. He then proceeded to explain how the victim's body had been left inside a construction dumpster at the back of a private property in Maywood. 'The body was already on its way to the coroner's when we got there. We should be getting the autopsy results and photographs anytime soon.' He double clicked something on his computer. 'Forensics sent us an email last night with all the shots they took of the body in situ at the "dump scene". I just haven't had time to print them out and pin them up yet.' He double clicked something again, and the printer at the edge of his desk came to life.

'Officially confirmed ID?' the captain asked.

Garcia nodded. 'The victim's wife and daughter live in Seattle. They were recently divorced. His parents live in Iowa, but we got access to his apartment in Bellflower through his landlord. Fingerprint analysis between items in his apartment and the body found in Maywood is a one hundred percent match.'

'So who is he?'

'His name is Ethan Walsh,' Hunter replied, handing her a copy of the photograph the pizzeria owner had sent Detective Perez.

Captain Blake's eyes moved to the picture and recognition was instant. She too hadn't been able to forget his face. Seeing him branding a timid smile like the one he had on the picture seemed too alien to her memory of his terrified face contorting in agony.

'What's the story on him?' Her voice almost faltered.

Hunter gave her a quick summary on everything they had found so far on Ethan Walsh.

Captain Blake listened to everything in silence, interjecting only when Hunter was done. 'Do we have anything on this ex-partner of his, Mr. Nelson is it? He's also an expert computer programmer, right?' She handed the picture back to Hunter.

'That's right,' Hunter confirmed. 'Brad Nelson. We're still gathering information on him, but chances are he'll be clean. He moved back to Canada ten months ago.'

Garcia retrieved the printouts from his printer and carefully pinned them onto the pictures board.

The captain stepped closer to have a better look. The close-up photos of the victim's face sticking out of the heavy-duty plastic bags made a sick acid taste travel up from her stomach, through her throat and into her mouth. She quickly reached into her pocket for a mint.

'You said that you've been to the victim's apartment,' Captain Blake said, finally turning to face her detectives. 'Anything?'

'We found his laptop,' Garcia informed her. 'But it's password protected. We left it with Dennis Baxter at the Computer Crimes Unit. They're trying to break it.'

Captain Blake nodded, unenthusiastically.

'But we also got this,' Garcia said, producing the notebook he found in Ethan Walsh's apartment.

'And what is that?'

'An old-fashioned address and telephone book,' Garcia explained. 'Apparently, the more into technology you are, the more you know that it can all go disastrously wrong. It looks like Ethan Walsh kept a hard copy of what I'm guessing are all the numbers in his cellphone's address book.'

Captain Blake nodded. She had one herself. 'OK, and ...?'

Garcia handed her the book, already opened onto a specific page. 'Fifth name from the top,' he said.

The captain's eyes scrolled down the list, paused, widened a fraction. 'Christina Stevenson?' She read the name out loud before her gaze shot up in the direction of both detectives. 'Is this the same Christina Stevenson?' She pointed to the pictures board. 'The killer's second victim?'

'The one and the same,' Hunter agreed. 'That's her cellphone number.'

'You do remember that we retrieved Christina Stevenson's cellphone from her house, right?' Garcia asked.

'His number is in her address book as well.' The captain phrased it half as a question, half as a statement.

'It is,' Garcia confirmed. 'We checked her phone's call log, but it goes back only three weeks. She hadn't made or received a call to or from Ethan Walsh's number during that period.'

'Do you have his cellphone?' she asked.

'No,' Garcia replied. 'It wasn't in his apartment. We've checked with the provider, and the phone has been switched off. We've already requested phone records for the past three months for both of them. We should hopefully have them by the end of today, or maybe tomorrow. At the moment we're not sure if they were friends, acquaintances, or if Ethan Walsh had, in any level, been part of any of Ms. Stevenson's reports.'

Captain Blake returned her attention to the phone book.

'I spent most of the night reading through every article Christina Stevenson wrote for the *LA Times* in the past two years,' Hunter announced. 'Six hundred and sixty-nine in total. Ethan Walsh's name isn't mentioned in any of them. I've already contacted Ms. Stevenson's ex-editor with the entertainment desk again. She's never heard the name Ethan Walsh.'

'You're thinking he might've been an informant?' Captain Blake asked. 'Like a source, I mean?'

Hunter shrugged gently. 'It's possible. I've also asked her for a copy of all the articles Ms. Stevenson wrote while she was with the crime desk.'

'Crime desk?' the captain asked.

'Before she became an entertainment reporter, Christina Stevenson spent nine months with the crime desk. I know it was a long time ago, but I'd still like to go through all those articles as well. I should be getting those sometime today.'

The captain started flipping through the pages in Ethan Walsh's phone book.

'If you're looking for the first victim's name,' Garcia said, 'Kevin Lee Parker, it's not there. We've looked.'

She paused, considering her thoughts for a little while. 'Yeah, but this shows that at least two of the victims knew each other. In a city where the population stands at around twelve and a half million people, this cannot be a coincidence. This killer isn't selecting his victims at random.'

Ninety-Three

Her first thought as she finally reawakened was that death felt nothing like what she had expected.

Next, as her senses slowly came back to her, she realized that death hadn't taken her yet, then came the pain – rushing through her like a drug overdose. It felt as if every bone and muscle in her body had been beaten up and then twisted out of shape. Her head throbbed so ferociously it was hard even to breathe. She could feel the blood thundering through her ears with such force she believed her eardrums would explode. She moaned slowly, while trying to find the strength to open her eyes against the pain.

That was when she heard his voice again, and the sheer sound of it sent a shocking wave of fear through every atom in her body.

'Don't fight it. Don't try to move. Just try to relax.' His tone was calm, emotionless, disembodied.

She was unable to hold back the fearful cry that escaped her lips.

The man waited.

She tried blinking her eyes open, thinking that she must not panic, but fear had already covered her like a shroud. She gasped in air, hyperventilating.

He spoke again.

'Take a deep breath, and try to remain calm.'

Another gasp of air.

'I know you're scared. I understand it seems difficult right now, but just breathe, and soon the panic will go away.'

She tried to do as she was told.

She finally managed to open her eyes, allowing them to drink in her surroundings, but the room was mostly dark. The only light came from a terribly weak corner light far away. The air was stale, heavy with the smell of old hay, disinfectant and something else she didn't recognize. Something sweet and sickly. She couldn't see the man, but she could hear his breathing, and she could sense his oppressing presence.

She slowly became aware that she couldn't move. She was sitting down in some sort of heavy, hard and uncomfortable high-backed chair. Her wrists were roped to the chair's arms – her ankles securely fastened to the chair's legs. Her torso and head weren't restrained, which allowed her to slightly twist her body from side to side. She did so slowly. First left, then right, trying to better understand the room. Only then she realized that she was naked.

Suddenly she was overcome by an abrupt despair at how vulnerable, exposed and fragile she really was. She wanted to stay in control. She wanted to show strength and determination, but at that precise moment fear was winning that battle, and involuntarily she began sobbing.

'You're not doing what I told you to do.' The man's cold voice came again.

The woman could not stifle her sobs. She felt tears welling up in her eyes and squeezed them tight, wishing the tears away.

'*Stay strong,*' the voice in her head said.

She had read somewhere that rape attackers thrived on fear, on the submission of their prey, but that thought only served to scare her more, and the uncertainty of what would happen to her next petrified her. When she spoke, the words left her lips as if spoken by a little lost child.

'Please, don't hurt me.' Her voice faltered. 'Please, let me go.'

Silence.

Her next words came out without any thought.

'I'll do whatever you want. Please, just let me go.'

No reply.

'Please . . .' In a moment of sobriety from her fear, she realized how useless that word sounded.

'Tell me what you want from me?' Her mind raced over the possible answers to her own question, but she forced herself to banish the gruesome visions.

The man breathed out slowly, and she sensed his movement.

For an instant she felt as if her heart had stopped.

The man stepped out of the shadows, for the first time hovering into the periphery of her vision. She craned her neck in his direction. Despite the different clothes, she immediately recognized him. It was the same man she had talked to in the supermarket, and then later helped at the parking lot. But gone were the easy approachable grin, the shy persona and the kind eyes. He looked taller, stronger, menacing. His face now seemed to be all edges and angles.

'Hello again,' he said.

His gaze grabbed hers like a giant claw, and she had the sensation that she was being helplessly sucked into a dark place. More tears came to her eyes.

'Crying won't help you.'

'Please, don't hurt me,' she said again. The words simply dripped out of her lips, unrequested, sorrowful, powerless. 'I'll do whatever you want.'

'*Whatever* I want?' He did not take his eyes from her naked body. The insinuation in his words and the rigidity of his gaze struck her like a blow to the temple.

She swallowed the lump that had formed in her throat, and heard the lost girl inside her reply, 'Yes. Whatever you want.'

He stepped closer.

She held her breath. 'Oh, please, God.'

'Stop praying.'

'Sorry,' she said quickly. 'Whatever you say. Please.'

'Stop begging.'

She began crying again.

'Stop crying.'

She breathed in through her nose and held the breath in her lungs until she was able to control her sobs.

'So, will you do *whatever* I want you to do?' he asked her one more time.

She breathed in again, courage coming to her out of thin air.

'Yes.' There was now distinct determination in her tone. '*You can do this.*' The voice in her head spoke again.

He stepped closer still, and she finally saw the glint of the knife in his hand.

'Oh my God . . . no.' The determination was all gone. Her mind became a single black sheet of panic, paralyzing her every move.

The man smiled in a way that told her that her fear pleased him. His eyes held hers as if they were connected. She felt the coldness of the steel blade on her skin, but was unable to break away from his hypnotizing stare. The blade pulled away fast, in a quick slicing movement.

The woman held her breath for a moment.

No pain.

She knew that a sharp enough blade could cut through human skin and flesh so subtly that sometimes no pain would come with it. She also knew that the tremendous amount of adrenaline rushing through her veins at that precise moment could hide even the most excruciating pain.

She waited.

Still no pain.

The man stepped back, breaking eye contact at last.

As if finally let go from a spell, her eyes moved down to her body, searching for blood, looking for cuts.

There were none.

Instead she saw that the man had sliced through the ropes that bonded her right wrist.

She was confused. Was he about to let her go? She didn't dwell on that idea for very long, because her ankles and her left wrist were still tied to the heavy chair. She brought her right arm toward her chest, and the sensation of being able to move it again was exhilarating. Blowing onto her wrist, she opened and closed her fingers into a fist several times to get the blood circulating again. It felt nice.

The man reappeared suddenly, moving from behind her, and placed something heavy and cold on her lap. Her eyes moved to it.

A pair of gardening scissors.

'Pick them up,' he said.

She obeyed.

He paused. Time seemed to hesitate with him. 'OK. I want you to cut off all the fingers on your left hand. Start with your pinky, and work your way to your thumb.'

She looked up, but he had returned to the shadows.

'What?' Her voice wavered.

'You said that you would do anything I wanted you to.' The voice came from behind her, now speaking very slowly. 'That's what I want you to do. I want you to cut off all the fingers on your left hand.'

The woman could not hide the terror she felt. The gardening scissors started shaking in her hand, and her lip quivered.

'I suggest that you put a finger between the blades, close your eyes and just clip it fast and hard, before the courage escapes you.'

She couldn't even form words.

'It will hurt. No doubt about that. There will be a lot of blood. No doubt about that either. You will certainly feel like passing out. But if you show me that you are psychologically strong enough to completely mutilate your left hand, I'll let you go, that's a promise. I'll even drive you to the police station myself.'

The woman fought the wave of nausea that came over her and looked down at the scissors.

'I am giving you a *choice*. Do this and you are free. Don't do it and . . .' He left the mystery of the consequences at the mercy of her already terrified imagination.

She took a mouth full of air, but this time courage did not come with it.

'Do it,' he said firmly.

Her gaze moved to her left hand, still firmly tied to the chair.

'Do it. That's the price of your freedom.'

Hesitantly she spread the fingers on her left hand wide.

'That's it. Do it. Show me you are strong.'

She placed the scissors' blades around her trembling left pinky finger.

'That's it. They are laser-sharp. Just squeeze the handles hard and fast and the blades will do the rest.'

She couldn't move.

'CUT YOUR FINGERS OFF.' His yell was so loud and surprising, she wet herself. The sound of his voice reverberated against the walls and ceiling for what seemed like an eternity.

Tears started coming down the woman's cheeks. The blades were so sharp that only brushing against them was enough to produce a cut. She saw a small drop of blood color the skin around her finger.

'DO IT.' Another loud and angry yell.

She closed her eyes and took a deep breath.

The man smiled.

The woman threw the scissors on the floor.

'I can't, I just can't.' She brought her shaking right hand to her face, sobbing. 'I can't do it. I can't.'

The man laughed. 'You thought that I wanted to rape you, didn't you?' he asked. He didn't require a reply. 'And that's why you said that you would do anything I wanted you to. You figured that all you had to do was lay back and spread your legs. Put up with this monster entering you for a few minutes.' He faintly came into view again. 'If I wanted to rape you, what makes you think I needed your permission or cooperation for it?'

The woman didn't answer. Her sobs became more intense.

'Relax,' he said. 'I have no intention of raping you.'

In her mind she was filled with agony and embarrass-
ment, exposed and lost.

'Wha . . . What are you going to do to me?' The little girl
inside her spoke again.

The man disappeared back into the shadows. His reply
came in a whisper to her right ear. 'I'm going to kill you.'

She gasped for air. Her body now convulsing with fear.

The man laughed. 'If that scares you,' he paused for effect,
'wait until you find out how I'm going to do it.'

Ninety-Four

The rain came in spurts as the evening began, falling heavily, with thunder blows and lightning strikes out over the ocean, before tapering off into a steady, irritating drizzle. As the storm passed, the temperature dropped a few degrees, giving the night an uncomfortable chill that seemed totally out of place in a city like Los Angeles.

By the end of the afternoon, Hunter and Garcia had received the phone records they had requested for Christina Stevenson and Ethan Walsh. The records went back only three months, and neither of the two victims had called the other during that period. At least not via their cellphones. Hunter was forced to request a new batch of phone records, this time going back a whole year, but it would be at least another day before they had those.

Instead of driving home at the end of the day and spend another night struggling with his thoughts and fighting insomnia, Hunter decided to revisit Christina Stevenson's house. He knew for sure that Christina had been abducted from inside her bedroom, and abduction locations, just like crime scenes, always had more to offer than simple physical evidence. Hunter had a gift when it came to understanding them, and maybe, being there alone, away from any distractions, would help him see something he'd missed.

He spent almost two hours in her house, most of it inside her bedroom. He tried to imagine what had happened that night, and role-played along with the images that came to him.

He positioned himself behind the flowery curtain in Christina's bedroom, exactly where he figured the killer had hid. Hunter knew that the killer hadn't attacked Christina immediately as she entered the room; her clothes scattered around the floor, together with the champagne flute and bottle, told him that. She was drinking alone. Judging by how expensive a bottle of Dom Ruinart was, Christina must've been celebrating something special. Probably her article making the front cover of the entertainment supplement that Sunday.

The killer took his time watching her, either waiting for the perfect moment to strike or enjoying the show as she undressed. Either way, the moment came when she squeezed herself under her bed to retrieve her watch, Hunter guessed. He had a feeling that while Christina was under the bed, she had spotted the killer's shoes as he hid behind the curtain. Then everything happened in a flash. Within a minute she had been dragged out from under the bed and subdued. The killer most certainly had a syringe with the appropriate dosage of phenoperidine ready. Christina had fought as hard as she could, kicking and screaming. Signs of her struggle were all over the room, but her attacker was strong, and the drug stronger.

Despite reliving the entire scene in his mind, and meticulously moving about the house, Hunter picked up no new clues, nothing that answered any of the many questions screaming at him from inside his head.

After leaving Christina's place, he sat in his car for a long while, wondering what to do next, wondering if they would be able to move even an inch closer to this killer before he killed again. And Hunter was certain he would kill again.

He checked his watch and decided that he still wasn't ready to go home yet. Instead, he drove around the city aimlessly, looking for nothing, heading nowhere. In West Hollywood the bright neon lights and the busy streets made him feel a little more alive. It was always good to see people smiling, laughing and enjoying life.

From there he drove east for a while, past Echo Lake and the concrete bulk that was the Dodgers' stadium, before heading south through central Los Angeles. All of a sudden, Hunter had an urge to go to the beach, see the ocean, maybe walk barefoot on the sand. He loved the sea breeze at night. It reminded him of his parents and of when he was a little kid. A happier time, perhaps. He turned west and headed toward Santa Monica Beach, deciding to avoid the freeways. For once, he wasn't in a hurry to get anywhere.

He passed the turn for the 4th Street Bridge and carried on down South Mission Road. Those streets were as familiar to him as the inside of his apartment, and he took no notice of any street signs, specially the large one overhead.

Then it happened, similar to a wayward domino that has suddenly lost its balance, tumbling against all the other pieces and triggering a great linked chain reaction. First, his subconscious registered it. Then, about a second later, as his subconscious mind communicated with his conscious one, a warning bell sounded inside Hunter's head. It took just another millisecond for his brain to send a signal down to the muscles in his body via his nervous system. Adrenaline rushed through him like a tidal wave, and Hunter finally slammed on the brakes, hard. His old Buick LeSabre swerved left before coming to an abrupt stop in the middle of the road. He was lucky that there wasn't another vehicle right behind him.

Hunter shot out of the car like a bullet. His breath catching on his throat as his eyes focused on the large green road sign he'd just driven under. His mind was working at a thousand miles per hour, searching for memories, trying to slot them into place. As he started recalling, his mind segmented the memory into pictures, and he felt a shiver gradually climb up his spine.

'It can't be this,' he said to no one, but his words had little meaning, because the more he remembered, the more certain he was.

All the clues the killer had thrown at them had been real.

Ninety-Five

Hunter drove straight back to his office in the PAB and immediately fired up his computer. The first thing he noticed after it booted up was that he had received an email from Pamela Hays, Christina Stevenson's editor at the *LA Times* entertainment desk. Attached was a zip file – Christina's crime articles he had requested earlier.

'Great!' Hunter whispered before setting those aside for the time being, knowing that he would soon be coming back to them.

His priority at that moment was to find an old incident file. He couldn't remember the victim's name, or the exact date, but he was certain of the year – that would be good enough. He called up the internal search engine for the LAPD Incidents Database, entered the year he could remember, the incident type and the officer's name. The single result came back in about 0.23 seconds.

'Bingo!' Hunter smiled.

He clicked on the link and read through the incident report. Adrenaline and excitement pumped through his veins.

Hunter went back to Pamela Hays' email and uncompressed the attached archive. There were two hundred and fifty-nine files in total, but just like the first articles archive he had received a few days ago, these also weren't searchable text files. They were scanned images of the newspaper pages with the published articles. No file titles, just published dates, but this time Hunter didn't have to read them all. He now knew the exact date he was looking for. The incident file gave him that. He quickly found the specific article and double clicked the image.

It wasn't a very long piece, only around five hundred words or so. The article also contained four photographs. Three of them were of poor quality; the fourth was a good-quality portrait, and absolutely shocking. The article had featured on the second page of the *LA Times* crime supplement on a Thursday morning, almost two and a half years ago.

The title of the article alone made Hunter pause for breath, forcing him to reread it a couple of times. Things were starting to make a dreadful kind of sense.

A side note at the end of the article revealed how the newspaper had acquired the three poor-quality photographs that accompanied the piece, and Hunter choked for the second time.

'No way,' he said out loud in the quiet of the room. The room echoed around him. Hunter felt almost dizzy at how quickly the pieces were now slotting into place.

He made a printout of the scanned image and placed it on his desk, taking another moment to think about what to search for next. Then he remembered the camcorder the killer had left inside the trashcan out in City Hall Park, and just like that his mind made the connection.

'Sonofabitch.'

He brought up his web browser and took a moment to think about what words to type into the search engine. He quickly decided on a four-word sentence. The result came back almost instantly – about 6 million results in 0.36 seconds.

Because he had used a four-word sentence as his search criterion, the search engine would first look for all the words together, and in the order Hunter had typed them in. Those results would be placed at the top of the results list. Once the search engine had run out of matches for all the words in that specific order, it would then automatically start searching for any of the four individual words, or combination of them, in or out of order. That's why it had returned so many results.

Hunter clicked on the topmost result, which took him to a specialized website. He spent some time there, browsing through its pages and searching its archives, but didn't find what he was looking for.

He returned to the results page and tried the second link from the top. Again, after spending several minutes searching the site's archives, he got nowhere.

He repeated the unfruitful process eighteen more times, until he finally came across an obscure website. The strange thing was that as soon as the website's front page loaded onto his screen, Hunter felt an odd tingle scratch at the back of his neck. He shook the sensation away and used the site's internal search engine, typing in a combination of key words and a date. It returned fifteen files. The site's search engine wasn't very good, and entering a date made no difference whatsoever. He decided that the easiest thing to do was to check all fifteen results.

He didn't have to. The one he was looking for was the fourth one.

He sat back and rubbed his face with both hands. The images on his screen collided with the memories inside his head with absurd force.

The file had been uploaded by someone who called him/herself DarkXX1000. Hunter tried all he could to find out the real identity for the person behind that Internet handle, but didn't get very far. He decided to go back to it later.

He spent the next hour and a half doing a combination search between the Internet and general-public-restricted files, which, as an LAPD officer, he was able to access. They didn't reveal much either.

His eyes were itching and watering from squinting at the screen for so long. He took a bathroom break before pouring himself another cup of strong black coffee. Pacing the room, Hunter allowed his mind to go through everything he had uncovered up to that point – a lot, but many details were still missing. What he needed was help. Disregarding the late hour, he reached for his cellphone and dialed Michelle's number. She answered after the third ring.

'Michelle,' Hunter said. 'My turn to apologize for calling you so late and out of office hours.'

Michelle chuckled. 'Well, the term "office hours" does not apply to the FBI. My shift started the day I was hired, and it's only due to finish in about—' she paused, as if calculating how long '—forty-five years.'

'That's a long shift.'

'You're telling me?' Another chuckle. 'OK, so what's up?'

Hunter told her about everything he'd found so far, and what he was still after. When he was done, Michelle was speechless.

'Michelle, are you still there?'

'Um . . . yeah. Are you sure about this?'

'As sure as I will ever be.'

'OK. I'll see what I can find out and I'll call you back. It might be late . . . or early, depending on how you look at it.'

'I'm not going anywhere.'

Ninety-Six

Michelle called back just before six in the morning. She had finally managed to find out all the information Hunter had requested, including the name of the person behind the handle DarkXX1000. By 8:00 a.m., Hunter was heading an urgent meeting inside the windowless briefing room down in the basement of the PAB.

The room was a rectangular concrete box that resembled an old-fashioned high school classroom. Sixteen desks were arranged in four rows of four, the first starting about three feet from the wooden podium at the front of the room, behind which Hunter was standing. To his left, a large, white projection screen; to his right, a large flip chart mounted onto a tripod.

Garcia and Captain Blake were sitting at both ends of the first row, two desks apart. Behind and in between them was Michelle Kelly, who had told Hunter that she wanted in. The two last rows were taken by a SWAT team, eight strong, all wearing bulletproof vests over black fatigues. The tense and uncomfortable murmur that spiked the air inside the room came to a complete stop as soon as Hunter coughed to clear his throat.

All eyes went to him.

'OK, I'll give you the entire story from the beginning,' he said, nodding at Jack Fallon, the SWAT team captain standing at the back of the room, just behind the last row of SWAT agents.

Fallon dimmed the lights.

Hunter pressed the button on the clicker he had on his right hand, and the portrait photograph of a teenage boy was projected onto the white screen. The boy looked to be no older than sixteen, with a prominent brow, distinct cheekbones and a delicate nose covered in freckles. His eyes, clear and pale blue, perfectly complemented his wavy, dark blond hair. He was a good-looking kid.

'This is Brandon Fisher,' Hunter began. 'Until two and a half years ago, Brandon was a student at Jefferson High in south Los Angeles. Despite being terribly shy and sometimes withdrawn, he was an intelligent kid, with the grades to prove it, mostly As and Bs. Brandon was also a very promising quarterback, with a much-talked-about left arm. His chances for a university football scholarship were very high.' Hunter moved from behind the podium. 'A few weeks after receiving his driver's license, Brandon was involved in a very serious collision at the junction between West Washington Boulevard and South La Brea Avenue. The accident took place at 2:41 a.m.,' Hunter explained. 'Even though Brandon was a novice to driving, the accident wasn't his fault. Other than the fact that three distinct witnesses testified to it, LA Traffic PD also had photographic evidence supplied by the red-light-infraction-activated camera at that junction. The other driver jumped the red light.'

Hunter pressed the clicker again. Brandon Fisher's portrait was substituted by a series of six photographs, positioned two by two in three rows. The sequence of events depicted on them clearly showed a dark blue Ford Mustang running over a red light and colliding with a silver Chevrolet

Cruze. The Mustang speed shown at the bottom right-hand corner of every picture was 55mph.

'The collision sent Brandon's car spinning twenty-seven yards into West Washington Boulevard,' Hunter said. 'There was no one else inside the vehicle with him. Brandon fractured his left arm, both of his legs, received severe cuts to his face and body and broke several ribs, one of which perforated his left lung.'

Another click and a new portrait of Brandon Fisher took over the entire projection screen. Murmurs and curse words came from the SWAT agents. Hunter saw Garcia cringe. He saw Captain Blake and Michelle Kelly gasp and bring a hand to their mouths in surprise.

Brandon's eyes now carried a sadness that seemed contagious. His once good-looking face was severely disfigured by two large scars and several small ones. The larger of the two scars had missed his left eye by a fraction, but it had cut across his small nose, brutally deforming it, before moving down to traverse both of his lips, tipping the entire left side of his mouth downward, as if it'd been melted into an eternal sorrowful smile. The second large scar started at the top left side of his forehead, just under his scalp, and moved unsteadily all the way across to his right ear, slicing through the top of his right eyebrow and stretching it out of shape, together with his eyelid.

'This picture was taken about twelve months after the accident,' Hunter explained, 'once the scars had pretty much healed. He'd also already had two cosmetic surgeries to try to lessen their effect, and this was as good as it would get. Doctors and more operations could do little more for him.'

'Poor kid,' Michelle whispered.

'You don't need me to tell you that such severe, life-changing facial disfigurement is something most people will rarely find a way to *completely* cope with,' Hunter said. 'No matter how much time passes, or how much support they get.' He paused for breath. 'As I've said, Brandon was an already shy and withdrawn kid. It's no surprise that the accident sent him down a bottomless depression dark hole. He wasn't able to play football anymore, or any other sport for that matter. Despite healing properly after the fractures, his legs and left arm weren't as fast or as strong as they used to be, and, after being perforated, his left lung worked in a reduced capacity. At first, the few friends he had tried to be supportive, but kids will be kids, and slowly but surely they began distancing themselves from him. It wasn't long before the gossiping, the jokes and the name-calling started happening behind his back. But things like that never stay "behind the back" for too long. He knew. His girlfriend also ended their relationship, and that devastated him.'

'Didn't he get any psychological help?' Captain Blake asked.

'He did. As soon as he was able to,' Hunter confirmed with a head nod and a half shrug. 'Three one-hour sessions a week, that was all.'

'Yeah,' one of the SWAT agents chuckled. 'How much do you think that's going to help?'

'And even if it does,' another one added, 'with only three sessions a week, how long do you think it will take?'

'Too long,' Hunter agreed.

Murmuring came back to the room.

Hunter pressed the clicker button once again. The image that took over the screen this time was that of a bridge in downtown Los Angeles.

'Twenty-nine months ago, on a Tuesday night,' Hunter proceeded, and the room quieted down again, 'Brandon kissed his mother and father goodnight and went to his room, but he didn't go to bed. He waited until the house was silent before exiting it through his bedroom window and making his way to the 6th Street Bridge in downtown LA, just a few blocks away from where he lived, in Boyle Heights.'

The briefing room was completely silent. Everyone had their eyes on Hunter.

'Brandon had been at this for weeks, maybe months,' Hunter moved on. 'He had everything planned out, including time schedules. When the correct time came, he jumped off the bridge.'

Captain Blake and Michelle Kelly shifted uncomfortably on their chairs.

'As you all know,' Hunter said, 'the 6th Street Bridge not only provides a crossing over the Los Angeles River but also over several train tracks. Brandon chose the tracks instead of the river.' Hunter paused and cleared his throat again. 'As I've mentioned, Brandon seemed to have had everything planned out to the last detail, including the train's schedule. He timed his jump to perfection. A split second after his feet touched the tracks, an oncoming cargo train hit him at full speed. His body almost disintegrated.'

Another button click and the picture on the screen changed to a section of the train tracks that ran underneath and just past the 6th Street Bridge. A forensics evidence marker had been placed next to something that looked like a human leg.

'His body parts were scattered over a fifty-yard area,' Hunter added.

More nervous chair shuffling. This time it came from everyone in the briefing room.

Hunter wasn't finished yet. 'Before jumping off the bridge, Brandon said that most of the world believed in the stupid misconception that everything we do in life is ultimately down to us. That we *always* have a *choice*, whether we want it or not.' Hunter paused and folded his arms over his chest. 'And then Brandon said, "What about the choices other people make that end up completely changing your life, not theirs? Where is our choice there, then?"'

'Wait a second,' one of the SWAT agents said, lifting a hand as if requesting his teacher's permission to speak. 'How do you know what the kid said on the bridge?'

Hunter took a deep breath before looking back at the room.

'Because I was there.'

Ninety-Seven

Twenty-nine months ago
Whittier Boulevard,
about twenty seconds away from the 6th Street Bridge
01.19 a.m.

Hunter had given up the fight against another sleepless night. As he had done so many times before, and was sure to do countless times again, instead of sitting at home and staring at his dull and faded walls, all in desperate need of a new coat of paint, he had decided to go for a drive. Once again, he drove around aimlessly, going nowhere, searching for nothing. The city simply washed past the windshield as he drove. Empty minded, he allowed the streets and turns to guide him.

For no particular reason, or maybe it was because he had done the exact same thing just a few days ago, and had then decided to drive down to Venice Beach, tonight he chose to drive around downtown LA.

With the financial district and the city supposedly asleep, the streets of central Los Angeles seemed disturbingly quiet, too alien to what most people were accustomed to.

Hunter had just driven through Boyle Heights, turned right on El Camino Real and joined Whittier Boulevard, heading toward the 6th Street Bridge, when the police radio in his car crackled loudly.

'*Attention any downtown units near the 6th Street Bridge. We just received a 911 call about a possible suicide attempt on the bridge. Subject appears to be in his teens. According to the caller, the kid looks like he's going to jump. We need immediate response. Is anyone close enough?*'

Hunter looked up from his dashboard, where his eyes had rested while he listened to the call from dispatch. The first thing he saw was the large green road sign announcing the bridge that lay straight ahead, less than fifteen seconds away. Though many call it the 6th Street Bridge, the official name, and the one shown in all the city road signs, was Sixth Street Viaduct.

Hunter quickly reached for his radio.

'Dispatch, this is Detective Robert Hunter, LAPD Homicide Special. I am practically on the bridge, approaching it from the east side – coming from Whittier Boulevard. I'll be there in about ten seconds. Is there any info on the subject?'

'*Roger that on location, proximity and ETA on the bridge, Detective Hunter, but on subsequent info on the subject, that's a negative. Caller was a passerby who spotted the subject on the ledge. There's nothing else I can offer at this point. I'm sorry.*'

'Roger that,' Hunter replied. 'I'm coming to the bridge now and I have visual on the subject. He's up on the north-facing ledge – west end of the viaduct. I repeat – subject is up on the north-facing ledge, at the west end of the Sixth Street Viaduct. Send backup in the form of the fire brigade, and a psychologist ASAP.'

'*10-4 on backup and medical help, Detective. Good luck.*'

Hunter reduced his speed and stopped his car halfway through crossing the bridge, blocking all westward traffic. He did none of that briskly. There was no screeching of the tires, no slamming of the doors, no loud sound or abrupt movement that could potentially worsen an already extremely tense situation. The dashboard clock read 01:21 a.m.

As Hunter had described to dispatch, the subject was standing on the north-facing ledge, at the west end of the viaduct. His back was toward Hunter, but instead of looking down at what awaited him if he jumped, he was looking ahead in the distance, as if waiting for something, or maybe contemplating a change of mind. That was a good sign.

Hunter moved quickly but quietly, trying to get as close as possible before the jumper noticed him. He got to about fourteen feet when the kid broke eye contact with the nothingness in the distant darkness and turned around.

Hunter stopped moving and looked at the kid, trying to establish eye contact, and as the kid looked back at him Hunter froze in place for the briefest of moments. At that precise instant Hunter cursed the lack of prep information on the subject. He knew nothing about who that kid was, or what possible motives had led him to be on that bridge, ready to end his life. That would've better prepared him for what he saw.

Then Hunter cursed *himself*, because with or without prep information, an LAPD Homicide Special detective, especially one with a PhD in Criminal Behavior Analysis and Biopsychology, should've been prepared for anything. Prepared to expect the unexpected, no matter how shocking.

During that split second of hesitation, Hunter became terrified that his face, his eyes, his demeanor, his expression, anything about him at all gave away how surprised he was. If anything did, he knew that his chances of talking the kid down were already dead in the water.

Hunter's surprise had come because when the kid finally turned and looked at him, Hunter saw that his face had been completely disfigured by heavy scars, as if he'd been thrown face first through several sheets of glass. It was the kind of disfigurement that would attract pitiful, shocked and even disgusted looks anywhere he went. The kind of disfigurement that gave bullies a buffet of abuse and name-calling to throw at him. A disfigurement that would scar much deeper than anyone could see – psychological scars capable of destroying self-esteem and throwing anyone into the deepest of depressions. The kind of disfigurement that could make anyone's life seem unbearable, let alone a teenager's.

If any surprise had been shown by Hunter, the kid didn't seem to notice.

'Hello,' Hunter said. His voice was calm and warm, but loud enough.

No reply.

Hunter gave it a moment. 'Do you mind if I step a little closer? It makes it easier to talk.'

'I'd rather you didn't.' The left side of the kid's mouth barely moved. Hunter guessed that the cut that had produced the large scar he could see traversing the kid's lips had cut through nerves and muscles, paralyzing part of his mouth, maybe even part of his face. The kid's voice was in contrast strong, determined.

'That's fine,' Hunter said, lifting both hands in a 'no problem' gesture. 'I'll stay right here.' A very short pause. 'My name is Robert.'

Nothing.

'Could I ask yours?'

A few silent seconds went by before the kid replied. 'Brandon.' He hesitated for a quick moment. 'Or you can call me *freakshow, slashface, scars-r-us*, or make up one of your own. Everyone does.'

Hunter felt a disconcerting sadness drown his heart. He slightly tilted his head to one side and tried to sound upbeat. 'Well, a lot of people call me idiot, imbecile, or my personal favorite – dumbass. You can use any of those if you like.'

Brandon didn't reply. Didn't smile. He simply looked back into the distant darkness.

Hunter took a step closer. 'Brandon,' he called. 'Look, I was just going to get some pizza. What do you say you come with me? I'm buying. We can talk if you want, and you can tell me what's going through your head right now. I'm a *great* listener. Actually, if there were a world listening championship, I'd walk it.'

Brandon looked back at him, and for the first time Hunter could clearly see his eyes.

Hunter knew that about seventy-five percent of all suicide attempts in the USA were preventable by the most simple of actions – listening and being a friend. One argued that most attempts are, in fact, a cry for help. In truth, those people didn't really want to commit suicide any more than the next person along, but at that particular moment in their lives they are experiencing a great deal of emotional and psychological pain. They might be feeling rejected, misunderstood, neglected, depressed, alone, abused, forgotten, scared or any combination of very strong sentiments, none of them good. The emptiness they felt inside grew to such an extent that they reached a point where they believed that they had no other alternative, no other way out. Unfortunately that usually happened because they were left alone with their dark thoughts for too long. They had no one to talk to, and no one was prepared to listen when they did. That made them feel unimportant, uncared for, unappreciated and insignificant to everyone. Most of the time they genuinely wanted someone to help them, but they just didn't really know how to ask for it. Nevertheless, if help were offered, they'd grab at it with both hands. They just needed someone to be there, someone who could show them that they mattered.

As Hunter locked eyes with Brandon, his heart seemed to stutter. Hunter saw none of that inside the kid's eyes. What he saw was extreme sadness, and total and utter determination. Brandon wasn't looking for help anymore. He was way beyond that. His decision had been made, and nothing and no one would change his mind. He had only one thing burning inside his eyes, and Hunter felt at that moment that not even God would be able to dissuade him.

No more sugar coating.

'Brandon, listen to me.' Hunter took another tentative step toward him. 'You don't want to do this. I promise you there's a better solution for whatever it is that made you believe that this is the only way out. Trust me, I've been there. I've been as close as you are right now . . . more than once. Give me a chance to talk to you. Give me a chance to show you that there are better choices than this.'

'Choices?'

If Brandon's eyes were laser beams, Hunter would've been dead.

Hunter nodded, and then said the words he would regret forever.

'We always have a choice, and right now you don't want to make the wrong one. Trust me on this.'

Brandon peeked at the distant darkness again. Only this time it wasn't darkness. Two headlights had appeared, coming fast toward them. Brandon's demeanor changed slightly – relieved of something that had been worrying him.

Hunter's eyes checked the headlights for a fraction of a second, and then he understood what Brandon had been waiting for. The oncoming train should've been passing under the viaduct at around 01:21 a.m. But a short delay caused by a late driver meant that it would now be at the bridge at 01:23 a.m. – *0123*.

Hunter tensed.

Brandon chuckled. 'People always try to feed others this bullshit about everyone always having a choice.' He put on a silly, childlike voice. '*We are in control of our lives, because no matter what, we always have a choice.*'

'Well,' Hunter said. 'You have that choice right now.' He checked the headlights again. They were almost at the bridge. 'Please, Brandon, don't make the wrong one. Come down from there and let's talk about this. I promise you there's a better solution.'

'Really?' Brandon was sounding angry now. 'We always have a choice, do we? What about the choices that other people make that end up completely changing your life, not theirs. Where is our choice there, then?' Brandon paused and swallowed hard as tears came to his eyes. 'He chose to run that red light, not me. He chose to be drunk and high that night, not me. He chose to not give a shit about what could happen, not me. He chose to be speeding like a maniac, not me.' Brandon wiped the tears from his face.

'His choices changed my entire life. They changed my entire future. They changed who I was. Things I knew I could accomplish, I physically can't anymore. Because of his choices, I have to face the world looking like this . . . for the rest of my life.' He punctuated the last four words with hand stabs toward his face.

The train was upon the bridge.

'His choices . . .' Brandon said, this time with no emotion in his voice whatsoever, 'led me to mine.'

Time was over.

Hunter saw Brandon's feet leave the concrete ledge and step onto nothing at all.

'NO,' Hunter yelled, taking a step forward and throwing himself at the kid, stretching his body, reaching with everything he had. His fingers brushed against Brandon's left shoulder as gravity did its job, dragging the kid's body faster and faster toward the train tracks tens of feet beneath them. Hunter closed his fingers fast and with all the strength he could muster, but all he managed was to pinch a tiny portion of the fabric on Brandon's shirt.

Hunter almost had him, but he didn't get there fast enough.

Brandon's body escaped Hunter's grasp and plunged downward like a rock.

The next sound Hunter heard was that of Brandon's body being disintegrated as it met the oncoming train.

The train number shown at the front of the engine car was 678.

Ninety-Eight

The briefing room had been absolutely quiet throughout Hunter's accounts, and the stunned silence persisted for a few seconds afterward. Everything now starting to slot into place – SSV, 678, 0123.

'I remember you telling me about it,' Garcia eventually said, surprise still showing on his face.

Captain Blake nodded. So did she.

'So the phone call to you at the beginning of all this,' she said. 'It wasn't by chance or because of your reputation, as we once thought.'

'No,' Hunter agreed. 'It was because I was the one on the bridge. Because I wasn't fast enough. And because I was the one who failed to dissuade Brandon from jumping.'

'But how do our three victims fit into this?' Garcia asked.

Hunter nodded, pressing the button on the clicker again. The image on the projection screen was substituted by three low-quality photographs. There was no doubt that the pictures showed the Sixth Street Viaduct on that fateful night. They were slightly out of focus and a little grainy, but on all three of them, though his face was obscured by shadows, everyone could clearly see Brandon Fisher standing on the concrete ledge at the west end of the bridge. In the second and third photographs, Hunter was easy to identify. He was also on the bridge, standing just a few feet away from Brandon, bathed by the yellowish light that came from a bridge lamppost. His demeanor showed signs of tension.

'These pictures were taken by the passerby who called 911 that night, using a cellphone camera,' Hunter clarified. 'As we all know, central dispatch general police radio calls are usually scanned by crime reporters looking for a scoop. The crime desk at the *LA Times* was scanning that night. I'm not sure if the passerby was persuaded to, or if he sold them of his own accord, but the pictures he captured on the bridge ended up with the *LA Times* crime reporter who came to the scene.'

Hunter paused and pressed the clicker button again. A new portrait photograph took over the screen. One that was now very familiar to Hunter, Garcia, Captain Blake and Michelle Kelly.

'The name of the passerby who made the call and took the pictures,' Hunter said, looking at the portrait. 'Kevin Lee Parker. Our first victim.'

Garcia filled his cheeks with air and blew it out slowly. 'Let me guess. Christina Stevenson, the killer's second victim, was the *LA Times* reporter who showed up to cover the story.'

'The one and the same,' Hunter confirmed. 'She was with the crime desk back then. She not only used the three photographs taken by Kevin Lee Parker that night but she also added this picture to her article, obviously looking for the "shocking" factor.'

Another click.

The same close-up photograph of Brandon Fisher's scarred face Hunter had shown them just minutes before, taken about twelve months after his accident, returned to the screen.

'Shit!' Michelle said. 'She exposed the kid's face and with it his entire internal struggle to *everyone*.'

Hunter nodded. 'Christina's article made sure that Brandon's injuries became public domain. Now anyone could pull pitiful, shocked or disgusted faces. Anyone could make comments, jokes or whatever about the "disfigured" kid who jumped from the bridge.' Hunter took a moment and had a sip of water. 'Maybe because Christina was in a hurry to finish the article, which came out a day after Brandon's suicide, it would be fair to say that her efforts into researching the story properly weren't her best.'

A new picture took over the projection screen – Christina Stevenson's article.

'I got this from her editor at the *LA Times* late last night,' Hunter said.

'I'll be damned,' Captain Blake exclaimed, before reading the title of the article out loud. '*The Devil Inside*.'

'What the killer left us on the glass door inside Christina Stevenson's bedroom,' Hunter reminded everyone, 'was the title of the article she wrote. The piece goes on to suggest that a bullied, rejected, cast-aside and troubled Brandon Fisher was unable to cope with *the devil inside* him. The devil of his injuries. A devil that had slowly but surely worked its way through Brandon's sanity, finally driving him to suicide.' Hunter paused for a beat. 'Christina also used words such as—' he pointed them out as he spoke '—"*another* teenager's suicide", which implies triviality, something unimportant, something that happens too often for anyone to really care. And "*disturbing* the quiet night", which suggests Brandon's death was nothing more than a simple burden that the city of Los Angeles could do without, like pickpockets or muggers.

'Unfortunately,' Hunter added, 'Christina's poor choice of words trivialized what happened that night. Just another sad story to be forgotten seconds after it's been read.'

No comment was made, so Hunter proceeded.

'And then we have this.'

One more click and once again the images on the screen changed, but this time they weren't static. They weren't pictures. They had a video.

The surprised expression was uniform across everyone's face.

The video showed the final fifteen seconds of Brandon's life. He was standing on the ledge facing south. Hunter was standing a few feet from him, his back to the camera. Brandon was saying something to Hunter the camera's microphone wasn't able to pick up. All they could hear was the loud sound of a train approaching. Then it all happened very fast. Brandon turned around quickly, but didn't jump as such. He simply stepped away from the ledge and onto thin air, as if stepping into a room, or out of a house. Gravity did the rest. At that exact moment, Hunter sprang to life, taking a step forward and launching himself in Brandon's direction, stretching his body like Superman in mid-flight. Then the camera panned fast downward, just quick enough to catch the moment of impact as the train rushed past beneath the bridge and struck the kid's small body with all its force.

The room was filled with curse words and anxious murmurs. Hunter saw everyone in the room cringe, including the SWAT captain.

Hunter paused the footage.

'This was captured by the driver of the next vehicle that came along onto the bridge, several seconds after I blocked the traffic. He so happened to have a camcorder with him. His name ...'

Click.

A new portrait photograph appeared on the screen. The same one Hunter and Garcia had on the pictures board inside their office.

'Ethan Walsh,' Hunter said. 'The killer's third victim.'

A few seconds of stunned silence.

'So that explains why the killer left us a camcorder in the park's trashcan right after Ethan Walsh's death,' Garcia said. 'Because he used one to capture Brandon's suicide that night.'

'Precisely,' Hunter agreed. 'Mr. Walsh was already facing serious financial problems then. He had put everything he had into his company, and had nothing left. I guess that Ethan Walsh saw an opportunity to maybe make some cash, because he sold his footage to Christina Stevenson at the *LA Times*, and that's why he had her number in his phone book. But she wasn't the only one. Mr. Walsh also sold his footage to a cable TV show called *A Mystery in 60 Minutes*. He probably tried others, but no major network would buy it because they just wouldn't show a teenager's suicide video on national television. The cable TV station, on the other hand, couldn't care less and used the footage a few days later as part of a special *Teenage Suicide* program. That particular cable TV station is only available in *California*. So no one else outside this state was able to watch it.'

Hunter returned to the podium.

'The problem is that the tragedy of a suicide never ends there,' he explained. 'Family and loved ones are left to deal not only with the loss of someone dear, but with the inevitable depression and psychological guilt that take over. *How come they didn't see it coming? Could they have done more?* But what really eats them inside is knowing that all that would've taken to save them was a listening ear, maybe a few comforting words and the reassurance that they weren't alone, that they mattered, that they were loved.'

No one said a word.

'But with today's technology and the Internet, that internal guilt and pain can be increased exponentially,' Hunter added. 'For some reason that I can't explain, Ethan Walsh wasn't content with just selling his video to Christina Stevenson at the *LA Times* and the cable TV channel. Using the Internet handle, DarkXX1000, he uploaded the footage to a specialized, shock-video website called *thiscrazyworld. com*. From then on it became a free-for-all, and the worst pain a family could endure became public domain, a joke, just a video snippet for millions of people to watch and laugh at, gossip about, comment on and criticize. And people did.'

Hunter quickly clicked through a few slides of screen prints showing pages and pages of comments that had been placed on the website. A few showed support, but most of them were terribly offensive.

'So who exactly are we after, then?' the SWAT captain asked.

'I was just getting to that,' Hunter said.

Click.

Ninety-Nine

The new photograph that took over the screen was of a woman who was probably in her forties but looked at least ten years older. She had straight auburn hair and a milky-white complexion. Not actually bad looking, except for a pair of deeply recessed eyes that gave her a slightly cadaverous appearance.

'Brandon Fisher didn't come from a large family,' Hunter explained. 'In fact, he was the only child of Graham and Margaret Fisher. His mother—' he indicated the photograph on the screen '—was a frail woman, who had developed multiple sclerosis just a few months after giving birth to Brandon. His death hit her hard. The shock-video website where Brandon's suicide footage appeared, coupled with the devastating comments made online, hit her even harder. Her son, together with all his pain and struggle, were now exposed to the entire world, ready to be judged by anyone with an Internet connection. She was unable to sleep and started rejecting food. Soon she developed anorexia nervosa, and quickly became addicted to sedatives, among other drugs. She wouldn't leave the house and was subsequently also diagnosed with major depression and severe anxiety disorder, all brought on by her son's suicide and how abusive some people remained, even after his death.'

Hunter moved around to the front of the podium before continuing.

'Her already delicate health deteriorated faster than was predicted based on her long-term illness. About ten months after Brandon's suicide, due to how little she ate, she had to start being fed via an IV drip. She passed away twelve months ago.'

The room remained quiet.

'And that brings us to Brandon's father, Graham Fisher,' Hunter said, moving on. 'At the time of his son's suicide, Mr. Fisher was a professor at UCLA. He taught advanced programming as part of the university's computer science degree. He holds a PhD in Engineering and Computer Science from Harvard University. One of his many areas of expertise is in Internet security. In the past he has even worked as a consultant for the US government.

'Not surprisingly, Mr. Fisher also took his son's suicide very badly, and with his wife's health and sanity fading so quickly he saw no alternative but to quit his job. He then dedicated all his time and effort to taking care of her. She was all the family he had left. Her death, together with Brandon's suicide, was much more than his psyche could withstand. My guess is that after Margaret Fisher's death, Graham found himself alone, hurt and very, very angry. Someone in that state of mind armed with his sort of intelligence and enough time on his hands would contemplate anything.'

More hushed murmurs.

'He methodically made a list of all the people he considered *guilty*,' Hunter continued, 'not for his son's death but for making a mockery of it. For exposing Brandon's most intimate psychological and emotional pain to everyone. For transforming his and his wife's personal loss into a side-show attraction ... a public entertainment. And certainly for contributing to the rapid decline in Margaret's health.' Hunter paused for breath. 'After identifying the parties, which I'm sure took some finding, he busied himself engineering and developing his torture and murder devices, before seeking out every name on his kill list, one by one. The problem we have is that there's no way we can know how many names are on that list. As we all know, three are already dead.'

'Do we have his picture?' the SWAT captain asked.

Hunter nodded and pressed the clicker button.

The photograph now showing on the screen was of an attractive man in his early fifties. His robust face suggested both trustworthiness and self-confidence. He had high cheekbones, a prominent brow and a strong chin with a subtle cleft. His light brown hair was worn just off the shoulders, pleasantly tousled. He looked to be broadly built, with sturdy muscles and wide shoulders.

'No fucking way.' Everyone in the room heard Garcia cough the words.

'Something wrong, Carlos?'

'Yeah,' Garcia nodded slowly. 'I know him.'

One Hundred

The man was putting the final touches to his latest torture and murder device. He had spent considerably more time developing this particular apparatus than the previous three, but his work had paid off. He considered this one to be a work of art – ingenious and evil in equal measures. Once the mechanics of it had started working, no one could stop it, not even himself. Yes, this device was something special. Something that would undoubtedly teach 'that bitch' an unforgettable lesson.

'That bitch' was sitting at the far end of the large open-plan room he was in, still tied up to the same heavy chair. He had to sedate her again, though. Her crying was driving him insane. But her time was coming.

The man had to admit that there was a tiny part somewhere inside of him that wished that she had taken his offer and used the garden scissors to butcher her own hand. He would really have let her go if she had done it. But the truth was he knew that there were very few people on this earth who were mentally and emotionally strong enough. Very few people on this earth who were capable of that sort of self-mutilation, even if it was to save their own life. And 'that bitch' wasn't one of them.

No matter, he thought. What he had in store for her was infinitely better than chopping her fingers off, and it would produce another fantastic Internet spectacle, of that he was sure. That thought brought a grin to his face.

He tightened up the last screw, connecting his device to the electricity supply. It was time to test it.

The man got up from the chair he'd been sitting on for the past two hours, removed his working glasses and gently rubbed his gritty eyes with his thumb and forefinger for a long while. The sensation was soothing. He drank a glass of iced water before reaching inside the groceries bag he had with him, retrieving a large watermelon he had bought that morning.

He'd smiled when the short and round lady at the grocery store told him that the two particular watermelons he was looking at weren't ripe enough yet.

'It'll be at least three days before those are good enough to eat,' the groceries lady had said. 'I have better ones right here, look. Nice and juicy, perfectly ripe, good for today.'

The man simply shook his head. 'These ones will do fine. It's the size I'm more interested in.'

Approaching his newly finished gadget, the man placed the large fruit on the correct spot before grabbing the remote control from the worktable. He stood back several paces, took a deep breath, readied his stopwatch and finally clicked the red button on the control.

A muffled mechanical grinding noise came from the device, as the many sprockets started turning, bringing his new monstrous creation to life.

The man watched transfixed, as every part worked just as he had designed, but there was one tiny problem. It all happened way too fast. The watermelon lasted exactly 39.8 seconds. True, the human body was much more resistant than any watermelon, but, still, he wanted this to drag on for as long as possible. He wanted his Internet audience to enjoy it, be disgusted and terrified by it, feel pity or anger, laugh at it, comment on it, joke and gossip about it, whatever, but most of all he wanted 'that bitch' to suffer.

He cleaned the device from the mess the watermelon had made and spent the next forty-five minutes tightening and loosening screws, adjusting the tension on different joints and springs, and calibrating pressured parts until he was satisfied. When he figured he had done enough, he reached for the second watermelon from his groceries bag and ran his device test again.

When, at the end of it, he clicked his stopwatch and checked the time, he smiled.

'Perfect.'

One Hundred and One

For a quick instant it felt as if Garcia's words were too surreal to make any sense.

'What?' Hunter and Captain Blake asked him at the exact same time.

'What do you mean – *you know him*?' Michelle tagged.

Garcia's eyes were still fixed on Graham Fisher's photograph that was being projected onto the screen at the front of the room.

'I mean.' He barely mumbled the words, clearly running something over inside his head. 'I know I've seen him before, but I just can't remember where.'

Hunter looked back at the screen. 'You've seen this face before?'

Garcia nodded slowly. 'I'm positive I have.'

'Recently?'

Another slow nod.

A brief tense moment of hesitation went by.

'Maybe it was at one of the crime scenes?' a SWAT agent suggested. 'As we all know, there are always curious people hanging around at the edge of the perimeter. Some killers love to hang back, mingle with the crowd and watch the police work. Some of them get off on that kind of shit.'

Garcia closed his eyes, urging the images to come back to him. What he got was a roller coaster of mental pictures shuffled out of order. The first memory that flashed at him was of his wife, Anna, and her friend, Patricia, in Tujunga Village, just after the killer had privately broadcast the two of them. Garcia tried to remember all the faces he'd seen that day – maybe in the coffee shop where Anna had been waiting for them, or across the road, or maybe even looking out through a shop window.

Nothing.

Tujunga Village wasn't where he had seen Graham Fisher before.

Garcia then mentally revisited the alleyway in Mission Hills where the body of Kevin Lee Parker, the killer's first victim, had been found. It had been before dawn, in a hidden-away back street. There were no curious onlookers hanging around that morning. No one except the homeless man who had found the body. Garcia quickly discarded those images as well and moved on.

Next came City Hall Park and the discovery of the camcorder. He and Hunter knew the killer was close by that day. He would've wanted to watch the police's reaction to his little joke. Garcia tried his best to remember everyone he saw around the park.

Rush hour – way too many people.

He pushed himself, concentrating harder. Graham Fisher's face wasn't among the ones he could remember.

The second dump scene came next – Dewey Street in Santa Monica. Christina Stevenson's body had been left by a dumpster in the small parking lot at the back of a two-story office building. Garcia could clearly recall a crowd hanging around the perimeter. Then he remembered the man who had caught his eye that day – tall, lean and spare, dressed in a black hooded sweatshirt and dark blue jeans. Garcia tried to picture his face, and that was when all the memories, except one, vanished from his mind and he finally remembered.

'Oh my God!' he whispered, his eyes reopening and instantly widening. 'The doctor.'

'What?' Hunter queried. 'What doctor?'

'The one in the park,' Garcia replied, almost numbed by the memory. 'I told you about it.' He addressed Hunter, before turning and looking at Captain Blake and Michelle. 'Anna and I went for a run in the park close to our apartment a couple of weeks ago, on a Sunday morning,' he explained. 'It was my day off. We were on our last lap of the park when some guy, who was riding a bike, had a heart attack right there and then. He was just behind us. Despite a bunch of people gathering around to have a look at what was happening, I was the only one who rushed to help. At least at first. I was just about to start CPR when this other guy turned up, weaving his way through the crowd. He'd also been jogging in the park that morning. I know because I saw him. Well, he *said* he was a doctor and took complete control of the situation until the paramedics got there. I helped him administer CPR. He wasn't kidding, or faking it. He *really* tried to save that man's life.'

'And that guy was Graham Fisher?' the captain asked.

Garcia nodded again, looking back at the photograph on the screen. 'It was him. No doubt about it.'

A new uncomfortable silence descended onto the room.

'Shit,' Garcia said. 'He was stalking Anna and me because he was already planning on going after her. That incident happened only a couple of days before he pulled that sick stunt of broadcasting Anna and her friend as they were out shopping.' Anger coated Garcia's words now. 'Fuck! I talked to him. I stood next to him. He shook my hand . . . He shook Anna's hand . . .'

'Wow, the motherfucker's got balls, I'll give him that,' a tall and muscular SWAT agent said.

'What are you, a fucking fan now, Luke? The guy is a psycho,' another SWAT agent shot back. This one was a little shorter but just as muscular.

New murmurs erupted.

'OK,' Hunter said loudly, quieting everyone down again. 'Graham Fisher still lives in the same house he shared with his wife and son in Boyle Heights. The address and the house schematics are all inside the folders on your desks. And we already have a warrant for his arrest. So how about we go take this sonofabitch down?'

One Hundred and Two

The police convoy was made up of two black SWAT SUVs, three unmarked police cars and two black and white units. Four SWAT agents occupied each of the SUVs. Hunter, Garcia and Captain Blake were in the first unmarked car, heading the convoy. Michelle Kelly was in the vehicle just behind them, together with two LAPD SIS agents. Three more SIS agents occupied the third unmarked car. The two black and white units were there just as a backup precaution.

The LAPD Special Investigation Section (SIS) was an Elite Tactical Surveillance squad that has existed for more than forty years, despite efforts from various human-rights and political groups to shut it down. Their kill rate was higher than that of any other unit in the department, including SWAT. SIS teams were mainly used to stealthily watch apex predators – individuals suspected of violent crimes who would not cease until caught in the act. Masters of surveillance, SIS officers waited to observe a suspect committing new crimes before moving in to make arrests. Lethal force was often used, and they were all expert marksmen.

The address they had took them to a small hilly street in the west quadrant of Boyle Heights, a working-class neighborhood just east of downtown Los Angeles.

All the houses were set back from the street but without any foliage. The street was devoid of trees. It was an unusually uninviting place. In the summer the heat probably turned the street into a relentlessly dusty place, where tensions and angers multiplied with the same intensity that bacteria did.

Graham Fisher's house, number 21, was tucked away right at the top of the hilly street. The house itself was much the same as all the others in that road, a medium-sized, two-story, three-bedroom home, with air conditioners hanging from a couple of windows. Three narrow steps led up to the concrete front porch. The house was painted a faded blue, with the number 21 hand-painted in white near the front door. All the windows were shut. All the curtains were drawn. All appeared quiet. The front yard had a neglected look to it, streaks of dirt sidling up against grass choked with weeds. A white, thigh-high steel fence circled the property. The back alleyway that serviced the entire street wasn't wide enough for any of the vehicles to drive down. The convoy parked at the bottom of the road.

'OK, listen up,' the SWAT captain said in an authoritative voice as everyone gathered by the two SUVs. 'Alpha team – Morris, Luke and myself – will blast in through the front door. We'll clear the living room, the dining room and the downstairs washroom, here.'

As he spoke he indicated the locations on the house schematics that he had spread open over the hood of one of the cars.

'Beta team – Johnson, Davis and Lewis – will come in through the back door that leads directly into the kitchen. They will clear that room first before moving on upstairs, where they will clear both bathrooms and all three bedrooms. Gamma team – Lopez and Turkowski – will follow Alpha team inside through the front door and then proceed to the basement.' He paused and looked up at Captain Blake. 'SIS agents and HSS detectives will *only* enter the house once *we* have radioed in that we're all clear inside. Is that understood?' He made harsh and determined eye contact with everyone who wasn't part of the SWAT team, hammering his point through.

'Roger that,' Hunter, Garcia and the SIS agents replied back.

The SWAT captain turned and faced his team.

'OK, badasses. We have everything in our favor this morning. This sick puppy doesn't know we're coming for him today. So let's hit the house fast and hard and give him the surprise of his sorry-ass life. We all know he's a psycho, but not the gun-slinging kind of psycho. So even though he might have a firearm in the house, chances are it won't be close at hand. Nevertheless, *watch your six*. No mistakes. No hesitations. This guy is as clever as they come, full of fucking surprises, and you all know that the only surprises I like are the ones we spring up on them. As soon as a room is cleared, radio it on. If anyone spots the target, arrest the fucker. Lethal force *only*, and I repeat, *only* if called for. No happy triggering today. Are we all clear?'

'Clear, Captain,' all seven SWAT agents replied in unison.

'OK, badasses, let's lock and load. I want this whole thing wrapped up in sixty seconds or less. Take positions, and let's bring Judgment Day to this piece of shit.'

Twenty seconds later the SWAT captain heard the first status update through his earpiece.

'*Beta team is in position. Ready to blast some doors, Cap.*'

Beta team was the only team traveling down the back alley. Alpha and Gamma teams were coming in through the front door.

To reduce the chance of pre-warning the subject, a SWAT agent slowly drove one of the SUVs up the hilly street. The remaining agents, forming teams Alpha and Gamma, crouch-ran together with the vehicle, hiding on the other side of it.

'Roger that,' the SWAT captain replied via his helmet microphone. 'We'll be in position in less than ten.'

'*Roger that, Captain.*'

'OK, let's move,' the captain ordered teams Alpha and Gamma.

They moved fast and stealthily. The captain took point while the other agents assumed standard 2x2 cover formation. They all cleared the steel fence by jumping it instead of going for the gate with rusty hinges – no noise, no warning.

At the porch the captain updated the teams' status.

'Alpha and Gamma are in position.'

'*Roger that, Cap,*' Davis from Beta team replied.

Agent Morris, Captain Fallon's second in command, quickly slid a small fiber-optic tube under the front door. The tube was a fiberscope, connected to a three-inch screen monitor.

Davis did the same at the back door.

There was no movement coming from anywhere inside.

'*Kitchen is dead,*' Davis transmitted. '*No one here.*'

'Negative for movement at the front room too,' Morris confirmed.

'*We've got a very sturdy lock back here, Captain,*' Davis reported. '*We'll need to blast the whole thing off with the breaching shotgun.*'

The captain quickly checked the lock and the hinges on the front door. So did Morris, who nodded back at Captain Fallon, agreeing with Beta team's assessment.

A breaching shotgun is nothing more than a regular shotgun loaded with breaching rounds, also called 'TESAR' or disintegrators. These are shotgun shells specially designed to destroy door deadbolts, locks and hinges without risking injury or lives by ricocheting or by flying on at lethal speed once they get through the door. The rounds are frangible, made of a dense, sintered material, most commonly metal powder, in a binder, such as wax. The round will destroy a lock or hinge and then immediately disperse. Jokingly, SWAT agents have nicknamed these rounds 'master keys' and their use is referred to as 'Avon Calling'.

'*Roger that and agreed,*' the SWAT captain replied, signaling Luke, one of the agents, who was carrying a breaching shotgun.

Luke moved forward, readying the weapon. From a distance of about six inches, he aimed it at the door's top hinge. A very subtle head nod told Captain Fallon that he was ready.

'OK, Beta,' the captain said into the microphone. 'Avon Call on my three count . . . three . . . two . . . one . . .'

BOOM.

One Hundred and Three

The shots exploded through the otherwise quiet morning, echoing off the other houses. At the front door, Luke had blasted off two hinges and the deadbolt lock in less than three seconds. As soon as the last shot was fired, Captain Fallon kicked the door hard, throwing it flying into the living room.

At the rear of the house, Johnson had also blasted the hinges and the deadbolt lock off the door in just as many seconds. Davis was the one who kicked the door in.

All eight SWAT agents were carrying Heckler & Koch MP5 submachine guns – a 9mm compact weapon exceptionally powerful and accurate in close-quarters combat. All eight of them had been expertly trained for such situations.

Still crouch-running, all three teams moved forward into the house with immense agility, their MP5s' red laser target sights bouncing around the room like disco lights.

The front door led directly into a small, rectangular-shaped living room. With the curtains shut, all the light came from the now wide-open door. Plumes of smoke and dust danced in the air, spotlighted by uneven streaks of sunlight.

In a three-man wedge-shaped assault formation, Alpha team stormed into the living room, checking every corner and possible hiding place with incredible speed and accuracy. There were two armchairs, a couch, a television on a wooden module and a low coffee table. The walls were bare, save for a single, stiffly posed wedding photo.

It took Alpha team four seconds flat to take control of the room.

'Living room is clear,' Captain Fallon announced through his microphone before crossing the room and exiting it through the door at the other side.

Gamma team simply followed them in.

At the rear of the house, Beta team took no time to clear the small kitchen, made even smaller by the square wooden table pushed up against the east wall.

'*Kitchen is clear,*' agent Davis called through his mike.

He and the two other agents in Beta team proceeded fast across the kitchen and through its door, which took them to a hallway, leading to the front of the house and the stairs that would give them access to the second floor of the property. As they reached the top of the staircase, Alpha team came through the door at the opposite end of that same hallway.

Alpha team immediately turned left into the dining room. The door was already open. This room was smaller than the living room, and most of it was taken by a square, four-seat, glass and steel dining table and two large bookshelves. More bare walls. The room was empty, and there was no place for someone as tall and as well built as Graham Fisher to hide.

'Dining room is clear,' the captain announced.

Morris, one of the two other agents in Alpha team, had already kicked open the door to the downstairs washroom, smashing it against the white-tiled wall. Two of the tiles cracked with the impact. The room was empty.

'Downstairs washroom is clear,' he called.

The staircase had taken Beta team onto a twenty-three-foot-long hallway upstairs. There were five doors – two on the right, two on the left and one at the far end of the corridor. From the house schematics, all three agents knew that the first door on the right gave them access to a small storage room. That door was closed. The second door on the right would lead them into the first of the three bedrooms, a medium-sized one, probably the one that used to belong to Brandon Fisher. That door was also closed. The first door on the left was the first bathroom. That door was open. The second door on the left would take them into a smaller bedroom. Door closed. The one at the far end would lead them into the master bedroom, inside which they would find the second bathroom. That final door was also open.

The team moved lightning fast, clearing the first room on the left – the bathroom – and the first room on the right – the small storage room – in two seconds. Both empty.

While Davis and Lewis pushed open the second door on the left side of the corridor, the one that led into the smallest of the three bedrooms, Johnson held fast on the hallway, covering their backs.

The room had been transformed into a simple study. It was a barren space – a pressed wood desk with a computer and a printer, a black-leather desk chair, a crammed bookcase and a beige-metal filing cabinet, nothing else. The room was empty.

'Bedroom one clear.'

Both agents exited the study and moved on to the second room on the right – bedroom number two. Johnson tried the door – locked. The lock didn't look too strong.

'Breach it,' Johnson said, stepping back.

Launching his body forward, Lewis rammed the heel of his boot against the door lock. That was all that was needed. The door slammed back hard, splintering the frame. The room was dark and smelled of age and disuse.

Johnson immediately reached for the light switch. As the light came on, he and Lewis entered the room, leaving Davis to cover their backs this time.

They'd been right. This was the room that had belonged to Brandon Fisher, and it looked like not a single thing had been touched since his suicide. The walls were covered with posters of music groups, cars, sport stars and girls in tiny bikinis. There was a large chest of drawers with a black stereo on it to the right of the door. Next to it, a two-door wardrobe. An old and scratched desk with a laptop computer and a printer was positioned by the window. A nicely made up twin bed had its headboard pushed up against one of the walls. Everything was covered by a thick layer of dust, as if the room hadn't been entered in years.

The agents quickly checked everywhere, including the wardrobe.

No one.

'Second bedroom is clear,' Johnson radioed it on.

From there Beta team moved with purpose toward the end of the corridor and the last bedroom. This one was much larger than the previous two, with a king bed, an ottoman, a leather armchair in one corner, an old-fashioned wooden dresser with a rectangular mirror by the window and a sliding-door wardrobe taking the whole of the west wall. There was a sweaty smell lingering in the air, as if the room hadn't been cleaned and the bedding hadn't been washed in months.

They checked every corner, under the bed and inside the wardrobe.

No one.

The en suite bathroom door was ajar, and it was hastily kicked fully open by agent Davis.

The bathroom was empty.

They had cleared the whole second floor of the house in less than twenty-two seconds.

'We're all clear up here, Captain,' Davis called down. 'The psycho ain't upstairs.'

One Hundred and Four

Team Gamma had followed team Alpha into the house, crossed the living room, and as team Alpha turned left into the dining room once they reached the corridor downstairs, team Gamma veered right. The door that led down into the basement was locked with a military-grade padlock.

'We need to blast the basement door open,' agent Turkowski said into his mike, alerting the other teams that a loud blast was coming.

'I'm on it,' agent Lopez, the second half of Gamma team, replied, readying the breaching shotgun he had strapped to his back.

Turkowski took a step back and held fast. 'Do it.'

BOOM.

The loud blast sent shock waves throughout the house.

The padlock disintegrated.

Turkowski kicked the door open, and they were immediately slapped across the face by a breath of musty, stale-smelling air. It had a fetid and sickly quality to it, aged and filthy, charred by the daily Californian heat. Despite the obnoxious odor, neither agent even blinked.

Wide wooden steps led down to the pitch-black basement.

'Lights, lights,' Turkowski called without lowering his MP5, his laser sight searching for a target at the bottom of the stairs, but finding nothing.

'I've got it,' Lopez replied, reaching for the thin light-switch cord that hung from the ceiling.

The light was terribly weak.

Crude brick walls ran against both sides of the staircase, creating an oppressing and claustrophobic down-running corridor.

'I've got a real bad feeling about this,' Turkowski said, as he and Lopez quickly took the stairs down in cover formation.

The steps were sturdy, but almost every one of them creaked under the strain of their weight. They cleared the last step and entered the dimly lit, wide-open basement room, their breathing labored, their laser sights doing a crazy crisscross dance everywhere, looking for the slightest sign of a threat, before finally homing in on the west end of the hall.

'Holy shit!' Lopez breathed out before radioing in. 'Basement is clear. Psycho ain't down here either.' He paused for a gulp of putrid air. 'But I guess you're going to want to see this, Captain. And so will the homicide detectives.'

One Hundred and Five

Graham Fisher waited patiently for the red light to turn green before turning right onto East 4th Street in Boyle Heights. The traffic was as slow as it'd always been at that time in the morning, trickling through like water through a funnel. A few seconds later he hung a left onto South St Louis Street, and as he did so he tensed. About seventy-five yards ahead, just at the bottom of the hilly street he lived on, he could see a cluster of seven vehicles hastily parked; two of them were LAPD black and white cruisers. Gathered in a tight group by the first vehicle was a crowd of law-enforcement agents.

Graham immediately reduced his speed, but not in a panicky way, and signaled a left turn onto the next street along. He calmly parked by the first house on the right before reaching inside his glove compartment for his sunglasses. Pushing his baseball cap low over his forehead, he exited his car and leisurely walked up to the top of the road, where a white van was parked. Using the van for cover, he peeked at the cluster of vehicles and at the tightly gathered crowd of agents at the bottom of his street.

The first person he recognized was Detective Robert Hunter. The second was Detective Carlos Garcia. Together with them Graham saw an eight-men-strong SWAT team, two females, four other intimidating-looking males and four uniformed police officers. Twenty people in total. They all looked to be heavily armed. They were clearly getting ready for a surprise assault, and Graham had no doubt which house they'd be storming into in the next few seconds.

Graham knew that this day was coming. In fact, he was expecting it. He just wasn't expecting it so soon, at least not before he was done.

With his eyes still fixed on the group, Graham's mind started going over his plan once again. It was still perfect, he decided. The only difference was that he now needed to speed things up, move things forward a little, and improvise, at least a little bit. But that would be no problem. He knew exactly what to do.

As he returned to his car, Graham broke into a slightly manic giggle, a high-pitched sound that joined nervousness and joy all at once.

'Let's see how prepared you are for what's coming to you, Detective Hunter,' he said to himself, trembling with excitement, before jumping back into his car and driving away.

One Hundred and Six

Hunter, Garcia, Captain Blake and Michelle Kelly all wrinkled their noses at the sickening smell that hit them as they started down the wooden steps that took them to Graham Fisher's basement. None of them could explain the strange feeling they got as they entered the house. As if they were all stepping into a house of horrors, where pain, fear and suffering were as much a part of it as its walls.

As they reached the basement floor, they all stopped dead. It was a large and damp room, surrounded by bare brick walls. There was a single glowing yellowish light bulb encased in a wire screen at the center of the ceiling. Its weak light struggled to illuminate the room, while at the same time casting shadows just about everywhere. The floor was made of concrete, and it was covered in stains, some new, some old and some larger than others.

Pushed up against the east wall was a long wooden worktable. On it, electronic components such as circuit boards, decoder modules, capacitors, potentiometers, microprocessors and oscilloscopes. A few blueprints had been matter-of-factly pushed to one end of the worktable. On the northeast corner of the room they found a large handmade tools cabinet, housing an impressive collection of tools, including several special glass-cutting drills and saws. But not every space or hook was taken. Some of the tools seemed to be missing.

The southeast corner of the room was taken by a smaller worktable with a vise at one end and a multipurpose table saw at the other. Placed next to the table was a large, faded green, chest fridge. But what made the hairs on the back of everyone's neck stand on end was what was at the opposite end of the room, against the west wall – something that all four of them had stared at and tried to analyze for hours on end on their computer screens.

Mounted near the left corner was the glass enclosure the killer had used to soak Kevin Lee Parker into his deadly alkaline bath. The heavy metal chair he'd been tied to was still there, right at the center of the enclosure, bolted to the crude concrete floor. A large gas canister had been placed on either side of the glass cage. They were connected to the two metal pipes sprinkled with holes on the inside of the enclosure via two thick, fire-resistant tubes.

'*Fire or water,*' the killer had said. '*Burned alive or drowned.*'

The images came back to Hunter in a hurricane of memories.

The metal pipes could either fill the enclosure with water or fire. The house's water system was connected to them at the top.

Hunter knew he had been tricked into choosing water that day; nevertheless, Graham Fisher had been prepared to burn his victim alive in case he had misjudged Hunter.

Next to the gas canisters were two fifteen-liter barrels of industrial-grade NaOH – sodium hydroxide. They were also connected to the metal pipes via thick, chemical-resistant tubes.

By the other corner of the west wall, mounted onto a surgical-looking metal table, was the glass coffin the killer had used for Christina Stevenson. As Garcia's eyes settled on it, he shivered and took two steps back, feeling an awkward panic start to gain momentum at the bottom of his stomach. Inside the glass coffin were hundreds of dead tarantula hawks.

Hunter sensed his partner's hesitation and gave him a subtle headshake before whispering, 'They're all dead.'

Still, the sight of it was enough for Garcia's memory to send him back to the day he was stung by four tarantula hawks. The day he almost died.

He took a series of steady deep breaths, fought the shiver that threatened to run down his spine and felt his heartbeat slowly return to normal. But he wasn't the only one feeling uneasy down in that basement.

Two people had been sadistically tortured and murdered in that dark and damp room. The instruments used for all their suffering were still there, stained with their blood, filled with their pain. To everyone, it felt as if the victims' terrified screams and pleas were still echoing around those brick walls. Graham Fisher had created a true torture chamber in his basement.

Just a few feet away from the glass coffin were an old wheelchair and two hospital-standard IV stands. Still hanging from one of their hooks, an old and empty plastic methyl B12 nutrient IV bag. No doubt one of the many different nutrient cocktails Graham had to intravenously feed his wife during her last few months alive.

'The rack isn't here,' Captain Blake said. 'That grotesque thing he used to dismember his third victim. It's not here.'

'He used a different location,' Hunter said. 'This place doesn't have the physical structure for it.' His eyes instinctively circled the room.

'It's certainly big enough,' the SWAT captain offered.

'Yes,' Hunter agreed. 'But the killer had a large and heavy slab of concrete hanging high above his victim, suspended by thick metal chains. He even said that he could control it. He said that he could slowly lower the rock onto his victim's body, adjusting the amount of pressure he was able to deliver, like a vise. He would've needed some very strong and probably large piece of machinery to do that.'

'Some sort of electronically controlled crane or something,' Garcia confirmed. 'No way he would've been able to get something like that down here.'

'So where, then?' Captain Blake asked.

'I'm not sure,' Hunter said. 'We need to check land and property registries to see if Graham Fisher owns any other properties or pieces of land. The problem is, even if he doesn't, he could be renting a large garage or a small warehouse or any other type of building big enough for what he had in mind. If he is, I'm sure he would've paid cash for a short-term lease. Finding him that way can take a long time.'

Captain Blake didn't look impressed.

'But it's now just a matter of time, Captain,' Hunter added. 'The house is lived in. There are freshly washed dishes on the dish rack in the kitchen, and the sponge is still a little damp. He wasn't expecting us here today, so chances are he hasn't taken all the necessary precautions. We now have a whole house to search here, including an office with a computer upstairs. There's got to be something that will give us a clue to where he might be. Meanwhile we need a citywide APB for Graham and his car, a black Chevrolet Silverado. We need to get his picture to the press and the media ASAP. We need his face *everywhere*. Let's close the circle on him. We also need a team of officers to knock on every door on this street and see if anyone knows anything.'

Captain Blake lifted both hands in the air in a surrender gesture. 'You've got a green light on whatever you need.' Her gaze moved from the glass coffin to the glass cage and then back to Hunter. 'Just bring this psycho in.'

She walked back toward the staircase again. The basement was starting to give her the creeps. She needed to get out of there.

Michelle had also moved, but not in the direction of the staircase. She was now at the worktable by the east wall, looking through all the electronic components and blueprints she found. The blueprints were detailed schematics of how both torture devices in that basement had been put together, and how they'd work. The blueprints for the rack used to torture and murder the third victim weren't there, but she found something else.

Something that made her blood run cold.

One Hundred and Seven

'Shit!' Michelle whispered, but down in the basement her whisper reverberated off the walls like a handclap. Everyone turned to face her.

'What have you got?' Hunter asked.

Captain Blake paused just before taking the first step up the stairs.

'Surveillance photographs of the victims,' Michelle replied, showing everyone the first of several photographs from the pile she had discovered. 'Kevin Lee Parker, the first victim,' she said.

The photo showed Kevin coming out of the videogames store he worked at. The killer had used a red marker pen to draw a circle around his face. Michelle put the photo down and reached for another one before announcing, 'Christina Stevenson, the second victim.'

This one showed Christina as she stepped out of her house. A red circle had been also drawn around her face.

'Ethan Walsh, the third victim,' Michelle said, displaying a new photograph to everyone. It showed Ethan having a cigarette outside the restaurant where he worked. Another red circle.

Michelle returned the photograph to the worktable and grabbed the next one from the pile. 'And this, I can only assume, is the next victim on his list.'

The photograph was of an attractive young woman, probably in her late twenties, sitting outside a coffee shop. She had a petite diamond-shaped face, framed by long straight blonde hair. Her bright blue eyes were a little catlike, and complemented her delicate nose, her small mouth and her shapely cheekbones very nicely. The picture was also marked with a red circle around her face. That new photograph seemed to electrify the air inside the room.

'Is there a name?' Hunter asked, quickly moving toward Michelle. Garcia and Captain Blake followed him.

Michelle checked the reverse side of the picture. 'No, nothing.' She handed it to Hunter.

Hunter checked it again before allowing his gaze to move to the worktable. 'Are there any more photographs of her?' he asked Michelle.

'Not of her.'

Something in Michelle's tone of voice made everyone pause for an instant and look at the FBI agent.

'This is the only other photograph I found.' She showed them the last picture she had with her, the one that had made her blood run cold.

Everyone tensed. Time appeared to slow down inside that basement.

The photograph was taken as the subject was crossing a busy road, but this time they didn't need to search for a name. They didn't even need to track the subject down. They were all looking at a photograph of Robert Hunter, with a red circle drawn around his face.

One Hundred and Eight

Garcia and Captain Blake paused mid-breath, their gazes drawn to the picture in Michelle's hands like insects to a blue light. Everyone inside that room seemed to be filled with an odd, disquieting fear, except for Hunter. He simply shook his head, unfazed, taking the picture from Michelle's hands.

'This is not a concern,' he said. 'In fact, it's not even surprising.'

'What do you mean, *it's not a concern*?' Michelle said.

'Because whatever Graham Fisher had planned for me, he'll now have to reconsider, readjust, readapt, because as soon as his picture hits the news, he'll know that he's not a cyber ghost anymore. We now know who he is. He'll know that we've been to his house, to his basement, and that we've found all of this.' He indicated the room and the pictures. 'Which means that he'll also know that now I'm the one doing the hunting.'

'Yeah, but we're talking about a highly intelligent and skillful killer here,' Michelle came back. 'You still need to be careful.'

'I always am. But I'm not the priority here.' Hunter showed everyone the photograph of the young blonde woman again. 'She is. She would've been the next victim on his list whether we had his identity or not, not me.'

'How do you know that?' Captain Blake asked.

'Because he would've wanted me to be last,' Hunter explained. 'It's part of his revenge exercise. He wants me to watch all the victims die in real time, without being able to help them. Just like I watched his son die, without being able to save him.'

'But that wasn't your fault,' Captain Blake said.

'To Graham Fisher, it was. In his mind, I could've saved his son. I could've done more. But all that doesn't matter. What matters is finding who this woman is.' Hunter indicated the photograph once again. 'She's no doubt somehow linked to Graham's son's suicide, or the aftermath of it, like all the previous victims.'

'Another reporter?' Garcia suggested. 'Or maybe the webmaster of that shock-video website where the video of Brandon Fisher's suicide appeared?'

'Maybe,' Hunter agreed with a firm head nod. 'Let's get some people looking into that.'

Garcia nodded. 'I'll get a team on it.'

Hunter addressed Captain Blake. 'We've got to get this picture over to the press together with Graham's ASAP. We need to find out who she is, where she lives, where she works, everything. For all we know, he might already have her.'

One Hundred and Nine

Captain Blake called Hunter an hour and a half later. She had returned to the PAB with the woman's photograph while Hunter, Garcia and Michelle stayed behind. They wanted to slowly go through every inch of Graham Fisher's house. Five experienced police officers and two forensics agents had also joined them.

The captain told Hunter that she had handed the woman's photograph to the LAPD Media Relations Office, with specific instructions. They had immediately flexed their muscles, contacting the city's press and media. The woman's photo, together with Graham's, were to appear on all major TV channels in a special bulletin during the lunchtime news, and then again during the afternoon and evening news. The photographs would also be published in the next edition of all city newspapers, but that wouldn't be until tomorrow morning. Radio stations had also been contacted. They were urging listeners to log onto a special web page that the LAPD IT Department had set up with both photographs. Special call-in lines were already in place. They were now just waiting for developments.

Back in Graham Fisher's house, Hunter and Garcia started with the basement, bringing in two powerful forensics lights to do away with all the shadows. Garcia worked his way through everything found at the east end of the room, while Hunter meticulously examined the glass cage and the glass coffin found by the west wall.

Neither of the two torture and murder devices could tell Hunter something he didn't already know. The craftsmanship had been exceptional, but he expected nothing less from someone like Graham Fisher. The glass sheets used to create both devices were a combination of polycarbonate, thermoplastic and layers of laminated glass, making them bulletproof and totally unbreakable by human fists. But Graham had told him that over the phone. Hunter didn't expect him to be lying. The smell inside both glass containers was a sickening mixture of vomit, urine, feces, fear and very strong disinfectant. In the glass coffin, the dead tarantula hawks added a new, distinct, sour layer to the overall odor. Despite wearing a nose and mouth mask, Hunter felt the urge to throw up a few times, forcing him to take several breaks.

'Do you think he already has the woman on the photo?' Garcia asked, as Hunter joined him at the west end of the room.

Hunter took a deep breath, allowing his gaze to settle on the large tools cabinet. 'I don't know,' he finally replied. He didn't want to say it, but the truth was that Hunter had a terrible gut feeling about all this.

'There's something I want to show you,' Garcia said, stirring Hunter's attention to a specific spot on the wooden worktable. 'Have a look at this.'

Hunter looked at the spot Garcia was pointing to, frowned, then crouched down to look at it from even closer.

'Can you see it?'

Hunter nodded. Regular house dust had settled on the worktable, probably two days' worth of it. At that

particular spot, it had settled in an uneven pattern.
Something that used to be on that table had been removed
– a rectangular object of about fourteen inches by ten.
Hunter moved closer still, examining a second uneven dust
pattern, this one thin and long, dragging all the way to the
edge of the worktable. He checked the brick wall on that
side and saw that about a foot from the floor a power socket
had been fitted to it.

'A laptop computer,' Hunter ultimately said.

Garcia nodded. 'That's exactly what I was thinking. And
if we're right, you know what that means, right? Graham
probably kept all his plans, drawings, names, timetables,
sketches . . . whatever in the laptop that used to be here, not
in the desktop computer upstairs.'

Michelle Kelly had taken charge of searching through the
desktop computer inside Graham's office upstairs. Not
surprisingly, the computer was password protected, but not
by the simple, relatively easy-to-break, original operating
system password application, but by a custom-made one,
no doubt developed by Graham himself. Trying to breach
that protection right there and then, without some of the
tools and gadgets she had back at the FBI Cybercrime
Division, was an impossible task. Hunter gave her the
go-ahead to take the computer back to the FBI headquarters and proceed from there. She would contact them with
news as soon as she had any. So far, nothing.

Hunter nodded his agreement to Garcia's suggestion.
'Let's hope we're wrong. If there's anything in that desktop
computer, even if it's only a residue of something, I'm sure
Michelle will find it.'

They finally moved from the basement, and both detectives unashamedly breathed a sigh of relief.

The officers who were tasked with the door-to-door around Graham's street, and some of the neighboring ones, came back with no news. Not every neighbor was home, but the few who were could shine no light on the identity of the woman in the photograph they found inside Graham's basement, or on where Graham might've gone. One thing was consistent, though. They had all said that since his son's death, Graham had become a different man – withdrawn, isolated, uncommunicative. Since his wife passed away, he had become a ghost, barely seen by anyone.

Hunter and Garcia spent almost two hours going through every scrap of paper, every book, every magazine, every note they found inside Graham's office upstairs. None of it gave them anything to work with.

By mid-afternoon Hunter received a call from Detective Perez. He explained that after the lunchtime news the call-in lines had already received several tips about the woman's identity. Detectives and officers were checking the veracity of those tips, and he would get back to Hunter as soon as they had something more solid.

Another hour and a half came and went without a single new piece of development. Garcia had gone back to the PAB to help Detective Perez with the call-in lines.

Hunter was sitting alone inside Graham's son's bedroom when his cellphone beeped, announcing a new text message. He checked the display window – *unknown number*.

Hunter opened the text message and was immediately filled with a disquieting anxiety.

Well done, Detective Hunter, you finally managed to put all the clues together. Unfortunately for you, that has only led you to my house – my empty house. I hope you are having fun. Found anything interesting yet? I have.

As Hunter finished reading the message, his phone beeped again. Part two of the text message had arrived.

I took the liberty to track your phone's location. I can see you're still in my house, so here's where this game gets really fun. You, and you ALONE, have 7 mins to make it to St Mary's Church on the intersection of E. 4th St and S. Chicago St. That's seven blocks away. Don't drive – run. I'm sending you something to persuade you.

Another beep.

Another message.

This one started with an image.

An image that sent the room spinning around Hunter, making him feel as if all of a sudden all the oxygen had been sucked from his lungs.

He was looking at a photograph of a woman gagged and strapped onto a metal chair. The same woman he saw on the photograph they'd found down in the basement. The message read:

'*7 mins, or she dies. You tell anyone, including your partner, and I will kill her so slowly it will take her a month to die. The clock is ticking, Detective Hunter – 6:59, 6:58, 6:57 – LOL.*

One Hundred and Ten

Hunter came charging down the stairs like a bullet train, clearing the hall, the living room, and exiting the house in three seconds flat.

The two police officers who were standing by the house's front porch were taken by complete surprise. It took them about 1.5 seconds to get over the initial shock and react, instinctively reaching for their guns before quickly turning on the balls of their feet and anxiously aiming at the open door and the empty living room beyond it.

'Wha . . . What's going on?' one of them called out in a nervous voice.

'Fuck if I know,' the second officer replied, resisting the urge to check the street behind him to see where Hunter had gone. If they were about to face any sort of threat, it was coming from inside the house, not from the street.

Five seconds passed and nothing.

Both officers began craning their necks to one side, in a quick jab motion, peeking into the house like chickens on drugs.

'See anything?' the first officer asked.

'Not a damn thing.'

After another couple of seconds the first officer stepped up to the door and looked inside. The second officer assumed cover position.

'There's nothing here.'

'What the hell?' The second officer holstered his weapon and swung around looking for Hunter. He was nowhere to be seen. 'What the fuck was that all about? That homicide detective just hauled ass down the street as if he were on fire.'

The first officer shrugged and holstered his weapon. 'Where is he?'

'He's gone, man, didn't you see? He was going faster than Usain Bolt.'

'Maybe he finally lost it. It's a common thing with Homicide Special detectives. You already need to be nuts to join that group.'

Hunter had used a back alleyway to cut through to South Chicago Street. As he reached the main road, he turned left and ran as fast as he could. A million questions were tumbling over inside his head, but he just didn't have the time to think about any of them.

He was about three city blocks from St Mary's Church, when he peeked at his watch. He had less than three minutes to make it.

As he reached the next intersection along – East 6th Street – Hunter paid no attention to the traffic or the red pedestrian crossing light.

A white van, driving east on that road, saw him way too late as he suddenly appeared out of nowhere, stepping directly in front of the van. The driver slammed on the brakes hard, killing the van's speed almost immediately, but not fast enough. Hunter collided with the front of the van and was thrown sideways to the ground, smashing his left arm and shoulder against the asphalt.

'What the fuck?' the van driver yelled, wide-eyed, jumping out of his vehicle. 'Are you trying to fucking kill yourself, crazy man?'

Hunter rolled over twice and quickly scrambled on his hands and toes, trying to get back up. His legs finally found the traction he needed, and just like that he was back on his feet.

'Didn't you see the red light, you crazy fuc—' the driver began, but as Hunter moved he saw Hunter's gun tucked away in his shoulder holster. 'Yo, it's all cool, dawg,' the driver said in a much less aggressive tone, taking a step back and showing Hunter his palms. 'My bad all the way. I should've been paying more attention. You good?'

Hunter didn't even look at him. He cut through the small, intrigued crowd that had already gathered on the sidewalk and moved on.

Hunter had handled the fall pretty well, but the collision with the van had hurt his right knee. He could feel it stabbing at him with every new step, forcing him to reduce his speed and limp awkwardly. But he wasn't far now. He could see the bell tower of St. Mary's Church just at the top of the road.

Out of breath and with his knee starting to scream at him, Hunter made it to the intersection in 6 minutes 53 seconds. There was no one there.

'What the hell?' he puffed the words out, while reaching for his phone.

No new messages, no new calls.

Out of the blue, a yellow cab pulled up right in front of him and rolled down its window.

'You Robert Hunter?' the driver asked.

Hunter nodded with a quizzical look on his face.

'Here's your phone, dude,' the driver said, offering Hunter an old, brick-like cellphone with a hands-free earpiece already plugged into it.

'What?'

The driver shrugged. 'Look, man, a guy paid me two hundred bucks to bring this phone to this exact location, at this exact time, and give it to some dude called Robert Hunter. That's you, right? So here's your phone.'

The phone the driver had offered Hunter started ringing, startling the driver.

'Shit, man.' The driver jumped in his seat before extending his arm again. 'It ain't gonna be for me.'

Hunter quickly took the phone and answered it, placing the earpiece in his ear.

'Great,' the caller said. 'You made it. Now hand your phone over to the cab driver.' The caller's voice sounded a little different from all the previous calls. Hunter knew that was because he wasn't using any electronic device to disguise it anymore. There was no longer a need for it.

'What?' Hunter replied.

'You heard me. Take this phone and hand your phone over to the cab driver. You won't need it anymore. Do it now or she dies.'

Hunter knew exactly what Graham was doing – getting rid of Hunter's police phone GPS, and any other tricks and warning signals Hunter might've had set up at the touch of a button.

He did as he was told.

The cab driver rolled his window back up and quickly drove away.

'Now, you have exactly sixty minutes to get to the address I'm going to give you. Don't use your car. Don't use a police car. Don't take a taxi. Improvise. If you don't, the killing begins. If you don't get here in sixty minutes, the killing begins. If you disconnect from this call during the next sixty minutes, the killing begins. Am I clear?'

'Yes.'

The caller gave Hunter the address.

'Go. The clock starts . . . now.'

One Hundred and Eleven

Hunter looked around himself, quickly evaluating what his next move should be. Directly across the road from him was a convenience store with its own small private parking lot at the back. At that exact moment, an overweight man exited the store, carrying a large bag under his arm and happily chewing on a Twinkie. Hunter got to him as he unlocked the door to his Chevrolet Malibu.

'Sorry, sir, I need to take your car,' Hunter said in a hurried voice, displaying his badge and police credentials.

'What?' the man said with a mouthful of Twinkie, eyeing Hunter's documents and badge, before looking straight into his eyes.

'This is a police emergency and I need to take your car, sir.'

The man swallowed down whatever was left inside his mouth with a gulping noise. 'Are you fucking with me right now? You're commandeering my car? That kind of shit only happens in the movies.'

'Well, that kind of shit just got real, sir.'

'You've gotta be fucking kidding me.' The man looked around, as if expecting to see a camera crew hiding somewhere. 'Am I being punked right now?'

'No, sir.'

'Did my ex-bitch-of-a-wife put you up to this?'

'I'm afraid I don't know your ex-bitch-of-a-wife, sir, and I don't have time to argue. I really need to take your car.'

'No freaking way. Are you for real? Is that badge real? Let me see that again.'

'It's real, sir. I assure you. And so is this.' Hunter opened his jacket, allowing the man to see his gun.

'Yup,' the man said, taking a step back. 'That looks pretty damn real.'

'Can I please have the keys now, sir,' Hunter said.

'Goddammit,' the man said, before handing the keys to Hunter. 'How the hell am I supposed get home now?'

Hunter wasn't listening anymore. He jumped into the car, started the engine and took off with the tires screeching.

Out of the parking lot, he immediately veered left onto East 4th Street, heading toward the Golden State Freeway.

'Great improvisation, Detective,' Hunter heard the caller say through his earpiece.

'Graham,' Hunter said. 'Listen to me. You don't have to do this anymore.'

'Is that so, Detective Hunter?'

'Yes,' Hunter replied with conviction. 'We all understand you're angry and hurt. We understand that all the people you sought – Kevin Lee Parker, Christina Stevenson and Ethan Walsh . . .' Hunter used their names in a futile effort to humanize the victims in Graham Fisher's eyes. 'They have all, in one way or another, made the already terrible pain of dealing with your son's death even harder, but revenge will not make the pain go away.'

'Harder . . .?' Graham cut Hunter short with a sneer. 'They bastardized it. They gave every freak out there a chance to turn my son's life struggle, and his death, into a joke. A chance for them to make fun of him, even after he was gone. Society has turned into something unrecognizable, Detective. A monster without respect or care for anyone's life. A monster whose values have been turned upside down. Haven't I proven it to you, Detective? Didn't you witness people voting on how to kill another human being, a complete stranger who they knew nothing of, as if it were a game? We're talking *real people* wanting to watch *real people* die live on their screens for pure entertainment. How messed up is that, Detective Hunter?'

'Graham, I understand.'

'No, no, no,' Graham interrupted Hunter again, his voice now lifting with anger. 'Don't tell me you understand, because you don't. And do not insult me by trying to psychobullshit your way through this. It will *not* work. I assure you. My mind is much stronger than yours, Detective Hunter.' There was a short pause, but before Hunter could say anything Graham spoke again, his tone back to being calm and serene. 'But look at the bright side of all this. Once you get here, this will all end . . . For both of us. You've got fifty-three minutes, Detective. And in the next fifty-three minutes I do not want to hear a word from you. If I do, every word I hear means she loses a finger. If I run out of fingers . . . well . . . I'll have to start cutting something else. Is that understood?'

Silence.

'Is that understood, Detective Hunter?'

'Yes.'

The next silent fifty-three minutes felt like forever. Hunter's mind kept churning possibility after possibility of what would happen once he got to his destination. None of them ended well.

Graham had calculated the trip, taking into account the obstacle that LA traffic posed at that time of day, with the precision of a rocket scientist, because Hunter reached the secluded destination in Sylmar, the northernmost neighborhood in the city of Los Angeles, in exactly fifty-two minutes. Hunter wasn't surprised by Graham's precision. No matter how tough he sounded, Graham didn't want Hunter to fail, because his revenge plan would never be completed without the last name on his victims' list – Robert Hunter.

By the time Hunter got to Sylmar, the day was disappearing over the Hollywood hills, with the sky taking an almost crippled brownish hue.

The address Graham gave him took Hunter to an isolated road near the Equestrian Arena in Sylmar, by the foot of the Angeles National Forest hills. There wasn't much there, except two small warehouses and an old, disused stable. Graham had told Hunter to drive to the back of the main stable building, where he would find a second, high-roofed construction.

'I see you have arrived.' Graham broke the oppressing phone silence, just as Hunter parked the car. 'The door is unlocked. Come right in, Detective Hunter. We have all been waiting for you. But unfortunately we couldn't wait. The show has already started. The clock is already ticking. And you don't have much time left.'

One Hundred and Twelve

Exactly five minutes before Hunter was due to arrive, Graham set the phone he was on to Hunter to mute and placed a new call to a different number, using a different phone.

Back at the PAB, Garcia was just about to call Hunter with some news when the phone on his desk rang. Captain Blake was in the office with him.

'Detective Garcia, Homicide Special,' he answered it.

'Detective,' the caller said. 'I have a very special show for you today. The last in the series. Something you might like to call – the grand finale.'

Garcia paused for a split, hesitant second. His gaze found Captain Blake's, and something in it made her shiver.

'Graham?' Garcia said, switching the call to loudspeaker.

'That's correct, Detective. And now that we have been properly introduced, would you care to log onto picka-death.com? I'm sure you will enjoy this last show.'

Garcia quickly got to his computer and typed the web address onto his browser's address bar.

Captain Blake joined him behind his desk in a hurry.

This time there was no green tint indicating night-vision lenses. The image was bright and clear. It showed the same woman they'd been searching for all day. The one on the photograph they'd found inside Graham Fisher's basement – the next victim. She had been gagged and securely strapped to a heavy metal chair, similar to the one they found bolted to the concrete floor inside the glass enclosure they'd discovered that morning. But this time there was no glass enclosure. Instead, the chair had been placed inside a large metal-bar cage, like the ones used to hold animals in a zoo. The woman's eyes were wide with fear and blood-red from crying. She had been completely stripped of all her clothes. Despite all that, she did not appear to be injured. But what frightened the hell out of Garcia and Captain Blake was the strangely shaped wire-mesh panel that had been placed directly in front of her face. It looked like some sort of odd, medieval, torturing metal mask.

'Oh my God. He already had her,' Captain Blake whispered.

'Do you see her?' Graham asked.

'Yes.'

'Keep watching.'

As in the previous broadcasts, the word GUILTY appeared in big letters, centered at the bottom of the screen.

'Where is Robert?' Captain Blake mouthed the words at Garcia.

He gave her a subtle headshake, while at the same time pressing a speed dial button on his cellphone. A second later there was a barely audible beep, followed by Hunter's 'unavailable' message. Garcia frowned. That meant Hunter's cellphone was switched off. Hunter never switched his phone off.

'I decided to change the rules yet again,' Graham calmly said. 'This time there will be only one death method, not a choice of two. You see, Detective, I want to test how benevolent the people of California are. If they care enough, she lives. If they don't, she dies. It's that simple.'

About halfway down the right-hand edge of the screen, the word SAVE appeared followed by the number zero and a green button. Directly underneath it, the word EXECUTE appeared, also followed by the number zero and a second green button.

'This will be a simple race to the finish line, Detective. Ten minutes, at the end of which we count the votes. SAVE – she lives. EXECUTE – she dies. Does that sound fair?'

No reply.

'All she needs is for the people of this great state we live in to care enough.' Graham laughed out loud. 'So what do you think, Detective Garcia? In the days of today, are people more inclined to give a complete stranger the benefit of the doubt, or condemn her to die simply because they see the word GUILTY on the screen? Can people really be that gullible?'

No reply.

'I guess we'll find out in ten minutes. But there's something else I want you to do. Are you listening?'

'Yes.'

'Exactly two minutes before time is up, I want you to use a different computer and log onto the following IP address.' Graham dictated the address to Garcia. 'Two minutes from time up, not a second before. If you log onto it anytime before two minutes, I'll know it, and the deal is off. I will kill her no matter what, and I will kill her slowly. Is that understood?'

'Yes.'

The line went dead.

The digital clock at the bottom left-hand corner of the screen started counting down – 9:59, 9:58, 9:57 . . .

One Hundred and Thirteen

Still with the hands-free earpiece securely in his ear, Hunter exited the car, unholstered his weapon and cautiously moved toward the door of the high-roofed building at the back of the disused stable. It was a medium-sized, unremarkable brick and cement construction, where unequal patches of green mold covered the walls outside. Old debris and garden weed surrounded the entire property. The only two windows Hunter could see from where he was had been boarded up, but the heavy wooden door he'd just approached on the east wall looked new. So did the two deadbolt locks on it.

Hunter moved closer and placed his right ear against the door. It was too thick and too solid for him to be able to hear anything coming from the other side.

'It's not a trick, Detective Hunter,' Graham's voice came through the hands-free once again, taking Hunter by surprise. 'I am not going to shoot you as you walk through the door. That's a promise. I really want you to see what's inside. Just push the door. It's open. And let me remind you – the clock is already ticking.'

Hunter had no other option but to trust Graham. He took a deep breath, cocked his gun and slowly pushed the door open.

The space inside was large and bare, like an empty family house stripped of all the walls. There was an odd smell in the air, a combination of disinfectant with something sweet and sickly, like dried-up old vomit. The light was uneven, coming from the north end of the room. Instinctively Hunter's eyes moved in that direction, and a suffocating knot immediately formed in his throat.

Pushed up against the wall was a large, solid, metal-bar cage. The bars were at least one inch in diameter. Sitting at the center of it, naked and firmly strapped to a metal chair, was the woman he saw on the photograph he'd found earlier in Graham's basement. She looked absolutely terrified. As her blurry, full-of-tears gaze found Hunter's, her whole being was filled with hope, electrifying her entire body. She tried screaming, but her weak voice, made even weaker by her tired and wasted vocal cords, made no impression through the thick gag in her mouth. She used whatever strength she had left in her to try to swing her body from side to side and rock it forward, away from the chair's backrest, but the straps that held her tight were too strong. Her eyes, though, communicated with Hunter in a clear voice.

Please help me.

A strange, metal-mesh mask had been attached to a mechanical arm and placed just a couple of inches in front of her face.

Directly in front of the cage, Hunter saw an internet camera. To the left of the cage, he saw a large computer monitor displaying the exact same images that were being broadcast over the Internet. The clock at the bottom left-hand corner of the screen was counting down – 6:05, 6:04, 6:03 ... The voting display at the right-hand edge of the screen read:

SAVE: 12,574.

EXECUTE: 12,955.

Hunter was about to take a step toward the cage and the woman when he heard Graham's voice again. This time he didn't need the hands-free. The voice came from a dark spot at the west end of the room, directly in front of him.

'Not so fast, Detective Hunter.'

Hunter immediately raised his gun in the direction of the voice, but shadows expertly cloaked that corner of the room.

'I'd be careful with that gun if I were you,' Graham said.

Hunter searched the darkness for a hint of movement, something he could use as a target. He found nothing.

'Allow me to explain to you what is happening, Detective Hunter,' Graham's voice boomed around the room again. Due to how it echoed across the walls, Hunter couldn't use it to pinpoint Graham's exact location. Still, he kept his gun firmly aimed at the west end corner.

In a calm and unexcited voice, Graham explained to Hunter exactly what he had explained to Garcia over the phone.

'As you can see, Detective,' Graham said. 'The hour of truth is almost upon us.'

Hunter peeked at the computer monitor again.

CLOCK: 4:18, 4:17, 4:16 . . .

SAVE: 14,325.

EXECUTE: 14,693.

Hunter slowly and subtly moved the aim of his gun from left to right, still looking for something he could use.

'Shooting me won't help you, Detective. The lock on that cage door is unbreakable and unbreachable. Bullets will have no effect on it. Nothing will. Actually, no one can unlock it. Not even me. It's on a time-release mechanism.

When that clock reaches zero, if SAVE is ahead, the door will automatically unlock, and she will be freed. If EXECUTE is ahead, the door will automatically unlock after five minutes, by which time my hand-made metal-mesh mask will have slowly compressed against her face, slicing through her flesh and facial bones like a piece of rotten animal carcass, before reaching her gray matter, finally killing her.'

The woman in the cage squealed in terror.

'You can't stop it from happening, Detective Hunter. You can't save her, no matter what you do. Her fate will be decided by the people of California in the next few minutes. It's their choice now.'

Hunter stole a peek at the woman again. She was shivering violently from fright and was about to pass out.

'But wouldn't you like to know who she is first before that clock reaches zero?' Graham asked. 'How she fits in with my plan?'

'Graham, don't do this,' Hunter pleaded.

Graham simply ignored Hunter's words. 'Her real name is Julie, but in cyberspace she goes by the handle MSDarkDays. She is what is known as an Internet troll, Detective. I am sure you're familiar with the term.'

Hunter knew exactly what an Internet troll was. Someone who deliberately posts offensive and derogative messages in online communities such as social networks, chat rooms, blogs, forums, etc. with the sole purpose of hurting others and provoking an emotional response.

'When the video footage of my son's suicide appeared online for the first time,' Graham continued, 'MSDarkDays was the first person to post a message. Would you like to hear that message, Detective Hunter?'

Hunter stayed silent.

'*The ugly fuck did the right thing. If my face were that fucked up, I would've killed myself a long time ago. Los Angeles has one less ugly freak to deal with. If all the ugly, fucked-up schoolkids who can't deal with their own problems followed suit and topped themselves, LA would be a much better place,*' Graham quoted the post word for word. 'Not content with what she wrote in that first post, MSDarkDays returned to the site several times over a period of weeks, adding several more posts. But I won't bore you with them all, Detective. We don't have the time.'

Hunter let out a deep breath. 'We all make mistakes, Graham. You, me, her – no one is free of them. Don't make another one now.'

Graham laughed a slightly crazy laugh.

CLOCK: 2:19, 2:18, 2:17 . . .

SAVE: 21,458.

EXECUTE: 21,587.

'I'm not making a mistake, Detective. But if you use that gun, you might. You wouldn't want to shoot the wrong person, would you?'

At that exact moment the clock reached 2:00. A new light came on, weak and yellowish but strong enough to make some of the shadows disappear, bringing Graham out of the darkness.

But Graham wasn't alone. He was crouching down behind another metal chair, hiding behind the person strapped to it.

Hunter immediately took aim, but as his eyes settled on the person strapped to the chair he felt as if his heart had shot up his throat, blocking his intake of oxygen and making him feel faint.

Graham was hiding behind Anna – Garcia's wife.

One Hundred and Fourteen

Using the computer on Hunter's desk, Garcia typed the private IP address that Graham had given him onto the browser's address bar and hit the 'enter' key.

Captain Blake was standing just behind him.

The screen flickered twice before the images loaded and, as they did, Garcia's world came crumbling down in front of his eyes.

The broadcasting camera had been positioned high, and seemingly at the northeast corner of the room. The diagonal angle allowed it to cover a wide area. Standing on the left of the picture Garcia could see Hunter. His weapon was drawn and firmly aimed at the two people across the room from him. One of those two people was Anna.

'Oh my God!' Garcia mumbled the words almost catatonically.

Anna had been gagged and strapped to a high-backed metal chair in the same manner as the woman who was sitting inside the metal-bar cage. The difference was, she hadn't been stripped of her clothes, and unlike the other woman Anna looked drugged. Her eyes were lazy and unfocused, her body depleted of all energy, her lips drooping to one side.

Cowardly hiding directly behind the chair was someone they couldn't clearly see, but who they could only assume was Graham Fisher. He was holding a gun to Anna's head.

Captain Blake was watching the images wide-eyed, her mouth half open. 'What the hell is going on?' She finally uttered the words like someone who had just awakened from a deep sleep, still groggy.

Garcia couldn't find the strength to answer back.

Suddenly and unexpectedly, Graham's voice came booming out of the small speakers on Hunter's desk.

One Hundred and Fifteen

'I must apologize for this crude improvisation,' Graham said to Hunter. 'This certainly wasn't how I had planned this final broadcast, but since I underestimated you and your partner, Detective Hunter, this was the best I could come up with in the few hours I had.' A very short pause. 'But enough with the apologies. I bet that you're wondering how on earth I managed to get to your partner's wife when she had a police unit following her everywhere she went.'

Hunter remained quiet.

'Well, knowing the exact police car identification number, how difficult do you think it would be for someone like me to hack into the LAPD radio frequency, pretend I'm dispatch and call off the police escort, Detective?'

'You've got to let her go, Graham,' Hunter finally spoke, his aim still uncertain. 'She's not part of your plan. She's never been part of your plan. I'm the one you want, not her. I'm the one you blame, not her. She had nothing to do with what happened to your son, before or after the bridge incident.'

'That's true,' Graham admitted. 'She was never part of my original plan. But as I've said, due to very late developments, I had to improvise, and if I'm honest I think it's going quite well so far.'

CLOCK: 1:27, 1:26, 1:25 . . .

SAVE: 29,783.

EXECUTE: 29,794.

Hunter steadied his aim.

'Go on, Detective, take a shot,' Graham challenged him. 'I know you want to. I also know how good a shot you are. I read your whole file. From this distance you can practically shoot the wings off the back of a fly. All you need is a chance, right?'

Hunter said nothing.

'What's wrong, Detective Hunter, confidence wavering a little? Not so certain of that kill-shot right about now? Oh, that's right. If you miss, you could kill your partner's wife. How would you explain that, then?'

No reply.

'I have one more surprise for you, Detective Hunter. The camera high on the wall to your right is also broadcasting. Not to the World Wide Web, but to your partner back at the Police Administration Building, and whoever else he has in the room with him.'

Hunter's attention didn't flicker.

'Oh, and he can hear us too. The microphone is on. So let me ask you this, Detective Hunter. What do you think your partner would say to you right now? Would he want you to take a shot or not? Bearing in mind that if you miss me, and by some miracle also managed not to hit his wife, then it will be my turn to pull my trigger.' He pressed his gun harder against the side of Anna's head. 'From this distance, I know *I* won't miss.'

Hunter tensed.

As if teasing Hunter, Graham shifted behind Anna for a split second.

Hunter held his breath. His left-hand grip tightened on his gun, while his right hand relaxed just a fraction, allowing his trigger finger to become more flexible, and his arms to better control the recoil. But the fact that Anna was Graham's shield played in Hunter's mind and he hesitated, giving Graham the chance to disappear behind her again.

CLOCK: 1:01, 1:00, 0:59 . . .

SAVE: 31,125.

EXECUTE: 31,148.

'Sartre once said,' Graham spoke again, 'that the only real choice a man has in life is whether or not to commit suicide. Are you familiar with that quote, Detective Hunter?'

Hunter felt an uncomfortable anxiety run through him.

'Yes or no, Detective?' Graham demanded.

'Yes,' Hunter replied.

Graham paused for an instant. 'Good, because I'm forcing that choice upon you right now, Detective Hunter. You want to save your partner's wife's life? Then I want you to put your gun to your head and pull the trigger.'

Absolute silence ruled over the room. Even the air seemed to stop moving.

'You have until that clock reaches zero,' Graham said. 'Not a second more.'

CLOCK: 0:47, 0:46, 0:45 . . .

SAVE: 33,570.

EXECUTE: 33,601.

'It's a simple choice, Detective Hunter,' Graham continued. 'An innocent life for a guilty one. If you put the gun to your head and pull the trigger, she lives. I guarantee it. No harm will come to her. But if that clock reaches zero and you are still standing, I *will* blow her brains all over this room with no hesitation and no equivocations.' He cocked his gun. 'What happens after that makes no difference to me. Like I said, MSDarkDays' fate isn't in your hands. There's nothing you, or I, can do to change it. But your partner's wife's is. Do you understand what's happening here, Detective? I want to know if you are prepared to save her in the same way you were prepared to save my son, or will you try harder this time?'

Hunter said nothing.

CLOCK: 0:28, 0:27, 0:26 . . .

SAVE: 33,888.

EXECUTE: 33,903.

'I want you to take your own life just like my son took his,' Graham said in an indignant, disgusted voice. 'I want to watch you do it just like you watched him do it.'

A million things were going through Hunter's mind at that moment, but he knew he had time to consider none of them.

'Police officers have to be prepared to put their lives on the line for others, isn't that right, Detective Hunter? But are you really prepared for it or is that just a bullshit motto? Would you give your life for someone else's, Detective? Would you give your life to save an innocent one?'

CLOCK: 0:16, 0:15, 0:14 . . .

SAVE: 34,146.

EXECUTE: 34,155.

Hunter knew he had run out of time. He also knew that he had underestimated Graham Fisher, because out of all the possibilities he had run through in his head of how his encounter with Graham could've ended up, blowing his own brains all over the floor had never been one of them.

He now understood that Graham had indeed played him all along. This had always been the grand finale to his master plan. As Graham had said, he wanted to watch Hunter take his own life, just like Hunter had watched his son, Brandon Fisher, take his. Only then would Graham's revenge be complete. And he played it to perfection. Even broadcasting the final act to Garcia so he could watch Hunter decide if his wife lived or died.

Hunter had no counterplan, no more time left, and in truth only one option. He knew Graham wouldn't falter. When that clock reached zero, he *would* end Anna's life right there and then. He had the same determination in his eyes and in his voice as his son did that night on the bridge. He wasn't looking for help, or salvation. His decision had been made a long time ago.

'Ten seconds, Detective,' Graham said.

Hunter looked at Anna, not an ounce of doubt in his mind anymore.

He brought his gun to him and placed it under his own chin, but didn't shut his eyes like most people would have. He kept them open . . . proud . . . staring straight ahead.

A 9mm bullet will enter someone's skull and exit at the other side in three ten-thousandths of a second. It will shatter the cranium and rupture through the subject's brain matter so fast the nervous system has no time to register any pain. If the angle in which the bullet enters the head is correct, the bullet should splice the cerebral cortex, the cerebellum, even the thalamus in such a way that the brain will cease functioning, resulting in instant death.

Hunter placed his gun in the best possible angle to achieve such a result.

CLOCK: 0:04, 0:03, 0:02 . . .

Hunter held his breath.

One Hundred and Sixteen

Neither Garcia nor Captain Blake could believe what they were witnessing through the computer monitor on Hunter's desk.

CLOCK: 0:10, 0:09, 0:08 . . .

SAVE: 34,146.

EXECUTE: 34,155.

'Is this for real?' Captain Blake asked, and for the first time ever Garcia heard fear in her voice.

He didn't answer, didn't move, didn't blink, didn't breathe. His eyes were cemented to the computer screen. Dread was pumping through his veins like poisoned blood. He didn't even notice his hands shaking.

CLOCK: 0:06, 0:05, 0:04 . . .

SAVE: 34,184.

EXECUTE: 34,196.

Hunter finally moved, and, as he did, time seemed to slow down for everyone.

First, his left hand let go of its grip to his gun. Then his eyes saddened in a way Garcia had never seen before, as if he knew there was nothing else he could do. As if he knew he had been outwitted and outplayed by a smarter opponent.

After that, Hunter's right arm folded back in the direction of his body, bringing his gun with him.

'Oh my God!' Captain Blake brought both hands to her face, covering her nose and mouth. Just like Garcia's, hers were also shaking.

Hunter raised his gun and placed it under his own chin.

The captain felt an enormous pit open up inside her stomach. She knew Hunter well enough to know that he *would* give his life to save someone else's, never mind someone he knew, someone as important as his partner's wife. She felt tears come to her eyes and squeezed them tight, wishing that when she reopened them she'd find herself back in her room, waking up from a terrible nightmare. But she knew that that wouldn't happen. That day was as real and as hard-hitting as she would ever have.

Captain Blake kept her eyes shut. She knew exactly what was about to happen. She didn't need or want to watch it happening.

Garcia, on the other hand, kept his unblinking eyes wide open, taking everything in. He saw the moment the look in Hunter's eyes changed from sad to serene, as he recognized and accepted that he really had only one choice.

CLOCK: 0:03, 0:02, 0:01.

At that exact instant, as if programmed by Graham, the images on the screen faded to total darkness. As it did, and just before the broadcast went completely offline, they heard the faint sound of a single gunshot being fired.

'No, no, no ...' Garcia jumped up and grabbed the computer monitor with both hands, shaking it. 'What happened? What happened? Where's the picture?' His heart seemed to stop beating for a moment. Desperation took over him, because there was no way he could be sure if the shot had come from Hunter or Graham's gun.

One Hundred and Seventeen

CLOCK: 0:03, 0:02, 0:01.

And that was when Hunter's gamble paid off.

Graham had been right. From that distance, Hunter only needed half a chance, and he would hit the target ten times out of ten.

Graham had said so himself – he wanted to *watch* Hunter take his own life. The problem was, from where Graham was hiding, his direct line of sight to Hunter was blocked by the high-backed metal chair that Anna was strapped to.

Hunter kept his eyes wide open, staring straight at the chair, waiting for his chance. As the countdown clock reached 0.01, Graham Fisher did exactly what Hunter was expecting him to do.

First, Graham shifted his attention from his own gun and from Anna. Then he subtly moved sideways, partially abandoning the safety of his shield. In doing that he was forced to expose just a little more of his body, while craning his neck to get a better glimpse at something that he just wouldn't want to miss – the closing act to his master plan.

That was all the chance Hunter needed.

As he dived right, simultaneously extending his arm, time switched to slow motion. In his head, all sounds ceased, being replaced by a vacuum. Hunter became aware of only two things: his target, and his own heartbeat as it pounded inside his chest and thundered in his brain. While in mid-flight, and as his eyes locked with Graham's, Hunter squeezed the trigger on his gun.

In real time it all happened way too fast for Graham to be able to react.

Hunter's shot hit Graham's right shoulder with pinpoint precision, rupturing muscles, shattering bones and slicing through tendons and ligaments.

Graham's hand instantly lost all its grip, and his gun dropped to the floor. The powerful impact of an ultra-high-performance, center-fire, fragmenting 9mm bullet projected his body backward, throwing him to the ground while a red mist of blood shot up, coloring the air. The bitter tang of cordite filled the room.

Hunter also hit the ground after the shot, rolling sideways twice but expertly keeping his aim on his target.

Graham let out a guttural roar and immediately brought his left hand to his right shoulder, which was now just a gooey mess of blood and torn flesh. He felt the room spinning violently around him, as dizziness, brought on by the tremendous pain and sudden loss of blood, took over. Only in Hollywood films can a person be shot with a high-velocity exploding bullet and still have the strength to dance a jig. A couple of seconds later, Graham fainted.

Hunter shot back to his feet and covered the short distance between him and Graham in a flash.

'Don't even think of moving,' he said firmly with his gun pointing straight at Graham's head, but Graham was down and out, at least for the time being.

Hunter lost no time in cuffing his hands behind his back, disregarding the new bolt of pain that undoubtedly shot up

Graham's right arm as he did so. After that, Hunter quickly checked on Anna.

She had been heavily sedated. Her pupils were dilated, making her eyes seem lost in time. Her body was unresponsive, but her pulse was strong, and she didn't seem hurt.

That was when Hunter heard the most terrifying and agonizing scream he'd ever heard. He swung his body around in the direction of the scream and the metal-bar cage, only then his attention returned to the computer monitor to the left of it.

CLOCK: 0:00.

SAVE: 34,471.

EXECUTE: 34,502.

'Oh God! No.'

He ran toward the cage, but the EXECUTE process had already started. The mechanical arm the metal-mesh mask was attached to had begun pressing it against the woman's face. The laser-sharp wires were already tearing through her skin and flesh, covering her face with a red mask of sticky blood.

Hunter took a step back, aimed his gun at the lock on the cage's door and fired twice. The bullets didn't even seem to scratch it. He fired two more rounds. Nothing.

The wires had now cut through the cartilage on the woman's nose. Unable to escape the most basic human reaction to pain, she began screaming. Her jaw and head movement only served to shift and grind her face against the sharp wires that had already dug deep into her flesh, making them not only cut horizontally but vertically as well, in a shredding action, mutilating whatever was left.

Hunter took a step to the side and looked around, desperate to help but not knowing how. He needed to find something.

That was when all of a sudden the metal-mesh mask stopped compressing against the woman's face and began retracting, bringing with it chunks of skin, flesh and cartilage. Hunter then heard a loud buzzing noise, followed by a lock click.

The cage door popped open.

Graham had told Hunter that if EXECUTE was ahead when the countdown clock reached zero, the time-release mechanism would release the door after five minutes, enough time for Graham's horror-mask to have put the woman through the most agonizing and torturous pain before killing her. But the whole process had lasted less than fifty seconds.

Something had malfunctioned.

Hunter pulled the cage's door open and quickly got to the woman. She was shaking uncontrollably, just about to enter shock.

Hunter still had the phone the cab driver had given him. He called for help, untied the woman and, cradling her bloody face in his arms, sat on the floor and waited for it to arrive.

One Hundred and Eighteen

Next day
Outside Garcia's apartment building
5.00 p.m.

As Hunter parked his car, he saw Garcia exiting the building's entrance lobby, carrying a suitcase.

Captain Blake had ordered them both to take a two-week break, effective immediately.

'Need any help with that?' Hunter said, stepping out of his car.

Garcia looked up and smiled. 'No, I'm cool. Why do women always have to over-pack?'

Hunter had no answer.

Garcia popped open his trunk, placed the suitcase inside it and turned to face his partner. He knew Hunter had spent part of the afternoon at the California Hospital Medical Center in South Grand Avenue.

'Any news?' he asked.

'The doctors have just operated on her again,' Hunter replied. 'The second surgery in less than twenty-four hours.' His eye had a sad gloom to them. 'And they believe that she will have to undergo a few more in the next few months. But even so, most of her disfigurement will be irreversible.'

Garcia combed a hand through his hair.

'It wasn't a malfunction, Carlos,' Hunter said.

Garcia looked at him.

'The metal-mesh mask stopping when it did,' Hunter clarified. 'It wasn't a malfunction. Graham Fisher programmed it that way. He lied when he told me that it would take five minutes for the door to disengage, by which time she should've been dead.'

'How do you know? Has he confessed?'

'No,' Hunter replied. 'He isn't talking . . . yet. But I know that that was what he wanted. He never wanted her dead. He wanted her disfigured.' Hunter leaned against the car parked next to Garcia's. '*If my face were that fucked up, I would've killed myself a long time ago. Los Angeles has one less ugly freak to deal with. If all the ugly, fucked-up school-kids who can't deal with their own problems followed suit and topped themselves, LA would be a much better place.*'

Garcia's brow creased.

'She troll-posted those words on the Internet,' Hunter confirmed. 'Referring to Graham Fisher's son.'

'Fuck,' Garcia whispered.

'Graham wanted her disfigured because he wanted her to go through everything his son went through. He wanted to teach her what having others stare at you, laugh at you, gossip behind your back, call you names and treat you like a monster for the rest of your life felt like. That was his final revenge, not her death.' Hunter looked away, shaking his head. 'Even though we caught him, he won. In the end, he got what he wanted.'

'No, he didn't,' Garcia shot back firmly. 'His final revenge involved you being dead, remember? And that didn't happen. Graham Fisher will now rot in prison. He's never coming out.' He looked away for a moment, regaining his breath. 'But that can't undo the fact that people voted, Robert.' He looked almost disgusted. 'Regular people out there, sitting in their homes, in their offices, in cafés, in schools . . .' He shook his head. 'They *voted*. Unlike the two previous times, Graham gave them the chance and the power to *save* someone's life, and a great number of them chose not to. They chose to sentence a complete stranger to death, just so they could watch it for entertainment. A human life in exchange for a few laughs – how's that for a bargain?'

Hunter breathed out.

'There's no two ways of looking at this, Robert. That's just fucked up. Some people out there have lost track of everything. Especially of how valuable a life is.'

Hunter's long silence told Garcia he agreed. 'How is Anna?' he finally asked.

'Alive because of you.'

Hunter said nothing.

Garcia drew in a deep breath. 'She's very shaken up, and still a little dopey from the drugs Graham pumped into her. But in a way that was a blessing. She doesn't remember anything that happened after she was drugged. If she'd been conscious throughout that whole ordeal yesterday, the psychological damage she'd be facing would've been far worse than what she'll already have to overcome. You know that better than anyone else.'

The next few seconds felt more awkward than it had ever felt between the two of them.

'So where are you going?' Hunter asked, indicating the suitcase.

'We're going to visit a few relatives up in the mountains in Oregon,' Garcia replied. 'Just get away from everything for a while, you know? It will be good to take Anna away from this city. It will be good to be just the two of us for two weeks ... No interruptions ... No phone calls in the middle of the night ...'

Another awkward silence.

'Will you be back?' Hunter asked.

Garcia knew Hunter was referring to the Homicide Special Section. He was pensive for a long moment. 'I'll be back to the force,' he finally said. 'I have to decide if I can come back to Homicide Special.'

Hunter said nothing.

'I'll be truthful with you,' Garcia said, meeting Hunter's eyes. 'I've never been as scared as I was yesterday, Robert. Anna has always been everything to me. Without her, I'm nothing. I've always feared losing her. But you know the kind of fear I'm talking about, right? The kind that happens to every couple in love.' Garcia shook his head. 'Not yesterday. Seeing Anna tied to that chair with a gun to her head made it real. It made me totally realize how fragile and vulnerable she really is. And you as well as I know that the only reason her life was put in danger was because I'm a Homicide Special Section detective. In other words, I put her life in danger by doing the job I do.'

Hunter studied his partner in silence.

'You know that threats to my life don't scare me. I don't even mind being nailed to a human-sized cross, as you well know. But this is the first time that a threat has branched out to Anna, and I won't lie to you, Robert. It's forced me to rethink things. To rethink my priorities.'

Hunter knew it would.

'I was so scared, that I wasn't thinking clearly,' Garcia admitted. 'If it had been me instead of you in that room yesterday, I don't think I would've seen the chance you saw, and even if I had I don't think I would've had the nerve to have taken it. I would've simply shot myself to save Anna.'

Hunter said nothing, and the silence stretched for several seconds.

'But I'm not making any decisions right now,' Garcia said. 'Things are still too vivid and fresh in my mind, and therefore I'm not thinking one hundred percent straight.' Garcia put on a brave smile. 'The break will do me good. It will give me time to sort my head out. It will do you good as well. Are you going anywhere?'

Hunter shrugged. 'I haven't decided yet, but I was thinking maybe Hawaii.'

Garcia smiled. 'That would *really* do you good.'

Hunter smiled back. 'Yeah, I really do need a break.'

'Whatever decision I come to,' Garcia said at last. 'You'll be the first one to know, partner.'

Hunter nodded.

Without any warning, Garcia took a step toward Hunter and hugged him as if he would never see him again. 'Thank you for what you did yesterday, Robert. Thank you for saving Anna.'

Hunter smiled awkwardly.

'Now why don't you come up?' Garcia said. 'I know Anna would love to see you.'

'Give me a minute,' Hunter said and quickly returned to his car. From the passenger's seat, he retrieved a bouquet of white and yellow roses before following Garcia into the building.

One thing Hunter was certain of. Whatever decision Garcia came to in the next two weeks, it would be the right one.

Acknowledgments

Many people have contributed in so many different and generous ways to this work and, though a simple acknowledgment page cannot fully express my gratitude, I'd like them to know that this novel would never have been possible without them.

My friend, and the best agent an author could ever hope for, Darley Anderson. Camilla Wray, Clare Wallace, Mary Darby, and everyone at the Darley Anderson Literary Agency for their never-ending strive to promote and sell my work anywhere and everywhere possible.

My fantastic editor at Simon & Schuster, Maxine Hitchcock, whose comments, suggestions, knowledge and friendship I could never do without. Emma Lowth for double editing, and making sure that everything makes sense (because it usually never does). My publisher, Ian Chapman and Suzanne Baboneau, for the tremendous support and belief. The amazing team at Simon & Schuster for always doing their best, and going way beyond the call of duty.

Samantha Johnson for patiently listening to all my crazy ideas, and for being there.

Most of all, thank you to all the readers and everyone out there who have so fantastically supported me and my novels from the start. This one, and all my novels are written for you.